ACKNOWLEDGMENTS

Sometimes we make up fictional places that end up having the same names as actual places. These are our fictional interpretations only. Please grant us leeway if our creative vision isn't true to reality.

ROCKSTAR BABY

A SMALL TOWN ROMANTIC COMEDY

CRESCENT COVE
BOOK 6

TARYN QUINN

Rockstar Baby
© 2019 Taryn Quinn
Rainbow Rage Publishing
Stock Photo by Shutterstock

Cover by LateNite Designs

First print edition: February 2021
ISBN: 978-1-940346-66-3

A great big THANK YOU to our Facebook group, the Word Wenches. You guys make us laugh and we're grateful to you for all your support.

Special thanks this round goes to Janeen P for naming Ivy's ice cream truck, as well as Barbara B & Tricia D for helping us out with a few fun ideas for Ivy's business!

And Crystal B for her baby name choice. ;)

You ladies rock!

ONE

**Rory**

Fuck me running.

I peered through the windshield at the blur of white coloring the world around me. The *thunk-thunk-thunk* of the wipers didn't do a thing for visibility. The sound just pissed me off.

If the plane hadn't been delayed, I would've traversed these back roads in the daylight. Or closer to it. Of course Kellan hadn't seen fit to tell me that he lived in the middle of nowhere.

His hometown was probably rustic and lovely in the summer. In this hell they called winter? It was complete shite.

Add in something called lake effect on the weather report—what the heck was that?—and I was already over Turnbull, New York before I'd even reached it.

My cell rang through the audio system of my rental car. *Kellan McGuire.*

The reason I was even here. The guy was lucky I liked him.

"Kellan, I'm almost there."

"Are you?" He didn't sound as happy as he should have considering the thousands of miles I'd traveled.

Hello, *I* was the pissed off traveler. He was the bloke sitting on his living room couch and twirling a pencil while he pretended to be productive.

"I think so. Maybe."

"What mile marker did you pass?"

"Come again?"

"There's mile markers on the side of the road. They're to help during winter conditions since we get some travelers passing through to Syracuse and Rochester."

I squinted into the snow slanting down in front of my headlights and wondered why I hadn't hired a driver.

It'll be more of an adventure this way.

Turnbull isn't far from the airport.

When else am I going to see the quaint bits of New York?

I was a fucking moron.

"I can't see a bloody thing out here," I muttered.

"They're there, trust me."

"I've been driving a good while and I haven't seen a damn thing but snow. What the hell is lake effect? I thought being near bodies of water was a good thing."

Kellan let out a low laugh. "Not this time of year around here. Look, it's getting late."

I glanced at the time. Past ten. Jesus. I hadn't realized I'd been driving this long. As it was, I'd be in town barely a day before I hopped on the red eye back to LA tomorrow night. Kellan and I were working on a song together and between both of our hectic schedules, a day was all we'd been able to carve out.

The hours were ticking by and I was driving in circles in a blizzard. It was a miracle I'd even made it across the country to New York when flights were being cancelled right and left.

"You're right, it is. My GPS says I'm on North Hollow. Isn't that the road I'm supposed to be on?"

"If you're headed to Turnbull, yes, but I'm just outside Turnbull. Remember I told you it was easier to go to Crescent Cove then program it for my address? Otherwise the GPS takes you the other way."

"The way with no mile markers?"

Kellan laughed. "Essentially. Sorry, man."

For God's sake, I could see nothing out here. Even a deer would be welcome company. And where were all the other vehicles? Surely someone else had to live in this godforsaken backwoods area.

Maybe not. Maybe this was where they'd find my body. I'd become the subject of one of those tragic dead guy music specials. Did they even do those anymore?

Fuck, I'd have had more sex if I'd known this would be my last stand. I didn't even have on proper footwear. The autopsy pictures would show my beat up Jordans with the hole in the heel and everyone would murmur about how I must have spent all my money on wine, women, and song.

More like beer, pizza, and recording equipment.

"Look, you're closer to Crescent Cove than you are to my place. With the storm, why don't you go back to town and get a room for the night? By morning, the storm should be easing up so you can make it out here. Or better yet, I'll come to you. Just text me where you're staying."

It took me a moment to decipher what he was rambling on about, since I was currently trying not to slide off the road in my small sedan. I should have demanded a truck at the very least. This car had no traction whatsoever.

"You must be joking."

Kellan cleared his throat. "It's late, man."

"So you already said. Is it your bedtime or something? Need I remind you that I traveled across country to help you with your first solo single? You're the one who wanted to make sure it was a success."

Kellan had basically begged me, but I wouldn't remind him of that yet. Unless he gave me no choice.

I was hotly in demand. It was simply a fact. If I took the time to work with someone, they had serious chops and there was a good likelihood of our collaboration being a hit. Or someone had requested a favor. That was rarer, because I didn't make a habit of putting myself in that position. I didn't like to be beholden to anyone. Ever. Or for anyone to be beholden to me.

Life was less messy that way.

"I did. I do. But Christ, man, we just got Wolf to sleep. He's the fussiest sleeper on the planet."

"Look, mate, I feel for you with your issues with your pet dog, but—"

Kellan laughed long and hard, filling the car with the sound. "Wolf's my son. Nice one with the dog though."

I frowned although he couldn't see me. "I didn't know you had any of those."

"Yeah, well, came as a surprise to me too, but it's a been a couple of years and here we are."

"I'm happy for you, but I'm not happy for me. For one, I can't even find a lane to turn around in." Or anything but trees. And snow. And darkness. And snow.

"If you're on North Hollow, go up to the old, closed Heaphy's gas station. Turn around there then follow North Hollow back to a 4-way stop and take a left. That'll take you right into Crescent Cove in about twenty miles or so."

"Twenty miles? Why can't I just program the GPS from here?" I didn't see any gas station. Of course it had to be an old, non-functional one when I'd just noticed my tank was stuck near E.

So much for the rental car place making sure the car was set to go. Sure, no problem, I can stop for gas out in the middle of the woods. Why not?

"You can but the amount of woods in this area sometimes gives it fits. Just follow my directions and you'll be fine. In this weather, you don't want to be taking the scenic route the GPS will try to take you on."

"Scenic, is it? Is that what they're calling this?"

Kellan heaved out a sigh. "Look, man, I'm sorry about all this. Try to find the gas station. If you can't, call me back in an hour and I'll come find you. If I try to leave now, Wolf will hear it and Maggie will pitch a fit."

It was my turn to sigh. "Along with the son, you have a girlfriend too?" It was only logical, but I didn't get too personal with the people I worked with if I could help it.

I was focused on the music. *Only* the music. I didn't give two figs about who was waiting—or not waiting—at the dinner table.

"Wife. Didn't we discuss all this already?"

We probably had, but I tended to tune out when it came to family and all that. It was a potential job hazard in my line of work. Not that I had any looming entanglements on the horizon, but I also made sure not to cultivate them. My happiness was found in the studio, not in building family units.

I'd spent enough time trying to put an ocean between me and mine.

My old man didn't get my love of music versus a good stable job like he had in the fields. My mum wasn't much better. She'd stayed home with her children and thought that a family was the cornerstone of life. My younger brother Thomas went his own way, as did my younger sister Maureen. Yet my mum behaved as if we were living in a Norman Rockwell painting. Even if her marriage didn't seem particularly happy and her kids weren't close, the idea of home and hearth was all she cared about.

Not me. I wasn't doing anything for the sake of tradition or appearances. And I was lucky enough not to have to please anyone but myself.

"Don't remember, sorry." I shrugged it off. "I won't be your best friend, but I'll help you get that hit single you're looking for."

"Fine by me. I've already got a best friend and no particular fondness for the warm and fuzzies myself." Kellan paused. "So, give me that call if you can't find your way back to the Cove, or else text me in the morning and I'll meet you before we come back here to use my studio. Hope you can find accommodations. See Sage at The Hummingbird's Nest if all else fails."

I grunted and disconnected the call. *Thanks for nothing.*

Goddamn rockstars. Always thought the world revolved around them.

The sad part was they were usually right. Especially the successful ones like Kellan McGuire. As the frontman for the rock band Wilder Mind, he made the girls scream and his songs climbed the charts. Until one of the members had quit and Kellan had gotten the itch to play on his own on the side.

I played music now and then, sitting in with bands for my own entertainment or if a song needed something the artist couldn't provide. But I was a part-time rocker at best. I treated music as art, but I also kept an eye on the business end. Whether or not my pop believed my work to be "artsy fartsy", his words not mine.

I kept driving until I found the gas station Kellan had mentioned. I didn't entirely trust his directions, and they were hard to follow in this inclement weather in any case. It was practically impossible to see anything. But somehow the huge sign for Heaphy's still partially worked, a couple of the letters gleaming in neon in the darkness.

After making a U-turn, I went back the way I'd come from. I drove and drove and drove until I was about to turn to the GPS out of desperation. I didn't see any 4-way stop. Maybe Kellan had been drinking. Maybe I'd become snow blind.

Struck incapable by lake effect, whatever the flying fuck that was.

Then a stop sign appeared out of the darkness like a battered red angel. The sign was moving in the wind. I would've said that didn't seem possible, but my rental car was too.

Definitely getting a truck next time. Or a battering ram.

I made the left turn. Barely. The car fishtailed and the ditch on the side of the road came frighteningly close before somehow the tires bore down and gripped the road.

Heart in my throat, I soldiered on at the brisk speed of...eleven miles an hour.

This place was a hellhole. I was not ever returning. I didn't care if Kellan bribed me with a million dollars and a lifetime of producing credits. I'd just stick to sunny California, thanks. When I needed a taste of cold, I'd go home to Ireland or visit my sister in Cheltenham.

It felt as if I was driving forever, although that might've been due to my reduced speed. I didn't trust this car. Certainly didn't trust the road. Weren't they supposed to be out sanding or salting or something?

They probably would've been had it not been approaching eleven now. No one was driving out here but me.

A colossal idiot.

When the small green sign for Crescent Cove swam into view, coming out of the snowy dark like an oasis in the desert, I nearly wept.

Sweet bleeding Christ, I was here. I'd found it.

Now to acquire lodging for the evening.

I peered through the windshield at the rows of tidy buildings and storefronts as I passed them, most of them dark and closed up for the day. Kellan had mentioned an inn. I'd have to turn on the GPS for that one. Small town or not, there were enough side streets that I didn't want to be circling around all night.

Assuming I didn't end up sleeping in my car. I'd probably freeze.

I scratched my chin. Huh, that'd be a new experience. Maybe I could get a song out of it.

One I wouldn't give to Kellan. He was on his own.

A sign labeled Main Street came briefly into view and I grinned. Thank God. The place Kellan had mentioned was probably near here.

I hoped.

My stomach growled as I slowed to a crawl near the famed lake Crescent Cove was known for, at least according to Kellan. The snowstorm made it seem like a huge dark bowl of wind-whipped water with spots that were flat and dense. Likely parts that were iced over. I squinted at the festively lit gazebo and tried to imagine this quaint little spot festooned for Christmas. Probably quite pretty, if one was into small towns. I'd grown up in one and had been eager to leave it as soon as I turned eighteen.

What was quaint to some seemed like a strait jacket to others. I'd had no desire to live in a snow globe, with or without the flakes.

A sign caught my eye not far from the pier that led down to the gazebo. The Rusty Spoon.

My stomach rumbled again. That would do just fine.

Small rural towns often had diners. And thank God for that. What else would be open at this time of night? Other than possibly some swanky place probably down to a dessert and drink menu at best.

I'd take my chances with the grease and a corner booth—after I found the inn.

It took me another fifteen minutes to find it via GPS and then to locate parking. I was tempted to do a sideways tilt off a snowbank but figured that probably wouldn't ingratiate me to this perfectly lovely town.

That I could not fucking *wait* to leave.

The Hummingbird's Nest bed and breakfast was church silent as I crossed the wide porch to the door with its cheery little bell. That might've been because of the innate quiet of a good snowfall or due to the lateness of the hour.

Going inside didn't change my assessment. I saw absolutely no one in the foyer, or the little gift shop to the left, or the fancy restaurant closed off behind pocket doors to my right.

Then a blond popped up from behind the wide cherry counter. "Hi, you look peaked!" Her curls bounced to match her infernally perky voice. "Weary traveler?"

I blessed myself because Jesus Christ, my heart had nearly stopped at the sight of her. "You could say that. Room?"

"Like room at the inn? Sure thing. What's your name? Do you have people in town? What brought you this way in a storm like this?"

Far too many questions, offered in a rapid-fire style that made my ears buzz. She was like a living white noise machine. Except her noise was pink, to go along with her brightly colored dress. "Come again?"

"I'm sorry, you must think I'm wacky."

That was one word for it.

"I'm Sage Hamilton. My husband and I own The Hummingbird's Nest—where you're standing," she added, as if I'd failed to notice the sign on the door. "We don't get a lot of out-of-towners this time of year, and definitely not this time of night during a storm. But your reasons for being here are none of my business. I'm just a nosy sort." She smiled and her looks veered from pretty into downright stunning.

"I was meeting an acquaintance near Turnbull but the storm delayed my flight. Then his baby was fussy and I didn't even know he had a baby. Named Wolf no less. Who names their child that?"

"Mine is named Star."

"So, it's a small town thing then." Made sense.

"Possibly." Her smile grew as she tapped keys on a sleek computer system. "So, how long are you here for?"

I glanced at my watch. "Twenty-two hours give or take."

"Aww, you're going to miss the Sap Fest."

I hated to be redundant, but... "Come again?"

"Maple syrup. You came at the perfect time to try some of our tastiest local concoctions. Like maple ice. If you're a fan of icees from the gas station, you've got to try these."

"Um. Shame to miss that."

"You have no idea what I'm talking about, do you? What country are you from anyway? I can't place the accent."

"America."

Rather than becoming offended, she laughed. Gaily. As if I wasn't a rude fucker who'd invaded her happy hushed sanctuary at damn close to midnight.

"Point taken. I have a nice room for you. The last one we have with a fireplace. Good for a night like this."

She leaned forward and tilted her head, peering over the counter at my hands. At least that was what I assumed she was looking at. Maybe my lack of gloves? Surely she couldn't see the hole in my sneaker from that height. It wasn't a big one. It hadn't even been the shoe's fault. I'd met a nail and lost. And stubborn fool that I was, I'd refused to stop wearing my favorite pair.

"No luggage?"

"A bag in the car." I gestured vaguely out the door. "I wanted to make sure there was room for me before I brought in my belongings."

"We always have room at The Hummingbird's Nest." Her voice was sober as she tapped her name tag. I'd not noticed it before.

And lookee there. It actually said that exact sentiment.

We always have room for you at The Hummingbird's Nest. You're not a friend, you're family.

"I'm not even a friend, but I'll take the goodwill. Let me go get that bag—"

"You haven't finished checking in yet. I'll send my assistant out to retrieve it for you." She pressed a button on the phone. "Yo, Hamilton, we've got a live one."

My eyebrows lifted. Was she truly having someone get my bag or would my rental car end up at the bottom of the lake, never to be found again?

Was this small town really like the one in the Richard Marx song? I was a bit west of the setting of that one, but there were crazies everywhere. Possibly ones with shiny blond curls and doe eyes.

A talk dark man in a business suit—at midnight?—came down the sweeping staircase a moment later. He said nothing to Sage, just cocked his head at me. "Vehicle make and model? And may I have the keys?"

"You say hello first." Sage let out a long breath. "He's not new here, but he acts it. Oliver Hamilton, this is...what's your name?"

"Rory."

"Last name?" When I hesitated, she tapped her keyboard pointedly. "Unless you're checking in with an assumed name, I'll find it out on your credit card. Unless you only have cash. Hmm. You don't seem like the miscreant sort. Are you in trouble with the law?"

"Don't mind my wife. She claims I'm the one with no manners, but sometimes she puts me to shame." Oliver held out his hand and I gave him the keys.

"Blue Honda parked in front of the flagpole at the white house down the street. Bag is in the boot. Trunk," I corrected automatically.

He nodded, moving in close for an instant as he passed me. "But if you touch a hair on her head while I'm occupied, I'll use your own vehicle to end you."

TWO

 **Rory**

I coughed into my fist. Weren't small towns supposed to be welcoming? I was pretty sure implied death threats didn't count as hospitality.

Oliver stepped back and smiled. "Have a pleasant evening. Enjoy your stay." The door shut behind him.

"Payment method, please."

I handed over my card. "Your husband seems nice," I said carefully.

So did Ted Bundy.

"He isn't. But he's a good lover and a wonderful father and he's easy on the eyes too. So, there's that. A temporary additional deposit of one hundred dollars has been placed on the card and will come off assuming there is no damage to your room during your stay."

"Okay." I didn't even know how much the room cost. It didn't really matter. I'd pay anything to get out of here.

Perhaps that was the Hamilton policy. Make potential guests so uncomfortable, they'll pay anything to escape the conversation.

I had to say it was working so far.

Oliver returned with my single bag just as Sage passed me my credit card.

"I'll show you to your room," he said ominously and I held up my hands before pointing at Sage.

"Her hair hasn't moved. See?"

"Don't mind him. He's testy at being awakened this late."

"Awakened? Does he sleep in a three-piece suit?"

"Only on special occasions." Oliver nodded at the stairs and I followed him up.

There was a good chance I was going to do bodily harm to Kellan when we met up tomorrow. First, he wouldn't let me spend the night at his place, then he sends me *here?* The guy was parked on a piece of ice so thin he could see his own reflection.

Oliver led me to my room and set down my lone bag, all the while commenting on the amenities in a brutally pleasant voice.

I didn't pay him much mind. The room itself was actually quite nice, with the aforementioned fireplace already going and the King sized bed turned down. I moved to the window and tried not to grimace at the snow. It still hadn't ceased. At least I could walk to the diner from here. Better to fall on my ass than to slide into another vehicle.

Assuming I saw any.

"Room service has ended for the evening but it resumes again at eight a.m. If you're up before then, there's a complimentary continental—"

"I'll be up and out of here by then." I smiled thinly. "Hoping to have my meeting first thing in the morning."

If Kellan cooperated. If not, I'd amuse myself in town until he was available rather than lay about eating sausage links and miniature boxes of cereal.

"Suit yourself. Hope you enjoy your stay at The Hummingbird's Nest." Without so much as another smile, Oliver was gone.

Clearly, I wasn't the only dour sort around.

I used the facilities—large clawfoot tub and separate shower stall,

I noted, along with piles of thick soft towels—and unpacked my toiletries. I left my glasses behind on the dresser and my clothes in my suitcase, although I put on a heavier sweater under my thin jacket. Then I was out the door again and headed downstairs.

Sage wasn't at the desk. Nor was she hiding behind it. In fact, a bell had been set upon it with a sign.

Ring for service. Desk will be staffed at seven a.m.

Did she have a room here herself? Did the bell somehow sound over her bed?

Shaking my head, I stepped out into the storm, drawing my collar in tight. I descended the icy steps and hurried up the street, my mind already on my stomach. The town itself was a postcard vision in icy white, with the soft glow of lights against windows here and there reminding me just how alone I was.

Starkly alone. Not just here, but essentially on the planet. If I disappeared, my family wouldn't realize for days or weeks. And I wasn't even sure they'd care if they did.

What the hell was it about this place, making me think such maudlin thoughts? That wasn't me. Then again, passing that partially frozen over lake in the hushed darkness could make anyone uneasy.

This was why I preferred the hustle and bustle of the city. Less room for me and my thoughts.

I rushed past the closed souvenir shop and another for women's clothing and accessories, then grasped the ice cold handle to the diner with a sigh of relief.

Finally. Maybe this place would have some life. A distraction for my far too busy brain.

I opened the door and glanced around at the tidy, well-worn booths. Empty, every one of them.

Great.

Elvis's *The Wonder of You* came from an honest to God jukebox at the back of the room. One of my father's favorites. Seemed to be an auspicious sign.

Despite my rumbling belly, I almost turned around and walked back out. I'd shifted to debate doing just that when a friendly voice rang out behind me.

"We're still open, don't worry. Sorry, I was in back making tomorrow's bread. Missed a delivery because of the storm. Table or booth?"

Her voice. Christ. It was like a melody, but a discordant one. A little husky, a little broken, with an edge of fatigue she couldn't quite cover with the layer of false cheer.

I pivoted back to face her and couldn't quite match up that raspy voice with the long red braids and pouty mouth slicked with pink gloss. She wore a tight top and tighter pants, the bellbottom kind that hung over her shoes. Platforms, I thought they were called. Not exactly work attire, even if she had a sloppily tied apron on over her outfit.

"Got called in unexpectedly," she said, correctly reading my thoughts. "No one else could make it in because of the storm."

"And you were on a modeling job when you were called away?"

She tilted her head. "Have you been drinking?"

I crossed my arms. "Hear the Irish in my voice and that's what you think, hmm?"

"Now that you mention it, yes, I do hear the Irish. I didn't at first. I meant because you accused me of being a model. I lost one of my false eyelashes in my margarita." She pointed to her naked eye and it made me laugh, because somehow I hadn't noticed she was missing one.

I'd been too busy noticing all the rest of her.

"A night out with your girlfriends, was it? Or your boyfriend?" I wasn't sure why my voice deepened when I said that, or why my hands tightened where I'd tucked them under my arms.

She snorted at that. "You're kidding, right? In this town? All the men are married or dating or old enough to be my grandfather. I have to widen my net." She licked her lips, probably a nervous habit. But that quick flash of tongue combined with her lush mouth had my muscles locking as if I was a predator in the woods, scenting my mate.

"How old are you?"

She let out a laugh. "Old enough. Would you like a seat? You must be hungry."

"Oh, I am." I just hadn't expected to be hungry for *her* more than I was for food. "You didn't answer the question."

She tucked her tongue in her cheek. "Neither did you."

"Yes, I'd like a seat. Usually when women don't share their age either they're too young or too—"

"Old?"

"Too tired of bullshit."

"Oh, well, I'm definitely tired of that. Booth or table?"

"Whatever you'd like to give me."

Her eyes flashed, and it annoyed me that without my glasses I couldn't as easily make out their color. I hadn't expected to need them for any fine details at the diner. Sometimes it was better if you couldn't see too clearly at a greasy spoon.

But here, I'd miscalculated. In more ways than one.

Silently, she led me to a booth. She leaned across the table to grab a laminated menu out of the rack and opened it in front of me. "We serve our full menu all night long, so whatever you'd like is available."

"Not sure about that," I said under my breath as I scanned the offerings. "Black coffee and the big boy breakfast with bacon, please." I winced and closed the menu. "Unfortunate name."

"Are you?"

I blinked. "Excuse me?"

She was scribbling so furiously on her pad I was almost certain I'd imagined the cheeky question—if not for the telltale twitch of her bedroom mouth. "I'll let management know you're displeased with the name of your food."

"Appreciate it. While you're at it, let them know I'm happy to compensate them for cutting your shift short." I met her shocked stare straight on. "And I'll answer that question of yours in private."

THREE

 IVY

I took the menu from him and tucked it back behind the condiments. Something I did a million times a day. Except everything inside me was jangling in a whole new way.

The jukebox kicked over to the next song. The Zombies and their groovy 60's rhythm filled the space between us.

He didn't mean what he'd just said. That was ridiculous.

"Do you need glasses?"

"That's neither here nor there."

"First, you thought I was a model. Then you think it would be okay to blatantly proposition me."

"If you're offended, I apologize. I misread."

My lips twitched again. "You didn't."

He narrowed his eyes at me. "Contrary girl."

"Very." I grinned and tapped his shoulder with my pad. "No harm. Unfortunately, I can't close the diner." I almost said I was the only one here, but he was a stranger. I might be a small town girl, but I listened to true crime podcasts. Far too many to be healthy sometimes, but they were so fascinating. The women from Vee's baby group had passed around names and episodes like prenatal vitamins. And the worst of the stories happened in a small town.

No thanks.

I rose. "Let me just put your order in."

"If you must. The idea of you for breakfast is far more interesting."

"Because you don't know me very well." My skin was tingling and I was sure my freckles were literally glowing under my long-sleeved top. I put an extra sway in my step as I walked away.

The Animals piped through the speakers. Mitch had just put the retro jukebox in the diner and the constant rotation of 45's wasn't annoying yet. Especially with the number of singles my boss had in his collection. The playlist was forever changing and the colorful machine made him smile.

Mitch in a good mood meant the rest of us were in a good mood.

Once I got to the swinging door, I rushed through and back to the small bathroom. A quick look in the mirror assured me the damage was as bad as I'd feared. "Good Lord, girl." I debated going back to my purse for my other eyelash, but it was fairly ruined. Damn margarita. I peeled the other one off and groaned. I really needed to start over. Glue and an uneven line of eyeliner belied my very steady hand.

"Fuck it." How many times was I going to have a hot dude in the diner?

Especially one who actually looked at me like I was more than just August Beck's little sister. His hotness factor clicked up a few simply because he didn't know me or this town.

I rushed back to my locker and dragged out my purse. Of course I didn't have my good makeup bag on me. I had my baby purse for the bar and I looked like a reject from an Elvis movie.

It had been 60's night at The Spinning Wheel. Music and games from that era. The entire town was bored as hell this time of year. Barely anything to do but watch snow fall.

And I was very sick of snow.

The Sap Fest was starting tomorrow, so at least there was that. Not exactly in town, but close enough to bring a few strangers into the vicinity. My customer didn't look like he'd ever gone to a festival in his life. At least not one that included maple syrup.

I dug around with a small prayer. "Yes!" I grabbed the black liner and rushed back to the bathroom. I ended up with a bit of a smokier look than usual, but it was better than the twisted *Alice in Wonderland* look I was rocking before. I freshened up the deep lip stain with some gloss and smoothed my hand over my tight shirt. It might not be the current fashion, but the green and pink records pattern was funky and the top kept me warm.

I quickly reached back for the strings on my stained apron. That had to go.

I washed my hands and rushed back into the kitchen to pull out the fixings for the big boy breakfast. Cooking was second nature to me. I didn't run the grill too often, but enough that I didn't have to think about what I was doing.

Normally.

It wasn't like there were no attractive men in the Cove, just none that actually made my heart race. I peeked out into the diner to make sure he was okay. He was holding his phone up close to the window. Good luck finding a signal in this storm.

Then I burned the toast and had to trash it.

Pay attention to the food, Ivy. Not to the dude outside.

I poured a juice and a water and backed out through the door.

"Here we go. Your food is almost ready." Only a little bit of a lie.

"Is there a big dude named Mick in the back?"

"Close. His name is Mitch." Except Mitch was probably sound asleep next to his fireplace right now.

"Of course it is." The way his accent slipped around the vowels of his words made something flutter in my chest. Energy, happiness... lust?

Maybe.

Interest more than lust perhaps.

Lust wasn't for girls like me. I was the forever girl. The one who would marry a teacher and pump out two kids.

The kids part intrigued me, not so much the teacher. Not that it had to be a teacher, but the only guy who had hit on me lately was one of my brother Caleb's friends. Mark was just like my brother and pretty much hit on anyone with a pair of tits. And those kinds of guys didn't interest me.

At least not right now.

I was used to being the buddy and that sweet girl from the diner. Old people patted my hand and left me a dollar under their coffee cups as if they were giving me the world.

Not *him*.

He looked at me as if I was a woman. I mean, I was, but being twenty-four and looking like a perpetual teen got old sometimes.

His golden lashes swept down as he took in the snug line of my polyester pants. I'd pregamed my trip to the bar with a few glasses from Kinleigh's perpetual box of wine at her clothing store. It had taken very little prodding for me to dive into her retro trunks at the back of her store. Sure, most of us used those particular trunks for Halloween, but we'd giggled our way into outfits and wobbled to the bar on ridiculous platform heels.

Kinleigh was one of my best friends, and she was forever trying to give me a makeover. I was suddenly very glad I'd listened to her clothing suggestions for once. The platform shoes were surprisingly comfy though. I might keep them. I liked the extra four inches without the accompanying pain as well.

Too bad the margaritas had mostly worn off on my walk to the diner.

I might need some of that courage to get through his meal. Mitch usually had an emergency bottle of whiskey stashed in the flour pantry.

Then again, I didn't want to rush my customer. He'd be gone and I'd be back to taking my frustrations out on bread dough again.

"Does that work back there?" He nodded toward the jukebox with a hopeful glint in his eyes. "Or just pre-programmed?"

"Nope. Fully functional. If you've got the quarters."

His eyebrows snapped down. "Who carries quarters?"

I patted my tiny pocket. The pants really weren't made for anything other than showing off my butt. "I don't have much in the way of tips, seeing as I was SOS'd from my boss to fill in for the usual night girl." I curled my finger around the two quarters I had in my pocket from my one drink at the bar. Unfortunately, I'd had to pay my way there as well. No one had bought me drinks. "However—"

He held his hand up. "I can pay my own way, love."

"You have quarters?"

"Well, no."

"Cash?"

"That I have."

"Good, then you can give me a nice tip." I slapped the two quarters on the table. "Good luck finding a song you like. Most of the songs are from the 50's and 60's. A handful of 70's."

"I'll make do."

Chubby Checker's anthem wasn't exactly the conduit for a sashay back to the kitchen, so I just double-timed it to get back before the bacon was well done.

As I was plating his food, I had to redo his toast—again. Talk about distractible Debbie.

"Re-fucking-lax, he's just a guy." I blew a flyaway bit of hair out of my eyes and grabbed the two plates. Perfect toast this time, thank you very much.

He was still standing in front of the juke when I returned. He had broad shoulders. The sweater was obviously well made—not a Target special. It fit his body far too well. He seemed athletic. The kind of guy who played football or...no, rugby. He seemed like he would play something a little more about contact.

Something that would leave bruises.

Lord, where did that come from? And why was that so fascinating?

He turned and caught me staring. His eyebrow rose and a slow smirk spread across his interesting mouth. Straight white teeth flashed and transformed his serious face into a mouthwatering collection of smile lines and rugged charm.

Cripes, my panties were in such trouble. And not just because they were currently drowning.

He gave me that unsettling once over again as I set the plates down.

He pressed a combination of buttons and "Bang a Gong" came through the speakers. He came back toward me with a little swagger in his walk before sliding back into the booth. "Thanks."

I pressed my lips together against a laugh. "Anything else?"

"Yeah. I hate eating alone."

I rolled my tongue along the back of my teeth. "I'm working."

He glanced around the room. "Think your boss won't mind."

"You don't know my boss."

"I'll pay for your meal."

"You keep wanting to pay for things for me. My time, my food..." I tipped my head. "Then you play this song."

"Are you telling me you're dirty and sweet like the girl in this song?"

"Maybe." My heart was going to bang its way out of my damn chest.

"Do you want to be my girl...for tonight?"

Yes! Holy shit, yes!

"It remains to be seen." I twisted on my heel and burst out laughing when the song changed to "Happy Together" by the Turtles.

A sense of humor *and* he was hot? Score.

Once I was in the kitchen, I used what was left of the bacon I'd cooked for him and dropped a basket of fries. The three minutes it would take would calm my freaking heart.

Did he really want to take me home?

Or to his hotel. That was probably more likely. He definitely wasn't from here.

I made myself some cheese fries and filled a cup with ranch, blew out a slow breath, and pushed through the doors.

He looked up from his plate and sat up straighter. "Change your mind?"

I peered through the window out into the storm. "Since they're not beating down the doors…"

"Do people actually come here this late? It seems like this little town probably buttons down at like half past seven."

I set down my plate and slid across from him. "A few years ago, you'd have been right, but there's a lot more people moving to the area these days." I dipped my fry into the ranch and popped it into my mouth. "Ugh, heaven. Mitch won't let me add it to the menu."

He glanced down at my plate. "That looks decadent."

"Better than chocolate."

His eyebrow did that arching thing. "Now let's not go that far."

"I'm more of a mint girl, though I don't mind some chocolate chips." I pointed a naked fry at him. "But you can't beat the perfection of mint ice cream without anything on it."

"Is that right?"

I nodded. "Especially mine."

He set his knife down on his plate and hung his fork along the edge. So unlike most of the people who came into the diner. Half the time, they didn't even use utensils. He lifted his napkin off his lap and blotted his mouth, then leaned forward. "Is this special ice cream?"

I dragged my fry through the cheese and bacon on my plate. "Kind of. My own blend."

"You make ice cream? How…quaint."

I narrowed my gaze at him. "How rude."

He laughed and sat back to cross his arms. "You got me. Sorry. I'm not from around here."

"Obviously."

"What? I don't fit in with the sweet Americana flavor of...where am I again?" He lifted his water glass to his mouth. "Crescent Cove, is it?"

"Yes, baby capital of the world."

He choked on his sip.

I laughed. "Sorry, that was mean."

"Yes, it was."

I picked out another fry that was loaded down with cheese and bacon. "It's not a real moniker for the town, though it might as well be. We're currently going through a bit of a baby boom. Macy blames it on the water."

He quickly put his glass down and shoved it away. "Is that right?"

I managed not to give him a cheeky grin. "So much so that she makes the most delicious shakes and drinks to avoid drinking it. But I think she's just a touch superstitious. Halloween is her favorite holiday after all."

He shook his head. "This town is odd."

"No doubt about that, but it's home and I love it." I really did. So many people from my class had moved away after college. They'd been dying to get out of this town. Me? I kept finding reasons to stay. Working at the diner didn't exactly give me a huge savings account, but living with my brother meant I didn't have a whole lot of expenses. Now and then, I picked up shifts at The Spinning Wheel and The Cove to pad my pockets. I was cute enough to get tips at least.

"So, are you going to give me a name?"

He looked up from his mostly empty plate. "Are you?"

The juke went silent, then the needle hissed before the quiet was filled by The Rolling Stones.

We broke eye contact and I laughed as "Paint it Black" filled the space between us. Another song with so much meaning. This time, it was the juke speaking to us since he'd only had two quarters.

I looked down. Since I wasn't wearing my usual navy shirt, there was definitely no name tag. "Sorry, I'm usually in uniform." I licked cheese off the tips of my fingers and debated holding my hand out. I wasn't quite sure I was ready to touch him just yet. "Ivy Beck."

"Rory Ferguson."

Yeah, good thing I didn't go for that handshake. That purring Irish lilt sounded way hotter than it should have. Who even named their kid Rory?

His mom.

His dad.

And they were smart. Because it was different enough to make me take notice. Unfortunately, it also meant I wouldn't forget it. Annoying. Then again, if the night went where I thought it was going, I wouldn't forget him anyway.

I was discerning about who I got naked with. In a town where everyone always knew your business, it was just good practice, but I also didn't often have the urge to do crazy things.

At least not anymore.

My one year in college had been filled with spectacular mistakes, but once I'd gotten that out of my system, men had seemed like way more trouble than they were worth.

Until now anyway.

Annoying. Did I mention that?

"You see the palace in which I work." I did a grand gesture with my arm. "What brings you in here on a dark and stormy night?"

"Only place open."

"And here I thought it was my sparkling personality."

He tapped his long finger on the handle of his knife. "You and your town are very unique. For me, that's saying something."

"Oh, and why would that be? Are you special, Rory Ferguson?" It wouldn't surprise me in the least. Beyond the clothes that surely weren't off the rack, I couldn't put my finger on just what made the air different around him.

I saw the indecision on his face.

Was he famous? I frowned. An actor, maybe?

I glanced down at his hands and saw the little callouses on the tips of his fingers. No. Unless an actor was suddenly doing something habitual beyond staring at their own face in the mirror.

He tapped his knife again. "Recognize me?"

"No."

"Refreshing. Not that I'd expect you to unless you have your sights set on something beyond this town. Say in Los Angeles."

"Definitely not. I have no designs on leaving New York, let alone heading for the other side of the country."

"Too bad. It's a big world."

I shrugged. "I like home. I like sameness. I like knowing what will happen every day."

"You get strangers in your diner during snowstorms?"

"No, not generally. Takes some doing to find Crescent Cove."

"Tell me about it."

I picked up my glass of water and leaned back in the booth to toy with the straw. "GPS failed you?"

"To say the least. My mate told me how to get here."

The skin along the back of my neck tingled. Mate. Such a simple word, but so alien here. Friend, buddy, teammate—that was the small town life. Football and basketball were gods here. That and the small businesses that made us who we were.

A small town. A safe town.

One made for families.

Not for Rory Fergusons.

"Who's your friend?"

His blue eyes went a little cool.

I held up my hands. "You don't have to tell me." Relief and a little annoyance filled his eyes. "If you want to leave alone anyway."

His gaze narrowed. "Is that right?"

I shrugged. "I don't know you from the doorknob over there."

"Not sure you'd know my friend."

"So, what's the deal with you being so cagey?" I started to slide out of the booth. "Look, if answering questions is a problem, then I'm good with just getting your check."

He reached across the table to close his hand over mine.

Nope. I was right. I definitely wasn't ready for him to touch me. Not because I wanted to pull my hand away, but because there was the *zing*.

I knew it was going to be there. Some things a girl just knew.

I also knew he was like a rich, sinful, caramel treat. He'd taste so damn amazing, but I'd pay for him for a good long while. The question was just how good was the caramel? Or was he even worse? Would he be like my favorite mint, so good I'd never be able to forget?

Wow, overthinking.

He could just be Ben & Jerry's.

My hand was still hot where he'd touched me. Ben & Jerry's, my ass. Not that there was anything wrong with store bought ice cream, I just knew I made better. Same as I knew he was going to taste far more decadent.

"No. I just..." He sighed and pulled his hand back. "I like this."

I twisted back into the booth. "Like what?"

He shrugged and looked down. "I'm no one here. No preconceptions."

"Yeah, for you, that's cool. For me, you could be married, a serial killer, a criminal..."

He frowned and looked up. "Wow, dark."

"Try being a woman in this age. That's nothing."

"You're right though. Being a woman in the industry can mean experiencing plenty of the dark. You're right to be careful."

Industry. What the hell was that supposed to mean? Sex trafficking? "Then why won't you answer me?"

"Whatever you're thinking is wrong."

"Who are you to tell me that?"

"Because I can see the wheels in your head turning. I think some of that is part of living in this damn town. The proprietress of the place I'm staying at couldn't stop interrogating me. Is there something I should know about Crescent Cove? Are you hiding a murderer here or something?"

"No. At least I don't think so. But if you listen to the podcasts I do, there has to be at least three murderers here somewhere. Maybe the next town over. Small towns are breeding grounds for murder."

"And yet you want to stay here? At least in Los Angeles, I'm ready for a carjacking or shooting."

I shuddered. "That's no way to live."

"But the pseudo-murderers in your mind are just fine. Maybe something's in the water here, and it's not baby-making juice. You're all crackers."

"Fair."

He frowned at me. "What?"

"That's fair. I mean, we're all kind of used to each other here. You probably think you dropped into the *Twilight Zone*. Speaking of, did you see they're rebooting that? God, I'm so excited to see it. I binge watch shows while I'm working."

"At the diner?" His eyebrow shot up.

"Oh, no. Sorry. I have a few jobs actually. Don't think I've forgotten the question about what you do, Lucky Charms."

"I beg your pardon."

I laughed at the horror on his face.

The bell over the door rang and the stomp of heavy feet made me leap out of the booth. "Mitch!"

"It's shit outside, ladybug. Get home."

My heart melted at the beefy older man standing in full snow gear. Fat snowflakes were melting on his Giants winter cap pulled over his salt and pepper hair. Mitch never called me ladybug unless he was worried. "I have a few more hours."

"You're not even supposed to be here. Damn Gina living outside of town. I never should have hired her."

"You love Gina." I turned to Rory and he waved me off. I crossed to Mitch. "Is it really bad out there?"

"It ain't good. The plows can't even keep up. No one will be going anywhere tomorrow. Freaking sales will be in the toilet." His deep voice was even grumpier. "Go on and get home." He slid his gaze to Rory. "Who's the outsider?"

"Mitch," I whispered. "What have we talked about?"

"What? Is stranger better?"

I rolled my eyes. "I started the bread. It's proofing in the kitchen. Should be good for the French toast special in the morning."

"If anyone shows up. Go on. Thanks for holding down the fort until I could get here."

"No problem. I told you I was just down the street."

"I figured I'd find Kinleigh in here with you." His bushy brows lowered even more. "Not some strange man."

"He's staying at the Hummingbird. Just got snowed in is all." At least I was assuming the Hummingbird based on his description of the owner. Sounded like Sage Hamilton all right.

Mitch grunted. "At least there was one sale tonight." He stomped into the kitchen. "Crash at Kinleigh's. It's a shit drive."

I saluted at the closed door and sighed as I turned back to Rory. "Looks like I'm off the clock."

He was reclined against the bench, his long legs crossed in the middle of the aisle. "And?"

"Where's your keys, Lucky Charms?"

Surprise lit his features, then his delicious eyes did this hooded thing that made me think all the impure thoughts. "No more inquiries, Ginger Fairy?"

I threw back my head with a laugh. "No. I think I'm just going on faith tonight."

I just hoped I wasn't being beyond stupid.

FOUR

 IVY

HE STOOD AND CAME TOWARD ME. "YOU SURE ABOUT THIS? A few minutes ago, I was trying to convince you I wasn't a serial killer."

I backed up a step. "Playing panther and prey isn't the way to go."

But there was no fear in my heart. Maybe a little below my non-existent belt, but it was more like I wasn't sure what to expect. In a good way. Because a man like Rory didn't come around very often.

Even if I didn't know he was probably famous in some way, he didn't quite vibe with the town. He was too restless and his brain seemed to be going a million miles an hour.

Not like the people who lived here.

The townsfolk weren't exactly sluggish, but they definitely were not constantly looking forward. Here, it was about the moment. At least it was for me.

And this was a moment I was going to soak in like a tub full of my favorite bath bomb.

He crowded into me and I put my hand up to...touch him? Ward him off? Pretend I just didn't touch cashmere for the first time in my damn life? Ugh. I smoothed my hand along his rock-hard belly to his chest.

I finally looked up and his eyes were carefully taking me in as I touched him. His hands were at his sides, easy as you please.

"Not here, my little fairy. I don't think your boss wants an eyeful of all the things going through my mind."

I swallowed. "Is that right? Who says he would know?"

He nodded lightly toward the kitchen door. "Those bushy eyebrows in the window of the door, maybe?"

"Dammit." I really wanted to know just what his first move would be. Was he a grabber? What kind of kisser? Intense and hard? A teasing brush of dry lips?

I refused to think about him doing anything I didn't like. This was my fantasy and I was going to think positively. Not like one of the frat boys I hooked up with in college, or my last boyfriend, whose technique in the kissing department left a lot to be desired.

As far as I was concerned, Rory was exactly the fantasy fuck I wanted him to be.

"Whatever is going on in that brain of yours, hold onto it for...like eight minutes."

"What happens in eight minutes? And hopefully, you last longer than that."

His laugh was harsh and delighted at the same time. Not sure how he managed that, but it made my toes curl. "Sweet mother Mary, you will be the death of me tonight."

My smile was quick and bright. "Is that so? I don't think I've been the death of any man."

"I find that hard to believe."

I pressed my lips together and backed out of his weird gravitational pull. Even with the platforms, he was a good head taller than me. The good kind of height that meant I could crawl up him and hang on for a good long bit of fun. "Let me just get my stuff."

"All right."

I swallowed and spun around, pushing through the door to the kitchen.

"Know what you're doing, ladybug?"

I paused at the lockers. "Probably not."

Mitch grunted. "Let me know if I have to castrate him."

I looked over my shoulder. "Did you get a bad vibe?" I believed in vibes. It was hard to hold onto faith like my parents. They were so certain in all the things. Church, life, raising their kids. I was the youngest girl with two older brothers. August, who was just as steady and sure as my parents, and Caleb, who thought the only sure thing was how fast he could get a girl naked. Then there was me, the baby, who never really knew where she was meant to fit.

But vibes helped lead the way for everything I tried. And they hadn't steered me wrong yet.

The first hint of doubt niggled at me.

"City boy. Isn't that bad enough?"

I tugged my purse out of the locker, then my hat, scarf, and gloves. I tugged my hat over my pigtail braids. For a second, I thought about taking them out, but my hair was...*ugh*. There was so much of it and it was so damn heavy.

Nope, he seemed to like me with them, so I wasn't going to go there.

I stopped in front of Mitch on my way out. I looped my scarf around his neck and pulled him down for a quick kiss on his beardy cheek. "Thanks for looking out for me, big guy."

"If you don't show up for work tomorrow, where should I start looking for you?"

I rolled my eyes. "The Hummingbird."

"Still don't like it."

"I love you, Mitch."

He grunted again. "Get."

I tugged my scarf free and wound it around my neck as I walked into the diner. I didn't have my good coat with me tonight, but if my neck was warm, I could manage just about anything. Central New York strong.

"Is that all you're wearing?" Rory's gaze narrowed as he zipped up his coat.

"As opposed to that windbreaker you're wearing?" I laughed and headed for the coatrack.

"Yes, well, I'm a dumb guy from California, remember?"

"Oh, I do." I tugged my puffy vest off the hanger. "But you have a car, right?"

"Actually, I walked."

"Oh. Well, I have mine." I tugged on my gloves. "Let's get moving, LC."

"That's not going to stick, is it?"

"Maybe." I patted his cheek with my thermal gloved hand, then sauntered out the door. "Whoa."

Rory came up behind me and whistled. "So, maybe a bit more than eight minutes, yeah?"

I peered up at him, then at the near foot of snow on top of my car. "Let's see what we can do about that."

"Your feet." He hurried after me as I stepped off the sidewalk.

"What about them?"

"Get in the car. It's too cold."

"Sorry?"

"It's freezing and snowing. You are not dressed for this."

"Baby, my blood is thick and hardy. You're the one who is probably dying a little inside." I'd already waded through a foot of snow from the bar to the diner tonight. My toes were just fine. Mitch was right though. No plow would be coming through for another hour or two. Easier to wait until just before work hours.

Rory grunted and brushed off snow halfheartedly with his sleeve.

"If we get stuck, we'll just call my brother. He's a few doors down. When it snows he crashes in his shop."

"I don't think your brother is going to like bailing me out to help his sister get lucky."

I laughed. "Getting lucky with Lucky Charms."

"Would you stop with that?"

I sliced my arm across the window of the driver's side door as snow dropped to the ground. I opened the door and grabbed my snow brush from the floor. I slammed the door shut and another pound of snow coated my feet. With economic movements, I made short work of clearing off my car. I peered over the roof at him. "Are you magically delicious, Rory?"

He came around the car, his hands stuffed into his pockets. The dummy didn't have gloves like I did. "The better question, my sweet fairy queen, is: are you?"

I straightened and slapped my gloves together to brush off the worst of the snow. "Wow, upgrade. Fairy queen?"

"Only the reddest of redheads are allowed the queen title." He flicked the end of my braid. "Or is this enhanced?" His gaze dropped to my mouth then lifted to meet my gaze.

I hooked my gloved finger into his belt loop. He hissed as my snow covered fingers hit the skin between his belt and sweater. "Are you asking if the drapes match the curtains, fine sir?"

"I don't care either way."

I peered up at him, thick snowflakes tangling in my eyelashes. I tried to blink them away, but the snow was coming down too hard. Just as I was about to step back to continue clearing off the car, he curled his arm around my back and dragged me against his chest.

There was no asking, no teasing.

He swooped down and covered my mouth with his. I could only grip his arms as I held on for the ride. I gave back just as good as I got. When his tongue brushed my bottom lip, I groaned.

Evidently, I was going to check hard and intense off on my internal checklist. He tasted of snow and dark corners that required a roaring fire to combat. I liked it.

I wanted more.

I went on my toes to get closer. My padded breasts felt too tight under the puffy vest. Too many layers, too much cold, too many minutes between us and the Hummingbird's Nest.

The air whooshed out of my chest as he bumped me up against the car door. His mouth was hot and wild against mine. I forgot where I was, how cold it was, and how long it had been since I'd been kissed. There was nothing but his firm, talented mouth.

His cool fingers slipped under the back of my vest and shirt to find my skin. The calloused tips were almost scratchy and foreign on my flesh as he tunneled up the stretchy fabric. His long fingers practically spanned the width of my lower back. Was he going for my bra?

God, right against the car.

Was I really this far gone? This hard up?

Maybe.

God, he felt good. Tasted better.

The very obvious ridge of something impressive pressed against my middle. *Please let that be him and not his phone.*

"Sweet Jesus," he said against my mouth, his accent thick and full of shadows like his kiss. "It's been too long for me."

"Really?" My voice was far too breathless. I definitely sounded very amateur-ish in this whole one-night stand business, but surely, I had to have misunderstood.

"Not very California of me, yeah?"

I laughed and went for his mouth again. God, he tasted divine. Better than mint ice cream. I didn't even care if he was lying to me. I liked the idea of driving him wild.

"As much as I want this right now," I molded my gloved fingers over his zipper and *hallelujah,* that was definitely not his phone, "we *are* on Main Street."

"Right." He went for my mouth again, then backed up. "Fuck, that mouth of yours is like a siren's." He cupped my cheeks and went in for another hot, mind-wiping kiss.

God, he was way too good at that. Obviously, he was lying about it being too long. Not if he could kiss like that. Again, I didn't really care. I just wanted more of it.

A car slowly came down the street, red and blue lights twirling. "Shit."

Rory's deliciously blurry blue eyes opened and then widened. "Fuck."

I fumbled behind me . I opened the driver's side door and pushed him back a step. "That's our cue."

"Get in." I waved to Sheriff Brooks as he slowly passed us by. Great. The only good thing about getting seen by the sheriff was that he didn't gossip like the rest of the town.

Small favors.

Rory gripped the edge of the door. "I'll finish—"

"Nope, get in. It takes a minute to start this thing in the winter."

His brows snapped down. "You'll break your neck in those shoes."

"You didn't seem to mind when you were kissing my lips off my face. Now get in the damn car, Lucky Charms."

The brake lights on the cop car went on, leaving me no choice. I pushed Rory into the car and raced around the back to brush off the back window. Then I hurried around to take care of the other side.

Catching Rory's annoyed expression, I couldn't resist a laugh as I cleaned the worst of the snow off the wiper blades.

He rolled down the window. "Get in, for fuck's sake."

"You want to drive in one piece?"

"It's freezing."

"Stop bitching and crank the heat," I called over the whine of the engine trying to warm up and the overworked blades.

"Get in the car, Ivy."

I opened the door and tipped my head to the side. "Hey, you do remember my name."

"If that cop comes back around... Tell me it's not your dad or something."

"Now that would be fun." I climbed in and turned the fan grates up to warm my hands. I pulled off my wet gloves and rubbed them together.

He shook his head and took my hands between his.

"And that's going to help? Yours are even colder."

He lifted his sweater and yelped as my cold hands hit his skin, but he held them tight against him. His very warm, very deliciously hair roughened skin. I couldn't exactly tell, but I was pretty sure he wasn't at gorilla status. He was a nice in-between over some seriously yum muscles.

The console was between us, but I was tempted to push my luck again. What was it about him that made me want to do all the wrong things?

"Ivy." His voice was deep and full of warning.

Well, that just meant I had to do it now.

I inched up farther to find his nipple, dragging my thumb across the ridge of muscle and around the tip. My other hand went down to his belt.

"Christ, you do try a man," he said, just before we started heating up the windows.

By the time we came up for air, the car was an oven and I was ready to strip down to the skin. The *whoop-whoop* of a siren had us breaking apart. I laughed like a loon as he scrambled for the gear shift and his seatbelt.

"What is so funny? You want us to get pulled over for indecent exposure?"

I fastened my belt and pushed my hat off my head. "Have some experience with that?"

"No."

His clipped voice made me laugh even harder.

He wiped at the fogged up window and grumbled something under his breath I couldn't quite catch, thanks to the loud fan.

"Do you need me to drive, California boy?"

"I got it. I managed to get to town, didn't I?"

"That you did." I sat back and tried not to passenger seat drive as he made the slow trek to the Hummingbird's Nest.

"How do you people live with this level of apocalypse?" His fingers were white-knuckled on the steering wheel and he was leaning forward with so much tension in his delicious body, I was pretty sure he was going to twang like a plucked string.

"Lake effect is always fun."

"What does that even mean?"

"Do you really want a weather lesson?"

"No."

I pressed my lips together at his grumpy tone. Laughing probably wasn't a good idea. I wasn't even sure why his grouchy tone made me want to needle him even more. It happened with my brother August too. Then again, I didn't want to pick *that* apart when I was still itching to get naked with Rory.

"Easiest way to think of it is the lake is warm and adds to the moisture in the air which increases the snow totals."

"In this cold?"

"Big lake," I said with a shrug.

"California makes sense."

"Oh, sure. Seismic shifts and tectonic plates that want to dump half—if not the entire—state into the ocean."

He spared me a quick glance. "Doom and gloom much?"

I shrugged again. "You can dig out of snow."

"Or die in a pile as tall as a building."

"Actually—"

He held up a hand before slamming it back down on the wheel. Back to his death grip. "Never mind."

Finally, the yellow glow from the porch light of the bed and breakfast came into view. The visibility was shit, but the swollen clouds seemed to be dissipating a bit. The storm would probably play itself out in the next few hours.

More than enough time to get Rory Ferguson out of my system.

I hoped.

FIVE

 IVY

He parked along the side of the building. I reached for my door and his terse, "stay," made my hackles rise and something a little more interesting bloom inside me.

"Ruff."

He glowered. Seemed to be his natural state. Why did that turn me on so much? Maybe I was a little more twisted than I thought.

I laughed at him to see what would happen. This was all for science, after all.

I didn't do one-nighters. Even in college, I just ended up hooking up with people in my circle of friends. Some stuck around, others drifted away. It had all been so light and easy.

Nothing seemed remotely light or easy with this man. And he was definitely not a boy.

"I don't know whether to kiss you or throttle you."

My eyes widened. I didn't know him well enough to know if he was kidding or not, but it didn't stop the delicious little shiver playing cross country track star down my spine. Should I be running for the side entrance to find Sage for safety?

Everything inside me screamed no.

Was I getting under his skin?

He was certainly making mine tingle and tighten in all the best places. A few others loosened and heated. I so wasn't used to that. Or I'd forgotten what attraction felt like. I knew everyone in town—mostly. Oh, there had been a few new people now that the town was expanding exponentially, thanks to our own private little baby boom, but so far, none of the locals rang my bell.

Yet here I was with a perfect stranger who would be moving on before dawn, probably. And my bells were clanging like the end of Christmas mass.

I leaned across the console and dragged him to my mouth. Better to remind him why we were doing this. Besides, this was his idea. I'd never have been so bold if he hadn't prompted me to wonder what he tasted like. About the accent that told stories without giving me any real information on the man.

He kissed me with the same intensity as before we got into the car, though his touch was soft. He tugged on the end of my braid, lightly playing with the end like a paintbrush. It was confusing and wonderful at the same time. Nothing made sense and yet this little moment felt righter than anything I'd experienced so far.

I fumbled with the belt to get closer to him. My gloves were gone due to the sauna level of the car. It allowed me to dip my fingers into his thick hair. His mouth moved to my neck and I tugged at his sweater with my other hand. I wanted more skin, more closeness, more everything.

Raking my fingers through his hair, I dragged him closer. He was ginger like me, but the deeper kind with lots of brown and blond mixed in. The golden glow of the lights around the bed and breakfast turned his hair to the color of an older penny. One that had been through a lot and somehow always ended up back in your pocket.

I groaned when his lips hit a certain spot on my neck. Most guys didn't care enough about the foreplay part before they were trying to get their dick wet. At least that had been my entire college experience. One wild year before I came home.

This? Yeah, this wasn't anything like the fumbling nineteen-year-old guys I'd been with in the past.

No, this was wild and wonderful.

I felt him smiling against my skin. So, he *was* able to smile. It was rare. Exasperation and interest often flared in his blue eyes, but not much laughter.

I'd have to change that. At least for tonight.

"As much as I'm enjoying all this foreplay, LC, I'd really like to get inside. I've heard Sage has very comfortable beds."

He drew back, those shrewd eyes blurry and confused before he seemed to come back to himself. He brushed his nose along mine. "All your fault, fairy queen. You make me forget myself."

"I thought I made you want to throttle me." My lips twitched as he wrapped my long braid around his palm.

"Oh, you definitely do that. I'll just have to find other ways to keep your mouth busy."

The laugh rolled out of me. "Is that so?"

He seemed to realize what he'd said and frowned. "I'm sorry, I—"

I shushed him with my finger to his lips. "I don't mind a cocky response now and then."

"I'm not that guy. At least not with women."

I drew the pad of my finger over the little wrinkle between his furrowed brows. "Neither of us are doing what we normally do tonight. Let's just be spontaneous and go with it."

"That's not—"

I kissed him hard. "That's what spontaneity is, LC. Not doing your usual. Now take me to bed or lose me forever."

He let out a strangled laugh. "Did you just quote *Top Gun* at me?"

I shrugged. "I watch a lot of movies. Especially the good ones. And if you can play the piano, then I definitely found my Goose."

"Not your Maverick?"

I felt like that might be a bit of a test. "Let's see if I get the best of both worlds then." I opened my door and he sighed. I leaned back in. "What?"

"I can't even be a gentleman for a moment."

"Oh, that's so cute." I nodded to the Hummingbird's Nest. "I'll race you to the door." I slipped a bit on the snow, but almost kept my footing. Until Mr. Helpful hooked his arm around me and we both went down like a pair of children.

Rory's face was covered in the cold, fluffy snow, and I couldn't stop the screeching laughter.

"Again, thwarted." He pushed himself up and almost lost his arm in the deep snow. I rolled him over with a laugh. His eyes were dancing as he looked up at me. "You do know it's like two in the morning..." He raised his hand out of the drift and checked his watch. "Make that three."

"Hmm. You telling me to be quiet?"

"I don't give a fuck. I just want to keep hearing that laugh. Even if it's at my expense."

I lowered myself on top of him. "Do you understand the difference between with and at?"

"I do." He pushed a few loose bits of hair out of my face. "My best mate definitely laughs at me."

I curled my hand around his wrist. "Then you should know this is definitely with. Sex should be fun. Especially the pre-sex stuff." I kissed him again, our lips slick and cool from the snow still falling around us.

Before it could get too out of control again, I rolled off of him into the snow and quickly opened and closed my legs to make a snow angel. I looked over at him. He seemed confused as he rolled up onto his elbow.

"Fun, LC. Remember?"

He sighed and dropped onto his back and followed suit.

Content to stare up at the sky and watch the snow globe level snowflakes swirling in the sky, we both stayed there for a few minutes. I looked over and he had a crooked little smile on his face.

DANGER!

Do not fall in love with this man!

A red flasher in the back of my head tried to turn on, but I stomped it out. I was wearing four-inch platforms. I could do such things.

I didn't want to hold anything back. There would be no tomorrow. Tonight was just us being us, no matter which way the dice fell onto the table. I found his cold hand in the snow and pulled him up with me. "Time for you to warm me up, LC."

The night sky matched his hooded eyes. He was actually looking at me as if I was a sexual creature capable of inciting desire. Me, with my braids and crazy sixties' outfit. August's little sister who had a little fence around her when it came to some guys.

Do not cross.

Do not mess with August's little sister.

Luckily, Rory Ferguson of California didn't know such things. And I was going to use that knowledge to the fullest. No holding back.

"Should I be worried about that expression?"

"Maybe."

"Queen fairy indeed."

I took his cold hand and dragged him behind me to the front door of the Hummingbird's Nest. He fumbled the key out of his pocket behind me and we both tumbled into the foyer. It was empty and silent. A note on the desk said no one would be there until morning—well, a few more hours since it was well past three at this point.

Rory steered me away from the desk to the stairs. I talked to Sage now and then, but I wasn't quite in her circle of people. Of course I talked to everyone since I worked at the diner, but Sage was always at the bed and breakfast, so she didn't come by that often.

That and she had her hands full with her husband and child.

Again, that pang hit me. The same one that compelled me to join the baby meetings at the café. How could I not get a touch of baby fever with all the coupling going on in the town?

I pushed that thought away. This wasn't about babies. This was about me taking something for myself that wasn't attached to work or my brothers. Or my ice cream plans, which were taking over my whole world.

Nope, this was just for me. To feel like a woman who was wanted. Heck, so I felt like a flesh and blood woman all around.

Rory turned back to me as we headed up the spiral staircase. A look of concentration was back on his face. Like I was a puzzle he was still trying to figure out.

I rushed up to meet him, curling my arm around his middle so I could get my cold hands under his sweater.

He gave a little yelp, but pushed me against the wall as we got to the top of the stairs. I smoothed my hand around his back when he eased his knee between my legs. I love how smooth he was along his back and the rough chest hair along the front of him. What would it feel like against my skin?

Would he leave me pink and abraded? Or would it just wind me up more?

"Being thinky," he said against my mouth.

"Haven't done this in a while."

The lines reappeared between his brows. "How long is awhile?"

I brought my hand back around to the front of his torso again. I found a necklace the higher up I went. I toyed with the disk before I tunneled my nails through the hair between his pecs. Thank God it was so late, because we were being improper in such a fancy place. "It's not my first time. I just haven't had much opportunity since college."

"How long ago was college? A second?"

I smiled. "Is that your way of trying to ask me how old I am, Mr. Ferguson?"

His gaze narrowed. "Should I be wondering?" He tugged on one of my braids. "It's not right for a grown man to be this lustful toward a woman with braids."

"Lustful? I like the sound of that."

He pressed his zipper against my belly. "You know what you're doing to me, Ivy."

I shivered. Hearing him say *Ivy* made me crazy. I rather loved the fairy queen moniker, but there was something about his accent and my name. A low rolling timber of music. I had always thought my name was old-fashioned, but it sounded lyrical on his tongue.

"Say it again."

His eyebrow shot up. "That you're near jailbait?"

I nipped his scruffy chin. "My name, sir."

"Oh, is that what you're after?" His accent got a little thicker. "Are you looking for this, my fairy queen?"

I rolled my lips behind my teeth with a soft groan. "Is it so wrong to enjoy your accent?"

"All you American ladies do seem to get off on it."

It was my turn for an eyebrow raise. "I'm not just one of your American chick hookups."

"Aren't you though?"

I kicked his boot.

He laughed and curled tighter around me. "No, Ivy Beck, there's been nothing and no one like you before. Or will be after, I'd wager."

Before I could unpack that compliment or statement or whatever it was, he dragged me back into the whirling sensations of his kiss. He rocked against me as he took my mouth into a long, slow turn of lips and tongue. He kissed me like he'd been doing it for years, not for less than an hour.

Thoughtful and restless with just the lightest hint of...*more*. I couldn't put my finger on what, but I chased it. Consuming and overwhelming, his taste burned my tongue and seared into my memories. He brought his hands up to cup my face and hold me there for him to plunder and own.

I shivered at each dip of his tongue and roll of his hips against me. My nails dug into his sides to ground myself, because I wanted to hold onto this moment and not think about the future, just live in the now. Tomorrow would be coming soon enough.

My heart raced as I went onto my toes to get closer to him even as he was backing up.

"Room." He swallowed as if he was trying to find oxygen. "I need you under me."

"Yes."

He walked backwards down the hall, watching me the entire time. His seductive eyes drew me forward, but the low light of the hallway didn't give anything away. Was he thinking about how quickly he could get me naked? It seemed like it was so much more than that.

Silly. It was just because we were alone and worked up. Nothing more.

He stopped at a door with sunflowers and a tiny family of sparrows nestled into a wreath. That was me, the sparrow that was used to doing her job, staying in the safe confines of her world.

Mercy, I was getting fanciful.

Maybe it was the wildness of the moment. The way he touched me like he couldn't stop. But it was just a moment.

And that was all this could be. It was enough. It had to be.

He opened the door and flicked on the light then turned to me with his hand outstretched.

I told myself that again and again as I put my hand in his and let him lead me into the softly lit room. The fire was going, flames licking up from a wash of colorless, glittering stones. This room wasn't as cozy as I'd been expecting.

It was cool and modern with touches of the sunflower on the door to warm it up. It suited the situation. Pretty lies wrapped over cool perfection. Neither one of us were bringing our truths. We'd just found a connection to hold onto.

It had been so long since I'd felt an instant connection with someone. I'd been working toward my future for so long, I forgot to look at the now.

I turned to Rory. His blue eyes were full of heat—for me. It seemed so overwhelming and alien, exciting and incomprehensible.

My fingers trembled a little as I unzipped my vest, tossing it on the warm yellow chair in the corner. Rory's gaze never wavered even as I slowly tugged the end of one of my braids free.

He walked toward me, the bulge in his jeans still as impressive as it felt against me in the hall. But there was no hurry in his step. All the rushing seemed to have been left outside these doors.

He drew me deeper into the room toward the fire. My fingers weren't trembling from cold, but it was sweet that he thought so.

Coming closer, he took my other braid and mirrored my slow unwind of hair. My one vanity. It wasn't practical to have it so long considering all the jobs I had, but watching him spear his fingers through it and lay it over my chest made me shiver all over again.

When both braids were done and the waves fell down my back, he leaned in and kissed me, filling his hands with my thick hair. He massaged the back of my head, and each kiss went deeper until I couldn't resist the urge to lean into his touch for more.

He tugged at my shirt and tossed it aside, his lips going for my neck as he tugged lightly on my scalp to keep my head tipped back. With his other hand, he softly drew the backs of his knuckles along my midriff to the line of my breasts, but never over them. I thanked all the gods I knew that Kinleigh had demanded a full treatment for the sixties' outfit I was wearing. The bra was a little more modern, but the smooth silk made my okay breasts look way better than the ill-fitting bras I was forever fighting with.

He dropped into the high-backed chair by the fireplace and drew me down to straddle him. My hair was a curtain of fire, thanks to the flames behind me.

Rory's hands slid down to my waist to tug me as close as possible, making sure I felt just how hard he was. I rolled my hips lightly as we kissed until we were both breathless with it. His fingers slipped up my back and undid my bra. The straps fell forward, but he didn't look at my breasts. No, his gaze was on mine as he slowly stripped everything away from me.

I wanted to feel him too.

I pushed at his sweater until it was up and over his head. We both hissed as my breasts swayed against his hair roughened chest. His fingers sunk into my hair, dragging my head back to get to my neck and finally, the tips of my breasts.

I let out a harsh, surprised groan as he sucked the tip of one. After all the sweet, soft touches, the harsh pull and tiny bite seemed to catapult me past the dreamy veil of lust into a technicolor reality. My nails dug into his chest, sliding down to his hard belly, to his pants.

He cupped my breasts and ravaged my mouth as I ripped at his belt and zipper. I needed him closer. Needed to know he was just as wound up as me.

He filled my hand as I finally looked at him. Finally met his gaze and found crackling intensity where there had been patience.

"It's been too long, Ivy. I'm hanging on by my fingernails here." He nudged my hair out of my face. "I want everything." He coasted his thumb across the hard tip of my breast, then pinched it until I gasped. "I want to take my time, but I think I'm going to go mad if I don't get inside you."

I stroked down the impressive length of him. "You're not the only one."

"Maybe we're not ready for you to get inside of me tonight, yeah?"

I laughed. "That's a whole different kind of evening."

His laugh was choked and rumbling. "Not that I wouldn't do just about anything you asked right now." He groaned. "Not that I should be saying that to a woman who has her hands around my cock."

"Then it's a good thing I want one thing right now." I slid off his lap and swallowed back a groan of my own at the reality of Rory sitting before me with his dick so hard it was pushing against his lower belly.

I kicked off my platforms and lost a few inches, but Rory sure didn't.

Dear Lord, I wasn't sure what I was going to do with all of that, but I was going to find out. I wiggled out of the tight pants, kicking them away with my shoes. "Sorry, the panties don't match the cute bra."

"You're fucking gorgeous."

My breath stalled and everything went warm. His voice rattled as if sandpaper and a storm were dueling in his chest. I took his hand and drew him in front of me. He towered over me now. The uncertainty in his eyes just wouldn't do.

I was tiny compared to his broad shoulders and athletically lean body. I liked that he wasn't all rippling muscle. He was real. There were plenty of muscles going on and he was fit as all get out, but it was more like a guy who liked to play sports than one who lived in the gym.

I drew my nail around the medal he wore. I couldn't quite make out the saint, but it was old and looked as if it had been handed down or worn forever. The chain was long enough that it was probably hidden more than shown in his life. My touch drifted lower to the line of hair that dipped to his open buckle.

The thick ridge of his cock pushed at the black cotton. I was tempted to hit my knees for the first time in...well, ever. Oral was rarely first on any girl's list, but something about the way he looked at me made me want to taste him. To have him watch me.

He lifted his hand to cup my face. "Sweet Christ, I'd die if you do what I think you want to do."

I stepped closer, pulling the band of his boxers away from his hardness. "Is that right?"

"Siren."

I grinned. "I thought I was a fairy."

"You're temptation in all its forms."

"I rather like the sound of that." But that was all I was able to get out. He swooped down and kissed me hard, wrapping his arm around my waist to lift me against him. We fell onto the bed in a tangle of limbs and laughter.

He lifted me up against him as he shoved pillows out of the way to get me on my back. His mouth was everywhere. My lips, my neck, my shoulder. I couldn't get up out of the hole we were making in the pillow-top mattress.

I wrapped my legs around his waist. The line of his smooth, hard cock slipped between my thighs to bump my aching flesh. His fingers fumbled between us to push my panties aside, and he groaned at what he found.

I pressed my forehead into his shoulder. I was slightly embarrassed at the state I was in. Definitely not one of the cool, calm girls he was probably used to. Posh and unaffected.

Me? All of the affected. I was going to go out of my damn mind if he didn't make me come soon.

No woman should be this wound up. It couldn't be healthy for this kind of crazy to settle into my bones.

I lifted my hips to slide him against me. Anything to get some friction going. The ridged maze of veins along his shaft hit me just where I needed him. I pushed closer. "Rory."

"Christ, you're so fucking hot." He knelt between my thighs, widening my legs so he could drape one over each side.

I was drowning in pillows. I wanted to see him. I pushed the remaining ones off the bed and got up on my elbows as he slicked his thumb through my folds. I drew in a deep breath and tried to stay in the moment as he found my clit and made maddening circles around it. His hair had fallen forward to tease his eyes. It gave him a younger, softer appearance until I looked a little closer.

There was nothing soft about the way he watched me. He stroked his cock with the same, slow sure way he touched me. As if he was figuring out a combination between the two of us.

He clenched his jaw as he tightened his grip on his shaft. I tried to reach for him, but he shook his head. "I'm too close, Ivy. Give me just a moment."

"I don't want you to wait a moment."

He groaned and pushed forward, replacing his fingers with the head of his cock.

"Yes. Yes, inside me." Just the tip slid past the lace and my own drenched slit.

"Fuck." He scrambled back.

"Rory."

He vaulted off the bed to kick off his pants and pull out his wallet. "Sweet Blessed Jesus. I don't even know if I have anything on me."

"Oh." I pushed my hair out of my eyes. I was so far gone I didn't even think about protection. God, that was beyond stupid.

"Please, please." He tucked his finger along the inside pocket of his wallet and held up a condom like it was a prize.

Right about now, it was. The best prize ever.

I crawled over to the edge of the bed. "Hurry."

With shaking fingers, he ripped open the packet and rolled it down his length. "Fucking orange."

I laughed and dragged him on top of me. "I don't care what color it is, just that you have one."

"Fuck yeah." He crawled between my thighs and took himself in hand. Our eyes locked as he settled against me and slowly, so slowly, filled me.

The laughter drifted away. I winced at the fullness at first. It had been a few years since I'd done this. How many times had I just been a means to an end by the time this part came to pass?

Rory slid his arm under me and tipped my hips up to take me deeper. I gasped at the angle and when he drew out, I gripped his ass to bring him back into me. "So deep."

"So good," he said and covered my mouth.

I curled around him as he built up the tempo until we were both gasping and driving toward a common goal. Each thrust was more perfect than the last until there was no space between us. Just his hips and mine moving in tandem.

His fingers tangled into my hair as he twisted me onto my side and came at me from behind. He dragged my knee up and out until the cloying heat between us was now gone and my sweaty skin was shocked by the cool air. My nipples went tight and I bowed back as his mouth skimmed over that place on my neck that only he seemed to know how to find.

He brought his hand down to where he was sliding in and out of me and gave me just what I needed. One arm was banded around me as the other played me like a song until my thighs were shaking and my throat was hoarse from my screams.

The low, harsh groan in my ear was followed by my name in a twisted phrase I didn't understand. It wasn't English. Just a mumble of words with the sweetest lilt of something more.

I was too destroyed to hold onto it though. I had to worry about sucking down oxygen as pure pleasure drowned me.

Rory pulled out of me, then gently tucked me into the sheets before getting up to deal with the condom.

"Is this what lust drunk is?" Even I could hear how dazed my voice sounded.

He climbed back into bed behind me, this time with his boxers on. "No drunk I've ever been has felt that good."

I smiled into the firelight. I liked the sound of that. "Me neither," I whispered into the quiet.

He drew little circles on my belly with his fingertips until I was just about ready to drift off. But I had one more thing to say. "If I don't see you before you leave in the morning, just know I loved every part of this."

It might've been my imagination, but I thought he murmured, "Me too."

SIX

Rory

ROLLING AWAY FROM IVY NEAR SUNRISE TO GO TO KELLAN seemed like cruel and unusual punishment.

He'd texted me a bit ago, saying the kid seemed better. Loosely interpreted to mean: *come now or don't come at all.*

So, I showered and got dressed and left a note behind for Ivy to enjoy the room while I was working. It still seemed like a dick move, ducking out with a note on the bedside table. But I couldn't miss this appointment. It was the very reason I'd come this far in the first place.

Being with Ivy had been fun. More than I'd had in a lifetime. I still had no illusions that she'd be there when I returned.

One-nighters weren't meant to extend past daylight. That was best for her—and for me.

She was a small town girl and I was a big city guy. By choice. By lifestyle. The walls of the town had been closing in on me since I arrived.

Even if everything looked a lot different with the soft light of morning and a night spent so pleasurably behind me. My muscles were still loose from the hot shower.

And from Ivy.

I scraped the snow and icy shite off my windshield with a credit card and my jacket sleeve. I might be in a better mood for obvious reasons, but I was no more enamored of snow.

Playing with Ivy in it had been entertaining. She was like a candle in the darkness. Snow itself, however, was vile.

I got behind the wheel and started the engine and the heater. I still needed gas and would take care of that before I set off for Kellan's.

Pumping gas when it was nearly subzero bloody well sucked. At least the storm had finally mostly ended.

Bright side? It was much easier to find Kellan's cabin in the woods when the road wasn't fully obscured by a curtain of white. Fancy that.

I parked at the end of the driveway behind a hulking Jeep and a mini SUV and got out to more snow pelting me in the face, this time from the branches of the tree above me. A peeved-looking squirrel shook the branch again just for spite.

I tipped my hand to him. "Try getting laid, mate. I've found it brightens the mood."

Something came flying at me and landed on my sneaker.

A nut.

I laughed out loud.

"Don't give up faith. I had to wait too. Gotta watch for opportunities."

"Who the hell are you talking to?" Kellan's voice boomed from the little porch behind me. I turned and found him looming in the doorway, massive and broad-shouldered and blue faux-hawked as always. Only difference from his publicity snaps was the baby clad in a snuggly sweater, jeans, and boots in his arms.

The kid was crying. Surprise.

"Does that child ever stop squalling?" It was a better question than explaining I'd just been conversing with a squirrel about sex.

At least the squirrel hadn't conversed back. That would've been problematic.

"He's sick. He's also two. Those things tend to cause babies to cry." His son picked that moment to cluck Kellan in the chin, who barely flinched. Must be used to such abuse.

I shook my head, glancing at the squirrel out of the corner of my eye. He had another nut between his paws, ready to launch.

Next one he threw, I was lobbing it back. I was in a good mood—hell, a great one—but that didn't mean I'd tolerate rudeness.

"Are you coming inside, or would you rather debate the behavior of children from the driveway?"

Kellan's even tone made me chuckle. He was such a father. How did that change happen? I had to imagine Kellan had been the typical rockstar, pre-wife and baby. Did a light just go on one day and the appeal of groupies lessened?

I didn't have such interactions with the fairer sex because let's face it, I did not look like Kellan. The guy probably weighed close to two-hundred pounds, most of it muscle. He also had swagger and killer pipes. I was more on the intellectual side of things, which meant my appeal to women waxed and waned depending on my rep. When I had my name on a few hits, the offers came fast and furious. When I was in a dry period, my phone didn't ring.

The time or two I'd sat in with my mate Ian's band, I'd nearly had to hire a goddamn bodyguard to keep the women away. But I didn't do that often. And even when the access was there, I rarely took advantage.

I had sex as stress relief. Relationships I barely had at all. The last time I'd been serious with a woman hadn't ended well.

Understatement of the century. So, I'd learned to steer clear.

Mostly.

God only knows how Ivy had viewed my unpracticed seduction routine. We'd been together, so I supposed I couldn't have done too badly. She'd had enough grace to forgive me in any case. I was hardly the slick rockstar, even if I had occasion to pick up a guitar and sing now and then. Usually when I'd had a few too many with Ian in the pub.

And Kellan was staring at me, probably hoping a Bluetooth headset would appear so he could feel more at ease that I had not been talking to the air.

"Squirrel," I said as I made my way up the neatly shoveled walk. "I was talking to the squirrel."

"Uh..."

"Never mind."

We went inside and the kid stopped crying long enough to knuckle his big blue eyes and stare at me, much as his father had. Did I have a sign on my head or something?

Noticing Kellan was in his socks, I removed my boots. The kid watched me the whole time, whimpering softly.

"Why is he looking at me?"

"Maybe he doesn't like Irishmen."

"Is that so, Mr. McGuire?"

Kellan grinned. "He's a baby. Didn't say he made sense."

"Uh-huh. How's he doing today? Minus the sniffling."

Kellan glanced down at his son. "He's still feverish and he's doing...that." He sighed as the baby rubbed his ear against Kellan's chest. "We think he might have an ear infection. If he's not better this morning, Maggie will bundle him off to—"

"Where is my child?" A beautiful blue-eyed brunette woman wearing jeans and a thick pink sweater rushed into the foyer, stopping dead at the sight of me. "Oh, hello. You must be Rory. I'm sorry you got lost and weren't able to make it last night."

I slid a look at Kellan, who was fussing with his suddenly quiet child. "Yes, it was a shame. Maggie, is it? Pleasure to meet you." I stepped forward and shook her hand. "You have a lovely home." Not that I'd seen much of it yet, other than the quaint porch with its pair of snow-covered rockers and the small foyer that opened up into a recessed, rustic living room with log walls, exposed beam ceilings, and a large fireplace.

The fireplace made me think of Ivy. And hope she wasn't dressed yet.

So much for a one-nighter, hmm?

"Thank you, but it's Kellan's place. Or it was. I just sort of stumbled upon it." She smiled in a wide, affable way that made me wonder if she was also a Crescent Cove transplant. "We've added on, of course. And I've put in my own touches."

"Like that thing." Kellan nodded at a colorful quilt that took up much of one wall near the door.

Unrepentantly, Maggie flipped him the middle finger. I did a double take.

Well, then, this was the kind of marriage I could get behind.

"You bang on your little drum all day and I make quilts." She tossed her hair and smiled at me again. "Can I get you anything before you get to work? Have you eaten?"

I hadn't, but surprisingly, I was more interested in seeing this dynamic at play than I was at filling my belly. I was a student of human interaction. Being a voyeur was helpful in my business, since knowing how people ticked was a cornerstone of writing songs. Not to mention figuring out how to deal with thorny personalities was an asset in my line of work.

I'd also never seen a marriage work quite like this. In my own home, my parents had rarely argued. Or spoken, period. They didn't have fire between them—at least not visibly, excepting the three children they'd made—and that was what I'd always sought. Or I had, until Darla.

I frowned. Since when had I sought anything? I was happily single. Unfettered. Unconcerned.

Horny as hell, even still.

Clearly, sex was dangerous to a man's way of life. Good sex was like mental gasoline. Great sex could burn down a psyche and rebuild it from the ground up.

Hmm, I'd have to work that into a lyric.

I smiled at Maggie. "I haven't, no, but could I trouble you for coffee? Black, please."

She smiled back with a nod before deftly snagging her child from Kellan and toting him down the hall.

Kellan watched her go, shaking his head. "Is it any wonder I knocked her up the night we met? She's hot as fuck."

I lifted my brows. Looked as if I'd be getting an education.

"You weren't in baby town, were you? I've heard it's easier there. Probably because there's nothing to do out here but shovel or screw."

Kellan laughed so hard I worried he'd dislodged a vocal cord. "Nope. We were here. Though we get water from Crescent Cove."

"Hmm." I wasn't going to dwell on that overmuch, seeing as I'd just spent the night with a lovely resident of Crescent Cove myself.

Next time, perhaps I should suit up in double-walled Latex. Did such a thing exist?

Of course there wouldn't be a next time. By the time I got back to town, Ivy would likely be long gone, her light minty scent all that remained on the sheets.

I smiled. But the memories of my sweet ginger fairy in firelight would always be mine.

"So, how about a tour? We're still adding on, as you can see." He gestured vaguely down the hall to where construction debris littered the doorway between the kitchen and dining room. "But we have another guest room now besides Wolf's room and we have the studio. All new additions. I built this place just for me."

I eyed his muscled biceps, nearly bursting through his T-shirt. "You built it? I'm not surprised."

He grunted and led me through the living room to the dining room. The open concept of the place made it seem bigger than it actually was. "I had help."

On our way past the kitchen, Maggie offered me a cup of steaming black coffee, nicely offset with a couple of scones. I bit into one as we entered the small studio on the other side of the kitchen and let out a sound that I'd never heard myself make before.

Unless I recalled last night with Ivy...

"Bacon and egg scones," Kellan said knowingly. "It's basically a breakfast cookie."

I'd eaten half the thing before I came up for air to see the studio. It was a nice one, equipped with far more than the usual home setup. A capable mixing board lined one wall. In front of it sat a couple of cushy chairs, strategically placed rugs for acoustics, and a damn near plethora of instruments. The other walls held a few framed gold records.

"Get those on eBay, did you now?"

"Smart ass."

"Are you planning on returning to your band?" I gestured at the gold records with the second half of my scone, before I ate it as swiftly as I'd consumed the first half. Maggie was a magician.

"I never left it. Those are my brothers. I'm just branching out while we're on hiatus."

I ran my fingers over the scone. They were the perfect texture for dunking. "Uh-huh."

"Before you consider trying to steal my wife from me, be advised that's one of the few things she makes well. Most of her meals come charbroiled—and not on purpose."

"I heard that," Maggie called from the kitchen, making us both laugh. "Remember that when you tell me you want an early bedtime."

"Who needs a bed?"

I would've responded in kind if I hadn't already resumed eating— well, dunking now. Whether they counted as one of her few dishes or not, these scones were a gift from God.

"Maggie, you're a goddess behind a stove," I called.

Kellan snorted. "He wants more scones."

I did not confirm nor deny, but I was quite pleased when Maggie brought in another plate of them after we'd sat at the console.

"Thank you, love. Much appreciated."

"Look at the manners on this one. You could learn a thing or seventeen, Kel."

"You adore me for my rough exterior."

"You mean despite it." She flounced out.

"It's embarrassing how she fawns over me." Kellan rummaged through a drawer for a pad and pencil, then set his latest model iPhone on a stand. Lyrics scrolled by on the screen. At least he'd come to play ball.

Me? I'd come to eat. Obviously.

"So, this is just a project to keep you busy while you're away from the band."

"No."

"Then?"

I expected sarcasm in return but he dipped back his head. "Guess I want to see who I am outside of the group. If I still have anything worthwhile to say."

Sadly, I took a bolstering sip of the rich brew and set aside the remaining scones. Then I took out my phone and found my recording app. "So, let's see what we have."

We put in a couple of hours—with Kellan on his guitar and some lyrics he'd been working on, and me at the board experimenting with different sounds and elements to complement what he'd come up with. We'd finally started getting somewhere when Maggie appeared in the doorway in her coat and scarf with her surprisingly quiet son in her arms. His cheeks were bright red. Unnaturally so.

"I have to take him to urgent care. He's so hot, Kel." The baby leaned his head on his mother's shoulder. He looked so miserable that even my chest squeezed.

Kellan was on his feet in an instant. "I'm coming too."

"No, no, you have work—"

"Work can wait." Kellan set down his guitar and glanced at me. "I'm sorry, man. I know you came all this way and how in demand you are, but I have to be with my son and my wife." He blew out a breath. "We were really sounding good though, and you actually gave me some ideas for where to go with this song. If you can't extend your trip, I understand. And I appreciate all you've done for me so far." He stuck out his hand.

I stared at it, shaking my head as I rose. "You must take me for a real tosser."

Kellan drew back his hand. "Say what?"

"Your son is sick. Your woman needs you. All of this," I gestured at the sweet mixing board I hadn't gotten nearly enough time to play with, "can wait."

"You'll extend your trip?"

"I can't do that." Although it troubled me how much a part of me desperately wanted to. And probably not because of Kellan.

Maybe I was a tosser.

"Oh." Kellan tried to keep his face expressionless, but he didn't quite achieve it. "Understandable. You're in hot demand."

"Keep talking like that, you'll swell my head. I'm busy, yes, but I'll be back. Once your boy is on the mend, we'll figure out a date."

I wasn't thinking about seeing Ivy again. A one-night stand was plenty.

Liar.

"Thanks, man. I can't tell you how much I appreciate it." Kellan pulled me into a quick hug. He nearly dislocated both my shoulders from his grip, but I maintained my cool and patted his back before he moved away.

The air tasted sweet as it again flowed into my compromised lungs.

"No problem. Working with you was fun. We're on our way to creating a hit." I drained the last of my cold coffee and pocketed the rest of the scones without shame. I'd eat them in the car if need be.

Drowning my sorrows in cookies as I drove back to my most certainly empty room at the bed and breakfast? Maybe. It seemed like a noble cause.

"Thank you for your delicacies and for sharing your home, Maggie. And I hope your baby is well soon." I leaned in to give

Maggie a hug, shocked into silence when she cupped my face and kissed my cheek.

"You're welcome here anytime. I'm sorry your plans were messed up. Next time, it'll be spring and this one will be better. Right, little man?" Her voice was cheerful as she jiggled her son in her arms, but there was no missing the fear pinching her mouth.

My chest squeezed again as Wolf knuckled his eyes and tried to smile. It was probably gas, but the gesture touched me almost as much as his mother's kindness.

Swallowing hard, I glanced at Kellan. "You're a lucky man. Keep me posted on how he is."

Shockingly, I meant every word.

Kellan walked me out. As soon as I'd pulled out of the drive, Kellan and his family followed in the small SUV.

I let out a long breath and reached for my pocket. I'd finished off my purloined scones before I reached Crescent Cove's town limits.

Snow dripped from every bough and eave and glistened in the now full sun. Townspeople bustled up the tidily shoveled sidewalks with their hands full of shopping bags or tugging on leashes that led to an assortment of dogs, both small and large. I'd figured this was the type of place where teacup poodles reigned, but there were just as many German Shepherds and Labradors.

It was a home, not merely a postcard, and though some people rushed, no one scowled. The weather wasn't ideal and no one seemed to notice.

Where the hell was I? Had I been dropped onto another planet?

People seemed so oddly happy here. Perhaps that was why the townspeople's reproductive organs operated at peak efficiency.

That was as good an explanation as any other.

I parked near the bed and breakfast and climbed out of the car to empty crumbs from my pocket. There weren't many. Maggie's scones were like gold.

I was still licking my fingertips when I stepped inside and found

Sage helping a couple of guests. I figured I could sneak up the stairs undetected, but no such luck.

"There you are!" Sage smiled brightly. "And here I thought you were still holed up in your room."

"No indeed, in and out for business."

Sage smiled knowingly. "As we realized when Lucy knocked for housekeeping. A lovely young lady told her to come back later."

My ears and neck were heating up, but they weren't flushed. That would be ridiculous. I was a grown man. If I wanted to entertain female company in my suite, I was damn well entitled.

Before I could come back with some snark, Sage continued.

"Ivy is a beauty, isn't she? Bright and sweet too. If you had to choose a welcoming committee to Crescent Cove, you couldn't find anyone finer. Have a wonderful time." Sage winked at me and turned to the couple that had just shuffled up to the desk.

"It's lunchtime," I sputtered.

"So? Any time is a good time for *amore*. Am I right or am I right?" Sage asked the couple.

I didn't stick around for their response.

It was only as I climbed the stairs that hope surged inside me. My step quickened. If Ivy had still been in the room when housekeeping arrived, might she still be there?

I stopped outside my door and knocked, just to be polite. "Ivy? It's me."

No reply.

I opened the door to the suite and let out a long breath at the destruction around me. Nothing too horrifying, but there was little doubt a female was still in residence.

Thank God.

A noise came from the bathroom and I cocked my head. She was singing. I couldn't help a grin. Her voice was pleasing, as appealing as the rest of her. Even if she wasn't exactly nailing the lyrics of the song she'd decided to attempt.

I moved to the doorway and came to a halt. She was in the tub, surrounded by fragrant bubbles. Her hair was up but some spilled free to her shoulders. Barely contained fire. Her eyes were closed and her breasts bobbed and swayed as she danced in place, her tight pink nipples popping through the froth to torment me.

My throat went dry, my pulse sped up, and my jeans suddenly got a size smaller.

Christ, she was going to kill me.

Did the morning-after—okay, afternoon-after—count as an extension of a one-nighter?

Guess we were about to find out.

SEVEN

 IVY

Bubbles frothed around my neck. Perhaps a bath bomb *and* bubbles wasn't the way to go. Then again, I'd never been in such a luxurious tub. Not quite the *Pretty Woman* size, but I was going with it.

If I was going to be treated to a swanky room for my one-night stand, I damn well better use it.

My first reaction had been to ball up his note and pitch it on my way out the door with a flounce. But I was alone, so the flounce was just stupid.

No sense in wasting me time. Living with my brother didn't allow for much of it. And I really didn't need to do the walk of shame just yet. So, tub, my bitchy playlist, and my AirPods it was.

Fuck Rory Ferguson for being such a good lay.

I didn't want to keep thinking about him. Charlie Puth in my ears certainly didn't help. Fitting song though. I smoothed the bubbles along my arms and sang about attention and the gossipy nature of a relationship.

Not exactly us. Gossip would require caring about what we did.

And I didn't.

Time to stop feeling sorry for myself.

I slowly sat up, the bubbles and water flowing over my shoulders. My nipples tightened at the change of temperature.

"You are a sight."

My eyes popped open. Rory stood in the doorway, his arms crossed over his chest, pulling at the sporty collared sweater he was wearing. My gaze raked down over his lean waist to the strong thighs making his jeans way too appealing.

Especially with the obvious bulge showing there as well.

I ducked back under the suds. "How long have you been there?"

"Long enough to hear you butcher Charlie's song."

I pulled out my AirPods. "Rude." He shrugged. Was that a smirk? Ugh, such a shit. "I wasn't singing for you."

"Pity. I was still enjoying it."

"What are you doing here?" All the bubbles I'd been so worried about were suddenly disappearing at a rapid rate. I tried to pull them toward me, but they were dissolving as quickly as I tried to gather them.

"Are you trying to hide from me, ginger fairy?"

"No."

He stepped into the room and the huge bathroom instantly felt smaller. I wasn't worldly enough to throw my shoulders back and invite him in. Besides, the water was already getting cold. And I wasn't sure I wanted another round with him.

Not when he'd left with a note.

Though it was probably more than most women got after a wild night of sex with a stranger. I mean, it was sort of wild. It had certainly been athletic and memorable. At least for me anyway. Probably another day at the office for him.

He took a fluffy towel off the rack and stood at the side of the tub. "I've seen everything."

"It's different when there's daylight. And when I'm pruny."

His eyebrow spiked. "Should I leave then?" He set the towel back on the rack.

I blew the little hairs that had come free from my messy knot out of my face. "Why are you here?"

He reached over to turn on the taps and unplug the drain. "My meeting had...complications." He unhooked the fancy rain hood and switched the lever to turn the flowing water to the shower setting.

I frowned when he held out his hand for me.

"You want the bubbles rinsed off, yeah?"

"Right."

He held out the shower head. "We don't have to do anything more if you're not interested. I can leave you be."

"You still haven't answered me." I stood and the water sluiced down off of me. Far too little bubbles were left to cover any part of me.

His eyes did that hooded thing like last night. Just before he fucked me into the mattress. I stood still as a gentle flow of water at the perfect temperature rinsed away the minty bubbles.

Truly, how could I resist my favorite scent waiting for me when I spotted the tub?

His Adam's apple bobbed hard. "Turn." His voice was harsh and gritty.

I slowly turned until my back was to him. I shut my eyes and swayed a little. His eyes felt so heavy on me. His breath was light on my neck as the water flowed over my lower back and the curve of my ass.

The water stopped and I was about to turn around when his lips brushed along my neck. He cupped my breasts, tugging lightly on the tips as he slowly sipped from my wet skin.

He tucked his chin over my shoulder. "You're the most beautiful woman I've ever seen."

I covered his hands. "I doubt that, but it's lovely to hear."

He nipped at my jaw. "I don't lie."

I couldn't help the dreamy smile. "I don't suppose you do."

"That's one thing you don't have to worry about." His hand slid down my belly, his short nails leaving the lightest trail through the moisture clinging to my skin.

"Good to know."

His touch slid lower again, teasing through the narrow strip of curls that framed my slit. I was still sensitive, but I ached for him to fill me up again.

"Is this your version of seduction?"

"Does it make up for me leaving?"

I leaned back against him. The fine blend of his sweater made me straighten. "I'm going to get you wet."

"Not if I get you wet first."

My laugh ended in a groan as he slid two fingers into me. I had no choice but to lean on him. Not when his fingers were that freaking talented. My thighs trembled and I arched away from him as the last of the bubbles swirled around my feet.

I reached behind to grasp his hair, his name a sigh and a half scream as black dots played like fireworks across my vision. He held me tighter against him, his cock digging into me, but he didn't let me go.

He swayed and moved with me as I rocked through one orgasm and yet another before I sagged against him.

Whoa.

He wrapped a towel around me and scooped me out of the bath, then carted me into the bedroom.

"Wait."

He frowned down at me.

My teeth chattered a little as I came back from the quick trip to Euphoriaville. I curled into the blanket-sized towel and tucked my face into his warm neck. "If this is going for another round, I thought you might be happy to know Sage outfitted the medicine cabinet."

"She is a wonder. Practically congratulated me before I came up to the room."

I laughed. "Sounds like her. I started at the diner after she left, but I've heard some serious stories about her."

He set me down on the bed and tucked me into the covers. He rubbed the back of his neck. "I don't want to assume anything, nor to have the town talking about you."

I snuggled into the fluffy and very warm duvet. "I'm a big girl, LC."

He grunted, but he damn well returned to the bathroom. He came back into the room and set the small box of condoms on the end table before making a pit stop at the fireplace to set the fire to blazing.

Now that I was under the covers and the winter sun was streaming in the window, I was warming nicely, but I appreciated the gesture. Especially with the look on his face. It said that I was going to be losing the towel momentously.

I shivered as he stood before me.

"Still chilled?"

I shook my head *no* as I bit my lower lip.

"You'll be the death of me."

My smile was slow and wide as my arm shot out to drag him onto the bed. His boots thumped to the floor. A rare laugh tumbled from his lips as he stripped out of his jeans and I pushed at his sweater and the thermal shirt under it.

"Poor California boy is freezing his ass off here in New York."

"Ah, but I have a sweet redheaded lass who is going to warm me up."

I laughed at the thickened bit of Irish he put into his voice. "Keep talking like that and I'll never let you go." His smile slipped a little, and my breath backed up. "I didn't mean—"

He covered my mouth with his. "I know what you mean, Ivy."

The thrill zinged down my spine as he said my name again. Why did that drive me so crazy? It was just a name. People said it a million times a day since I was usually waitressing at three different places some weeks. When he said it?

It wasn't like anyone else.

And then it really didn't matter what names were being said, because most of the next string of words were curse words and deities in quick succession.

Sweet mercy, the man had a talented mouth. A devilish one that had no business making me scream out for God, but boy, did I.

He rolled me under him, above him, and finally, in what was becoming his favorite position—and mine—he spooned me as he splayed me open to his every touch.

I arched and his long, delicious fingers stroked me from clit to neck before he turned my head to meet his lips as he thrust into me again and again. I was surrounded and bared at the same time, cherished and displayed in ways I'd never been before.

His teeth sunk into my shoulder as a stifled groan ended in a sweet sigh. I didn't remember drifting off, but my body was sweetly swaddled into the covers as Rory slipped away to take care of the condom.

Just like last night, he returned to gather me close.

If I drifted off, would he be gone again?

The worry of it wouldn't let me slip away as I'd almost done only moments before. He would be leaving, I had no doubt of that. I just wanted to be awake and aware of it this time.

I rolled in his arms until our legs were a tangle and I could rest my cheek against his chest. Words felt like too much just then, but he seemed to be good with the silence. Part of me wanted to ask what he was thinking, but the other half of me didn't want to know.

Was he counting the minutes before he could escape?

As gruff as he was, there was a steely spine of politeness inside of him as well. Such a crazy combination. And he didn't reach for his phone every three minutes either. Most guys rolled over and checked their phones about thirty times.

Heck, I usually did as well.

It seemed too important to be fully present for once. To soak up this little moment to hold me through the seemingly endless thaw of spring until I could get my summer plans in order. To finally make my little truck a reality.

I toyed with the medal resting on his chest. I nearly missed the small cross threaded onto the chain behind it. "Saint Christopher?"

"Good eye."

I grinned up at him. "I worked at a little card shop when I was sixteen. Had a bunch of these kinds of medals in a display case. Grandmas usually bought them."

He laughed. "Well, you can add Irish mothers to that list as well. Even went so far as to get the holy father at Saint Peter and Paul's Church to bless it before she gave it to me. That was after she made me promise I'd wear it on every flight."

I rested my chin on top of my hand. "Patron saint of travelers."

"It's a comfort to her, so I wear it."

"Not a comfort to you?"

He shrugged. "Easier to wear it than to remember to grab it for every flight. Then again, I'm always on a plane going somewhere."

The questions burned my tongue. Just who was this man who didn't seem to belong anywhere and yet was comfortable wherever he was?

His face closed off a little. "Just spit out whatever it is you have to say."

Now I wanted to bite my tongue even more. It didn't matter. It was just today between us. I settled with the easy. For me as much as him. "What happened with your meeting?"

He visibly relaxed, fluffing the pillow behind his head. "My client's child fell ill and he and the boy's mother ended up heading to the urgent care center."

I propped myself on my elbow on the mattress. "Oh, no. Is he okay?"

"Seemed like a normal child's malady. Ear infection and fever perhaps? I'm not sure. Obviously, that ended our meeting."

"That was nice of you."

He sat up. "Just being human. Not sure why everyone is so surprised that I'd be okay with postponing our work."

I tucked the sheet around my breasts. "Well, you traveled from across the country."

He raked his hand through his hair. "Yeah, but I'm not a monster, for fuck's sake."

I sat up next to him. "Didn't say you were. You're getting a little worked up about it. Kids get sick all the time."

"Yeah, well, when it's your own I guess you get a little more upset about it."

"Oh, I'd have kicked you to the curb if the baby was mine."

He huffed out a half-laugh. "And yet you're surprised that I'm the one who's being magnanimous?"

"Oh, magnanimous."

"Ah, for feck's sake."

I laughed as his Irish temper roughened his voice and his frustration mounted. "So touchy. I was just saying it was nice of you." I climbed over his lap and let my sheet free.

His jaw flexed, but he didn't unfold his arms.

I cupped his face and smoothed my thumbs over his scruffy jaw. "Ah, LC, you're just mad that people know you're actually a nice guy under the grump."

"I am not."

"Aren't you though?"

He grabbed a condom, hooked an arm around my waist and dumped me on my back, rolling between my thighs. "Would a nice man do this?" He snapped the condom on and eased himself inside of me.

I arched at the quick invasion, but I was embarrassingly ready for him.

He buried his mouth in my neck. "Fuck, why do you feel so damn good?"

I groaned and adjusted my position to take more of him. I hissed out a breath as he drew back and sunk into me again and again. Sweat pooled between us as we grappled with each other. Teeth and lips clashing as he tried to prove to me that he wasn't a sweet and giving lover.

Instead, he was showing me he was just the opposite. Before he got off, I was always treated to at least one orgasm, if not two. And this time was no different. Even with just an evening and half an afternoon between us, he knew my body better than any boyfriend who'd come before him.

My nails clawed down his back to grip his ass to pull him deeper, ride him harder as my feet dug into the bed to rise up to meet each of his thrusts. By the end of the power play between us, my head was hanging off the end of the bed and my chest was heaving with the need for oxygen.

Rory's cheek was pressed to my belly, and I was pretty sure I'd just learned an entirely new language.

"What is that language you keep muttering just before we...you know."

He lifted his head. "You know?"

"Come our brains out."

He nipped the skin next to my belly button. "Shouldn't be doing it if you can't say it."

"Shut up."

He laughed. And rolled off me to flop onto his back. "I didn't realize I was saying anything."

"Evasive maneuvers, sir." The blood was rushing to my head. I inched down until I was next to him then noticed the time on his watch. "Oh, shit."

"What?"

I scrambled off the bed. "I can't believe we've been fucking for almost three hours."

"Well, there was a shower in there, but huh. Yeah, I guess so. Quite the nooner, my little ginger fairy."

I flipped my hair back and groaned at the rolled up state of my shirt. "Thank God, I've got a spare uniform in my locker." I shook it out, but it was nearly hopeless.

He rolled onto his side. "My shirt will be miles too big on you, but you can borrow one if you'd like."

"You don't mind?"

"Not a bit." He slid off the bed and went to his battered leather weekender.

I followed him, clutching the sheet against me. I snagged my bra hanging off the footboard of the bed. How did that end up there?

He pulled out a fresh pair of boxers for himself and tugged them on. Which I was grateful for since I didn't seem to have any impulse control when it came to this man and his dick.

"Not sure this will go with your snazzy pants, but..." He held up a well-worn fisherman's sweater.

"No. You're going to let me wear that?" I snatched it out of his hand. "Is this..." I brought up the material to my cheek. It was destined to make me itchy, but it also happened to be the most perfect gray I'd ever seen in my life. I'd always wanted one of the famous sweaters from Ireland. They were so out of my price range.

He tossed me a white shirt. "You'll probably need that under it."

I almost hated to do it since I'd probably only get to wear the sweater for a few hours, but it *was* pretty scratchy. "Are you sure?"

He nodded. "You can probably wear it like a dress."

I laughed. "Almost." I rushed over to him and went onto my toes to brush a kiss along his cheek. "I love it."

He scrubbed his hands into his hair again, ruddy color climbing his neck. "No big deal."

I dashed to the bathroom, then stopped at the threshold and turned back. "Do you need to go?"

"My flight's not out until tonight."

"Oh." I nibbled on my lower lip. "If you don't have anywhere to be, maybe you can come to the diner with me? I'll feed you. You know, since I depleted all your electrolytes."

His lips twitched. "It's the least you can do."

"Right. I'll make you the very best club sandwich and fries. Everything's better with bacon."

He snapped out a pair of dark washed jeans. "That it is."

"Okay, cool. I'll be right back." I snatched my pants off the chair by the bathroom door and went to get dressed.

I wasn't quite sure what the hell I was doing, but I was glad to have a little more time to figure it out.

EIGHT

 IVY

THE DRIVE TO THE DINER WAS A QUIET ONE. WE WEREN'T exactly sure what to say to each other.

Maybe that was just me.

Maybe I should have driven my car. Parking on Main was at a premium during the day. It was smarter to leave it where it was.

More like a red flag that I'd stayed at the Hummingbird to get laid, but whatever. It was done.

I couldn't even distract myself with my phone. It was currently so dead that it was taking a few minutes to charge up enough to turn on.

As we pulled into a spot outside the diner, his fingers flexed on the steering wheel.

I unsnapped my belt and turned to him. "Look, it's okay if you—"

He released his belt and dragged me in for a hot, hard kiss. His gaze blazed into mine when he leaned back just enough to speak. "I know it doesn't really make sense, but I do want to be with you. I *like* being with you."

His lips kept brushing mine as he spoke and I had a hard time following what he was saying. "Right. Me too." Too much. I didn't understand why it was so easy and so hard to be around him.

This part was easy. The hot flash of attraction blanked my brain, but the rest...not so much.

Because I wanted to know everything and was too afraid to ask? Perhaps.

Or was it just worse that I'd actually met someone I wanted to talk to and he was going to be leaving in less than twelve hours? That, of course, was my luck.

I forced my lips to curve up into a smile. *Relax. Enjoy. Keep your planning for the future focused on the ice cream truck.*

That should be easy, since it was my longest held dream and the one closest to coming true.

I leaned in for one more scorching kiss, then slid back to my side of the car, unhooked my phone from the charger, and pushed open my door.

"Dammit," he muttered behind me just as I closed the door.

Whoops. I'd forgotten to let him open the door for me again. At least that was what I thought the *dammit* was for.

He caught up to me on the sidewalk and held open the door for me. I patted his cheek as I strolled into the diner to find it nearly empty. I frowned and dug my phone out of my pocket.

Gina came out with a smile, her perky smile fading to her regular one when she saw it was me. "Hey, girl." Her gaze slid back to Rory with an arched brow. Probably because he was nearly on my ass.

I kinda liked it and yet I wondered if I should make some space between us.

There were going to be a lot of damn questions. People were nosy as freaking hell in this town.

"Sorry, I'm late."

She tipped her head. "Didn't you get my text?"

I pulled my phone out and noticed the three texts loading. One from my brother and two from Gina. "Dammit, I didn't have the phone charged."

She played with the end of her fat braid. "As you can see, no one is really up and around today. I think I've had four people all day."

"Really?"

She swung her braid over her shoulder. "Not sure what the hell's going on. The Cove is usually much hardier than this. It was even a pretty nice day."

Rory stuffed his hands into his pockets. "Shouldn't the snow be gone? It's spring in like...two days or something."

Me and Gina both laughed.

"Oh, honey. Snow is forever here in Central New York." Gina tucked her thumbs into her apron pockets, then looked from me to Rory. "So, who might you be?"

"About that text?" I needed to steer her away from asking questions. Mostly because I had no answers.

Gina narrowed her eyes.

Rory pressed his lips together, then sighed. "I'm—"

I put my hand on his chest. "A friend. And if you don't need me today, I'd love to have a rare day off to go hang out with my..."

"Friend," Rory finished.

"Right." I smiled brightly.

Gina grabbed my arm and dragged me over to the counter. "Girl."

"I'm fine."

"You got laid is what you got."

Was there a scarlet letter on my chest or something? Hmm, wrong analogy, but honestly, how could she tell?

"You're wearing a dude's sweater."

"Oh. Yeah, that's true."

"And you have walk of shame vibes, which you shouldn't have. We're adults and dammit, he's fine."

"Thanks." I glanced over to him. He was on his phone, but it was that bored scroll I could spot on a male from fifty paces. "It's just a one day thing. He's not from around here."

"Um, that's obvious. His shoes alone cost more than my rent."

I spared him another look. They just looked like boots to me. Not ones that would get him up a mountain since they were brand spanking new and he'd have blisters for days, but they were just boots. However, his jeans... I was pretty sure those were designer.

"You know what you're doing?"

"No."

"Well, at least you're honest." Gina shook her head. "I expect details, in all forms."

"Maybe."

"Girl, there's no maybe. You *will* give me all the details," she said in a whisper that so wasn't a whisper.

I winced and couldn't help notice the side eye from Rory.

"Just be careful and have fun. You deserve to have some fun. All you do is work."

"I'll see you tomorrow."

"That you will." She looked over my shoulder and waggled her fingers at Rory. "Nice to meet you, stud."

"Jeez, Gina. It's not like it's a secret."

"Then what's his name?" she asked out of the side of her mouth.

"Rory. Okay, his name is Rory. I'll be fine, Mom."

"Have fun and make sure you keep some raincoats in your pocket."

"I'm leaving."

I stopped in front of Rory. "Ready?"

"We're not eating?" His gaze dropped to my lips then back up to my eyes. "Kind of worked up an appetite."

I swallowed hard. We sure did. And everyone in this town knew who I was. And I'd be answering questions all day if I took him anywhere else. Except...

I held up my finger, then took out my phone and quickly texted my brother back.

> Where the hell have you been?

AUGUST

> Do I ask you these questions when you are out late?

Yes.

Okay, so that was true. Rory gave me a hard look.

Something came up. I ran into a friend and
passed out at their place.

Their? Her?

Are you working or home?

Obviously, you're still not home, but no, I'm
at the shop,

K. Heading home, just didn't want you to
worry. Didn't need me at the diner, so I'm
going to work on some new recipes.

Sounded like a good enough excuse for him not to rush home. He
hated when I took over the kitchen to try out ice cream recipes.

Please, for the love of all that is holy, make
something other than mint.

No promises.

GIDEON

PITA.

Love you too.

When I got the middle finger emoji as a response, I knew all was
okay in my world.

"Okay, let's go to my place. I'll cook you dinner."

"Why don't we just get some food to go?"

I looped my finger into his jeans. "You really want me to cook."

"Do I now?" His smile was slow and delicious in a way that made my stomach do a little flip.

I could feel eyes on us. Gina was rudely staring and I was absolutely done with that. I turned Rory around and pushed him toward the door. "Bye, Gina."

"Bye. Remember raincoats."

"Ugh."

Rory glanced over his shoulder. "Do I want to know?"

"I'm sure you can infer."

He gave me that winged brow. "Lovely."

"Better than the alternative."

"That is for certain. Not that I don't think you're clean as a whistle."

"Yeah, yeah." The bell above the door made its usual jingle, but it still seemed weirdly loud. As if it was ushering me out the door and into a huge change.

"It was more the kid thing."

I suddenly wanted to yank my arms into the huge sweater and hug myself. *The kid thing.* He'd said it with such derision.

Instead of the full withdrawal, I just hid my hands. "No kids, huh?"

"I'm not the family sort."

"That's it? Just not the family sort?"

He shrugged. "I didn't have a bad home life or anything."

"And yet still no?"

He shoved his hands into his pockets. "I just don't think I'm suited for it. You have to be very selfless, and I'm definitely not that."

"Selfish people aren't usually that aware, LC."

He sighed. "Don't you think this is kind of a heavy topic?"

"Agreed. That's not what today is about, right?" I pushed the little bit of wistfulness down back where it belonged. Maybe it was all my own issues popping up. Not sure why it was happening around this man.

Okay, that was a lie. It was because we had connected during naked time.

At least I had. I wasn't quite sure how he was feeling. As soon as he was touching me, he was all in. Otherwise, he could be standoffish.

I really didn't know what to make of him or us.

Hookups in college were one thing. The next day, you went to class and maybe you saw the dude again at a party.

This?

Weird.

Different.

Addictive.

I just needed to stay in the moment. No matter how hard it was.

"Give me your keys?"

"Are you on my insurance?"

"Um, no."

"Then you cannot have my rental keys." He held open the door. "You can direct me to your place."

I sneered up at him. "It would be faster if I drove. Or better yet, we get my car and you follow me."

"Where's the fun in that?" He cupped the back of my head and drew me up on my toes. "My pushy fairy queen. Guess that title is quite fitting, yeah?" His lips hovered over mine before stepping back.

My heart raced and damn those stupid black dots danced again. I got into the car and he closed the door for me. I fiddled with my phone again, plugging it back in just in case.

"Where are we headed?"

"Go straight. Take a right at the end of the street."

"Not so hard."

The journey was quiet, save for my instructions and the low murmur of the radio. A Wilder Mind song came on and I turned up the volume.

He gave me a bit of side eye. "You like these guys?"

I nodded. "Sucks about the keyboardist. I hope they don't break up over it."

"Remains to be seen."

"Are you president of their fan club?"

He laughed. "No." But he didn't volunteer any more information.

I tapped my leg to the rhythm and hummed the lyrics under my breath. Wilder Mind was a semi-local band. I'd followed them simply because they were from the area, then fell in love with their sound along with the New Yorker pride element.

My brother's duplex was on the fringes of town. He'd been forever in fixer upper mode. The plan had been to rent out the other side of the duplex, but it had become a sort of showcase for all his furniture. A virtual storefront of sorts as long as no one picked up on the fact that the area wasn't zoned for businesses.

Then again, things were very gray on that front since many people worked from home. I didn't mind the two kitchens, however. Or the fact that I could have a super large freezer in the other half of the house.

August's truck was gone and I blew out a relieved breath. I got out before Rory could come around and open the door for me again. Chivalry be damned. I waited on the porch for him.

"Nice place for a waitress."

"Got a filter to go with that mouth?"

"No."

I rolled my eyes and twisted a stone behind the large glider bench that was currently tarped against the winter elements. Soon, it would be spring and I could sit outside with my ice cream instead of huddling under a blanket.

I unlocked the door, returned the key, and held it open. "Welcome to Casa Beck."

He crossed the threshold and the foyer felt smaller. Which was ridiculous since my brother was approximately the size of a rugby player and we came home together all the damn time.

I shrugged it off and flicked lights on as I walked through the small living room to the kitchen. "I currently live with my brother.

Both of us are single so it seemed stupid to pay two rents when we work opposite shifts."

"You don't need to explain yourself to me. In Ireland, it was rare for a woman not to live with their family until she was married."

"And you said you were American."

He curled his fingers around the back of the stool at the kitchen island. "I've been in the States for a while. Left as soon as I could. It's actually easier to get out and work in the US than it is to go the other way around. I was grateful for it."

That was probably the longest string of information I'd heard from him about who he was. And I had to remember it wasn't necessary. We were here for one thing.

Me to have a little more time with him and not get all twisted up into some awkward conversation that would make him want to head out faster.

Or maybe that was the right track. Maybe this was a—

He stepped in front of me and brushed my hair behind my shoulder. "Was bringing me here for food a euphemism? Or are you actually going to feed me?"

I laughed. "Little bit of both." I looped my finger into his belt. "When's your flight?"

He lowered his nose to brush along mine. "Midnight."

"Well, then. We have plenty of time to do both."

He nipped my lower lip. "When does this brother get home?"

I shrugged. "Aug tends to get lost in his work. A Beck trait."

"And what do you get lost in, my little ginger fairy?"

"You," I said against his mouth just before I covered it. I hadn't meant to say it, but it was true.

I dragged in a deep breath as storm Rory moved in for its second level destruction. He pushed me up against the kitchen island, then lifted me to the counter. I was a little taller than him, thanks to the island's custom height. It didn't seem to bother him though. He had greater access to my tits, which wasn't a bad thing in the least.

He stripped me out of the borrowed sweater and T-shirt to cup my breasts together as they flowed up out of my bra. I hooked my legs around his middle, pulling him closer.

This kitchen island action looked so easy in the movies. In reality, there was no way to get clothes off easily. We laughed and tugged at our clothes until he pulled me down off the counter.

"Bedroom," he muttered against my mouth as my bra disappeared.

I turned him toward the back of the house and we bumped our way down the darkened hallway. The day's brief sunshine had faded into a watery gray. We were just lucky another storm hadn't hitchhiked with the first one.

Finally, we got to the end of the hall. I fumbled with the doorknob before he pushed me through the doorway. I tripped over my laundry basket and we both went down hard on my bed, but it didn't stop us. We were both too far gone.

He didn't even get his jeans down around his thighs before I was gripping his shaft.

"Fuck, Ivy."

"Yes. Yes, more of that."

He unearthed a pair of condoms and I smiled wide.

"I nicked them from the medicine cabinet."

"Smart man."

"Not sure about that." He huffed out a groan against my throat as I gripped him tighter.

"Suit up, LC."

He reached for the condom on the edge of my bed. "I've never known a woman like you."

"That's a good thing."

"Working for me." He ripped open the package and sheathed himself quickly. Then he was inside me.

Thank freaking God.

Our hands both held onto the headboard. It was hard, fast, and relentless.

We were both up and over the edge before I even had time to consider anything crazy.

Like God, did my boobs look like shit this way? I didn't have any makeup on. Did I seem too greedy? The whole host of usual worries while having sex.

Nope. Not today. Not with him. When Rory got near me, I forgot about everything but pleasure and the wild ride past thought to pure feeling.

I hooked an arm around his neck as he touched his forehead to mine and a low, slow groan rumbled between us. Then he actually pinned me to mattress for a few seconds.

There were no words, just the marathon gallop of my heart as I slowly came out of the euphoria clouds. I looked down between us to see my pants dangling off one ankle, along with my panties. Who the hell knew where my bra had landed.

Somewhere in the kitchen. Maybe. I'd have to go look for that before August came home.

I so didn't need that conversation.

"Apologies," he muttered before sliding away to deal with the condom. He returned to curl around me. There wasn't a whole lot of room on my full bed for a man like Rory.

I laughed. "Only you would say 'I'm sorry' after amazing sex."

"Would you rather I be a dick and just roll off?"

Maybe. Then I wouldn't want to rewind and do this again three, four, twelve more times.

I slipped from the bed, then leaned down to remove the rest of my clothing. I gathered my hair up into a messy knot and forced myself to look him in the eye.

It took a minute since his gaze was roving over my body. All five-feet-three-inches of me. Not a long perusal, but I couldn't deny the flush I felt climbing up my neck. No one had ever looked at me like he did.

He had given me a lot of my firsts.

Just figured that a man who was rushing to leave town would

make all my girl parts stand up and take notice. As well as my brain, because I really liked sparring with him too.

"Fuck me, you are a vision."

"Glad those yoga videos really work."

"That they do. You put the women in Los Angeles to shame."

"Oh, now you're just blowing up my skirt."

"You're not wearing one." He held his hand out. The corner of his distractible mouth tipped up. "Come back here."

I wanted way too much to roll back into his arms. "I need to use the ladies. I'll be right back."

The smile in his eyes faded. "All right."

Ugh. I was so stupid. I was the one making it weird now.

Thankfully, we had a Jack and Jill bathroom, and I didn't have to sprint across the hall naked or something stupid. But I needed a second to gather my thoughts and put myself back together.

Obviously, getting naked with someone was way more intense than I'd thought it would be. I just needed to chill out a second and I'd be fine.

I'd never been so glad to have a load of clothes in the stackable washer and dryer in the bathroom. I pulled out my favorite jeans. There was nothing I couldn't do with these babies on.

My first batch of ice cream.

My first job.

My first date with a boy.

I tugged on a few more layers of armor—bra, underwear, long-sleeved T-shirt with a rude, dripping ice cream cartoon, and my mint chocolate chip socks. There was no way he would want me when I was wearing *this.*

I twisted my hair up into two twists on top of my head because it was so beyond snarled from all our...fun.

Yes, fun. That was it.

We could totally have a very late lunch and do the banter thing, and then he'd go on his merry way. I'd be left with a little soreness—because holy crap, that man knew how to fuck—and a great memory to get me through the next few months until I could get my truck ready for summer.

Easy peasy.

I slid back into the room to find Rory at my large window. He'd pulled his jeans back on, but they were still unbuttoned. He was shirtless and the afternoon light showcased his wide shoulders and lean hips. I was halfway across the room before I thought about it. What the hell was I going to do, cuddle up to him and look out the window like we were in some rom com come to life?

He turned to me with a hesitant smile. "Can you tell me why there's a large white lunch truck in your backyard?"

"That's soon to be my ice cream truck."

"Is it now?"

"It is."

"What? Like the ice cream man?"

I narrowed my gaze at him. "Not quite."

I picked up his shirt from the end of my bed and tossed it at him. Much safer if he was fully dressed. That way I wouldn't toss him back down on the bed.

"I'll show you."

He caught it against his chest. "All right."

I walked out the door and down the hall to the back door.

"Ivy?"

"This way." I called from the back door. I stepped into my snow boots and crunched my way across the yard to my future. I reached for the handle and hauled myself up into the rusted-out truck. I'd convinced my brother to help me strip it down to the bare parts just before winter hit. I'd lowered the windows to get the taco smell out of all the crevices. The brisk winter winds that whipped through the back of our property had done the trick.

A long whistle dragged me out of my musings.

I turned around with a big grin. "Like it?"

He folded his arms across his chest. "It's big."

I laughed. "I know it looks like something out of a bomb shelter right now. Me and my brother ripped out all the rusty grills, and I've ordered a huge double walled freezer to go right here." I widened my arms to take up the empty section. "It'll have room for all my ice cream tubs, and on Sundays, I'll have gelato. A lighter ice cream for after the big family picnics and dinners."

He lifted his arms up to hang on the handle above the old ventilation area. "And will you be wearing a cute little striped apron?"

"Shut up. I'll be wearing a T-shirt and shorts because it will be a million degrees in the summer."

"Short shorts?" he asked with a lot of hope in his voice. Way more than he should have since he probably wouldn't be seeing me in said shorts, but I was willing to play along.

"Easier to wipe ice cream off my legs if I keep them short."

He swallowed. "Is that right?"

Slowly, I moved to where he was. His sweater was a little raised due to his long stretch. "You have any idea how to keep my legs from getting sticky?"

"Jesus."

I grinned up at him. "Well, I'm only taking my cues from you, sir. I seem to remember a few thoughts you had." His belly trembled under my nails as I scored the light fur just above his jeans. I went onto my toes to nip his chin. "You have a very talented tongue, LC."

"Christ."

I traced little circles along the tight muscles of his abs. "What color do you think I should do?"

"Color?" His eyes went blind as I flicked the tail of his belt through the loops.

"I'm thinking bright, summery colors with a cool chalkboard on the side of the truck." I unzipped his jeans and lowered myself to the metal bench that still remained in the shell of the truck.

"Ivy."

"What? I don't even have to get my knees dirty."

His grip tightened and so did the muscles in his arms. Even under a sweater, they were deliciously impressive. "It's cold as fuck."

"You won't be cold in a minute."

"We're in a fucking truck."

"My ice cream truck." I pulled him free of his boxers and licked his shaft. I grinned up at him. "Want me to show you how I stop any drips?"

He shut his eyes and let out another string of words I couldn't understand.

I swiped my tongue along the flared head of his very interested cock. "That's a yes?" I took him into my mouth and released him with a little pop. "So, what's your favorite flavor?" I bit my lower lip as I gripped him a little harder. "Salted caramel?" I gave him a careless lick. "Or wait, is that mine?"

"Sweet bleeding Jesus."

"So many churchy references. Your mom would wash your mouth out."

"Can we not mention my mum right now?"

I licked my way up the underside of his cock, winding the path of a vein with the tip of my tongue. "Well, then tell me," I took a long, slow mouthful of him and let him free, "what your favorite flavor is."

"Peppermint."

"Like a candy cane?" I twisted my fingers around him. "Interesting."

"Like those sweets." His voice was strangled.

I could take pity on him, but where would be the fun in that? I took him deeper until I couldn't take anymore. Then I let him free with a gulp of my own. He really was an impressive specimen. "Which sweets?" I stroked again.

"The dark chocolate ones with the... Christ, how do you do that?"

I grinned around a mouthful of him. Making him forget words was very good for my ego. I made a light humming sound, and he let go of the handle above us to fist his fingers in my hair.

I took him deeper and he grunted before pulling me away from him and urging me to my feet. "Those York Peppermint Patty things." His blue eyes were flame-bright as he kissed me hard. There was no room for niceties.

It was messy and harsh and wonderful.

Distantly, I filed away the information and let him sweep me from my thoughts into just feelings. Wild, turbulent ones that only had one outcome.

Us naked.

And I was very okay with that.

He swooped me up in his arms and tossed me over his shoulder. "That's it. I'm freezing my bollocks off and even your impressively beautiful mouth can't combat that."

I laughed as he hopped down onto the snow, and wobbled his way to the house.

"Have those boots ever seen snow?"

"They have now." He brought his hand down on my ass and I screeched out a laugh. He put me down just before the door and we tumbled across the threshold in a tangle of legs and arms and kisses.

Laughter was only beaten out by moans as we stumbled our way down the hallway again to my room to try out the last condom he had with him.

Oh, how we made good use of it.

When I was fairly sure I'd never be able to walk again, we raided the kitchen for a frozen pizza. I even convinced him to try a few of my ice creams.

He showed me a few different concoctions that I'd never have thought of without his input. Between the two of us, we managed to make a batch of salted caramel and chocolate swirl.

A text from my brother gave me the last reprieve of the day. He was buried in a project at the shop and wouldn't be home until late.

I wasn't even ashamed of stealing one of his condoms from the medicine cabinet. He wouldn't miss it. Maybe.

By the time Rory had to leave, there were no awkward pauses. I couldn't even be mad that he was leaving. I was lucky enough to have a wonderful memory to pull out when I was old and gray.

When I was a crazy single woman who'd enjoyed an intense fling with an inventive Irish lover.

He kissed me at the door. Long, lingering kisses that made my lips tingle and my chest ache.

Maybe *his* chest ached a little too. I would probably never know.

And then he was gone.

I didn't even mind that I had to SOS my best friend to get my car the next day. It was that worth it.

NINE

Approximately one month later

THE TEXT FROM KELLAN CAME ACROSS MY RENTAL CAR'S dashboard screen—and yes, I'd rented the same model car from the same place, out of some misguided sense of sentimentalism. There was no snow in Crescent Cove now, thank God, but the scenario was already setting up the same.

I was late due to no fault of my own. Plane issues, missed connecting flight, lack of cars at the rental place. When I'd noticed this little dreamboat was one of two cars still available, how could I say no? It wasn't as if I was depriving anyone else of it. The rental clerk had shoved me toward it as if she couldn't wait to see it go.

To me, it was a sign that this trip would be as eventful as the last. And I'd brought a box of condoms this time just in case.

Tapping the wheel, I slid into an open spot near the Rusty Spoon and turned off the engine. My blood was already humming at the idea of seeing Ivy—

No. Wrong. I was merely anticipating another productive session with Kellan. Which was why I'd cleared my calendar this weekend when he'd contacted me and asked if I was available. Professional courtesy of course.

The condoms didn't mean I was thinking about Ivy. Naturally not. But I certainly wasn't thinking about any other women, in Crescent Cove or elsewhere. In the month I'd been gone, I'd barely even noticed any of the other females in my midst. That was saying plenty since I worked with rockstars who paraded around enough beautiful ladies to make the mind spin.

But not mine. Only one woman had registered with me.

I reached across the seat to grab my leather portfolio, flipping it open to scan the sheet on the top of the pad inside.

> Surrounded by fire
> Soaked in her glow
> Be with her tonight
> Before I go
> Tomorrow I'll be on a plane
> Gone far away
> A lock of flame in my pocket
> The words I couldn't say

My excuse before was that we were thousands of miles apart. I didn't have contact info, although that was probably partially my fault. Now I would have no such excuses.

Not that I had a handle on my emotions. I had barely come to terms with even having some, outside of the ones I needed to access to write a good song. Identifying them was way beyond my paygrade.

I just knew I was looking forward to seeing her again.

After grabbing my phone and my portfolio, I climbed out of the car and glanced toward the lake. I couldn't see most of the water from this vantage point, but it looked so different without a layer of ice and frost. The April day was sunny and windy, with a nip in the air that necessitated a light jacket for those who weren't hot-blooded.

As used to California as I was, I was fucking frozen. It couldn't have been more than forty-five damn degrees, but a woman in shorts rollerbladed past me on the sidewalk.

She smiled at me, but I didn't smile back. I didn't know what to make of this small town charm thing. The friendliness of Crescent Cove's citizens always slid over my skin like an ill-fitting suit. Some found California welcoming, but I was too busy working to even look around most of the time.

Here, it was impossible not to. Slowing down wasn't optional. It was imperative.

Holy shite, there was a sailboat bobbing across the lake. Not a speedboat. A sailboat with its colorful mast billowing in the wind. My da would love such a thing. It would be a whimsical bit of fun for a man who rarely took time for anything but work. I should look into getting him one—

I tucked my portfolio under my arm and gripped my phone. What was I doing? First off, thinking of him as my da rather than simply calling him my father, even in my head. Then pondering buying him a fanciful gift. As if he'd know what to do with a sailboat. He'd probably laugh and clap my shoulder while he gently chided my impulse.

Hope you didn't spend too much on that, boyo. You know I don't have time for such things.

This damn town. It made a person wish. And pretend their life could be different than the way they'd purposely designed it.

The way that had worked just fine for them—nay, worked *perfectly*—for more than half a dozen years.

My phone buzzed in my hand. Another text from Kellan.

KELLEN

I see you standing outside. You
sightseeing?

I sent him back a middle finger emoji and crossed the sidewalk to
go into the diner.

The jangle of the bell made me swallow hard. I glanced around
the place, filled to the brim with patrons on this sunny afternoon.
Elvis wasn't playing on the juke. Snow didn't dot the windows. And
Ivy didn't come toward me wearing a smile and braids that made me
think of altogether filthy things.

"Hello there. Can I help ya?" A smiling waitress—so not Ivy—
rushed up to me.

My gaze drifted over the packed tables and landed on a hulking
man sitting alone. He was crammed into the booth, his hood up, big
can headphones over his ears. Shades and a beard disguised half of
his face. No one paid him any mind as he tapped on the table with
one hand and read his phone with the other.

"Meeting a friend. Thanks though."

She followed me to the table, chattering brightly about the
weather and the menu and oh, yes, had I been by the tulip fest at the
Fairgrounds yet? It was such a happy little bloom of spring.

"You all have a damn lot of festivals," I muttered as I joined
Kellan.

She took my drink order and hustled off. Only then did Kellan
slip off his glasses and look up.

"Finally."

"So says the bloke who made me wait a damn month."

We bumped fists across the table and Kellan quickly lifted his
menu again when a gaggle of giggling teenage girls walked past our
table. I laughed into my fist. "Nice disguise."

"You think it's funny. Not all of us can stroll around freely."
He tightened the strings of his hood and I laughed, louder this
time.

"Did it ever occur to you that no one will care? You live close by. Surely you venture out now and then."

"We order in a lot. Maggie's been watching the Food Network when we can't stand another taco."

"Or your waistline can't." Kellan was rock-solid, the behemoth. "How's the kid?"

He'd been diagnosed with an ear infection and an upper respiratory ailment, so he'd been on the mend soon after our visit a month ago. But it was nice to ask. Wolf had been a relatively cute child.

This town had cursed me.

"He's finally better. The doc thinks with his history, we should look into putting tubes in his ears."

"A relatively minor procedure, yeah?"

Kellan shrugged. "For the most part. Maggie is worrying herself sick. The guys are talking about maybe doing a couple of one-off shows in the fall and I'm already dreading telling her I gotta go. Then if I do some dates solo in the meantime..." He released a long breath. "Balancing act, man."

"It's hard with children and a spouse."

As if I had any clue. I didn't even have a cat. Or a houseplant. I'd bought one off Amazon and forgot to water it and it died.

"You can say that again. You seeing anybody?"

The question hit me low. "Why would you ask that?"

"Uh, I dunno, being polite?" He waved it off. "Never mind. Forgot you were Rory the Inscrutable."

"Pardon me?"

"You gotta know that's your rep. Untouchable, remote dude. Hit maker but doesn't make friends."

"That's entirely untrue. I have friends."

Kellan nodded. "The Kagan dude, right?"

"Yes, Ian, but not only him. I have others." Even I could hear the defensiveness in my tone.

Kellan held up his hands, palms out. "Hey, I get it, man. Work comes first. I respect that. I respect even more that you don't use people right and left just for thrills. Unusual in our business."

"I'm focused."

"Understandable. I respect that," he repeated. "You've done well for yourself."

"As have you."

"Yeah, but I started off on the A & R side of the table myself. It's different when you're representing talent versus being the commodity. Gives you a new perspective."

"And there's Maggie and Wolf to do that as well."

"Yes." He smiled, so quickly that it would've been easy to miss if the effect hadn't lingered in his eyes. He might not go on about them to a near-stranger, but his family provided him with a solid foundation that had changed his view.

A month ago, I hadn't understood it. Not that I did fully now either. But here I was in Crescent Cove again, looking for Ivy around corners and peering toward the kitchen for any random glimpse of flame-red braids.

Polly, the waitress, returned with our drinks and asked for our orders. I had to get a big boy breakfast, even if Kellan cleared his throat about six times.

Whatever. At least I wasn't wearing can headphones large enough to make Dumbo jealous.

We made small talk about how Kellan's songwriting had been going and his current talks with his band. They hadn't jammed together in a while, but he'd invited them all out to the cabin this summer. He also invited me—and Ian, who I hadn't realized he knew on any more than a casual basis. The rock business was pretty damn incestuous. That was how I'd met Ian in the first place, after all.

"His fiancée is pregnant, so I'm not sure how he'll be with traveling this summer. She's due soon, I think." Even as I said the words, they shocked me all over again.

Ian was younger than me, and he hadn't even drawn a short straw in Crescent Cove. He'd actually—wait for it—planned and hoped for and actively tried to plant one in his not-even wife. And he'd succeeded in remarkable time.

"So, he can bring her along too. And the kid. Wolf could use a pal." Kellan shrugged, pausing as Polly returned with our food. Quick service in this place. "We keep adding on. We'll need more guest rooms at this rate."

"You can actually meet his fiancée before you invite them to stay for a week. Zoe's family owns Happy Acres." I circled my finger over the table. "In your milieu here, isn't it?"

Kellan dropped a French fry in his cup of salad dressing on the side and didn't seem to notice. "No shit? Wolf loves that place. We do the hayrides up there in the fall."

"I've never been. Ian is there now spending time with his new family-to-be. Said it was kismet or some rubbish that I was meeting you here." I rolled my eyes and forked up sausage. I sampled it, deciding right away it wasn't as good as Ivy's.

Surprise, surprise.

"So, you're going up?"

"I didn't make any plans. I came here to work with you, not run off on jaunts to the country." Not that Crescent Cove was exactly a metropolis.

Kellan chuckled. "Dude, I respect your work ethic, but you know, loosen your shorts now and then." He saluted me with his coffee cup. "Life's more enjoyable that way."

"My shorts are not too tight."

At least they wouldn't be until I saw Ivy again.

A low hum buzzed under my skin. Where was she? Day off? Vacation?

Had she met some new man and run away to Paris?

Gee, fanciful much?

After plowing through his salad, Kellan shoved the plate aside and went to work on his sandwich. He didn't say anything while I poked at my potatoes and wished they'd been made by a red-haired siren rather than a kindly older woman.

"You know what I did last time I was here?"

"Yeah, you worked with me."

"Before and after. Let's just say I wasn't alone." I stabbed a sausage. "My shorts were all the way loose then, let me tell you."

He winced and held up a hand. "TMI, bro. It wasn't an insult. Really. Just saying you come across the country, you should make time to see your buddy if you're able to." He jerked a shoulder. "If not, no harm, no foul."

I forced down some sausage. It had a nice flavor, but I wasn't thinking about food. I was thinking about Ivy, and how I was in her town and had no fucking way to contact her unless I sat here in this diner day and night. And that was if she even wanted to see me again.

A lot could change in a month.

Your fault, genius. You were the one who wanted to keep it simple.

I tended to do that too often. I didn't know how to foster connections with people outside of a work sphere. Even Ian was only my friend because he'd practically shoved himself into my life. I certainly hadn't opened the door. Although he had a family of his own now, he still made time for me, but I usually didn't feel it necessary to return the favor.

I didn't like family scenes, and Happy Acres pretty much screamed family. Hayrides, for feck's sake? It wasn't autumn, but that wasn't an activity that stirred me in any case. The spring equivalent was probably riding ponies and looking for Easter eggs.

God save me.

"We could go there to work, if you'd like." This person speaking was not me. I'd been invaded by a Crescent Cove body snatcher.

Right now, my alien invader was gaining strength from Polly's sausage. Which sounded wholly inappropriate.

Kellan sat back in the booth, probably to catch his breath. He'd demolished his food in the same amount of time it had taken me to eat some sausage and a few potatoes. I grabbed a piece of bacon and bit in, sighing inwardly. Definitely not Ivy's bacon either.

I was becoming obsessed with that woman, and it probably wasn't due to the deliciousness of her pork products.

"Sure."

"That's it? No artistic hissy fit about needing your space to compose?"

Kellan tipped back his head and laughed. "I brought some stuff to get your input on, but we're still in the early phases yet. It was cool that you got to work at the board during our last visit, but we'll have time for that later. Besides, I wouldn't mind meeting Ian. Assuming you'd be willing to introduce us."

So, he *didn't* know Ian. Yet he'd extended an invitation to stay with him sight unseen. Oh, to have so much faith.

"That could probably be arranged. I should probably check with him before I invite you out. Hang on." I pulled out my phone and was halfway through typing a text when a flash of red moved past the corner of my eye. My head jerked up and another part of me jerked to life.

It couldn't be her. A million women had red hair. But not that exact shade. Not those long braids hanging down over her kelly green coat.

The woman walked past our table, not glancing our way at all. I didn't think. I reached out and snagged her back pocket with two fingers—tearing off the patch of fabric with a rip that seemed to sound through the diner.

Well, hmm, it never happened like that in the movies.

On the positive side, I could now see her underwear, since her pocket had a hole in it. Just a tiny little peek of pink. Christ, I should be jailed.

She whirled, a fist coming up. Her deep brown eyes flared wide and then her mouth dropped open. "Lucky Charms?"

Across from me, Kellan's expression changed from shock to

amusement. "Thank God you know her, because I don't have enough cash on me for bail."

"Lucky Charms?" Ivy repeated, stepping forward. Her gaze lingered on my face for a beat too long before dropping to my plate. "You're eating a big boy breakfast."

I nodded mutely. This second meeting was not going like I'd planned.

Or hoped.

"That Polly made you," she said accusingly, and I blinked.

"Sorry?"

Laughter broke out behind our booth and Ivy looked over her shoulder, wrenching her neck to check out her own very fine ass. She sighed. "Least I'm wearing undies," she said loud enough for half the diner to join in with her laughter.

Even I laughed. This woman was a wonder.

Instead of yelling at me as she had every right to do, she leaned across the booth and wrapped her arms around me in a quick, unexpected hug. I reached up to hold on, shocked at how much I didn't want to let her go.

She felt right in my arms. I hadn't realized exactly how perfect until I'd gone four weeks without her.

"Next time," she said against my ear, "just say hi." Her tongue flicked over my neck a second before she eased back and was gone.

I cleared my throat and sat back, barely able to resist cupping a hand over the wet spot on my throat—or shifting to alleviate the pressure down below.

Kellan was stirring his coffee, as calm as could be. Neither of us spoke. Then I picked up my phone to complete my text to Ian.

Looked like I'd be inviting someone else to Happy Acres too. If she would be interested in coming.

Jesus, I needed to make her come again.

To the farm.

Just the farm.

"So, Lucky Charms, I'm gonna guess she's the one."

"Come again?"

I was too busy staring at my screen and trying to get my thumbs to work enough to compose a message.

"She didn't even look at me."

I glanced up. "So?" I stared at Kellan for a long moment and got his drift even if I didn't like it. His disguise didn't hide the rockstar bad-ass persona oozing from his veins—or his massive size.

"It's a good thing," he continued. "Just saying it doesn't happen often. She only had eyes for you."

I set down my phone. "She did, yeah?"

Without another look at my phone, I sent my message. And looked down to see I'd texted the following to Ian.

> Hey, Kellan McGuire and dii390dn might want to come with.

I had to grin at my thick thumbs. If anyone could make me forget how to type, it was Ivy.

Ian's reply was almost instantaneous.

> IAN
>
> Dii390dn wants to come? Sounds like a screen name. Visiting Tinder again, mate?

> Jackass. Typo. My friend's name is Ivy.

> Oh, is it now? And she wants to come, does she?

He was such a smartass. I was tempted to give him a middle finger emoji and just forget asking Ivy, except I wanted her with me. I wanted to spend more time with her. And if I had to get straw up my ass, I wanted her to be the one who caused it.

There was a sentiment one didn't often find on a greeting card.

> You'll still be there tomorrow?

> Yes, question is, will you be? Don't you keep your trips to see Kellan short?

> This one is a day longer.

> Ooooh, wild man. Look at you go.

> Keep it up & I'll deny you the pleasure of my company.

IAN

> In all seriousness, I'd love to see you. It's been too long & we're always headed in opposite directions lately. Not sure when we'll be able to get back to Flynn's for some R&R.

I blew out a breath. Ian and I had spent some time with another guy I'd worked with on occasion, Flynn Sheppard, last summer and it had cemented our friendship.

Since then, we'd seen each other here and there, and I'd sat in with his band a few times when he needed an extra hand on the guitar. But I hadn't made the time.

I hadn't wanted the expectation that I was supposed to.

"Problem with Happy Acres?" Kellan's affable tone set my teeth on edge.

"No. Everything is coming up fucking roses."

The song on the jukebox changed. As soon as I heard the first notes of "The Wonder of You" and saw Ivy's grin as she snapped on her apron over a fresh pair of pants, my irritation at...what, I wasn't even sure, vanished.

I switched apps on my phone and brought up a notepad one, writing in big block text. Then I held up the phone in her direction.

SEE YOU AFTER WORK?

She squinted for a moment before nodding and grinning.

I returned her grin and glanced at Kellan, who was turning back from the direction I'd been looking in with his own smile.

"Don't say a word," I said, pointing at him.

"Wouldn't dream of it. So, what time should I be at Happy Acres tomorrow?"

"Noon." Seemed reasonable enough. I knew Ian wouldn't mind regardless, no matter how much shite he tossed my way.

And I was far more focused on tonight.

TEN

Rory

THE MINUTES PASSED LIKE HOURS BETWEEN THEN AND WHEN I was due to see Ivy again.

How had I made it through a month without her?

Work. Always work. It was my savior and my crutch.

I ended up going with Kellan to his home recording studio after lunch, despite our plans to visit Happy Acres the next day. At best that would just be an inspiration sort of trip, since a farm wasn't exactly equipped for serious work.

Or serious anything, except perhaps picking wild, growing things.

Kellan seemed excited to meet Ian, which was a bit of a surprise. But Ian was an up and comer on the rock scene who had already been making waves, so maybe it wasn't so shocking. Kellan had his ear to the ground and obviously had an open mind when it came to exploring the possibilities.

Seemed like that was a trait I needed to acquire too. When I was with Ivy, it had seemed easier somehow.

Kellan and I made our way through the song we'd worked on last month, hammering out lyrics and melodies and arrangements. When that one seemed to be coming together, we shifted into a second one that, to me, would work better as a duet. And not with me, although I'd seen the light of interest in Kellan's eyes.

The guy was like a damn sponge. Eager to try anything I suggested.

In this case, I suggested we call it a day. If he wanted a duet partner, well, then, we'd just see if Ian had a gap in his schedule. Ian's pipes were as pretty as the rest of him, and I was no singer.

Maggie made more scones for me, and I filled my pockets with them like the beggar she'd turned me into. I even held Wolf, who was in much finer form than the last time I'd seen him.

He also tried to rip out a hank of my hair, but I was assured that was because he liked the pretty copper penny color of it.

His mother was probably a liar, but she was very sweet.

I didn't leave until shortly before eight, which was when Ivy had requested I meet her at the diner. By then, scones were inadequate to fill my belly, no matter how delicious they were, but I bypassed the offer of dinner in case Ivy was hungry.

It was almost easy for me to find my way back to Crescent Cove now. The roads were just as winding and lacking in appreciable landmarks, but I was beginning to find my way around. The lack of snow didn't hurt either.

I parked down the block from the diner, slipping into the last available spot. It offered me a gorgeous view of the lake and the gazebo strung up with fairy lights that twinkled in the darkness. Sunset came later this time of year, and it seemed as if half the town was out and about. Coming and going in and out of pubs and restaurants, wandering through little shops while carrying even tinier shopping bags. Most were in groups or couples.

Normally, I didn't notice stuff like that, but this was a place for families. Between the town itself and spending time with Kellan, Maggie, and Wolf, I was paying attention to things I usually did not.

Then there was Ivy, who made me pay attention as well.

I hadn't had a relationship in years. Didn't know how to have one, truthfully. What had happened with Darla had soured me on them.

And how.

Not that Ivy and I were in true dating territory. But I wasn't a dummy. Repeats meant it mattered.

The scent of steak on the grill wafted toward me as I walked past a surf and turf restaurant and down the block to the diner. Passersby smiled at me, and without thinking, I smiled back.

Crescent Cove was infectious. It sneaked into your blood and before you knew it, you weren't a grouchy, aloof, serious music dude anymore—minus the few times I got a little too deep into my cups. Exactly why I rarely imbibed.

Here, I didn't even have to. I had a sense of humor anyway. My step was just a little lighter. LA seemed like it was on the other side of the world.

The bell jangled as I opened the diner door. A harbinger. Of what, I wasn't sure.

Something country was on the juke. Conway Twitty maybe? Not my usual style of music. The place was half full with families and couples clearly fueling up for a night out. Polly, the waitress who'd waited on us earlier, was nowhere in sight. Neither was Ivy.

My heart started to beat too fast. Probably in the back. She hadn't skipped out.

"Hey there. Back again?" Gina, the waitress I remembered meeting with Ivy the last time I'd visited Crescent Cove strolled toward me. "Let me guess. You're looking for something special tonight." She winked and I narrowed my eyes to keep from flushing like a kid.

"Maybe I just want a chicken fried steak." I didn't exactly know what that was, but it didn't sound appealing.

"Oh, I just bet. Prepared by our sweet Ivy?"

"Perhaps. Is she around?"

"Ah-ha. Trying to play it cool. Don't worry about that with me. I'll keep your secret." She grinned. "If the price is right."

Something about her joke made my hackles rise. I moved past her and walked down the aisle between the booths, heading straight through the pass-through door into the back of the diner. People were calling to each other, and the guy manning the grill swore a blue—no, purple—streak.

I waited for someone to notice me and toss me out, but everyone was preoccupied. And Ivy was nowhere in sight.

Needing a quick escape, I headed toward the back door. I pushed it open and stepped out onto a small raised patio that fronted the lake.

Bingo.

Ivy was leaning on the railing, her long, flame-red ponytail whipping in the wind.

I came up behind her and wrapped my arms around her waist. She stiffened and craned her neck to see who was behind her, but she didn't relax when she saw it was me. If anything, she braced even more.

"You know better than that, Aug. There's no such thing as being friends with your ex. At least not when it comes to you and Serafina."

Serafina? That sounded like a Disney princess.

"I didn't say I was an expert, just warning you to be careful. And you shooing me out of the place tonight says to me that you aren't planning on keeping it platonic. You know how thin the walls are."

Hmm. A little late to find out considering our prior romp at the Becks' place, but good to know. Seemed like sex there was extremely risky.

So, why did that make my cock even harder?

Yes, harder, because I'd gone to stone the moment I'd seen her firm little ass pointing upward as she leaned on the rail. Pity those pants didn't have the hole in the pocket so I could shamelessly ogle her underwear.

Pervert.

Also, I'd probably better loosen my grip on her waist, since she didn't believe exes could be friends.

Not even "special" friends? Hmm.

We weren't exes though. Not exactly. Were we friends with benefits? Strangers with benefits who'd become friends?

This was why I didn't have relationships. I was such an analytical guy. Exactly why the production side of music suited me so well. It had mathematical aspects that many lay people didn't realize. Sure, creativity was a big part of it too, but oftentimes mine took a backseat as I figured out the best way to help someone else shine.

Ivy's hair blew against my face in the breeze and it took everything I possessed not to bury my face in it. In her at the rail where she stood.

So...no labels. We'd just enjoy the moment. That had held us in good stead last time, right?

"Okay, okay, fine, Aug, you do what you want. Me? Uh, why do you want to know?"

Ivy's apron dipped just enough to allow me to see her tank top and the pink bra strap that matched her panties. I tugged the bra strap aside with my teeth, kissing her shoulder in the process. Freckles exploded over her skin. They were everywhere. A dusting of cinnamon on the palest snow.

Huh, I'd have to integrate that into my song.

The song I'd written for the woman I'd had a meaningless hookup with.

My teeth scraped her skin, more roughly than I'd intended. She gasped, although she quickly hid it under a cough.

Since that wouldn't do, I reached around and slipped my hand under her apron, dragging my knuckle between her legs over the seam of her trousers. Rather than closing me out, she opened her thighs and tipped back her head.

I transferred my kisses to the side of her neck, climbing higher until I could suck on her earlobe. Her delicate earring tapped against my teeth. I rubbed my knuckle harder against the fabric, wondering if I was imagining how damp it was already.

Voices sounded below us as people strolled on the sidewalk to the pier that led to the lake. Behind us, someone dropped a plate in the kitchen and a curse rang out.

But Ivy didn't stop me. She just arched against me and slid the phone away every time she couldn't hold back a moan.

"You're going to come for me," I murmured against her throat.

I told myself her brother couldn't hear me.

And even if he could, I still wouldn't stop.

I shifted my hold on her, bringing her more tightly against me so my cock imprinted her back. She whimpered and held the phone away, dangling it over the water while she rocked into the determined movement of my fingers. Still through the cloth. It didn't matter. Already I'd begun to learn how to touch her. To give her what she needed.

She brought the phone back to her ear. "I'll just hang out with a… friend tonight." She barely managed to get the words out before she shattered, gasping and bucking into my palm as she moved the phone between her breasts.

I whirled her around and covered her mouth with my own, needing to taste her first few breaths as she came down from the high. Enjoying far too much how she softly moaned, letting the sound free as if I'd given her permission.

"Say goodbye to your brother," I said against her lips.

She nodded and lifted the phone. "Sorry. Bad connection. Have fun with Serafina. We'll talk later." She clicked off and stared at me with glazed dark brown eyes. "He could've heard."

"He didn't. You're very quiet when you come. We have to change that." I slanted my mouth over hers again, sliding my tongue against hers with the same kind of slow friction I'd use when I drove into her body.

Not that first stroke. The first would be wild and uninhibited, just enough to hurt. Then I'd slow it down, delaying my pleasure until she found hers.

Okay, that was the ideal scenario.

Reality? At this rate, I'd probably come in my pants before she stripped.

"God, I want you." She wrapped her arms around my neck and we fed off each other like animals, hungry and desperate.

Until the door behind us opened.

"Ladybug?"

Ivy jerked away from me and slammed backward into the railing. I reached around her to rub her back and she flailed, shoving me away.

"Yes, Mitch. Sorry. Just clocked out. I'm off the clock," she said loudly, as if she expected to be fired at any minute.

If she was going to be let go, I intended to make the reason worthwhile. I'd fuck her against the railing before we left.

"You again. You came back for her?"

I shifted, slipping my hands into the pockets of my trousers. "I came back. Nice to see you again, Mitch."

He grunted. "A gentleman doesn't maul his lady in the back of her workplace."

"Good thing I'm not a gentleman," I said at the same time Ivy answered him.

"He didn't maul me."

Ivy glanced at me. "You so are a gentleman."

"Whatever he is or is not, we can't have public displays back here."

"Yes, the ducks might get jealous. *Quack, quack.*"

Ivy shot me a look.

I slid my arm around her waist. "You're right, sir. We'll just be on our way."

Mitch nodded. "I think that's best. Just for your information, I keep a shovel and a shotgun in the trunk of my car."

"And a concealed carry permit, I hope."

He grunted at me again and held open the door to the kitchen, ushering us inside.

Ivy gathered her things and quickly said her goodbyes to a few coworkers. Gina waggled her brows, but Ivy didn't stop to chat.

We made our exit and gazed at each other as we stood on the sidewalk, basically cutting off the flow of Friday night foot traffic.

"The inn?" Ivy asked.

Just as I asked, "Your place?"

She frowned. "You heard me on the phone. August has a friend over."

"A friend you don't want him to fuck. He won't, if he's too worried about you hearing him fuck."

"Yes, but *I* want to fuck. Hello." She stepped forward and grabbed me by the lapels of the light jacket I'd put on after visiting with Kellan. "Did you miss the part about me wanting you?"

"No, and the feeling is definitely mutual." As if we weren't on a busy sidewalk, I grabbed one of her hands and discreetly brought it down between us. She gripped me shamelessly, moving so close that no one could see.

Maybe.

"You're a little exhibitionist."

"You're a big one." She licked her lips. "So, let's go somewhere and show each other...things."

I laughed and she blinked up at me as if the sound was foreign. It almost was. Away from Ivy, I definitely didn't grin and laugh and feel all the things she so effortlessly brought to life inside me. She made me feel young again, in a way I'd never been. Outside of cutting up a few times a year with some mates, frivolity wasn't a part of my life.

Except with her.

"We can't go back to the bed and breakfast yet."

"Why not?"

"I'm afraid of Sage."

Ivy stared at me for a long moment before letting go of my cock to cover her mouth. She laughed so hard her face turned a shade of red not commonly seen in nature.

I crossed my arms. "Go on, enjoy yourself at my expense."

She dropped her hand. "Afraid of sweet Sage Hamilton. Why?"

"She says things."

"Oh my God, no." She touched my arm. "I'm so sorry."

I shook her off. "She'll make all sorts of insinuations if I bring you up to my room."

"Insinuations she's already made?"

"Well, yes."

"That are actually true." She moved closer to me and lifted her hand to my cheek. "I didn't get a chance to tell you I like the thicker scruff."

I covered her hand with my own. "I didn't get to shave."

"Don't." She inched up on her tiptoes and rubbed her nose against mine. That move should not have been hot, but it definitely worked for me. Especially when she followed it up with, "I want to feel it between my thighs."

"Christ. I'm never shaving again."

She grinned up at me. "One little victory. I liked our room at the bed and breakfast."

The word *our* made me itchy between the shoulder blades. And surprisingly happy.

I shouldn't encourage her to think of us that way.

Shouldn't encourage myself.

It was just an accident of timing that I was back in this town with her.

That you asked Kellan to meet you at the diner, because she was your first thought.

"We'll go back under the cover of darkness." Then again, Sage had been manning the desk at midnight last time. "Super darkness," I added when Ivy tipped up her head to stare at the star-speckled night sky.

"Whatever you say, LC." She slipped her arm through mine and I led her over to my rental car. She grinned and patted the roof as if she'd missed it. "Got her back again, huh?"

"Why are all vehicles female?"

"Because they purr when they accelerate."

"This one does not purr. More like rumbles."

"Same difference." The vehicle unlocked and she slid inside the passenger side before I had a chance to grab her door. Then she stuck her tongue out at me.

Shaking my head, I came around to the driver's side and slipped inside. "Where are we headed? Since you won't go home."

"And since Sage is so super scary."

I arched a brow and waited.

"I know a place. Do a U-turn here and make a left at the blinking light."

"Uh-uh, you're not directing me back to the bed and breakfast, ginger fairy. Also, seatbelt."

She sighed heavily and put it on. "So suspicious. Just trust me."

I waited for a break in traffic and did as she asked, sliding a look at her when I came to the blinking light. I turned left, cruising past the bed and breakfast.

"Keep going."

After about five minutes, during which I followed the curving road past increasingly larger and larger homes—some damn near mansions—and a golf course, I finally reached over and pinched her thigh. "Are you leading me into the woods?"

"Better. Stop up there." She pointed.

I squinted into the darkness. The street lights were few and far between up here. "Where?"

"See those two huge trees? Veer left between them. But be careful."

"Because I'm driving into the fucking forest?"

"No, because if you go too far, you'll drive into the fucking lake."

I hit the brakes with a loud squeal.

Ivy doubled over, laughing. "Seriously, it's easy. Just coast off the road. You have plenty of warning where to stop. It's a clearing. There's just no fencing on that one tiny part."

"No fencing. Right. If I sink this car, I won't be getting my deposit back."

She laughed harder.

I obliged her, and lo and behold, she was right. The clearing was tucked away enough to be unobtrusive to passing cars, but if one was careful—and I was nothing if not that—it wasn't hard to figure out how far to go.

The sign my headlights flashed over that warned about the boat launch helped as well.

I turned off the engine and turned to her. "Now what?" I was pretty sure I knew, and I was okay with it. Chilly spring weather or not, I was certain we'd keep each other warm.

Then again, I could just turn the car back on. This was worth wasting gas.

She clicked off her seatbelt and my cock jerked. *Down, boy.* "Now we get out."

"Pardon?"

She was already on her way out, so I followed. At that point, my dick would've followed her into the bowels of hell.

She jogged forward, coming to a stop by some hedgerow that served as a poor blockade for the lake. I was about to say just that when I glanced upward and my words got stuck in my throat.

Just here, the canopy of trees separated and the endless dark blue sky opened up, covered in a carpet of minute diamonds. It was as if someone had poked holes in the night to let slivers of light through. They danced and shivered on the gently rolling water.

She turned toward me, her lips parting, and I forgot everything but cupping her face and bringing her mouth to mine.

Warmth exploded through me. I scarcely felt the cold as she slipped her cool hands under my shirt, lightly scraping my belly.

"Beautiful," I whispered, and I didn't mean the sky and the lake.

I meant her. This.

Us.

When she drew back and started to drop to her knees, I gripped her elbows. I knew where she'd been going, and my much less altruistic cock didn't like the change in direction. "No. Not here. I need to be inside you."

Later, I'd wonder what logic dictated a blowjob was too intimate for a public place while fornication was just fine, but that was lust for you.

I took her hand and led her back to the car. This was a romantic spot, but it was lacking certain amenities. And as far away from LA as I was, the media-savvy part of me would never allow us to openly do something so risqué.

Inside a car though? That was private.

Kinda.

She tugged open the back door of my rental sedan and crawled inside. She shifted to face me and held out her arms in a welcome I couldn't have resisted if I tried. Especially when she also spread her legs. Pity she wore trousers instead of a flirty little skirt.

"I'm not dressed for this," she said as I slid inside. "I had no idea how my day would end."

I shut the door behind me and ranged over her on the seat. The lack of room back here would be a problem. Good enough to break the tension, but not for long. "Some things are best kept a surprise."

"Especially since you don't have my phone number." She wound her legs around me and her arms around my neck.

"I have another combination." I reached between us to undo her trousers. "You're going to have to take these off. I need to see all the ginger parts of you."

"It's dark."

I dug out my phone and turned on the torch, making her laugh. She grabbed my cell and flicked it off again, tossing it aside before she smacked my ass. "Get a move on, Ferguson. We don't have all night."

No wonder I kept coming back to her. *For* her. She was unlike anyone I'd ever known.

"Yes, we do," I said between kisses. "As if I'd rather do anything else."

She made quick work of my trousers, as I did the same with hers. We didn't pull them all the way off, just out of the way. Shoving her jacket off her shoulders, I latched my mouth onto her neck and slipped my hand between her legs, finding her wet and hot for me. The elastic of her panties kept snapping back when I pushed them aside to get at her, and she laughed every time I cursed and moved them out of my way. Her clit rose under my fingers, so stiff and proud, and she didn't hold back her moans as our mouths met again and again.

"So. Not. Fair. You're supposed to be inside me."

"I am." Deliberately, I pushed two fingers into her, deep and hard. She only tilted her hips upward and pushed back against me, asking for more. I licked her throat up to her lips, tugging her lower one between my teeth while I nudged her up to the edge again. "Feel that?"

"As if I can feel anything else." She reached behind me and hauled up my shirt, scraping her nails down my spine. Christ. Then she gripped my ass, pulling me against her so that my fingers went even deeper. At her gasp, I started to pull away, but she dug in with her hands, keeping me in place. "Don't you fucking dare."

I'd never laughed during sex before. Not when I was so hard I couldn't think. Yet there was still room for amusement inside me, tangling with the need.

I drew out my fingers and she hissed, quieting when I lifted them to my lips. I tasted them thoroughly, and she watched me the whole time. Rapt. Openly aroused.

There was nothing hidden with Ivy.

She leaned up to take my mouth again. I twisted her nipple between my wet fingers, absorbing her whimpers like oxygen. I yanked her tank and bra down to get at her skin, and the same thing happened as with her panties. The fabric snapped back, trying to keep me out.

But I couldn't swear now. I'd lost the power to do anything but shove her underwear aside as she freed me from my boxers. She tugged on me with long, forceful strokes, her fevered gaze locked on mine in the darkness.

And when I couldn't stand another second, she just parted her thighs and moaned while I ripped the material guarding her sweet pussy.

Inside her. I was mindless with the need for it.

For her.

I slid into the heart of her and groaned. It had been a lifetime since I'd felt that particular heaven. I couldn't go that long without it again. Fucking could *not*.

"Jesus, Ivy. Ivy." It was the only thing I could manage to say as I pulled out and drove into her again. The angle was weird, my neck was cramped, and I'd probably be in traction tomorrow.

Didn't matter. I had to bury myself deep. Over and over until she was as mindless as I was, one leg locked around me and her foot thumping on the door behind us.

At least I thought it was her foot thumping.

Until a light bounced over the backseat and I realized two things at once.

One: I was not wearing a goddamn rubber.

Two: Ivy's foot did not have a light attached to it.

"This is the police. Cease and desist immediately."

ELEVEN

Rory

BEING INTERRUPTED BY THE POLICE SHOULD'VE BEEN THE biggest, coldest bucket of water ever.

Only problem? My dick needed a hearing aid.

It kept right on thrusting without conscious direction from me, as I stared at Ivy and wondered if my illustrious career would come to an end in a makeout spot in East Bumfuck, NY.

Or maybe I'd get even more famous. It wasn't as if she was married. Or I was. Or some other equally taboo scenario.

Minus the fact my bare ass was pointed at the window, I was sure there were far worse scenarios to be caught in.

Except I still hadn't gotten off. And Ivy's pussy apparently had better hearing than my cock.

"Rory, stop. Hello, stop. I'm not looking to get arrested."

"But I'm not done." Who was this petulant asshole talking? It certainly wasn't me.

Especially since the door behind me was not locked, as demonstrated by the fact the cop opened it and tapped my...back with his nightstick. Not gently either.

"Did you hear me? This area is not zoned for public nudity."

I almost asked which areas *were* zoned for such, but wisely, I shut the hell up.

"Let's go. Pants on and IDs."

I shifted and glared at the cop. I didn't move fully off of Ivy, however, as I was not going to expose her naked bits to his prying eyes. Until she punched me in the gut to give her enough room to pull up her trousers.

All righty then.

I dealt with my own clothing and rued the day I'd ever agreed to this plan. Even a nosy Sage was better than being frisked by the police.

Ivy dressed quickly and dug out her wallet from her pocket. She withdrew her license and leaned over me to thrust it out the door to the cop.

The side of her breast brushed my chest and I nearly groaned.

Never had an orgasm seemed so unattainable.

"Ivy Beck? Is that you?" The cop bounced his flashlight over us again and she ducked her head, her gorgeous hair coming down to shield her face. I wasn't sure when it had come out of its ponytail, but it was swinging free and wild now.

Similar to me, except there was no free. I was trapped in my pants like a snake in a vise.

"Yes, sir."

"You work at the Rusty Spoon with Gina?"

Her again. Was this man connected with Miss "Name your price"?

It was nearly impossible to know who could be trusted. Everyone was out for a story and a payday.

"Yes, sir."

The cop returned her ID. "And August is your brother."

"Yes, Sheriff Brooks."

The sheriff. Of course. God forbid we get a beat cop. Did places like this even have those?

"Look, can we get on with this? Clearly, you know she's a local and I'm fairly certain there must be real crimes for you to attend to. Isn't Woodstock happening near here again this year? What happened to free love?"

Ivy jammed her elbow into my shoulder.

"Where exactly are you from, hippie?" The cop tapped his baton on the top of the vehicle. "This is a rental car."

It was a miracle I didn't say *duh*. "LA."

"LA, huh? What brings you to the woods in Crescent Cove, NY?

"I had work."

"Oh, really. Sure you didn't get lost on your way to Woodstock? Should I search this car?"

"You do whatever makes you happy. You'll find nothing but some clothes and some rubbers." They were still in the boot since I'd phoned in my reservation at the bed and breakfast and hadn't even officially checked in yet. "Unless sex isn't allowed in your fair little town."

"Rory, shut the hell up." Ivy lifted her brows at me before turning her beseeching expression on the unworthy cop. "He's just... disoriented. Don't mind him. Please."

"Disoriented? Have you been drinking? Either of you?"

"Oh, for fuck's sake. No drinking. Fucking? Yes. Which we weren't allowed to finish."

The cop shone his light directly into my eyes and nearly rendered me blind. "Let's see that ID. Now."

"Fine by me. Then you'll realize who the hell I am."

I didn't know why I said it. I wasn't the sort to throw around attitude like some entitled rockstar. Perhaps I'd hung out with too many of them just recently. Either that or perpetual denial was doing bad things for my personality.

I handed over my license and didn't reply when he said to stay put while he ran it. Then he glanced at Ivy and said something in an undertone about her older brother being disappointed in such antics.

Since I was still "disoriented", I figured that was why she crossed her arms and stared straight ahead while the sheriff went back to his vehicle to see if I was a felon on the lam.

My mouth probably hadn't helped matters.

"I'm sorry, love." I reached across the seat to cup her fisted hand. She didn't react. "I don't know what got into me. I've never been in trouble with the law before."

"Or if you have, they knew who you were and let you off?"

I frowned. "Pardon?"

"I heard what you said. Don't you know who I am?" She turned toward me on the seat. "Traveling back and forth from LA as if it was nothing. Checking into a fancy bed and breakfast and barely even using it. All your work here. That's not normal."

"Says who?"

"Me. I should've just Googled you, but I didn't want to betray your trust."

I didn't respond.

"I have a daily shift in a diner, Rory. Most of the other people in town keep regular local, daily hours. They don't jet across the country for a few hours of work multiple times in a month."

The other shoe was dropping at a most inconvenient time. Courtesy of my flapping jaws.

I locked my hands behind my neck. "I didn't get to invite you to Happy Acres tomorrow, but I was going to. I want you to meet some of my people." It sounded as awkward as I felt.

"Some of your people? Like your family?" Shock lined her voice. "Are they visiting the country?"

"No. My mates." Kellan wasn't exactly that, but it seemed as if we were on the path to becoming friends.

Maybe. Hell if I knew. Quite frankly, I wasn't used to having so many personal connections crowding in on me.

It was this town.

Or having sex more often than once a millennia.

Or having sex more often than once a millennia *in* this town.

Or it was just Ivy.

Some combination of those factors had caused my current situation. Along with my own thickheadedness. It was one thing to think I could keep the fame business at bay when Ivy was just a hot hookup.

The problem was she'd never been that to me, not from the first moment. Even after I'd left, some part of me had been counting the minutes until I could come right back to her.

As if time would sit suspended until I picked up the hourglass again. And I'd probably believed I could do the same thing after this trip. Just leave this gorgeous, smart, funny woman on a shelf like a doll I could take down when it was time to play. Otherwise, my life didn't have to change.

But taking her to meet my friends was different. Inviting her into my world was different.

"Look, I don't know what I'm doing. Or what *we're* doing. For God's sake, I didn't even use a rubber just then. I didn't even think of it. I don't do these things."

Her finger jabbed me in the chest. Right then, I welcomed the pain. "Do you think I do?"

"No, I don't." I held her hand to my heart. It was beating far too fast. "I think we're both acting out of character, and it's probably not only because we enjoy seeing each other naked."

"Jeez, don't flatter me so." She tried to tug her hand back, but I couldn't let her go.

That was becoming a recurring problem for me.

"I'm messing all of this up. I'm sorry. All I know is I didn't want to leave you on the shelf."

Just then, the door opened again. I had only an instant to see the puzzlement and hurt warring on Ivy's lovely features. Because of me.

Because I'd kept things from her and forgotten a rubber and fought with the police like a common...rockstar.

The next few minutes went by in a blur.

Surprisingly, Sheriff Brooks let us go with a warning. A stern one, but we'd definitely gotten off easy. He also tacked on that he'd have his eye on me, which was more than a little disconcerting. At least he left before I could talk myself into a summons—or worse.

Ivy said nothing.

"I'm sorry." I brushed my knuckles over her cheek. "My ma would skin me alive if she knew I'd allowed you to be caught in a compromising position. No matter what, she didn't raise me that way."

Ivy's chin came up. "You didn't allow shit. I brought *you* here, remember?"

Somehow I still thought puffing out my chest and pulling the man card was a good idea. "Yes, but I'm the male and—"

"Rory Ferguson, if you tell me that you're responsible for my actions, you might as well call the sheriff to come back here because there is about to be a homicide in the woods."

From the glint in her eyes, she wasn't kidding.

I held up my hands. "Let's go back to the bed and breakfast, yeah? Everything will become clearer tomorrow, I promise." There was an edge to my voice I couldn't hide.

It mattered to me. All of this did.

Especially Ivy. Hurting her didn't sit well with me, and not because my mum would be horrified at my behavior. Not only that anyway. I wasn't particularly close to my parents, but their opinion of me counted for a lot.

Hell, maybe that was why we weren't that close. I'd always felt I was lacking by not picking a more usual job and sticking close to home like my siblings. Rather than risking seeing disapproval in their eyes, I stayed away.

Far simpler to focus on what I could control and not worry about expectations I couldn't meet.

Ivy looked out the still steamy window before blowing out a breath. "I'll drive."

"Why?"

"Because I'm the woman and I said so. Now let's go."

I stayed behind an extra couple of seconds after she climbed out and rounded the hood. I wasn't smiling, but it was almost impossible not to.

She was one hell of a woman, my Ivy.

Even if she wasn't mine for real—if she couldn't be—I could pretend. She couldn't hear my thoughts.

And thank God for that.

We pulled up near the duplex where she lived with her brother a short while later. She parked along the side and reached over to close my lips when I started to speak. "We'll go in the other door and go up the back stairs. He'll never know we're here."

I was tempted to argue, but I didn't want her to tell me to go back to where I'd come from.

We headed inside the back way and she was right. We weren't caught. Of course the place was as quiet as a temple, so I had my doubts August was even there, never mind his Disney princess.

Ivy didn't take me to her bedroom.

I hadn't earned the right to be there tonight. She deserved so much more than what I'd been giving her. Even if most of my sins were of omission—and as a result of severe blue balls—the fact remained.

I was a toad.

As evidence, I watched her fine ass bounce as she moved from room to room. She didn't even bother tiptoeing. I was certain all her fucks were gone.

I didn't expect her to cross the kitchen to the freezer. She took down a pint of ice cream and opened a drawer with the stealth of a horde of teenagers.

Handily, her brother didn't emerge from a hidden crevice and demand to know whom her lover was. I'd had enough awkward conversations for one evening, thank you.

She stuck a spoon in the ice cream and thrust the carton at me. "Try it," she demanded.

If she'd told me to crawl across a fiery pit of snakes, I would've done her bidding.

I scooped up the ice cream and tasted it, nearly groaning as the perfect mix of chocolate and mint hit my taste buds. "Christ, are you kidding me?" I didn't wait for an answer before diving for more.

"While you had me on a shelf, I was perfecting that." She gripped the counter behind her as I forced myself to lower the spoon into the most incredible ice cream I'd ever tasted. "I didn't even know if you'd come back. I figured you didn't intend to, since you didn't even want my phone number. But I did it anyway. It was a way to channel all of *this*." She gestured vaguely between us. "I spent hours getting it just right. How many hours did you spend on me, Rory?"

Her voice had dropped to a near whisper and it wasn't because she was concerned about her brother.

I set the carton aside and moved to her, framing her face with my cold hands. She didn't react, just watched me with her all too knowing eyes.

"Far too many," I said roughly. "I came back here because of you."

Her lower lip trembled. "You said you had work."

"Work has never consumed me as you did. As you are."

She sucked in a deep breath. "Don't think I don't know you still want to get into my panties—well, pants, since I've had the shredded pieces of my underwear stuck up my butt for the last hour."

I laughed. I didn't mean to. But once started, there was no stopping it.

Having her join me was the sweetest relief I'd ever known.

I tipped my forehead to hers. "Please come with me to Happy Acres. I want you to meet my mates. I want to spend a day with you."

She swallowed hard and swiped her thumb over the corner of my mouth before she licked it. "Sure." I could see the effort it costed her to shrug casually. "Why not? You're already here."

I gripped her hand and brought it to my lips to kiss her knuckles. "I'll take you to get your car at the diner before I spend the night at the bed and breakfast. But I'll be back tomorrow."

I'll always come back for you, Ivy.

But I didn't know if I was man enough to make it true, so I didn't say it.

Her gaze clouded before she nodded and picked up the carton of ice cream. She scooped up some and pushed the spoon between my lips. This time, I couldn't hold back my groan.

Slowly, smugly, she smiled. "I'll be waiting."

TWELVE

 IVY

"Hey Siri, what's the weather in Turnbull?" I called from my closet.

The British voice of my Siri chirped out that it would be unseasonably warm. Never knew what you'd get in April. Layers were safest.

Should I wear something that included easy access? I snapped hangers from one end of my closet to the other. Skirt? Cute jeans and a top?

Ugh.

Why was I overthinking this whole thing?

Because it was Rory and everything seemed precariously pinned on *don't have too much fun, don't think too much,* and *are we dating? Is this just another extension of our fling?*

Should I pack condoms? Be very millennial and have one in my back pocket just in case?

Ugh.

Ugh.

Ugh.

I flicked a denim skirt off a hanger. It had a patch of cherries on the back pocket with a bit of rockabilly flavor. I added a sparkly pink top with a small skulls print. I didn't get to wear my own style too often because I was almost always working.

Since we were going to an orchard, I went with matching cherry socks that peeked out of my battered Doc Martens. I wasn't sure if we were going to be coming back late.

Instead of overthinking everything, I rolled up a pair of stretchy jeans and stuffed them into the bottom of my purse. There, all bases covered.

My phone chirped with a reminder alarm. It was almost time for him to get here for our not-a-date-date.

Picking me up like a boyfriend would.

Stop.

It was stupid to think about him like that at all. It was just a fun day.

What? Like the bed-banging fun we'd had on his last visit?

Okay, I really sucked at this easy breezy hookup stuff. It seemed so different than when I did it in college. This felt like a date.

I put on makeup and did my damn hair, for fuck's sake. It was a damn date, no matter what Rory wanted to label it.

And he was going to show me off to his friends.

I stared at myself in the mirror behind my door. "Calm the fuck down, Beck." I pulled a hairtie off my doorknob and snapped it on my wrist, spritzed on my perfume, and grabbed my purse and phone.

"Aug!"

My brother peeked his head around the corner at the end of the hall. "Yo."

"I'm not sure when I'll be home. I'm going out to the orchard with a friend."

"A friend?" He crossed his arms as he leaned on the kitchen island. "The same friend we talked about earlier?"

I rolled my eyes. "Dad, my how you've grown younger."

"Shut up."

I went onto my toes and gave him a quick kiss on the cheek. "Don't wait up."

"You have your backup charger?"

"Yes," I called as I opened the closet.

He followed me down the hall. "Emergency fifty?"

"Yes." I pulled out my denim jacket just in case it got cooler later.

He stuffed his hands into his pockets. "Protection."

"Aug."

"What?"

"Do you really want to know how many condoms I have in my purse? I mean, I can show you."

His eyebrows snapped down. "No. You didn't steal my fucking stash, did you?"

I laughed. "I bought my own, thank you very much. It is 2019."

His cheeks flushed. "I don't want to think about it, but at least you're being safe."

My phone buzzed in my hand. "He's here."

"And he isn't coming to the door? Rude."

"It's not a date. We're just going to hang out with some of his friends. If you stop being an overbearing older brother, I'll even bring you back something from the shop at Happy Acres."

"Oh. Can you bring me turnovers?"

I laughed. "Maybe. If you go away."

"Going." He headed back to the kitchen. "Be careful," he shouted at me as I slipped out the door.

"I will." I shook my head as I rushed down the stairs.

Rory's car was waiting at the end of the drive. His head was bowed, probably looking at his phone.

I slapped the hood of his car and his head jerked up. I smiled at him and for once, waited for him to open the door for me. His eyes went wide as he quickly climbed out out of the car and came around to meet me. His arms went around my waist and I went on my toes to meet him in a feverish kiss.

So much for keeping things friendly.

He gripped my ass, tucking one of his hands into my back pocket. The hard line of his cock bumped against me. He was just as ready for me now as he was last night.

Of course we'd both been denied. And then the moment had been gone.

Evidently, it had come back.

Our kiss spun hotter than the spring sun overhead. His other hand lightly threaded through the waves I'd spent an unhealthy amount of time creating in my hair. Each little pull spurred me on to deepen the kiss until we were both panting.

"You're gorgeous." He lifted his thumb to my lower lip I'd stained a deep cherry red. "That mouth is going to get me into so much trouble today."

I probably should've reminded him—and myself—that we had so much more to learn about each other than which sexual position we liked best. Especially after the little famous bomb he'd dropped in the back of the police car. But being with him was too precious.

And fleeting.

I slicked my tongue over my abused lips. "I don't see a problem with that."

"You wouldn't. How the hell am I going to manage to keep all the freaking Manning brothers away from you?"

My smile widened. "Who are the Mannings?"

"They run the orchard side of Happy Acres. Their sister, Zoe, is my mate's...well, mate. They haven't managed to get a ring on each other." His eyebrows furrowed and I resisted the urge to smooth the wrinkle away. "They don't work well in the confines of any boxes."

"Nothing wrong with that."

"Except the baby part. They're having one."

"Oh." I tapped his decidedly scruffy chin. He still hadn't shaved, and I still hadn't had his face between my thighs on this trip.

Naughty Ivy.

There was also more than a bit of fatigue around his eyes.

Perhaps he'd been up as late as I was, tossing and turning. "Are you a traditionalist?"

"No. Definitely not. Just the Irish in me comes out sometimes, I guess. My mum would cuff me behind the ears if I didn't put a ring on a girl before a baby came."

"Wow. So baby means marriage?"

"Why there aren't any babies in my future."

My smile faltered. How could I be so into a man who was the opposite of me in every way?

And that forced me to put this day into a special little box. It couldn't be more than just this. A spring day with a man who made my heart race and my body sing. It would be enough. It had to be.

I patted his chest. "Let's go before my brother comes out and embarrasses me."

"Right." He slid his hand down my back to urge me forward.

After I settled into the car, I took a few seconds to calm the hell down. Rory's phone was linked to the radio and a song I didn't know was playing.

The voice was oddly familiar.

He got in on his side and flicked to the next song via his steering wheel. "Seatbelt."

"Right." I gave him a bright smile.

"I got you a tea on my way over." He nodded to the large green tea in the cup holder.

"How did you know?"

He shrugged. "I notice things."

"You certainly do." I lifted the cup and took a quick sip to swallow down the suspicious lump that kept forming.

Do not get attached to this man.

It wasn't a long drive and we spent most of it laughing over the control of his radio. I forced Ariana Grande on him and he brutalized my ears with a particularly obnoxious Eminem song.

It was nice enough that we rolled down the windows when we hit the backroads that led to the orchard. Rory's hand strayed to my lap and he drew circles along my inner thigh to the slower 90s jams we'd compromised on.

"Waterfalls" indeed.

I tried to ignore the urge to widen my legs to see what he'd do, but our recent brush with the law wouldn't quite let me pull the trigger on another car makeout sesh.

I was so wound up by the time the large Happy Acres sign came into view that I was ready to drag his hand under my skirt damn the consequences. I opened my mouth to ask him to find a space behind a tree when two men came into the clearing.

One was rippling with muscle. His hair was in a blue faux hawk and he wore aviators against the noontime sun. The other was lean and startlingly familiar with a baby on his hip.

Rory parked and I threw open my door before he could come around. He got out too, then rubbed the back of his neck as I glanced from him to the other two men.

Very fucking famous men.

The leaner man—Ian fucking Kagan—held out his hand with a wide, affable smile. "You must be Rory's Ivy. Now I see why he was so anxious to bring you along. Way to go, mate."

I shook his hand mutely.

The little boy attached to him like a monkey rubbed his nose against his shirt. Ian didn't seem fazed at all.

"Right. Um, yes. Kellan McGuire, Ian Kagan, meet Ivy Beck. The little one is Wolf." Rory cleared his throat. "Guess you two met easily enough."

Kellan shrugged. "Maggie is forever worried she'll turn into one of those mothers who is late for everything so I'm perpetually early for every-damn-thing. Ian's been super welcoming."

"Talking shop is easy, especially when there's a cute little rocker to break the ice." Ian bounced a toddler on his hip. "Isn't it, little mate?"

Surreal didn't cover it.

A prickle of sweat teased between my shoulder blades. "Nice to meet you," I said through gritted teeth.

Ian laughed. "Oh, man. This is priceless. I'm usually the one in hot water." He caught the child's flailing hand and lightly swayed back and forth like he'd been doing it forever. He was wearing paint splattered jeans and half laced boots caked in mud. A white thermal shirt was pushed up to show off well-toned forearms.

Ian Kagan.

Singer.

Famous brother of yet another huge rockstar, Simon Kagan.

"I'll just..." Rory nodded to the car. "I need my guitar out of the boot."

Kellan grinned. "My wife will be stoked that there's another girl here—woman, sorry. Then again, she and Zoe have been bonding over babies and the like."

Ian brushed a kiss over Wolf's hair. "I can't wait to have one just like it. Soon." He danced lightly with the baby and started singing "Baby Shark."

"Not that song." Kellan groaned.

"I can't help it, man. It's infectious." Ian's eyes crinkled with joy as the kid babbled back at him, singing along.

"Oh, you'll learn when you have to hear it thirty-seven times a day."

I swallowed hard. Things were becoming all too clear regarding Rory. That flash of entitlement with the sheriff, the money, the strangely detached way he was with people—all of it made more sense now.

"Jam sessions are my favorite."

"We are not doing 'Baby Shark'." Kellan's voice was firm.

"We'll see."

I smiled at the two international rockstars and took my leave to rush around the car to where Rory had the trunk open. "Are you kidding me?"

He lifted out a guitar case and portfolio and set them on the grass. "I told you we were meeting my friends."

"*Friends?* Friends are the guys you went to college with. Ian Kagan and Kellan McGuire aren't just friends."

"They are actually."

I punched him in the shoulder. "Don't be obtuse. You could have warned me. Given me some sort of information about this before you just sprung this all on me."

He stepped into my space, drawing me closer to him. "They're just my mates. Nothing special about them except for the famous part. Ian's usually got more paint on him than Zoe because he's forever getting into her stuff. He's annoying and overwhelming."

"Famous."

"Just a guy."

"*You're* famous too."

He set his guitar next to him on the gravel. "In certain circles, yes."

"In certain..." I spun away from him and headed for the grove.

"Everything okay?" Ian called after me.

I couldn't even pretend to know how to answer. No, everything was *not* okay.

Not knowing anything about Rory had been a thrill—at first anyway. Now I couldn't help wondering if he'd been laughing at me the entire time.

"Ivy." Surprise laced his voice.

I kept on walking. Better that than to kick him in the shin or somewhere slightly more soft.

He caught my hand and tried to turn me around, but I wrenched it away. "I need a minute."

"You're not going to stomp off like a two-year-old."

I whirled around. "What you think this is, some sort of tantrum? You lied to me."

"I did not."

"You were not forthcoming with details. Was it fun to kick it with a small-town girl who didn't know any better? Did you get off on that?"

"What? No."

The quick flash of horror on his face mollified me slightly. The hurt couldn't quite be fixed. And it shouldn't hurt. He shouldn't matter that much. Which meant I was in so much more trouble than I'd thought.

Being attracted to him was one thing, but this?

The rush of emotion choked me and tears burned. Nope, I would *not* let him see me cry. I ran deeper into the grove of trees full of their pink and white spring blooms.

Rory's longer stride passed me and he came around in front of me. He grasped my upper arms. "Christ, don't cry."

I shook my hair forward, so very glad I didn't have my braids in today. "I'm not crying about you."

"Then why?"

I tried to shake him off again. Mostly because I wanted to bury my face in his chest so much. His leather and just pure male scent was addictive. I couldn't tell you what the scent was exactly, but it made me want to crawl into him and stay. "Because I'm mad. I cry when I'm angry and it's very inconvenient."

When he laughed, I punched him in the gut and walked around him.

"No, I'm not laughing at you."

"Could have fooled me."

He raised his voice. "I don't want you to be pissed off. I just want you with me. I wanted you to meet my people. I have very few of them."

I dashed away my tears. "What do you mean very few of them? You have tons of people you work with."

He invaded my space to cup my face. "Emphasis on work, Ivy." He brushed the last of my tears away. His intense blue gaze bore into mine. "I have plenty of people I work with, but getting close to people isn't my thing. Not until..."

"Until what?"

He covered my mouth. The kiss was hard and fast. Intense on a level that usually left me missing clothing. Just as suddenly, he tore his mouth from mine and pressed his forehead to mine. "You're not supposed to be more than fun."

"Gee, thanks."

He hung his head. "Bollocks, I can't do any of this right."

This time, it was me who laughed. "I get it." I curled my arms around his waist and stepped into him.

He wrapped his arms around my shoulders until there was no space between us. "I never expected you."

I flattened my cheek to his chest and listened to his heartbeat. "Ditto."

He took a step back. "But I didn't mean to hurt you. I just wasn't ready to let you go."

I swallowed down the hope flaring to life inside me. He didn't mean it that way. And even if he did, Rory's basic makeup was completely opposite from my own. He was a musician, or a producer —heck, I wasn't even completely sure what he did. But none of it included a small town. Or a family.

For pity's sake, I'd been saving up to open an ice cream truck in the summer. I was small town. I wanted a baby so bad I'd actually gone to a meeting of like-minded women who were willing to do the baby thing alone. I wasn't exactly ready for the baby part yet, but it had always been in my plans.

A little girl or boy running around the truck with me, helping me pass out ice cream and create crazy flavors. I could see it all.

What I *couldn't* see was him.

Rory would be across the street watching. Forever watching and separate. He wasn't the guy who would climb into the fray and pick up a sticky, screaming kid and kiss away his or her hurts.

He kissed away yours.

I ignored that little voice. He wasn't a monster. He just wasn't my future.

But he could be my right now. He could be a bright spring day in one of my favorite places on the planet beyond the Cove.

"Let's go see your friends. You have work to do, right?"

"Only if that's okay with you."

I rose onto my toes and kissed his scruffy chin. "It's a real hardship to deal with you, LC, but I will survive."

He hooked his arm around my shoulders and dragged me back toward the car. "A magnanimous woman. I'm not sure *I* can survive the day."

I bumped my hip against him. "So, I get to see you play that guitar? Do you sing?"

His cheeks went ruddy. "I can play any instrument you put in front of me, but singing isn't really my forte. I leave that to the Kellans and Ians of the world."

"But you can?"

"I can hold a note, yes."

"I expect to hear you sing, LC. Today."

He rolled his eyes. "We'll see."

THIRTEEN

IVY

WE MADE IT INTO THE CLEARING AND IAN AND KELLAN WERE waiting for us.

This time, there were a few more men with them. A tall guy—well, they were all kind of on the tall end, to be honest—was playing airplane with Wolf. Another one stood nearby with a definite familial resemblance. Both men were enamored with the very happy child. A pretty dark-haired woman was filming on her phone as Wolf went for another zoom.

"There they are." Kellan kept an eye on his kid as he spoke. I was pretty sure Wolf was his anyway. Everything had gotten jumbled after I'd been sideswiped by the Rory information deluge.

So many things made more sense now, but it was still a lot to digest.

"Hey. Sorry about that." My chest, neck, and face had to be blazing.

"No worries. If Ian isn't tossed out of the barn at least twice a visit, then something's wrong." The woman who spoke made me feel like an Amazon. Her voice was husky and filled with humor. She was leaning against Ian's chest as his arms encircled her. He was lightly tapping some internal beat on her rounded belly. She had silvery hair gathered in an intricate braid I'd only ever seen in YouTube videos. She wore overalls and a sunny yellow tank top splattered with paint.

"Hey." Ian pouted.

She batted his hands away and came across the grass to me. "I'm Zoe Manning." She pointed behind her. "Those are my brothers. Hayes is the spotter and the pilot is Justin."

I shook Zoe's hand. "Thanks for letting me crash the rocker club."

"Please crash it. These guys get going and all we do is play audience."

"You love my music, Magic." Ian came up behind her and kissed her neck. "She likes to pretend we're a pain in the ass."

"Oh, you are."

Ian snaked a hand around her belly. "But I'm your pain in the ass."

She rolled her eyes, but put her hand over his. "Yeah, you are."

"Ugh, we're leaving if it's going to get all couple-ish in here." Justin swung the toddler through the air and handed him off to Kellan. "Flight's over, little dude."

Wolf's gleeful laugh filled the air. "More!"

Kellan sighed. "Now I'm going to be playing airplane all day."

The dark-haired woman came up beside him. "As if you don't do it already." She waved. "I'm Maggie."

Justin motioned his brother over. "Give them the keys."

Ian perked up. "Keys?"

Justin's tanned face was a mass of beard and wrinkles. He seemed young, but there was a lot of hair going on, so I wasn't sure. He was wearing a black T-shirt and jeans covered in...tree sap, maybe? But he was definitely on the manly-woodsy end of the spectrum. It was quite appealing. Especially his bright blue eyes that gave me an appreciative once over.

He glanced at Rory and cleared his throat.

I looked over my shoulder. Rory's face was set in that reserved, blank expression again.

So, he'd been right about the Manning brothers swarming about.

"Right. Keys." Justin clapped his hand on his brother's shoulder. "We finished the little stage in the distillery. If you guys want to try it out, we'd appreciate it."

As Hayes dug a set of keys out of his pocket, Ian rushed over and tried to snatch them.

"Hey, try it out, not trash it, rockstar." Hayes thumped Ian's forehead with with his middle finger.

"Bloody hell." Ian snatched them just the same. "If you didn't want me in there, you wouldn't have offered." His eyes were bright with excitement. "They've been teasing us with that stage for months. I can't believe my band's not here to try it out."

"Handily, we are," Kellan said.

Rory frowned. "We have work to do too."

"We've got all day, right?" Kellan handed off Wolf to Maggie and gave her a quick kiss on the cheek. "I'm going to get my guitar."

Maggie shook her head. "He's been dying to play with people. Thanks for inviting us. He's going to be like a..." She glanced at Wolf and kissed his neck until he laughed. "Well, like his kid."

I resisted the urge to ask to hold him. His face was so sweetly chubby and perfect.

Rory slid his hand into mine as the group of people started moving. I was herded with instruments, baby strollers, and general revelry. Everyone seemed at ease with each other.

Sometimes too at ease. It was a little weird that Ian Kagan was running back and forth between the groups of people like an antsy three-year-old.

Ian Kagan who had recently been on a billboard in Times Square. The billboard I'd seen with my own eyes during my annual trip down to see the Christmas windows with my bestie.

Yeah. Weird.

But Rory was right. He was a guy with energy to burn—bless his girlfriend/fiancée /lifemate—but just a guy.

Ian had the door open to a huge barn. He was waving his arms to get us to move faster. Hay was strewn across the floor, lending a rustic charm to the room. Large steel silos lined one side of the space, and a big bar was stretched in front of it with various taps. The bar top was steel and glass with half built stools situated against it.

The steel was the super industrial kind, but the stools seemed to be made from repurposed barrels with rich red cushions waiting to be fashioned to them. The rafters were high and three huge fans were lazily spinning.

It smelled like cider and hay with a bonus blast of floral notes from the blooming trees lining every square inch of the property.

Rory tugged me toward the stage and my mouth dropped. It was made of reclaimed wood polished to a gleaming shine with an apple tree coming from the far side of the stage. They'd actually built the barn around the gnarled old tree. It was gorgeous and each branch looked like it held a story.

"This is the coolest place I've ever seen."

Hayes was standing in the corner looking from the small group to the stage and back again. He was biting his lower lip and cracking his knuckles.

"Don't mind my brother," Zoe said in a whisper.

"He looks like he's about to throw up."

"Probably a close thing. This has been Hayes's baby for awhile. He's been working on it nonstop since before I got pregnant."

"Well, he did an awesome job."

"I've been painting tiles that I'm going to put behind the stage. He doesn't know it yet." She grinned. "I've been itching to do a huge puzzle piece of a painting, but I've got this basketball hampering me from climbing on my usual scaffolding."

I glanced down at her belly. It was pretty sizable. "Scaffolding?"

She shrugged. "I'm an artist."

"Best artist ever in the history of artists." Ian's voice behind me made me jump.

Zoe rolled her eyes. "Go play with your friends."

"Just making sure you have somewhere to sit, Magic."

"I'm fine. We'll be fine."

He frowned and kissed her then bent to kiss her belly. "Okay, but you'll tell me if you need anything."

"I'm a big girl."

"You're perfect."

"Just because I'm bearing your spawn doesn't mean you have to keep laying it all on so thick there, pal."

He started to run to the stage before coming right back to her. "I need to steal her for a minute."

I smiled and nodded to them.

Zoe laughed. "I'll be right back. It's easier to just let him show me whatever he's got to show me than to say no."

I watched them go, trying to hold down the wistfulness that was trying to grow inside my chest. "He's a bundle of energy."

Rory rolled his eyes. "He's like this all the time. It's a wonder we ever get work done when we're in the studio. He's like a butterfly on speed."

I laughed. "He's fairly adorable."

"You would think so."

"Oh?" I bumped his shoulder. "And why's that?"

Rory shrugged. "Everyone does. Why he has legions of women panting after him. And yet he only has eyes for his fair Zoe."

"As it should be."

He met my gaze. "For some."

I wasn't sure what to do with that little comment, but before I could come up with a reply, Kellan called for him to come onto the stage.

He dropped a quick kiss on my mouth and jogged off to oblige him.

"Have you ever seen him play?"

I turned toward the voice behind me. Maggie was swaying with Wolf in her arms. "I didn't even know he could until today."

"That one plays it close to the vest in all things." Wolf tugged on her hair and she patiently unwound his chubby little fingers without missing a beat. "He and Kellan have been working together for a bit. I've never seen someone with such innate talent who doesn't want to be on stage."

A different sort of wistfulness took root inside me. I wanted to know more about Rory. Especially about the parts of him he squirreled away. "No?"

"Rory? He definitely isn't interested."

"Hey guys, we can sit over here. My ankles are balloons."

We both turned toward Zoe's voice. Hayes was beside her, setting up chairs. He lifted a small cooler and set it on the table. "Gotta keep you ladies hydrated."

Zoe rolled her eyes. "I'll be glad when I'm not pregnant anymore and you start treating me like your sister again."

Hayes pushed up his dark rimmed glasses. "I am treating you like my sister."

"No, you're being nice to me."

"Well, you have my innocent nephew in there. Have to make sure he knows I'm the very best uncle."

"Ah, now that makes more sense." She grinned up at him, then dragged him down by the tail of his shirt to give him a hug. "Lemonade?"

"Maybe."

"Yes." She flipped open the cooler, then wiggled her fingers. "You ladies are in luck. This is the best lemonade in the state."

I sat down and peeked over the edge. "I'll take some of that." It felt like I could drink a damn lake. I was parched.

Maggie laughed. "I don't know. My mom's recipe is pretty amazing."

"Oh, let me get the stroller." Hayes jogged to the doorway and returned with the huge stroller laden with everything a little boy could want.

"Thanks." Maggie set Wolf inside and handed him his little cup with two handles.

He instantly tossed it past the table.

"Whoa." Hayes glanced from the kid to the cup a few feet away. "Impressive. You're on my team, bud." He retrieved it and gave Maggie a horrified look.

Maggie snapped out a baby wipe and handed it to him. "Every eventuality. Go-go-Gadget-Go."

Wolf waved his arms. "Go!"

"Is that a thing? I thought Mr. Gadget was like...ancient."

"All the good cartoons are recycled. He loves that show." Maggie accepted a cup from Zoe. "Just you wait, you'll be all about the television shows too."

"I'd love to say I won't use the iPad, but I know myself." Zoe filled another glass and handed it to me. "I mean, I'll have the most paint-splattered child, but there's a time for sanity."

"Smart lady." Maggie took a sip and her eyes widened. "Okay, your mom wins."

"Her cooking isn't as good as Aunt Laverne's, but she knows how to make anything in liquid form."

"And Dad started us on moonshine." Hayes grinned. "I took it a few steps further, but he taught us everything we know about the groves. Would you like to try some?"

I nibbled on my lower lip. "Is it going to knock me on my ass? I'm more of a tequila in a margarita kind of girl. Sometimes some wine."

Hayes pulled out another smaller bottle in the cooler. "This one was made to be a mixer with my mom's lemonade."

Maggie covered the top of her glass. "I'm still breastfeeding. Little bugger won't quite give up on the source."

"Guess it's just you and me." Hayes grinned at me and splashed some in my glass.

I lifted it. "Cheers." The drink was sweet and tart with a little something extra. "I was expecting it to taste like gasoline."

"Backwater moonshine maybe, but not ours. That's the problem. You can't even taste it, and then you're on your face."

I held up my glass to Zoe. "Maybe a bit more lemonade. I don't want to miss anything today because of too much alcohol."

"Smart lady." Zoe laughed and refilled my glass with straight lemonade.

Hayes stayed for a few minutes, but kept pulling out his phone. "Work just isn't going to wait. I'm heading out, guys. Maybe you could record a few songs for me so I can hear how it sounds once they get going?"

"Sure." Zoe grinned up at her brother. "I'll make sure they don't hurt your baby."

"I didn't say anything."

"You didn't have to." She elbowed him when he smushed her into a hard hug.

"I'll see you at dinner later."

"Sounds good." She watched him leave then eased back in her chair. "I love my brothers, but all they do is hover. Add in Ian and I have precisely seven minutes alone a day. And that's generally peeing." She pushed her chair out. "Speaking of. I'll be right back."

I twisted my glass in the little puddle of condensation on the table . I could easily get used to this kind of lazy afternoon. My boyfriend playing with his friends, making new girlfriends.

Only Rory definitely wasn't my boyfriend, even if he felt like he could be one sometimes.

The strum of guitars dragged me away from my thoughts. Wolf gave a happy shriek.

"He'll be out in ten minutes. The minute Kel starts playing the guitar, he's soothed right to sleep."

My eyebrow rose. "They're playing Metallica."

"It doesn't matter."

"Impressive."

"Handy having a husband who provides an instant lullaby, in between the overstimulation of course." Maggie gave me a wink. "For Mama too."

"It's got to be hard to have a musician as a husband."

"Sometimes." She bent down to get one of Wolf's toys. "For the most part, he's just a regular guy. When he gets a big head about certain things, I usually kick him or drag him back down to Earth. Kind of my favorite thing to do, but don't tell him that."

My attention slid to the stage. Rory's guitar was worn in that way that made me itch to get a closer look. Little nicks along the body where his hand rubbed with repetition. An odd smudge further along the outside of the body, away from the strings.

He watched Ian, taking cues from him, changing the song slightly to suit him. He didn't lead, which surprised me. He was so forthright when he was around me. Seeing him fall back into a supporting role was puzzling.

As the often played "One" from Metallica blended into... I frowned. What was that song? I loved music, but it was more of a whatever-is-on-the-radio love. I enjoyed the old songs on the jukebox at the diner, some of the country-type music that played at the Spinning Wheel, and even some of the rock my brothers listened to.

But this felt more groovy. Before our generation.

Rory wasn't that much older than me, maybe a handful of years, but this music felt older. Finally, Ian's vocals rose to the rafters. His voice was velvet-smooth with an almost seventies' flavor.

The guitars were layered and seemed very skillfully done. I listened to music, but I'd never picked a song apart in my life. Rory's fingers were sliding up and down the neck of the guitar, making it do all sorts of things I'd never noticed one could do before.

It was far hotter than it should have been.

"Oh, don't start that crap," Zoe called out behind us. "Freaking Eagles song. As if he hasn't already gotten me knocked up," she muttered.

Ian lifted his hands in exultation. "For you, my sweet wife-to-be."

"Get a life. You haven't asked yet!"

"Yet is the operative word, Magic."

"The Eagles?"

Zoe shrugged. "His brother was here and they got on a classic rock tear. 'One of These Nights' is my favorite Eagles' song."

I grinned. "That's sweet."

"Yeah, he likes to think he's adorable."

Maggie snorted. "Oh, he knows he is."

"Why my life is never boring. Besides, I don't really mind bringing him down a peg or two when necessary."

"I hear that, girl." Maggie held out her fist and Zoe bumped it.

Ian gave Zoe a saucy smile then turned to Rory. He said something to Ian and they started another song, this one more current. They both strummed their guitars faster, as if they were in some sort of race.

Kellan joined in and his rumbling voice growled out the words to "Animals" from Nickelback.

My mouth dropped open. He did *not*.

Rory's mouth tipped up into a sly grin as the song got dirtier and grittier. Ian's voice matched Kellan's and they sang the gunfire-fast song in a weird tandem.

Maggie gave a delighted laugh beside me and Zoe whooped.

I was ready to strangle Rory.

The song was a little too close to our previous evening. I finished my lemonade and threw my cup at Rory. He tipped back his head with a laugh, then hopped to the floor and swung his guitar around his back as he headed right for me.

As Kellan got to the part about getting caught in the car, Rory pulled me up into a quick, hot kiss before letting me go as fast as he'd grabbed me. Then he threaded his way through the assembled crowd back to the stage.

"Whew." Zoe fanned her face. "I didn't know Rory had it in him. At least without a beer or seven first."

My cheeks were flaming, but not because of the kiss. Somehow there was a lighthearted Rory hidden in there who felt the need to show me affection. Okay, so it was a very hot kind of affection, but still, so not him. I mean, when we were naked or alone, he was quite handsy, but in front of people? Yeah, no. He was almost reserved.

The three rockers were laughing like lunatics by the end of the song. Then they had their heads together, iPhones out.

"Oh, this will go on for awhile." Zoe kicked out her feet.

Maggie nodded. "Someone got an idea."

My gaze strayed to the stage. Ian was peering over Rory's shoulder at his phone. He was bouncing lightly as they muttered and hummed, then stopped to tune their guitars.

"We've lost them."

"What?" I turned to Zoe.

"That's the oh-my-God-where's-my-notes-app look." She rubbed her belly absently.

"You okay?"

"Oh, sure. I just finally popped. Before it was more like, I don't know, slightly inconvenient. You know, like when you indulged for Christmas way too much? Maybe ten pounds? That's what it was like for the longest time. Now?" She patted her belly. "Now there's this thing in the way all the time that *everyone* wants to keep touching."

"Oh, it gets worse." Maggie laughed. "Complete strangers will be coming at you with their hands out."

"Someone's going to get decked."

Maggie laughed. "You get used to it. Around the eight and a half month mark you will probably need to stay out of public."

"I could beat a murder rap. Probably."

I grinned at that one. "Do you want to marry him?"

"Oh, I'll be marrying him. I haven't seen the ring yet, but I know he bought it with his brother while we were in St. John's for the holidays."

St. John's. The Virgin Islands were a port in like half the cruises I'd looked at longingly on cold winter nights. Like traveling to a place like that was just a usual thing.

I tried to drag my chin off the floor, but the story Zoe was telling about Simon Kagan's wife having a baby in the middle of a hurricane didn't help my shock factor.

"I'm hoping to do things a little less dramatically." Zoe stroked the side of her belly. "Then again, I'm having a Kagan. It's probably out of the question. Not to mention my mother is on me to get married before the baby comes."

"Do you want to?"

"I'd rather have a really cool ceremony after the baby is here so I can actually drink during my toast—hello, my family makes to die for moonshine—and I don't know, maybe enjoy the party and not fall asleep in the corner. You know, little things like that."

"Some cool venue in the city?"

Zoe laughed. "No, we're doing it up here. The orchard is in my blood. My man may be from London and think he's a rockstar, but some things you have to do at home."

I glanced up at the stage at Ian's effortless rocker vibe. "He is."

"Yeah, he is, but he's also the annoying love of my life."

I had to smile. "I don't think the saying goes like that."

"Live with Ian for five minutes and it does."

"Yeah, living with a rockstar is just like living with any other man who won't put his freaking socks in the laundry." Maggie lightly rocked the stroller with her foot. "I met Kel in the middle of a snowstorm."

"Really?"

"Yeah. One wild night and my life was forever changed. I may want to strangle him with his damn socks some days, but I wouldn't trade him for the world."

"That's how I met Rory."

"Strangled socks?"

I laughed. "Snowstorm. That doozy we had last month."

Maggie grinned. "Twinners." She lifted her lemonade cup in a salute. "I keep forgetting you guys have only known each other a little while."

You and me both. "All this is a little overwhelming. I had no idea who Rory was. I didn't exactly ask, but I assumed he was some hotshot in Los Angeles."

"He is." Zoe refilled her drink and grabbed another cup for me. "Want this one leaded too?"

"No, I think one shot of your brother's moonshine is enough."

"Smart girl."

"You know, if you want to get your mom off your back, looking at wedding dresses is a good first step."

"You do see this belly going on?"

I laughed. "More like a place to find ideas. You don't seem like a traditional girl."

"What was the first clue?" Zoe flipped her braid over her shoulder.

Maggie grinned. "Maybe the rainbow streaks of paint in your hair?"

I laughed. "My bestie owns a shop in Crescent Cove called Kinleigh's. She stocks vintage clothes. She's always finding really cool wedding dresses for people. She kind of backed into it when she did her trunk parties for fun."

"Trunk parties?" Maggie turned toward me. "What's that?"

"Literally these huge steamer trunks. She used to pack them full of crazy clothes she picked up on her hunts. She found more than she could ever wear and started selling them by doing YouTube and Facebook live parties where she showed them off. Eventually, she did so well that she ended up opening her own shop."

Maggie dug into the diaper bag next to her chair and tugged out her phone. "What's her name again?"

Zoe pulled hers out of the pocket of her overalls and they both waited.

"You don't have to really look her up. I know she's—"

"Shut up." Zoe rolled her eyes. "That sounds way cooler than going to some frou-frou place my mother wants to drag me to. You know, the ones that sell prom dresses by the truckload?"

I laughed. "Kinleigh's is the name. Also her name—shocker."

Zoe typed quickly, as did Maggie.

"Holy shit." Maggie twisted her phone around to show off a sundress. "When can we go?"

Zoe leaned over to look then grinned at me. "Yeah, when can we go?"

I took Zoe's phone and plugged in my info, then did the same when Maggie handed over her phone too. "Sounds like a date to me."

"I have a gallery thing next week, but I'll definitely be in touch after that."

"You work at a gallery?"

"No, a showing. I'm pretty much ready to barf on a daily basis and only half the time it's because of the spawn. It's my second showing and I really don't want to be a one-hit wonder."

"Wow."

Zoe shrugged. "It's scary as hell, exhilarating, and insane. And I'm also unbearable before a show. Ian's a fucking saint."

I glanced back at the stage where Ian was plucking strings on Rory's guitar. "Are you sure he's not a two-year-old?"

She followed my gaze. "Well, he's that too, I swear." She shook her head, but the smile on her face was definitely indulgent. "But he's also amazing and so supportive. And he misses Rory. They became really good friends while writing his album. But then Rory was onto his next project."

"What does he do?"

"I'm not sure how to describe it." Zoe laughed. "Jack of all trades kind of dude."

Maggie leaned forward. "He's like a music doctor of sorts. Writes, produces, rips apart—and does some playing. It's more that he knows the ins and outs of songs. Kel is soaking it all up and talking about him constantly. If I didn't know better, I'd wonder if he was in love with him."

"About Rory?"

"Yeah, he's a little standoffish sometimes, but then he gets like that." Maggie nodded at the stage.

The three of them were sitting a circle, completely oblivious to us. Each of them was trying to play over the others to put their own spin on the song. Not in a one-upmanship kind of way, but more of an excited brainstorming style.

Like the way I got with an ice cream recipe. I recognized the signs.

Rory was passionate.

Intense.

Fascinating.

Just watching him in his element was intoxicating. This whole day had been so far. I felt as if I was discovering yet another intriguing side to him—and there were already so many.

So, how the hell was I going to get over him when he left?

FOURTEEN

**Rory**

Supper at Happy Acres was an experience. I still wasn't sure if it was a good one or bad.

Much like the day itself.

I had to give Ivy a lot of credit. She'd rolled with the rockstar hits all day long and had scarcely blinked. For someone who hadn't guessed what my career was, she'd adapted remarkably well. She'd barely squealed or fangirled at all. Except for her rightful indignation at my omissions, she'd been cool about everything. So much so that it was hard not to feel like a moron for thinking she couldn't handle our differences.

And she hadn't swooned at the sight of either Ian or Kellan, who, let's face it, were easy on the eyes. Or so I'd been told. I couldn't claim to fancy them myself.

We'd definitely worked up an appetite. Handy, since the folks at Happy Acres ate early. And they ate a lot. The huge farmhouse table was weighed down with enough plates and dishes to feed a small country. Which was saying plenty since Ian alone could clear half the bowls without help.

"I'm eating for three."

"Three?" I nearly choked on my slab of apple-peach pie. It wasn't a piece. I swore Laverne, the proprietress of Happy Acres, had served me roughly a quarter of it. "Zoe, you didn't let him plant twins in you."

Zoe rolled her eyes. "No. There's just one, although he's roly-poly. But Ian likes to claim he's eating for all three of us."

Laverne patted Ian's shoulder as he sprayed whipped cream on his second piece of pie. "He's a growing boy. We love feeding him here."

"Glad you do, since our grocery bill can barely handle him." Zoe shook her head.

"The baby is a boy?" I don't know why the question stuck in my throat. Or how I'd missed that information.

Ian rolled his eyes. "I already told you. Probably five times. He does not listen. Ivy, I hope you have patience with this one. He lives in his head and doesn't invite guests."

Ivy smiled weakly and poked at the crust of her pie. She'd barely eaten a thing. "I can play things close to the vest too, so I'm okay with it."

That was what she said, but I was fairly certain she wasn't truly okay with any of this. Despite her smiles and laughter, and how she'd enjoyed the music and spent time with my friends, I could tell she had a lot on her mind.

Maggie snorted and fed a spoonful of apple goo to Wolf in his high chair at her side. "You think he's tight-lipped, Ivy? You didn't know Kellan a couple of years ago. At least Rory is polite. Kellan just grunted and growled."

He slid his arm around the back of her chair. "Is this where you tell them I was changed by the love of a good woman?"

"Or a bad one." She fluttered her lashes and made the whole table laugh.

Even me.

It was hard not to relax around this group. If it wasn't Ian's antics or his impromptu jam sessions, or Kellan cutting up with his son, it was Laverne chasing the family dog, Lola, and trying to pry shoes out of her mouth. She'd welcomed all of us at some point in the day by snatching a sandal or sneaker and bounding off.

Every time Ivy laughed, something twisted inside me. That sound made everything better. And she wasn't doing it enough.

Because of me. So, it was up to me to make this right.

Hurting her had never been part of the plan. If I'd had one beyond just wanting to get lost in her. Anything to forget that our lives were so different.

But now I was wondering if the miles between us were as many as I'd first believed.

"I can't say Ian was ever grouchy. Well, minus that first night on stage. He insulted me in front of the world." Zoe pointed with her fork. "That was his wooing technique."

"You interrupted my show. And tried to steal my very large thunder."

"You had no thunder then. Except in your own head."

Ian shrugged and shoveled in more pie. He was already almost done with his second slice. "Positive thinking leads to positive results. That's what Anthony Robbins says."

"Anthony who?" Justin asked, scooping ice cream onto his pie until the thing nearly collapsed under its weight.

"He's on a self-improvement kick." Zoe leaned back in her chair and rubbed her truly mind-boggling belly. It had been a couple of months since I'd seen her, and in that time, her waistline had expanded to dangerous proportions.

Either she was carrying a giant human baby or a couple of aliens.

"I have a family now. I have to be all I can be."

"Isn't that the slogan for the Army?" Hayes wondered, retrieving some squeaky thing Lola dropped at his feet.

"Oh. Huh. Maybe."

"I feel the same way, by the way," Hayes said on the other side of Ivy. The way he smiled at her made me grip my fork that much tighter.

He was just being small-town friendly. That was what they did here. But Hayes was exactly the sort of man who'd stick around for the long haul. The kind of man Ivy deserved. Not one who'd come and go as he pleased.

A decent man wouldn't begrudge her finding someone—someone who wasn't me. But fuck if I didn't want to dig Hayes's eyes out with a rusty fork.

Christ, I should've been chivalrous and stayed away this time. I'd only thought of seeing her again, of spending time with her and burying myself inside her. I hadn't considered what it would be like to draw her closer only to leave again.

Justin chuckled. "Since when?"

Zoe's eldest brother Beckett leaned over the table and snatched the last slice of pie from the serving plate. "Right. So says the guy who woke up this morning with rug burn on his face."

"That was Justin, not me," Hayes protested.

Zoe sighed. "Some things never change. Males are like frat boys until they're senior citizens."

"Not me. I haven't had a drink in..." Ian glanced at his watch. "At least an hour. More pie?" Ian grinned up at Laverne as she stopped beside the table.

She laughed and shook her head. "There's another one in the oven. Good thing I planned ahead." She glanced around the table at each of us. "Anyone else? The fresh one will be ready soon."

I scraped up the last forkful on my plate. "Not for me, thanks, but it's delicious."

"What about you, Ivy?"

"No, thank you, I'm stuffed. It was all so good." She smiled at Laverne and suddenly, I couldn't wait any longer to be alone with her.

"We're going to go for a walk, if that's okay." I drew my chair back from the table. "Ivy mentioned wanting to see more of the grove."

"I did?" When I raised my brows, she delicately wiped her mouth with her napkin. "Oh. Right. Yes. The grove."

I moved behind her to pull out her chair. "We'll be back soon."

"Too much family time makes him itchy. Or else something else needs a scratch." Ian stuck his tongue in his cheek, making everyone laugh.

I discreetly flipped him off out of Laverne's line of sight. The bastard just grinned.

Ivy rose. "Let me just go freshen up first. Be right back."

She'd no sooner disappeared that Ian shook his head at me. "She's lovely. I hope you don't fuck it up."

Immediately, my hackles rose. "Excuse me?"

"You're clearly out of your element here, but underneath, you're an okay guy. I know that. My sweet Zoe probably knows that." Zoe poked him, but Ian didn't falter. "Ivy, however, may not realize under your porcupine shell, you're actually made of marshmallows and pudding."

"Says the man who consumes his weight in sweets on a daily basis."

Ian patted his rock-hard abs. "I train as hard as I eat. Work as hard as I play. F—"

Zoe covered his mouth. "Stop while you're ahead. Unless you want to get divorced before you're even married."

Everyone at the table chuckled while Ian nibbled the tips of her fingers and on up her arm. Zoe pretended to sigh, but her face was prettily flushed. She was enjoying every second with the loon.

"Ugh, not again. Can we not at the dinner table?" Hayes stood up with a stack of plates in his hands then walked away in disgust.

Ian shrugged. "Your brothers are sorely in need of female companionship, Magic."

"I'd rather not think about that, thanks." Zoe wrinkled her nose and drew her arm back, but I didn't miss the smile she flashed him.

They were insanely in love—emphasis on insane. Didn't they realize how much control a person had over you once you invested that much in them?

Pity that I never forgot.

I always told myself I'd never had a serious girlfriend, mainly since my first real relationship had ended so spectacularly. It hadn't lasted long in any case. We'd been young and foolish. Me even more so since I'd figured I could travel back and forth from the States to our tiny village near Dublin.

One day, I'd returned to find my girl in bed with one of my mates. And that had been that.

Since then, I'd done just fine single file. I rarely even thought about Darla. So, why was she on my mind now?

One guess. And her name was Ivy. But Ivy wasn't Darla, and she hadn't betrayed my trust.

Yet.

"Thanks again for a wonderful dinner," I said to Laverne before I escaped.

I went upstairs to where we'd stashed our instruments, took care of business, then picked up my case on my way back out. Ivy was waiting at the bottom of the stairs.

"I wondered if you'd skipped out." Her tone was light, but her deep, dark eyes were heavy with all the things she didn't—wouldn't—say.

We were a pair, me and my ginger fairy. She wasn't mine, but it was getting harder and harder to remember that.

Rather than reply, I dragged my guitar case in front of me.

Her eyebrows lifted. "I get a private show?"

I walked down the stairs to her and shrugged, channeling some of my best mate's easy charm. I would never be as effortless as Ian, but I'd picked up some pointers after all these years spent with rockstars. "Maybe. If you play your cards right."

She hit me lightly and I laughed, drawing her in for a hug and a quick kiss on top of her head. She didn't detangle herself as we said goodbye to the others still lingering around the table with coffee and gossip. Nor did she move to separate us outside as we headed up the meandering gravel path toward the grove.

It wasn't sunset yet, but from the soft golden light spearing between the budding and blooming trees, it wasn't too far off. The crisp air skated over my skin, but nothing could touch the warmth from Ivy's sweet body curved against mine.

She fit me just like my hand fit my Epiphone. There was a groove from my fingers where they notched just right. Somehow Ivy and I locked together in the same way.

As if it was meant.

As if we had known each other so much longer than the sum of the few hours we'd spent together.

It was the type of thing for which stories and songs and sonnets were written. Usually with a tragic ending, because how could anything so sudden and perfect be fated to last?

But that was for later. Tomorrow. Right now, she was still at my side. Sharing my air and smiling up at me with the rosy glow of the sun on her cheeks.

"So, you like my friends? Not that Kellan is one, exactly, as we're just collaborators for now. But Ian—"

She came to a halt. Just like that, the easy moment between us vanished. "Why do you do that?"

"Do what?"

"Pretend not to care. Diminish what matters to you. Try to be so blasé about everything."

I went cold. Inside, outside. I didn't drop my arm from around her, but I definitely loosened my grip. "I didn't realize I was doing that. Or that I'd done it enough for you to label it a trait."

"And now the snooty Irish tone. Jesus H. Christ." She moved away from me and threw up her hands. "You're so frustrating, LC."

Part of me rejoiced that she could still call me by that ridiculous nickname despite her irritation. The rest of me was peeved she was irritated, period. As if she had any right to be.

Okay, so she had plenty of right. But I'd never insinuated we were going to be a long-term thing. My mistake was in coming back to her again.

Your mistake or your salvation?

I gripped the neck of my guitar case. "My apologies."

She stared at me, her eyes catching the dying rays of the sun and turning them into fire. If this was a super hero movie, I would be lying dead in the dirt while she waited for the wind machine to blow back her flowing locks. "Your obnoxious attitude should not turn me on."

"No. It shouldn't."

"Yet it does. What's wrong with me?" While I pondered that, she stepped forward and fisted her hands in my shirt. "It's the accent," she muttered. "Gotta be the accent."

Then her mouth covered mine.

The craziest part was I could taste her anger. And her frustration. And underneath both, her sadness. They were layered with the sweetness from Laverne's pie and Ivy's natural essence.

"I'm really mad at you," she said between kisses, slipping her fingers in the gaps in the buttons along the front of my shirt. Her nails teased over my skin and made me hiss.

"Fuck." I nearly dropped my case in my urgency to tilt her head toward mine. Our tongues tangled, hot and needy. "I've been dying to get my hands on you again all day."

Even as I said it, I dialed myself back. She was worth so much more than just this. Yet I kept falling back on my base nature to avoid the tougher conversations.

I drew away from her and let out a long, shaky breath. "But we should walk first."

The hurt registering in her eyes nearly undid me.

"You have a right to more than I've given you." I rolled my thumb over her lower lip. "I didn't expect you, Ivy. No matter how many times I think or say that, it's not enough. I don't meet people like you. I don't—"

Fall for someone that easily.

Fuck easily. It was like crash landing without a parachute to break your fall.

She turned away. "Yeah, I get it. You live in a different world. I'd figured you did, just knowing the LA part, but now that I understand the rest?" She laughed quietly. "Maggie and Zoe came from here, and they made it work. I don't know how."

I gripped her shoulder in my free hand. "It takes effort on both sides. I don't have that in me." Not again. "Not because of you. But because of—"

"Because of you. Right. Standard line. Besides, who's to say I'm any different than you? I like fucking too, you know. Just because I have a pair of ovaries and a fine set of tits doesn't mean I'm one period away from needing to settle down."

Laughing right then couldn't have been wise. I just couldn't stop myself. "Christ, you're a sight," I said as she whirled to stab her finger into my chest.

"And *that*. That isn't fair. You wind me up and then you compliment me and deflate any argument I might have. You know why? I have no reason to argue. You never lied to me. It was always just sex and you'd be gone in the morning."

I tried to keep from checking out of the corner of my eye if we were being overheard. Not important. She was entitled to her feelings—including how loudly she was currently conveying them. So what if this was a farm meant for families and children?

It wasn't as if a telephoto lens would come through the trees of this bucolic scene and catch something unsavory for a tabloid. I wasn't a true rocker, after all. I just played one now and then when it suited my aims.

As I did most things. This weekend, I'd played the role of boyfriend.

Soon enough, I'd play the role of the asshole who couldn't commit and hop on a plane without a care in the world.

Right.

I nodded toward the grove ahead of us. "Let's walk, yeah?"

She gave me a healthy dose of side eye, but she did as I asked. She made no move to get closer to me, so I gave her some space. It was better for her at least, if not for me.

We wandered along the path, passing only a few people coming out of the grove. The deeper we went, following the beams of the descending sun, the more alone we became. After a bit, no one passed us, and I would've sworn it got chillier.

The scents of fresh earth and flowers I couldn't name filled my head. We were surrounded by trees, cushioned in a silence broken only by occasional songs from the birds overhead.

We might have been the only people left on earth.

The property seemed vast. Endless. As if we walked forever. Then she surprised me by taking my hand and veering off the path, rushing so fast that I had to chuckle as I picked my way over exposed roots and around rocks and greenery. She seemed to know where she was going, and I definitely did not.

We emerged into a clearing that led to a short rise. I followed her up it and caught my breath as we stood together viewing the countryside in all its rose-gold splendor below us. Trees bursting with new life, miles and miles of land. Farms and quaint country churches with their steeples mixed with sprawling ranches and businesses in the hills and valleys below. I couldn't take it all in and had to shield my eyes from the last of the sun. But the air seemed even clearer up here, as if it wasn't my imagination we were closer to the sky.

Fanciful sot, aren't you?

But I wouldn't have said I was particularly. At least not before Crescent Cove and Turnbull had gotten their hooks into me.

Before Ivy.

I unfolded the spread I'd tucked in my guitar case, then sat in the grass and patted the spot beside me. She joined me on the ground, her knees bumping mine. I smiled in silent thanks.

She always eased the way.

Swallowing the knot in my throat, I pulled out my Epiphone. I could feel her shock as if it was a tangible thing.

I wanted to make a joke. *Thought I was carrying this as a prop, did you?*

But I said nothing so as not to diminish the moment.

The words I'd written for her came easily to hand as I strummed the opening chords. I'd toyed with the song here and there, but it was still very much a work in progress. Still, new lyrics came to me, aided by the soft flutter of the breeze through her hair and the gentle, insistent press of her leg to mine.

A steady reminder.

Light in her eyes, not meant to go out
Broken by me, never
Not a doubt
But places inside me
She has laid claim
To go on with her
Or without her
I'll never be the same

I stopped, my fingers falling still. And chanced a look at her in the fading light.

Her eyes were damp with tears.

"That's..." Her throat moved. "You really wrote that for me?"

"Do you think there could be another ginger fairy?" *Ever?*

I didn't say the last part aloud, but it echoed through my head.

Her lips curved. "Just as there could be no other Lucky Charms."

"Not true. I ate some just last week."

On purpose. To remind myself of her.

As if I ever forgot.

"You ate yourself?"

"This conversation is veering dangerously close to perversion. Alas, I'm not that flexible."

Her smile grew and the constriction in my throat lessened.

"I wrote that for you weeks ago. I'd tried a few times and nothing came out right." Idly, I strummed the strings. "Today the last verse just seemed to flow. It needs more work of course, but—"

"It's perfect. No one's ever written anything for me." She dashed at the tears dripping off her chin, laughing self-consciously. "Well, an old high school boyfriend did. But no one who—"

She broke off and stared at me. I stared right back.

I needed to know what she'd meant to say. But I didn't have the stones to ask.

Rather than completing her thought, she leaned forward and took the guitar out of my hands. She traced the sunburst pattern on one of my most treasured instruments, her touch reverent. Carefully, she set it in its case and turned to me.

I cleared my throat. "Easy enough to string some words together."

Anything to fill the silence.

She pressed her finger to my lips. Then she sat back on her haunches and drew her quirky skull-patterned top over her head.

No warning. No time for me to prepare. Not even a lifetime would be enough.

The last of the sunshine shimmered over her skin. I tried to keep my gaze on her lovely face, on the ends of her red hair trailing in the wind, but I couldn't stop from taking in the sight of her perfect breasts encased in lace.

Lace that dropped away to leave only pale flesh and tight pink nipples.

My mouth went dry. I could only stare, my heartbeat throbbing in my head, as she straddled my lap.

Someone could see.

The protests inside me were weak. Practically nonexistent. And I didn't think to shield myself as I wrapped my arms around her. All I could think about was Ivy.

She coiled her arms around my neck and rocked into me as our mouths met. This kiss wasn't like any of the others. The same desperation fueled it, but there was more. Gentleness. Affection. Maybe even some regret.

A lot on my side, for sure.

She tipped back her head to give me access when my mouth slid to her throat. I nipped at the pulse just under her jaw, enjoying how it sped up for me. She was so responsive. Tuned to me in a way I'd never experienced.

Not because I was famous. Just because I was me, and she was her, and together, we made wild, wonderful music.

Her fingers drove through my hair to hold me against her as I focused my kisses on the tops of her breasts. I drifted lower to suck on her hard nipples. Her hair flowed around us like water, a silky cocoon. Not much protection from prying eyes, but there was a barbaric part of me that didn't want to hide. She was mine in this time and space, and I ached for the world to know it.

A scrape of my teeth and she shuddered. A twist of my fingers and she rocked against my rigid length.

Waiting for her any longer required more patience than I possessed.

I took her mouth again as I slipped a hand beneath her flirty skirt to tease the insides of her thighs. She was wet already, and my mind scrambled at just the brush of my thumb over her soaked panties.

"I'm sorry," I murmured between kisses.

"For what?"

"I need you. So much. I can't wait."

"Don't apologize for that." She reached down between us to unzip me and free my cock. For just one illicit second, she coated me in the wetness from her slit. I groaned and remembered last night.

I'd been inside her bare.

Again. I could have that again.

No, you can't, you idiot. Is it really worth risking everything?

She, too, must've come to her senses because she drew me away from the inferno slickness of her and held me to her belly. Rubbing me there so that the mixture of us branded her pale skin. She licked her lips and squeezed me hard before slipping her hand below to caress my sac.

"Christ, Ivy, you have the devil in you."

"Not yet," she panted, her eyes sparkling, "but I'm ready for him." Another swipe of her tongue over her full lips. "So ready. Can't you tell?"

Jesus.

I slipped two fingers inside her. Quick, deep thrusts made her clutch my shoulders and drop back her head to expose her throat. The long, creamy line of it begged for my kisses. As I dragged my teeth over her neck, I knew from her cry that I'd marked her.

I didn't care. The animal side of me had no compunction.

"I'm gonna ruin another pair," I warned before I rent the fabric in two.

"God, that's hot." She bounced against me, teasing me again with those wet little swipes of her greedy pussy. She caught the tip of her tongue between her teeth. "Such a tough man you are."

"About to show you."

But before I did, I withdrew the condom I'd tucked in my pocket when I went back to our room. I hadn't known what this walk would bring, but being prepared was how I lived my life.

Swiftly, I suited up. Well aware she watched my every movement.

She made a noise deep in her throat as I pulled her down onto me, sliding her down my shaft. She gripped me perfectly, enfolding me in a blinding blast of heat. I drew her up and down again, faster now, and she dug her nails into my shoulders through my shirt. Bearing down when I would've driven up, offering just enough of a push and pull that the need inside me wound even tighter.

"Not gonna make it easy on you, LC," she said breathlessly.

Bloody hell, this woman was unmatched.

Or worse—she was *my* match. Fire wrapped in sweetness wrapped in a smart mouth that tasted like pie and sex.

I rolled her beneath me on the spread on the grass, cursing the trousers and boxers that impeded my efforts. I started to shove them down, then recalled, oh yeah, bare ass, fucking outside.

What had I become? And better yet, how could I ensure I stayed this way forever?

Without ending our kisses, I shifted and rolled her on top of me, using her skirt for cover. Although her gorgeous breasts rose and fell with every goddamn thrust, so it wasn't as if it wasn't fully obvious what we were doing.

"Put your shirt back on," I gritted out.

She stretched her arm above her head and rocked her hips. "This is better." She cupped one of her breasts and toyed with the nipple, nearly making me cross-eyed. "Don't you think so?"

It was basically dark now. Just the faintest light remained. No one was out on this part of the property. We were safe.

Except nothing with Ivy Beck was safe, and I fucking loved—

It.

Not her.

Christ.

"To hell with it." Furious at myself, I rolled her beneath me again. She squealed at the sudden position shift and I caught her hands above her head as I hammered into her. Couldn't. Get. Deep. Enough. I was going to fuck her straight through the condom and pour myself inside her.

No barriers. Nothing between us.

"Rory." She curled her legs around my hips and clutched my torso hard enough that her nails practically sliced through my clothes. "Coming. God, coming."

"Yes. Hell, yes." I bit down on her lower lip. "Squeeze me as tight as you fucking can."

She didn't disappoint. I groaned as pleasure streaked through me, white-hot and overwhelming, and let the fraying wire around my control snap.

I drained myself into the condom as I buried my face in her hair. "Ivy." Just that, over and over again like a song.

A plea.

We didn't move for the longest time. It was the breeze tickling my bare ass that made me turn my head. And chow down on a mouthful of grass just beyond the spread. I sputtered and lifted my head, blades still stuck to my lips, while Ivy laughed.

"Crushing me. Ow. Ouch. But oh, God. You look like a cow."

I poked her in the side and she just laughed harder. So, I started laughing too.

When I rolled over, she climbed right back on top of me. She nuzzled my neck and wrapped herself around me like a content kitten. All she was missing was the purr.

"Gotta deal with the condom," I muttered. I couldn't imagine the mess we were making.

Actually, yes, I could. And I didn't really care.

"Don't worry." She licked my earlobe. "I'm good at getting you clean."

"You're going to be the death of me, Ivy Beck."

"Possibly. Just as you might be the same for me." She lifted her head, her wicked eyes glowing in the darkness. Must've been my imagination. "But for the next day, we're going to live."

I tucked her windblown hair behind her ear. "Taking it day by day is how I get by. You understand that, right? With my schedule, I need flexibility. I travel all over to meet with artists—"

"And you have a girl in every port. Gotcha." While she smiled, her voice turned cool.

"No. No other women. Just you. You're the only one in a long time."

"But?"

"But I live in LA and you live here. And bloody good sex can make people see compatibilities that aren't there. I'm not an easy man to be with," I added, turning her face back to mine when she shifted it away.

"As if I'm easy? You've never seen me during PMS. Or when I have Aunt Flo."

"Aunt who?"

"Never mind. You've definitely never seen me when I can't get a flavor right. I'm a raging bitch then. But that's people. We have a million different sides and half of them suck. You just hope to find someone with less suckage than the others. And if not, a really nice dick that makes up for the rest."

"Thank you. I think."

She didn't laugh, just rubbed her chilly arms. "I like you. A lot. We have fun. If that's all it is, then that's all it is. I won't try to rope you into anything."

"I don't know what to do with ropes. Or ties of most any kind. I'm used to living out of a suitcase and liking it. This..." I trailed off, gesturing to the wilderness around us, suddenly alive with chirps and rumbles and noises that I could not identify. I nearly shuddered. "Let's just say I'm not the sort to bond with nature and pitch a tent. I live in a place of glass and it suits me."

"And this suits me. But lots of things might. How will I ever know if I don't experience them?"

She was right. So right. As I'd seen during my short time in Crescent Cove.

"Trust doesn't come easy to me."

"No kidding?"

"Look, I don't want to bring up the past, but I've dealt with some things that make me wary. But I like being with you. To be honest, the idea of never seeing you again is painful." I touched her silky soft cheek. "And not just because I nearly dropped to my knees after tasting your—"

"Shh. This is a family show." Even in the dark, I could see her grin.

"Ice cream. Wow. Filthy mind." After I removed the condom and wrapped it in a tissue from my pocket, I pulled her close. "I have to go tomorrow night, but we have the rest of tonight. And I'd like to come back. I just don't know when."

I had tons of work waiting for me, with a list of prospective clients as long as both arms. I also wasn't sure how long it would take me to get some distance.

Some perspective on how to live my life with Ivy as only an occasional guest.

"Okay," she said after a few moments. "But I want your number. And I want you to have mine."

"Okay," I echoed, stroking her hair. "You have to make me a promise though."

She lifted her head.

"If you ever meet someone else and get tired of waiting on me, you'll be honest. Just call me and tell me the truth. I won't hold it against you."

"Rory—"

It was my turn to cover her lips with my finger. "Just that one promise."

She exhaled a heavy breath and nodded. "I promise."

FIFTEEN

 IVY

May

I RESTED MY CHIN ON MY ARM AS I STARED AT THE INGREDIENTS for my next creation. I was trying to make something exciting out of vanilla without it being too sweet. Oh, and without making me nauseated. Taking the cap off my vanilla extract made me want to hurl.

Probably because I'd been making everything vanilla for the last few weeks.

I reached for my phone and read the text one more time.

Kinleigh.

That was usually code for *let's do something crazy*. Usually that included far too much wine and too little self-control. Then again, the last time I'd lost control, there hadn't been any alcohol involved.

Just lust and a handful of condoms. Oh, and an Irish accent that I kept dreaming about.

No big deal. Even if time kept slipping away with barely a handful of texts between us.

My wild Irish fling. He was the drifter and I was the small town girl who was his port in a New York storm.

How very rockstar of him and very stupid of me.

Didn't stop me from looking for his blue eyes in the crowd.

I set my phone down and spun it in front of my supplies. I sighed, then stood and gathered them all to tuck into my storage bin. I slid it back into the cupboard and picked up my phone.

> Trying to make vanilla exciting.

KINLEIGH
That's not possible.

> So I'm learning. I'll crack it though. What's up with you?

I'm bored. The rain has chased away all my customers. I also have to update my website and I'm avoiding it like Mrs. Conroy. Entertain me.

I snorted. Mrs. Conroy liked to make everyone in town crazy. Busybody with a capital B. I should be working on the backup flavors on my list, but I didn't feel like getting my blenders out to make sorbet.

> Meet me at BA in twenty.

Yes! Cya in a few.

At least I'd get coffee out of the deal. And the drive into town usually cleared my head when I hit a wall.

I stuffed my feet into my outrageously pink galoshes that matched my slicker, then grabbed my keys and purse on my way out the door. If I didn't change out of my bum clothes, Kinleigh couldn't talk me into going to the bar. Then again, if I kept taste-testing my ice cream, I'd need to hit up my bestie for a new wardrobe of elastic-waist pants for the summer.

Flowing tops for the win.

My brother's truck pulled up just as I got to my car.

"Hey."

August reached back into his truck. "Hey. I got that spray paint machine you asked me for last week."

Excitement brewed despite the late spring soaking we were getting. "Finally."

"Hey. It takes time to order these things. Not like Home Depot is around the corner."

I wrinkled my nose and flipped my hood up on my slicker. "I know. Thanks for getting it for me. It's supposed to be gorgeous tomorrow. Maybe you can help me do a base coat?"

He tapped the low brim of my hood. "Maybe."

I went on my tiptoes and gave him a kiss, then tugged on the worn brim of his ever-present baseball hat. "Thanks, Aug."

"Where you headed?"

"Kinleigh's."

"Oh. Tell her I said hi."

"Sure. I might drag her back here for pizza later. Want?"

"Nah, you guys have fun. I have a sub from Robbie's."

"Okay, text me if you change your mind. Maybe I'll stay at Kin's." I shrugged. "Depends on my mood."

"Well, if you get home before ten tomorrow, I can help you paint."

"I'll be here."

"Bye, brat."

I waved at him and rushed over to my car. Finally, I was getting something done on my truck. Summer was right around the corner. I didn't really want to drive it all around town, but finding a spot to set up in was tricky.

Licenses and town ordinances were hard to navigate for mobile food businesses. I'd been going blind looking over all the paperwork, but it did keep my mind occupied. I itched to get to work on the truck again, but the rain was definitely putting a damper on that.

I could work on the inside, but I was still waiting on the custom freezer I'd ordered. It was stupid to do too much when I'd have workmen tromping through it, getting it all muddy.

Doing a running tally of my to-do list made short work of my trip into town. I parked a few doors down from Brewed Awakening. I'd worked the sunrise shift at the diner, so it was still fairly early in the day. The sun—when it was actually in the damn sky and not covered by the eternal mist from the lake—was making for longer days as May was quickly dissolving away.

I'd wanted to get the truck done by Memorial Day, but that didn't look like it was going to happen even if I had a fleet of fairies to help me. Maybe the Fourth of July would be a good stretch goal.

I waved to Kinleigh as I shook off the rain and stomped my boots on the scatter of rugs just inside the doorway. I tossed my bag into the empty chair across from my bestie. "Hey, girl."

She gave me an arched brow. "What's going on there?"

I rolled my eyes. "Not everyone can be put together all the time like you." I dug into my bag for my project notebook.

"Yes, but at least I look like I didn't pull my clothes off the floor."

"Shut up."

"Jeez, Ive."

"I was working." These jeans had been on the end of my bed when I'd dragged them on after work. Not exactly on the floor.

"Right, vanilla."

Just the word made my stomach roll. "Yeah, I'm about to admit defeat. I'm switching to sorbet recipes. That and gelato."

"Okay, call me for that part."

I laughed and sat down. "August picked up my paint sprayer."

"I know."

I looked up from my checklist. "You do?"

"Yeah." She twirled one of her strawberry curls around her finger. "He keeps bugging me about the busted lock on my front door. He made me come with him so I could pick out a new one."

"Oh. Cool." Not sure how they'd ended up making that hour long trip without killing each other. "Yeah, you definitely have to make sure your door works, idiot."

She rolled her eyes. "We're safe as kittens in this town."

"Dude, if you listened to my podcasts, you would not agree with that sentiment."

"I do not need to hear about death and dismemberment in a small town, thanks."

I made a few more notes about paint then stuffed my pen into my notebook and tossed it back in my purse. "It's fascinating and you know it."

"Only for freaks like you."

I stood. "What do you want?"

"I'm hungry. I figured I'd drag you down to the Spinning Wheel, but since you look like that, I'm thinking no." She narrowed her eyes. "Your plan all along."

I pressed my lips together. The problem with besties was they knew all your tricks. "Caramel or Strawberry?"

"Surprise me."

I patted my ass to make sure my debit card was still there and wound my way around the couches and chairs that made up the eclectically cute café. A towering pile of romance novels butted up against horror novels in the reading nook. It was a Friday night, so the projector was set up in the far corner with a pile of teens watching an old school horror movie.

Looked like Freddy Krueger was on the menu tonight.

Wonder what kind of popcorn would go with that? I could go for something salty.

My stomach growled as I waited in line. Macy, the owner, was barking orders to her minions. The espresso machine was working just as hard as the blender. A bin of popcorn was stirring in Macy's special cheddar and butter blend.

I was going to expire if the line didn't move a little faster.

Finally, I was next in line behind a teen.

"Do you have milkshakes?"

Internally, I groaned. She obviously wasn't from Crescent Cove.

"Are they on the menu?" Macy's voice was pleasant, if you didn't know her.

"Um, no."

"Then I don't have milkshakes." Macy sighed. "I can do my caff-smoothies and I have coffee blended drinks."

The teen in front of me put her hands on her hips. "But I don't do caffeine. It's not good for you."

"Then why the hell are you in my place, blondie? It's a café."

I smothered a snort.

"You don't have to be rude."

"Have you met me?" Macy barked an order over her shoulder. "How about a Coffee Shake minus the coffee. That's the best I can do."

"So, a vanilla shake?" The girl twisted the pop socket on her phone.

"Sure, but you're paying for a coffee shake."

"That's fine."

"Add some orange juice and pineapple juice and it's perfect," I said.

The girl turned around. "Really?"

"Surprisingly."

She turned back to Macy. "Can you do that?"

Macy narrowed her gaze at me. "You gunning for a job, red?"

I laughed. "I've got enough of those. But I do know my ice cream."

"Huh." Macy moved to the blender and eyeballed a few ingredients then set the blender to spinning. "Get over here, red."

"Ivy."

"Right. Whatever." She poured some of the drink into a mug then plunked it in front of me. "Taste it since you came up with it."

I came around the side of the counter. It looked magical. I took a sip. "Have any coconut milk?"

She folded her arms. "Now we're making a tropical shake?"

I shrugged. "Add in some coconut milk, a few coconut shavings, and voila, new menu item that doesn't cost you a thing."

Macy followed my recipe then put the blender back on the base. She dumped the rest of the concoction into a to-go cup and set it in front of the blond girl. "On the house."

"Really?" The girl shoved her cash into her pocket. She took a straw out and pierced the top. "Oh, wow." Her eyes were almost comically wide with her winged liner. "Yeah, make more of these. My boyfriend will want one." She took a bigger gulp. "Can I get another free one?"

"Don't push your luck."

The girl smiled tightly. "Right. I'll pay."

Macy stepped back. "All right, red. Show me what you got."

"You made it fine."

"You're the ice cream expert."

"I didn't say that."

"You didn't?" She gave me a bland look.

"I said I know my ice cream." But I quickly lined up the ingredients she had and made a few alterations, then set the final product in front of her. "There you go."

Macy flipped over a mug and poured some for herself. "It doesn't suck."

I laughed. High praise from the thorny proprietress. She was definitely a *take it or leave it* sort.

"I'm looking to do something fun for the summer. Interested in a job?" She poured the shake and handed it to one of the café girls. "Charge for a small coffee."

"You sure?" The dark-haired girl asked.

"Yeah, it's an experiment."

"You got it."

Macy turned back to me. "So, how about it?"

I nibbled my lower lip. It was tempting to take the job, but I really wanted to do something of my own instead of always working around someone else's idea. "I'm actually trying to get an ice cream truck going for the summer."

"Like a Mr. Ding-A-Ling?"

"Not quite. More like specialized, homemade ice cream. I'm looking for a spot to park my truck." I twisted my fingers. It was the first time I'd actually told someone about it beyond my friends and family—and Rory. "Lots of paperwork."

"Well if your ice cream tastes anything like that concoction—"

"Better," I blurted out.

"We'll see."

Breathe, Ivy.

"How big is this truck?"

My stomach flipped, excitement and nerves twisting together. "It's a repurposed taco truck."

Macy tapped one long finger on her folded arms. "I'd have to see it."

"I just started painting it."

"How long do you think you'll need?"

I blew out a slow breath. "I'm hoping for July 4th."

"Maybe we can work something out. I'd have to test the product. Try it out here and see if people are into it."

My heart raced. "I can do that. I've been testing flavors. I have a few gallons I can bring over to try."

"All right. If you don't poison me, we'll talk about it."

I laughed. "Wow. I didn't—I mean, thanks."

"Someone took a chance on me, I'm just paying it forward. Besides, then people will stop fucking asking about ice cream."

I grinned. "What if you love it?"

"One step at a time. Bring some by tomorrow at seven? My evenings are less crazy."

"I can do that. How many would you like me to bring?"

"Half a dozen of your best."

I swallowed. Holy shit, this was really happening. "You got it."

"Great." Macy turned without another word as I tried not to do back-springs. I mean, I hadn't done one since I was like twelve, but right now, I was pretty sure I could do one.

I was halfway to Kinleigh before I remembered I hadn't gotten our food or drinks. She gave me a *what the fuck* look and I spun back around to get in line once more. I wasn't even sure what I ordered. I just took the tray full of food and drinks back to the table.

"What the hell were you doing over there? And were you making a drink for Macy?"

"Yes."

"Oh, no shit. Really?" Kinleigh took her strawberry smoothie off the tray. "Are you saying I need to change my eating habits?"

"What?"

She held up the fruit cup.

"Oh, sorry. I was distracted. Macy wants to try my ice cream."

She paused while popping off the plastic top. "Are you serious?"

"Heart attack level."

She leaped out of her chair and tackle-hugged me. "Oh my God, you're actually finally telling people."

"Shut up, idiot."

Kinleigh sat back down. "Girl, you've been hiding this little idea in your home freezer for ages. Not that I mind having the best ice cream ever being in *my* personal freezer, but it should be shared."

"I'm going to. It's just not ready yet."

"Well, it better be. Macy Devereaux doesn't give second chances."

"I know that."

"Do you though?"

Kinleigh's blue eyes were serious. The same gaze that I got when

I was waffling about buying the truck. Tough love Scott style. Pretty sure that was why we were best friends. She willed it to be so.

Not that I was one to blend into the wallpaper, but I sucked at the whole *let's set stuff up* thing. Unless it came to my future. For that, I had a notebook full of plans. But I got tunnel vision and all other things could fall away.

Kinleigh didn't allow such things. She made me go out and have some fun in between having three jobs at any given moment. Being a waitress made me indispensable in high season. Being a great waitress meant I was on everyone's autodial when they were in a pinch.

The fact that I never said no never helped my cause, but it sure added a lot of favors to my tally list.

"I'm starving. This fruit cup isn't going to cut it." She put the empty container on the tray with a pout.

I got up and slid my coat on. "We can get a pizza from Robbie's. And maybe you can help me with some flavors tonight?"

"Sold." Kinleigh laughed. "I had thinky thoughts about your truck actually."

I dumped our tray and set it on the shelf above the trash. "Oh?"

Kin slipped her arm through mine. "Tell me you brought an umbrella."

"Just my slicker."

"Dammit."

The door opened and a gust of rain and wind slapped me in the face.

"What are you doing here?" She wiped the wet off her arms in disgust.

"Nice to see you too, Kinleigh." My brother's deep voice filled the space. He shook off the rain from his Carhartt jacket.

I glanced at my best friend. Her cheeks were flushed and she wouldn't look at him. Not her usual response to my brother.

"We were just leaving." She brushed by me to the door.

"Where's your jacket?"

"It's nearly summer."

My gaze jumped from my brother to Kinleigh like a tennis match. She fisted her hands. "I'll be fine." And she flew out the door.

"Something I should know?"

August laughed. "Just her pissed at me as per usual."

No, what usually passed between them was more like snark. I wasn't sure what the hell *that* was. "I suppose."

"She's just mad at me because I installed her lock without telling her."

"Okay, now that makes sense." Kinleigh really hated when anyone did anything for her. Especially August.

But August's heavy brow furrowed over his bright green eyes. He handed me his umbrella. "Here, go get her."

I went onto my toes and kissed his cheek. "Thanks, Aug."

"Yeah, yeah. Are you going to be home tonight?"

It was as if he'd forgotten what we had already discussed. But I didn't think I'd be crashing at Kinleigh's. I was exhausted and needed my own bed. "Just like usual."

He shoved his hands into his pockets. "Not always."

I tucked my fingers into my slicker sleeves. "Yes, well, you can rest easy. No wild sexcapades tonight. I'll be home making ice cream with Kinleigh."

He held a hand up. "Why do you have to say stuff like that?"

"What? That I had a little spring fun with a guy? Like you're a monk. Though I'm not sure that's far off. All you do is work."

At least Serafina hadn't been around. Nor had he mentioned her. She was an okay girl, but I had a feeling he could do better.

He was my big brother, so of course he could.

"You should talk."

"Considering I'm getting your help tomorrow, I will own up to my workaholic tendencies. However, Macy wants to try my ice cream. Eeep."

August's eyes went wide, then he hauled me in for a hug. "That's awesome."

I patted his arm, but relaxed into him. The familiar scent of fresh wood mixed with rain made me hold onto him a little longer. "Yeah, it's pretty awesome."

"Make sure you bring her some of that toffee coffee stuff."

I stepped back. "Oh, sure. Bring my coffee ice cream to the coffee queen of the Cove."

"Helluva introduction. Especially if you use her coffee." He waggled his eyebrows.

"Sneaky. I like it."

"Oh, we'll have to do the truck another day." I bit my lip. "I'm not sure how long my meeting will be."

"No big deal. I'm always here for you, sis."

"I know." Far more than anyone else in my life. August never let me down. I waved the umbrella. "I better get out there before she drowns."

He frowned as he craned his neck to look outside. "Yeah, you better."

Yeah, he was being super weird. I rushed outside and caught Kinleigh under the awning, gnawing on her thumbnail.

"Yo, Scott."

Kinleigh turned and caught the umbrella I tossed her. "Who'd you steal this from?"

"My brother."

She clicked the button and the bright yellow umbrella popped open with my brother's logo on it. She rolled her eyes, but held it over her head.

"You're just mad because you didn't think to put your logo on one."

"I'd have to have a cute vintage parasol and it wouldn't be cost effective. Although..."

"Oh, here we go."

"I can't help it if I have a marketing brain that won't turn off. But seriously, I can look for old umbrellas and put my logo on it—you know, those iron-on vinyl kind? Or," she snapped her fingers, "I can make a vinyl for the handle, that way it's the first thing they see when they grab the umbrella. Thought the parasol part would be free advertising. I'll have to think about it."

I just let her babble on because that was Kinleigh. She was born a boss babe. She'd been creating small businesses since I'd met her. She was forever bugging my brother to make her signs—which he did, because it was easier to let her steamroll us than to fight storm Kinleigh.

My phone buzzed with an alert. I glanced at the screen and quickly stuffed it back in my pocket. I wasn't proud of the fact that I followed Rory on every one of his social platforms, but I couldn't help myself. It wasn't like he was mentioned often, but I had his Instagram on notification status.

Rory Ferguson. Producer, musician, word doctor.

Even his bio was light on info.

Nothing personal.

No, I wasn't going to look. Later, when I was alone, I'd pore over whatever picture he'd decided to post. And okay, so maybe I'd make sure he wasn't on my coast. Just in case.

"Hello, earth to Ivy."

"What?"

"You're staring off into nothing. I mean, not like we can see much in this deluge, but I was talking here."

"Right. Sorry. Just thinking about the truck."

Lies. But better a little white lie than to tell my best friend I was mooning over a hookup. I could keep my stupidity to myself, thanks.

She reached over and squeezed my hand. "So exciting."

I pushed thoughts of Rory away. This was my dream. He was just a fantasy. "Let's get that pizza. If we're going to be working all night, at least I can feed you."

"I can so get behind that."

Moving forward. It was all I could do now. Going back wasn't good for anyone.

SIXTEEN

 IVY

"I SAID HALF A DOZEN." MACY STOOD IN THE DOORWAY, HER arms crossed as she held the door open for me.

"I know." I lugged in a second freezer tote. "It's only eight."

"Is that your version of six?"

I set the tote on the table to the side of the front door then pushed a curl out of my eyes. I had my hair in a single French braid instead of my doubles, but my hair just wouldn't stay tamed. I straightened my black button down shirt over my khakis. "Yes."

"You do realize it's a little early to gorge on ice cream?"

"This is the time you wanted. You'll eat it all. I even brought one that you could scoop into coffee."

"Did you?"

Yes. I'd finally perfected the vanilla. Even if I wanted to die each time I tasted it, I'd achieved the flavor I wanted. For others. I wouldn't be eating it again now that I knew it was as good as I could possibly make it.

Macy frowned. "You okay? You look a little peaked."

I waved her off. "No. I'm good."

"Good. I saw you at Vee's baby club meeting. Figured you got the job done like every other freaking woman in this town."

I laughed. "No. I was just curious about it all. I've got plenty of time to do the kid thing after I get my business started."

"That's my motto."

"You want kids?" My mouth dropped open.

"God, no. I just mean my business is the focus."

"Right." I discreetly tugged at my waistband of my pants. I'd had to do the hair tie and button trick today to keep them closed. Way too much ice cream tasting lately. "And that's why I'm really grateful you're willing to give my product a shot."

"We'll see."

I unzipped the tote and pulled out the long, thin metal bins I'd packed up with colorful lids. They were just wide enough to make a scoop. Technically, they were designed for my gelato flavors, but they seemed perfect for today's taste test. "I'm still working on the names of the flavors, but the actual product is going to be on a rotating schedule to keep interest up."

"Flavors of the week?"

"Yes. I'll have a few base flavors and change out half a dozen to a dozen others based on how the truck does."

"That's a lot of changing up."

I pulled a small cup out of the outside flap. "I'm going to use a chalkboard on the outside of my truck to keep costs down and stick with that homemade, small town feel."

"They do appreciate that around here."

"Exactly." I took out my small scoop and dragged it down the vanilla. "Do you have some coffee I could try this in?"

She narrowed her eyes. "Funny."

My lips twitched.

She wound her way through the empty tables and disappeared behind the counter. While she was getting the coffee, I scooped out four toddler-sized servings. My Toffee Coffee, Strawberry Dream, Dark Night of the Soul Chocolate, and signature mint.

My gaze drifted to the Peppermint Patty. I'd debated bringing it at all, but it really had turned out to be one of my best flavors. Even if its inspiration was less than worthy.

Macy came back with two large mugs of coffee and a creamer peeking from her apron. She set them down and I scooped the vanilla into each.

I could get it down one more time.

Hopefully.

Macy gave it a dubious look, but shrugged and picked up her mug. She took a careful sip, her face inscrutable. She put down her mug, still tight-lipped as she moved on to one of my tasting cups. She tried the strawberry, then the dark chocolate, and finally, the mint. Her gaze flew to mine at the mint, but she still didn't say a damn word.

Finally, she tried my Coffee Toffee. Her eyes narrowed, then one eyebrow winged up. "Did you use Brewed Awakening coffee to make this?"

"I sure did. Figured I couldn't use just any coffee."

People were walking by and craning their necks to see what we were doing. The growly and narrow-eyed gaze from Macy stopped people from pausing for too long. Or asking a question.

She was kind of my hero. I knew I was far too nice when it came to customer service. But I just couldn't be any other way. Probably my waitress training.

I gnawed my lower lip as she folded her arms and tapped one long finger against her forearm. Her nails were super short and painted black with some sort of red fleck to them. It suited her personality down to the ground—and hid coffee stains. Pretty much why my nails were painted a bright pink. The raspberry sorbet stained the shit out of my hands.

Macy cleared her throat. "These are really impressive."

"I have a gelato, a sorbet, and a yogurt as well."

"I'm already sold. I'd like to try some out in the store." She pulled out a sheaf of papers from her back pocket. She dropped it on the table next to us.

"You just happened to have that on you?"

She shrugged. "I had a feeling."

"Do you get those a lot?"

"Enough." She nodded to Rylee, who was returning an armful of books to the book nook.

"What's up?" Rylee Kramer, Macy's second-in-command if that was such a thing, tucked a dark lock of hair around her ear. "Oh, hello there, ice cream of glory."

"Our resident sweet freak should try some."

"Don't mind if I do." Rylee tapped her lip as she looked over my offerings. Her gaze landed on the coffee. "Whatever that is, I want it."

"Coffee Toffee."

"You may want to rethink those names, but I am here for a taste."

I scooped a serving into one of my taster cups and handed it to her with a little spoon. "I've been playing with some, but none have quite gelled."

Rylee's dark eyes rolled back in her head. "Yeah, you need to come up with some gimmicky thing. People love that stuff." Rylee thumbed away a little bit of ice cream from the corner of her mouth. "And this is too good not to push."

"Good." Macy tucked into the dark chocolate flavor. "Because we're going to be carrying it. You can help with the naming for the board."

"I can, can I?" Rylee's eyes sparkled. "Well, until you come up with something anyway." She glanced at me with an excited smile.

"That is, if you're amenable to those terms. A two-week trial."

Amenable!?!

I managed not to scream it. I picked up the papers and looked them over slowly. The words were dancing on the page.

Get it together, girl.

Breathe.

Read.

Don't freak out.

I blew out a breath. It seemed to be a standard contract and her cut was sizable, but considering I didn't have a platform yet, her taking thirty percent wasn't terrible. It was more than I'd made before. El zippo.

I signed the bottom of the contract. "You have yourself a deal for two weeks."

"If it goes well, we can talk about your truck. I just bought the storefront next door, but I'm not going to be doing anything with it quite yet. I'm mostly using it for the huge parking lot right now, but it would be a good spot to set up your truck if things work out."

"Really?"

I struggled to drag my jaw off the floor. I'd been fighting with town hall on where I could possibly put the truck. They wouldn't even let me pay for space in the park. Something about zoning and taxes and nineteen other roadblocks.

"Baby steps, Bob. We'll figure it out after we see how this goes over."

"Right. Thank you for the chance."

"Your product stands for itself, Ivy. I'm making out the most on this deal. Now let's see if you can keep up with the demand."

"I have fifteen gallons in my freezer. And an industrial ice cream machine due at my house any day now."

"It's going to be busy." Macy held out her hand.

I shook it. "I hope so."

I helped her pack up what I'd brought, then she and Rylee took it into the back.

All the while, I happy danced in my head.

I floated out of the café into the fading rays of sun and wandered across the street. I needed a few minutes to digest it all. The lake always calmed me down.

I passed the gazebo—which was being used as lover's lane at the moment, yikes—and headed down the pier. The lapping water evened me out. A few boats were out for a sunset cruise.

It was unseasonably warm and the scent of grilling meat drifted out from a few of the docked boats. Usually, that was a comforting smell. A belly-growling scent even, but right then, all it did was make my stomach churn.

Maybe I'd passed the point of hungry. I'd been working my ass off all night and exhaustion was overriding the high of Macy's offer. Had I eaten today? Other than taste-testing ice cream, I was pretty sure that was a no.

I dug out my phone to text Rory, but paused before I unlocked the phone. It wasn't like he was my boyfriend—obviously. There was a text waiting there. I'd had my phone on silent while I met with Macy.

Not from Rory, but one from Zoe.

I read the text.

> **ZOE**
>
> Hey, me and Maggie are dying of boredom. The boys are playing in the studio. Think we could come by and see that store you talked about?

I quickly typed a definite *yes*. Zoe must have been sitting on top of the phone because the little bubbles of a reply popped up right away. I gave her the address and promised to meet her there.

I texted Kinleigh.

> What are you doing?

> **KINLEIGH**
>
> Staring at the wall. Debating closing early to put myself out of my misery. How'd it go with Macy?

> Good.

> Dude, don't tease me. Good—what the hell kind of reply is that? Get your butt in the damn store. I have box wine chilling.

I laughed and rushed down the pier. Kinleigh's shop was a few doors down from where I was.

> My friends Zoe and Maggie are going to come by the shop.

Tell them to bring wine.

> One of them is preggers.

Okay, apple juice.

> I'll tell them. I'll pick up some snacks at the grocery. I'm freaking starving.

Nah, we'll DoorDash something. Chinese?

> Girl, yes.

KINLEIGH

K. See ya in a few.

My thumb hovered over Rory's contact name. Well, LC—even in my phone I couldn't use Rory. He'd been interested when I told him about my ideas for the truck.

I sighed and stuffed my phone back into my pocket.

I took a right at the end of the pier and passed the diner. I spotted Zoe climbing out of a SUV in front of Kinleigh's.

"Hey, that was quick."

She flipped her braid over her shoulder. "We were actually heading out this way when you texted."

Maggie came around the front. "We were super bored." She pulled a bag off her shoulder. "I have wine though."

I couldn't imagine being bored with two rockstars in my life, but it was probably old hat for them. "Kinleigh will be psyched."

"I can't wait to see the clothes she has. Nothing fits right since I had Wolf."

"I can't wait to look at clothes I might fit into by fall." Zoe laughed.

I laughed. "I might be looking at a bigger size." I patted my belly. "Too much ice cream testing."

"Oh, man. I could go for some ice cream." Zoe rubbed circles along the side of her belly. "This one really likes sweets. Much like his dad."

"I have a few gallons of tester ice cream in Kinleigh's freezer. I tend to have it all over town since mine is perpetually overfull."

"I will help you fix that."

"Deal."

I opened the door for them. "I didn't know you'd be back in town so fast."

"After the gallery opening, I kind of just wanted the quiet of the farm. My family was thrilled. Now I have a bunch of people hovering." She sighed. "I didn't think that idea through."

"I have an older brother too. I hear you."

Maggie climbed the stairs ahead of Zoe. "This place is so cool."

The bottom half of the building was my brother's furniture store, but Kinleigh had a separate entrance with winding stairs. The walls were papered in silk with fun photos of people in Kin's vintage clothes. Some were for Halloween, some were set up for a dress-up party where Kinleigh took pictures for marketing purposes. There were children, adults, even a Red Hat Society get-together. My best friend was a genius at playing up the fun of a vintage shop. People came from far and wide to do her trunk parties. She even did some live on Facebook.

As we got to the top of the stairs, music was blaring. Kinleigh had her camera out and lights set up. She had a trio of wedding dresses on her mannequins and had even brought out her extra fun girls, as she called them, which were mannequins in dirty poses. I didn't know how she had found them, but I also wasn't sure I wanted to either.

Kinleigh's Google search history had to be seriously interesting.

"Hi." She popped up from behind a mannequin that was bent at the waist. She was wearing a very Marilyn Monroe-esque outfit with high-waisted panties and a sturdy, yet sexy bra. "I was just teasing my boudoir trunk party for tomorrow."

Maggie's eyes were huge as she looked around the warehouse-sized space. Kinleigh had partitioned two of the corners with trifold dividers. Dresses and slips hung off them as if someone was mid-change. Mannequins were set behind them with a light showing to make the shadows seem evocative.

The rest of the place was set up with various trunks and racks full of clothes. A hat rack stood half empty, thanks to the recent Kentucky Derby. She made a killing in the spring due to all the people who hadn't shopped in advance.

Zoe silently crossed the room to a vintage dress form on wheels. An ivory lace wedding dress was half pinned, with the shoulder drooping. Kinleigh often got damaged dresses that needed to be fixed. Her seamstress skills were unmatched by any of the tailors in the area. "What's this?"

"Oh." Kinleigh blew a curl out of her eyes as she finished snapping the bra on the mannequin. "That's a new dress I got in last night. It's in rough shape."

"I want it."

"Oh. It's really damaged. I have to do a lot of work on it."

Zoe touched the edges of a sleeve. "It's gorgeous."

"I can alter it to fit."

Zoe laughed. "Sorry. I mean, he technically hasn't even asked me to marry him yet—my baby daddy." She patted her stomach. "I'm pretty sure he's going to ask soon though. He keeps playing with something in his pocket."

"Sure it's a box?" Kinleigh quipped.

"With Ian, you can never be too sure."

"Ian..." Kinleigh's gaze slammed into mine. "These are the girls you met at the orchard?"

"Kinleigh, meet Zoe Manning and Maggie McGuire. Rockstar wife—and girlfriend, though she and Ian act like they're already married."

"That's the truth. He annoys me like a husband." Zoe held out her hand to Kinleigh. "Pleased to meet you. This place is amazing, and I want this dress. I don't care how much it is."

I could see the dollar signs in Kin's eyes. "She has fair prices," I said.

"Within reason," Kinleigh said quickly.

"This is an art form and I don't mind paying for art. Considering that's exactly what I expect when I sell a painting."

"Oh, man." Kinleigh rushed to Zoe and hugged her. "Girl, you get it. I can't tell you how many people want me to sell them my stuff for less than twenty bucks. I revamp almost every piece I find."

I left them to talk about the dress and alterations. Maggie was wandering around the store, touching jeans and tops, then finding something she fancied and draping it over her arm.

"Sorry, we lost them to shop talk."

Maggie waved me off. "No worries. This place is ridiculous. I could wander in here for hours." She pulled down a sheer blouse. "Kellan might like this one."

"Pretty sure any man with a pulse would."

Though Rory did seem to enjoy me in my skirts and punk shirts. And I really needed to put a stop to that way of thinking. My phone burned in my pocket with the need to share my news with him.

Maggie touched my arm. "Are you all right?"

The urge to hold all my shit in was ingrained. I wasn't exactly the sharing type. More of a *get it done and don't complain* sort. I had goals and chased them. I'd been pursuing my dream for so long, nothing else had fit in my life.

But I wanted him to fit. And that was foolish.

The quick wash of tears horrified me. I tried to blink them away, but they just kept coming faster.

"I miss Rory." I tipped my head back to staunch the tears. "It's so stupid. I promised myself I wouldn't get attached to him. I don't want to be attached to him."

"Oh, honey." Maggie gathered me in, the clothes crushed between us.

A tentative hand brushed my hair. "Are you crying?" Kinleigh's voice was distressed. "You don't cry."

"I know. I don't know what's wrong with me. Must be my period." I let out a creaky laugh. "It has be."

I didn't ever really know when it was coming. Where Kin was as regular as the sunrise, I was a busted calendar.

She rubbed my shoulder. "Must be." But she didn't look convinced.

Maggie steered me over to the wide velvet hassock that dominated the dressing room area. "Did he do something?"

"No." I brushed away the tears with a frustrated sigh. "No, it's me. I knew what I was doing when I got involved with him."

Kinleigh's features hardened. "Fuck him. He can't get his head out of his ass to be a man about things."

I gave her a broken laugh. "It's not like I'm begging for him to be my guy. It was just nice, you know. More than nice. When we were at the orchard, everything was so good between us." My stupid eyes wouldn't stop leaking. "And I've got all this good news and I want to tell him. I want to share everything with him and it pisses me off."

Zoe sat on the other side of me. "He's an idiot. I don't even know what his deal is, but he's got this mile-high wall around him sometimes, then others..." She shrugged. "It's like he's two different people."

"Exactly." Our time at the grove, at the bed and breakfast, even at the diner, had proven how sweet he could be. When he wasn't over-thinking, he was so present. So absolutely in the moment. Then he just wasn't.

I huffed out a breath. "I'm sorry. I didn't mean to—"

"Shut up. We all have our moments." Zoe patted her rounded

belly. "You should have heard what Ian and I went through. Literally a war zone of emotional crap plus a crazy mother-in-law."

Maggie laughed. "I love my mother-in-law."

"Mine's literally insane. Ward and all."

"Oh." Well, my shit didn't seem so bad next to that one. "I want that though."

"A crazy mother-in-law?"

I laughed. Finally, the tears seemed to be fading. "No, the baby and the crazy guy in my life. Maybe it's not going to be Rory." It killed me to say it. My chest constricted and tears stung the backs of my eyes again. Slowly, I exhaled. "Maybe it won't be him, but I want the whole package."

Kinleigh crouched in front of me. "You deserve it and if he doesn't see that, then he's an idiot. As for the babies..." She fell back on her butt. "I get it. All these babies in the Cove have me thinking about them too."

"You?"

Maggie smoothed the shirt that was bunched in her arms. "Wolf is pretty amazing. I didn't think I was ready for it, but he decided otherwise. Totally unplanned. Same with Kellan."

"Ian was never in my plan. I'm going to keep him. At least today. He didn't piss me off today."

Maggie laughed. "How I live my life with Kellan too."

I glanced down at Kinleigh. She was playing with the laces of her Chucks. "Men are stupid."

"Well, that's never going to change." Maggie set the clothes down and moved to the box of wine on the refreshment station. "But alcohol helps."

Zoe sighed and rubbed the side of her belly. "Soon, my body won't be an incubator for the footballer I'm carrying. Ian's words, not mine. I'd say soccer, but then he..." Her cheeks flushed. "Well, let's just say he reminds me why I enjoy the British side of him."

I laughed. "Can't say the Irish in Rory is a detriment." I slid on the floor next to Kinleigh and crossed my legs. The makeshift button expander on my pants pinched. "Ugh, I'm going to have to have to alter my damn clothes."

"Guys have it so easy, they just push their belts lower." Zoe leaned back on her elbows with a sigh. "There you go, little one. Stretch out a little."

"Is your metabolism finally slowing?" Kinleigh asked me. "I thought for sure it was permanently set on high."

"I suck at dieting, but maybe I'm going to have to start. Nothing fits right."

Zoe rolled onto her side on the hassock. "Bra?"

"Ugh, definitely the bra. I swear, my boobs grew a whole size. Where was that when I was in high school?"

Maggie paused before she held out the glass of rosé. "Super sensitive?"

I blushed. The last time I was with Rory, that had definitely been a factor. Everything felt over-sensitive.

Maggie swung her hand to Kinleigh and handed her the wine instead.

I frowned and sat up straighter. "Oh, no."

"Oh, shit." Kinleigh's eyes widened and she downed her wine like a shot.

Digging out my phone, I flicked open my medical app. I was never regular so my gynecologist convinced me to track my period just to make sure nothing was too out of whack. I'd forgotten about it between shifts at the diner and the ice cream thing.

I swiped back two screens. "Oh, no."

I was two months late—at least.

SEVENTEEN

 IVY

"Are you sure you want to go all the way—"

"Yes. God, yes."

Two towns over, maybe even four. God, buying a pregnancy test in the Cove was asking for my damn name to be on the front of the newspaper by morning. Not to mention The Cove Facebook group. I'd seen exactly how that had worked with Vee from Brewed Awakening. And she wasn't even pregnant at the time.

The viral gossip-fest heated up the minute someone had the stomach flu, for God's sake. Flu or baby flu? The whispers started immediately. Even more than a few years ago.

Now it was a near pandemic in this town. And I was pretty sure I had it.

My hand slid over my still very flat belly. Yes, I'd gained a few pounds, but it was more of a...suck it in in and zip those pants a la high school. Okay, so I'd done the button expander thing, but it wasn't like I had to buy a whole new wardrobe.

Yet.

That little voice needed to be squashed.

Zoe and Maggie had been very understanding—especially Zoe. She even told me I could ask any questions I had.

And more importantly, she said she wouldn't tell Ian or Rory.

It might be a false alarm.

It might be gas.

It might be ice cream.

It might be denial.

Kinleigh reached over and took my hand. "Everything is going to be fine."

I nodded. "I know."

Sort of. The terror was abating the farther we got out of town. Now it was just knots of nerves and confusion. We'd been careful. Had it happened in the car? That had been wild and careening toward insanity.

All it took was one swimmer. Didn't every teacher say that to strike terror into teens in high school? I knew my teachers had. Enough that teen pregnancy was barely a thing in town. I could count the number of them on the fingers of one hand.

We didn't speak for most of the drive. We went to the one lone 24-hour pharmacy halfway to Syracuse. I bought two tests. I was tempted to buy the entire aisle of offerings, but I knew in my heart I already was. This was just a formality.

So many things made sense.

By the time Kinleigh pulled into my driveway, I'd shredded the bag handles. I looked up with a puzzled frown. "I thought you were bringing me back to my car."

"Pretty sure you shouldn't be driving at the moment." She unbuckled her belt.

"I think I need to do this alone."

Kinleigh's eyebrows snapped together. "Bad idea."

"I just...I kinda just need to—"

"Fall apart alone? No, ma'am." She opened her door and stalked up the driveway.

Sighing, I shoved the bag into my purse and followed. The light was on, but August's truck still wasn't there.

Maybe it would be better if she did stay with me. I wasn't ready to keel over about this anymore, but I was suspiciously numb. As if it was simply a foregone conclusion.

I lifted my chin and breezed through the door. I dumped my keys in the bowl on the table inside the door just like always. The kitchen light was on and Kinleigh was sitting on one of the bar stools with her arms crossed.

"I'm not leaving."

I walked over to her and hugged her. She pressed her cheek to my shoulder. "I'm supposed to be hugging you."

"So, hug me back."

Her arms came up around me. "It's going to be all right. I'm here for you. Every step of the way."

"I know. It's not like it's dire. I want a baby." I even wanted *his* baby. I wasn't ready to say that out loud though. Because one-sided love wasn't really enough. Enough to make a baby, evidently, but I wasn't sure about the rest.

"Yes, we both want kids. You're supercharging our timeline there, woman."

I laughed. "We don't know yet."

But I did.

I dug into my bag and took one of the tests out. "I'm going to go do this."

"You want me to come in there with you?"

"And watch me pee? I love you, girl, but not that much."

She laughed. "Okay. I mean I wouldn't like it, but I'd do it."

"Because you're my rockstar." The lump in my throat made my eyes burn. I had to use that phrase? Really?

"You better believe it. I'll be out here waiting. But you know, wash your hands."

I laughed because she needed me to. And I needed it as well.

The test was quick. Even quicker than I thought. It felt like it should require more than just a stick. But that was really all it was.

"How many minutes?"

I jumped a little. "Were you waiting for the flush, for God's sake?"

"Sort of. Well, the sink too."

I shook my head and washed my hands dutifully. I wasn't sure what to do with the freaking test. I didn't want to leave any of the trappings in the bathroom for my brother to find. In the end, I just tucked it all in the box and carried the wad out.

"Three minutes."

I bit my lower lip as we went back into the kitchen. I didn't know what else to do, so I went to the freezer and took out a pint of peanut butter chocolate swirl. I scooped out two small bowls and set one in front of Kinleigh.

The only sound in the room was spoons lightly tapping along the sides of the bowl. I didn't even really taste the ice cream. Every second felt like ten minutes until finally Kinleigh's app chirped.

I set the bowl down and walked around to the end of the counter. I scrubbed my palms down my thighs, then shook my fingers out before grabbing the test.

Sure enough, a big fat plus sign was staring back at me.

I bowed my head and Kinleigh rushed round the counter to me.

"Holy shitballs."

"Yeah."

She linked her arm with mine. "I'm going to be the best damn aunt in the freaking world."

"I know you are." I tipped my head to touch her shoulder.

I wasn't sure how long we stood like that, but I do know my ice cream was a melted mess by the time I gathered up the box and test and stuffed them in my bag. I didn't think shoving them at the bottom of the garbage would be enough to hide the evidence from my brother.

I might have to bring them to the next county.

Kinleigh crossed her arms over her middle as she slumped back into her chair. "So, you want to do a sleep over?"

"Chocolate and wine is off the menu. At least the wine."

"I'll drink all the wine for you."

"You're all heart."

"I know." Her smile was extra bright. "I'll go find *Pretty in Pink* on iTunes."

Things were extra dire if she was pulling out Molly Ringwald and Duckie.

But the movie did take my mind off things. Kinleigh fell asleep on the couch before the credits rolled. I couldn't settle my brain.

Was Rory my Blane?

Or even worse, was he my Steff? The snarky, damaged guy who could never be the one I deserved even though he was infinitely more interesting than Blane.

And in the end, I should have found a Duckie. The safe guy who would always be by my side and would be thrilled to make a family and a very lovely life.

I struggled out of my favorite comfy chair and padded back into the kitchen for a drink. I stared at my purse and the other test in there. Maybe I was being crazy. Maybe I wasn't really pregnant.

Maybe it was all a big joke.

All the things I'd ever wanted were in front of me. My ice cream was going to be sold at Macy's, and if I had my way, it would be in that ice cream truck before the summer was over.

Some time ago, I'd gone to that meeting Vee had put together at Brewed Awakening with all the women who were willing to do the baby thing alone. Now here I was.

Maybe it was just fate. I was supposed to do this on my own. Perhaps everything was going the way it was supposed to go.

Then again, maybe I wasn't really pregnant.

I grabbed the other test out of my bag and ran down the hall to the bathroom. I took the test and sat on the edge of the tub as the minutes ticked by. This one was a five-minute test and the stupid purple tester kept blurring.

I didn't even know I was crying until my brother crouched in front of me. The Jack and Jill door to the bathroom was open from his side. Yet again, tears had taken over and decided they were coming out, whether I wanted them to or not.

"Auggie."

"Oh, shit. You don't call me that anymore." Then he must have seen the box because his green gaze flew to mine. "Ah, Ivy Rose." His voice was gentle even as his hands went to fists. "Who is he?"

I curled my fingers around his huge, calloused hand. I could feel the rage under the calm. My brother was good at that. As the eldest of us, he was always the most responsible. The most reliable.

Our rock.

"No one you know."

"Are you all right?"

"I don't know."

He swore and sat down right on the tile floor. "Does he know?"

"No."

"How the hell is he supposed to step up if he doesn't know? Or..."

I blew out a long breath. "It's complicated."

"Uncomplicate it."

I laughed. "It doesn't work that way."

"You have his number, right?"

"Yes, Aug. I just know he's not interested in starting a family."

"Well, he was interested enough to get you horizontal."

"Okay, can we not go there? It's just weird to talk to you about sex."

"Yeah, well, I don't like thinking about it either. But he still needs to know."

"He won't—"

He twisted our hands until my smaller ones were enveloped by his huge ones. "He still deserves to know." His eyes were serious and steady. "Then it's on him. And if he doesn't help at least monetarily—"

"No. I'll take care of this baby. Somehow I'll make it work." I didn't realize just how much I wanted it until I said that. Because it was true. This baby was mine.

I might have been in love with Rory, but I could survive without him. It would suck and a little piece of me would always be sad, but the baby was non-negotiable.

"It's not just the responsibility angle, Ive. It's doing what's right. If I had a kid out there, I'd want to know." He let my hands go. "But I'm here for you. Whatever you need."

I nodded. "I know."

Keeping this from August would have been impossible. Hiding a pregnancy test was ridiculous. As if I wasn't going to tell my big brother. Not like I'd be able to hide it much longer anyway.

Did I mention flowing shirts for the win? Guess I wasn't far off on that one.

August got to his feet and tugged on one of my braids. "Tell him."

"I will."

He narrowed his gaze at me.

"Soon. I just need some time."

He nodded. "Get some rest. Your partner in crime is snoring on the couch."

I laughed. "Yeah, she took me to get the test."

His gaze was unreadable, but he gave me a small smile. "Are you all right?"

"I will be."

"Good enough. But you have to tell mom."

I swallowed a groan. Barely. "Yeah, I'll need a day or so to get ready for that."

"You and me both. Night, brat."

"Night."

I waited until he closed the door, then slid my hand over my barely there curve of a belly. "Just you and me."

At least for now.

EIGHTEEN

 **Rory**

June

"You know I can't do it without you."

I rolled my eyes and kicked my feet up next to the mixing board in my bare bones home studio. "You can and you have until this point."

"That is a lie. You helped me with my first EP. Don't you recall working with me and Flynn? Hijinks in the woods in Tennessee. So many woods." I imagined Ian shuddering.

Like me, my mate wasn't the biggest fan of bonding with nature. Although I'd gotten much closer to nature than I'd ever anticipated that night with Ivy...

A night on constant replay in my head, much to my consternation. It was over a month now since I'd seen her. Even that long had been torture. Going beyond it would test me.

It already was.

Sure, we'd texted a few times. Some nights more than a few. I was usually flying across the damn country and living out of my luggage and her long hours at the diner and working on her truck seemed to leave us at cross purposes. But an emoji from her could brighten my whole day.

Once or twice, I'd weakened and nearly called her. Yet I knew I couldn't open that box. It wouldn't make the distance easier. Just the opposite. And I'd made her promise to call me if she found someone else, so maybe she figured I'd do the same.

I didn't want to rock the boat. It was already damn close to capsizing.

With a sigh, I checked back into the conversation with Ian. "I do recall. I also remember you learning to enjoy those woods. You were up fishing every morning."

"It was nice being out there on the water. A good way to clear my head. Also, I drank a liquid breakfast, so there was that."

"I imagine a liquid breakfast makes most things better."

"Not really. Just dulls the edges so nothing is as vivid or as sharp. I'm not a happy drunk like you most of the time. You're the table dancer, not me."

I snorted and dropped my feet to the floor. Clearly, I was too restless to sit. "I have pictures that say otherwise."

"Those might as well have been a lifetime ago."

"Right, back when you were a single lad and footloose and fancy free."

"Footloose? I was a bloody mess. Women tossed me their numbers and I couldn't even consider taking them up on their offers. I'd gone to banana."

"What?"

"You know. Soft serve. Couldn't get it up for anyone but Zoe."

I did know. All too well. And it royally brassed me off. Not that I wanted to get it up for anyone else. I couldn't even look at other women. Every one I passed, I compared to Ivy and rejected. Too tall, too short, too thin, not ginger enough.

Just not Ivy.

"Must you rub in your love life at every turn?"

"Who's rubbing? Sounds like you might need to though. You're crankier than usual."

"Hell yes, I'm cranky, because you think I can just pick up and run to New York whenever you get the yen to bother me. I have clients, you know, and work that doesn't include you."

"I get that, and I have songs with others that I didn't intend to include you on either. But I wanted you to be part of this EP just as you were the last. If you're too busy, that's fine. I'll make do."

I stabbed my fingers into my eyes. They were gritty and hot from too many long nights spent fiddling with melodies and writing pages of lyrics that didn't go anywhere. "Look, I'm in a mood."

"What else is new?"

"Worse than usual. I appreciate you wanting my input, truly I do, but Jesus, there's a million other producers who could—"

"A million others who aren't you. If you don't want to come back to New York, why don't you just say so?"

I slammed my hand against the side of the console and swore under my breath as it wobbled on its legs. Shoddy workmanship. When I got my real place, I'd make sure—

Right, because this was all temporary. I'd moved into this apartment two years ago, thinking I'd be gone in a year. Instead, it had stretched into another while I searched for my dream home. Even with plenty of money at my disposal, and a mind full of ideas, I couldn't seem to find what I wanted. LA and its surrounding suburbs had everything I could ever imagine. It didn't make sense I couldn't find a place to suit.

Unless I hadn't been meant to find a place here at all. Searching forever in the wrong spot wouldn't lead to the fucking pot of gold, no matter how many hours I invested.

"It has nothing to do with New York. Wait a second, you're back there already?"

"Yes."

"Why?"

"Because my fiancée's family is here, perhaps? Did you fall out of bed while reaching for your Pepto and hit your head on the floor?"

I laughed before I could stop myself. It was encouragement Ian didn't need. Ivy might've called me Lucky Charms, but Ian was the one who made people happy. Not me.

I rubbed the stitch in my side. I was a dour bloke who probably would need Pepto if I didn't stop mainlining coffee like it was water and not getting any rest.

And let's not forget the medicinal qualities of sex. I missed those too.

"We just left there weeks ago."

"It's been more than a month. Heading toward a month and half. We went home, handled what we needed to there, and came back to the farm. Zoe wants to be here for the baby's birth and she can't be flitting about until the day of, you know."

No, I didn't know. I wasn't an expert on childbirth. Why would I need to be? I didn't even intend to have kids. Or a wife.

Why would I need any of those things? Obviously, I was ridiculously happy all on my own.

Right.

A thought occurred to me. "Which others are you doing songs with?"

He grew quiet. For about fifteen seconds, Ian's max. "Finally heard that, hmm? Your mind is half a dozen steps behind, mate."

"I have a lot to think about."

"Do you now? So envious. And here I am, with absolutely nothing in my head."

I laughed again and stared up at the ceiling. "Why do you like me, Ian? Seriously. I can't see why you cultivate our friendship. What's in it for you?"

"The truth."

"Pardon?"

"You don't snow me, ever, and we both know how rare that is in this business. You also don't kiss my ass. If you're nice to me, it's because you want to be, not because you expect something in return. Plus, you're oddly good at Karaoke, even if it takes a few pints of Guinness to get you to that point."

"You've never heard me sing Karaoke."

"The recording feature on my phone says otherwise."

I sat back down in my swivel chair and braced my elbow against my knee. Rubbing my face didn't begin to erase the exhaustion. I feared nothing could.

At least not on this coast. Right now, New York felt like another planet.

Almost at once, I realized who Ian was working with. That canny fucker. "You've been sneaking around with Kellan."

His silence spoke volumes. Especially since he hadn't ever been silent in my presence for more than thirty seconds, unless he was sleeping.

"Kellan mentioned something about a new piece he wanted me to hear when it was ready. We've been hammering out ideas over the phone, finding the slant for—hell, why am I telling you this? You probably know more than I do."

Ian chuckled. "Yeah, sure, I do. Kellan is like you. He grunts more than he shares. I guess I like a challenge. But our voices are complementary, and Lord Lewis likes what we're coming up with. He mentioned bringing in Connors and Goldwaith to—"

"Connors and Goldwaith? He never uses them."

"Right, but he said you already said you were busy. Too busy for your best friend, but whatever."

"I never said you were my best friend."

"No, but you can't stop me from making you mine."

The laughter rolled out of me and ended in a groan as I leaned back in my chair. "Seriously, I'm too tired for this conversation."

"So, just say yes and you'll get the triple bonus of me, Kellan, and Ivy. And Ivy will make you feel much better. There's something about redheads, isn't there?"

I hated that he was right. On all accounts. *"Your* lady is blond."

"My lady has been every color of the universe and probably will be again once she gives birth."

"You talk about that kid enough, you'd think it was the Christ child."

"I'm excited. So, sue me."

"If only I could. Sure you don't want Kellan to be your new best friend?"

"He's grouchy enough for the role, but you know I can't resist your baby blues."

"You are well and truly a jackass." Though I grinned just the same. And it wasn't just at Ian's typical antics.

I could go back to New York. To Ivy. I didn't have to linger around here, missing her. A few phone calls and a couple of altered arrangements, and I could—

The other line beeped. "Hang on."

But I didn't click over to take the call, just checked who it was.

Ivy.

Calling me at—I checked my watch—past midnight, her time. When she hadn't yet answered my text from earlier. My three texts actually. She'd had the day off, so I'd been persistent.

For that matter, she'd been slower and slower to respond to texts in general, so I'd started spacing them out. Except I hadn't today. Not that it had made a difference in her response. But I hadn't fully realized how far apart her replies had become until right this instant.

Now she was calling for the first time ever.

Fulfilling her promise, maybe? She'd probably been out with her new lover today. Guilt kicking in before bed.

Better tell old Rory to stop fussing at me so much, as my new man doesn't like it.

My stomach twisted in tandem with the vise around my heart. I sat up straighter and sent the call to voicemail.

Like a coward.

"Not all of us are like you," I said to Ian, once I could speak around the lump in my throat.

"Are you referring to your lack of flowing tresses? And it is a lack, but you still got yourself a mighty fine woman just the same. She's been hanging around with Maggie and Zoe, you know."

Even in the midst of my own confusion, I was happy to hear it. Ivy had meshed well with the other women, enough that they'd developed lasting bonds.

Ivy was able to do things like that. Me? I overthought and groused and generally pushed people away.

"Of course she has. I'm to come back there and it'll be just like it was that day in April. One big, happy, dysfunctional family."

"I put the fun in dysfunctional, thanks though."

"Aren't you assuming an awful lot? Just because Ivy is friends with Zoe and Maggie doesn't mean we can just pick up where we left off. Her life continues despite me being out here. I can't expect her to just hit the pause button and wait for me."

Except I did. In my head, in my heart, I couldn't help it. Because every fucking part of me was waiting for her.

"That's true. She may be shagging the high school football team even as we speak. I imagine she could still fit into one of those tiny cheer uniforms too. Just like Britney Spears."

Now I had that picture of Ivy in my head, complete with pigtails and pom-poms. Sometimes I hated that bastard.

"You aren't funny."

"Tell me, mate, what is it you're afraid of? That you'll come back here and Ivy will demand you drop down on one knee and produce a ring?" He waited a beat. "Or that she won't?"

"That's ridiculous."

"Which?"

I started to reply, then stopped. Of course she didn't expect a ring. Even if things had gotten far more intense than we'd expected, she wasn't looking to settle down yet.

Just as I wasn't.

But wasn't that like finding your next big hit? You might be looking or you might not, but when you stumbled upon a gold record, only an idiot would put it back on the shelf.

Bloody shelves again. I was going to ban that word from my vocabulary.

"How's Zoe?" I asked instead of continuing along that line of thought. Ian was relentless, and at heart, he was a good soul. But I didn't want to be counseled or guided. I just wanted Ivy, and having her in my life wasn't so simple.

Ian sighed. "She's fine."

"And the baby?"

"He's perfect. Kicks up a storm hard enough for me to feel it most nights."

"Is that because you're on top of her at the time?"

"Goes to show how much you know. At this stage, she's on top of me."

I shook my head. "Have you picked a name?"

"No. Our lists have lists. You're going to come out for the birth."

It wasn't a question. "Is this your new way to try to get me to work with you? And Kellan?" I couldn't hide the touch of sarcasm in my tone.

Sneaking around working together and inviting me to join in after the fact. I saw how it was.

"No, it's my ongoing way to demonstrate you're family to me, and as someone who had to fight for his, that's important."

I blew out a breath. "Low blow. Very low blow."

"I play to win. So? Flynn's already sent his regrets, but only because he'll be out of the country for some shows and can't rebook them."

The third spoke of our trio was a crafty one, I had to give him that. Not that I thought he was lying.

Probably.

"You know I'll be there. But don't expect me to boil any cloths or help with any weird breathing exercises."

"Think we have that covered. Also, we have access to hospitals in Turnbull, just in case you didn't realize."

"Jackass. I'll talk to you later."

"Yeah, yeah. Think about what I said. I don't want you to pass up a chance with Ivy. She's a lovely girl, and lovely girls aren't alone for long. Someone wise told me that when Zoe and I weren't together—not you, because you aren't—and I'm paying it forward."

"Yes, Anthony Robbins. I hear you. Loud and clear." Nothing I hadn't told myself a million times.

For all I knew, it was already too late. Ivy could already be in love with someone else. Just because Ian didn't know didn't mean it hadn't happened. Ivy would probably be circumspect when she was around the other women.

My mate certainly had been when he'd told me not to worry all those years ago that Darla seemed distant. Little had I known he was handling the problem just fine—literally and figuratively.

"Thick as a brick," Ian muttered. "Watch the mail."

Then he hung up before I could.

Watch the mail? For what?

I didn't have time to ponder that right now. I put my headphones on. I had a song to finish.

Alas, I still did at past eight the next morning when I finally looked up again. The sun was agonizingly bright and my stomach had sent up a roar deafening enough to wake the neighbors. I made coffee using my trusty tumbler and stumbled into the shower, leaning against the tiled wall as I poured the heavenly brew down my throat.

It didn't help. Nor did the water jabbing icy needles into my scalp and shoulders.

The song I'd been working on for the new Ripper Records artist who needed a surefire hit—good luck there—wasn't quite done. I'd made some progress before switching over to an equally thorny composition.

The song I'd written for Ivy.

I couldn't figure out how to end it. The last few lines had me stymied. Wondering why she'd called me and not having the stones to return her call didn't help.

> Carrying you in my pocket
> When I'm so far away
> Your scent in my mind, flavor on my tongue
> Let's live while we're still young
> Knowing it might end
> Has to end
> Won't make me not stay

But I hadn't stayed. I hadn't gone back when every part of me felt called to her. It had to be the timeline. It had been more than a month.

And her voice was on my phone right now. All I had to do was press play.

I just couldn't do it.

Not yet.

I got out of the shower and toweled down with one hand while I checked the rest of my voicemails. Work, work, and more work. I had a call from someone in Dublin, oddly enough, and I'd been wanting to get home to see my folks. If I could make the two coincide—

Or I could just hop on a fucking plane and make it happen. I didn't have to make it a write-off worthy expense. Family was more important than profits and losses.

Running from Ivy, are you? Now even the opposite coast isn't far enough away?

I wasn't running from. I was running to.

Sure you are, buddy.

After I got some goddamn sleep.

Blearily, I rubbed my eyes and put in a quick call to my travel agent. I'd let her handle it. I needed ten hours down.

"When do you want to go?" my travel agent asked.

"What's today?"

"Thursday, Rory." She was used to me.

"Friday night." It would require some shuffling—all right, a lot of it—but all of a sudden, I was certain I needed to be home.

Even if I'd never been certain of that before in my life.

"Can you make that happen?" I asked into the silence.

"Give me a couple hours. No guarantees on what class."

"I don't care. I'll take coach if need be."

Good thing I'd been so open-minded, because that was exactly what I got.

Once I finally arrived in Dublin what felt like a century later, I also took the most rubbish rental vehicle I'd ever encountered.

But less than seventy-two hours later, I was standing on the moss-covered stoop of the cottage where I'd grown up, drawing in great breaths of sea-tinged air. The scents of nature surrounded me. Flowers I'd been given names for since I was a child and had never bothered to commit to memory. And behind me, children shouted and laughed as they wheeled up the uneven street.

I lifted my hand to knock on the rounded door my mum had painted an eye-searing red. It swung open and the woman in question stared at me, her soft blue eyes more lined, her perfect bow mouth slack with shock.

"Rory Michael."

It made me smile despite the fatigue from the trip that hung heavy on my shoulders. "Ma."

She hauled me in for a hard hug that rattled my ribs and settled my heart into a more regular rhythm. I hadn't even realized how out of whack I was until I felt her arms around me.

Worse, I wouldn't have said I even derived comfort from her in that way. Was I so unaware of my true feelings? Could I be that daft?

She drew me back and cupped my cheeks. I towered over her, but she'd always closed the distance between us as if will was enough to make it less. "You're too thin."

I scuffed my sneaker. "I haven't lost more than half a stone."

That wasn't exactly accurate. I hadn't been eating. I wasn't close to wasting away, but my appetite wasn't what it had been.

I definitely couldn't go near ice cream.

"Your mum knows. Now you come in here and take a load off." Before I could argue, she stepped back into the small foyer and called up the stairs. "Padraig, we have a visitor."

I stepped over the threshold and dropped my bag. I'd traveled light as always. "Oh, Ma, he's probably busy—"

My da appeared on the landing, his halo of bushy salt-and-pepper hair whiter than I remembered. How long had it been since I'd been home? It shamed me that I couldn't remember.

That if not for my turmoil over Ivy and what that blasted town Crescent Cove had done to me, I might not even care.

"Son." He didn't ask me what I was doing here, or why I hadn't called to warn them, just thundered down the stairs and pulled me into another bone-crushing hug. "You're too thin."

I had to laugh as we eased apart. "Is there a script?"

"No, we have eyes. You look good otherwise. Tired," my mum declared after another inspection. "And you need a haircut. Don't you have a barber in California?"

The way she pronounced it always made me smile. To her, LA might as well have been located on the sun. "I do. Haven't had a chance to visit one recently."

"Or eat." My mum shook her head and waved me down the hall to the kitchen. "I just made lunch. You're in luck."

"You don't have to go to any trouble—"

"It's no trouble, boy. Didn't you hear her say she just finished making lunch?" My father dropped his beefy arm around my shoulders. "Besides, it's not often our oldest boy comes around. How long's it been?

"Not more than a year."

"Don't lie to your father," my mum admonished as she moved to the little stove and ladled out big stoneware bowls of soup. "Closer to two."

"I think three. Maureen wasn't even seeing Kevin then and she's already pregnant with their first."

"What? Maureen's pregnant? She didn't call me." I scrubbed a hand over my face and tried to cut through the cobwebs enough to remember. Had she? I wasn't the best at returning non-work calls. "I don't think."

"She called you. Six times."

"No. That can't be so."

"She has the call log to prove it. She showed it to your mum." My da jerked his thumb at my mother, and I hurried to help her with the bowls of stew. The smell of the rich, meaty soup made my stomach growl.

"I don't think it was six," I muttered as I carted them one by one to the cozy round table set by the windows. A sprig of yellow flowers sat in the middle of it, cheery and quaint.

"It surely was. It would've been more if she didn't know better than to waste her coins on transatlantic calls you wouldn't take."

"I would've taken it had I known, but I was working—"

"You can't take it with you. All your money and your gold records and your fancy house won't keep you out of the grave."

"Padraig," my mum snapped. "Can you let the boy alone for an hour before you start in on him?"

"Start? I've been saying the same things since he flew out of here. Barely a man and gone to a country where he knew no one. Didn't want his roots. Had no use for them. Now you're back at our door." He sat down heavily at the table and stabbed his spoon into his stew, splashing it. "Being happy to see him doesn't change the fact I still have half a mind to paddle his behind."

This was why I came home so readily. Five minutes in and threats of violence ensued.

And I hadn't even had lunch yet.

I accepted the loaf of fresh bread my mother offered, but I didn't sit. I couldn't. "What would you have me do then? Stay here and beat my clothes on a rock and grow a vegetable garden?"

The quick flush in my mum's cheeks made me rue the words. Yes, she did those things. Not out of necessity, but because they made sense to her. Air-dried clothes were so much nicer than those from the dryer. Homegrown vegetables tasted better in her stew.

When I stopped ranting long enough to taste it, I had to agree.

"You have talents we don't. There's a reason the world listens to you. You have something to say. Now sit if you're going to eat my stew."

I sat. And I ate like a starving man.

The next time I looked up, my mum was watching me from the other side of the table. I hadn't even noticed her take a seat. I'd been too busy inhaling her stew and swallowing her glorious brown bread nearly whole.

"Padraig, go fish."

My father's head snapped up. Like me, he'd sucked down his stew and was breaking off another piece of bread. "Pardon?"

"You heard me. Take the boat and go cast a line."

The boat? He had a fecking *boat*?

Maybe I really hadn't visited for three years. My younger sister round with a baby, my father with a boat. My brother might've run off with a harem of pole dancers for all I knew.

"Is Thomas married?"

My mum frowned at me. "He's in university. Don't you even remember the age of your own brother?"

The disappointment in her voice knocked me down half a dozen pegs. I reached out to cover her hand with my own. Her skin was soft enough to tease out more memories than I could stand from the hope chest I'd buried them in. "I remember. It just seems so much has changed."

My father rose. "Maybe you should come around more often."

"Yes." I swallowed deeply. "I should. I will."

He grunted. "Promises. Don't make ones you can't keep."

"I won't. I *don't*." Which was why I never made any, unless I was absolutely certain I would never break them.

My father finished off his piece, then shoved the remaining heel of bread in his pocket, nearly ripping it from my mouth. He'd gone halfway down the hall before he came back and set it on my napkin. I stared at it as if the thing might bite. "You need to eat," he said gruffly before he stomped off and shut the front door behind him.

"He loves you."

"Not so sure about that." But I tore into the bread just the same. "You clearly thought he must be serious about the paddling, which is why you sent him away."

"No, I knew you'd never tell me about the girl if he didn't leave."

I choked on the bread and a chunk of it splattered in the remnants of my stew. Precious few bits were left, mostly just detestable carrots. "Girl? What girl? I don't see any girl."

My mum cocked a brow and dug into her own stew. "You were always a rubbish liar."

"It's not a lie. I don't see a girl here, do you?"

"Rory Michael."

I fished out the piece of bread, dunking it more thoroughly before I chewed and swallowed. "How did you know?"

"Because you came home," she said simply.

"Is there anything to drink?"

"Milk on the door as always."

I ducked my head, a little embarrassed she still thought I preferred milk over any other drink. Mostly because it was true.

No wonder I'd fallen for my dairy queen.

I retrieved the glass bottle of milk and got down a glass, filling it to the brim. Then I returned to the table and took out my phone.

It contained two things that preyed on my mind. One, the voicemail I still hadn't listened to. And...this.

I scrolled through my picture app and found the right one. In it, Ivy was laughing at something Maggie and Zoe had said. I'd taken it right before we'd played Nickelback's "Animals" on stage. She was so beautiful I'd just had to save the moment. To have tangible proof she'd existed in my life. With one glimpse, I could hear her laughter and carry it with me as if I'd never left.

"This is Ivy." I pushed the phone across the table.

My mum picked it up and sighed. "Oh, she's lovely, isn't she? Irish? She must be, with that coloring."

"She's never said. Her last name is Beck."

"Irish," she proclaimed. "Do you love her?"

I didn't even hesitate. "Yes." I rubbed my throat to get it working again. "Is it possible to fall in love in one night?" In one hour? "It must be, because I've done it." I let out a rusty laugh. "And I didn't even realize until you just asked me. At least not to put a name to it."

She set down my phone, still smiling faintly. "You never put a name to much. You just keep your head down and work while life passes you by."

I drained my milk. It was easier than acknowledging she was right.

Also, nothing was quite as good as milk from home.

"Does she love you back?"

"I don't—we haven't ever—I think she may want to let me down easily."

My mother just waited for me to make sense. I was waiting too.

I tried to explain what had happened between us, more or less. The way we'd met and how I'd left and then returned a month later. I probably slightly exaggerated how well we'd gotten to know each other and minimized exactly how many times we'd learned about each other in a...carnal fashion. But really, what was more intimate? And I wasn't in a habit of falling in love with women I shagged, so that wasn't a consideration. Our time together had been accelerated certainly, but everything else between us had been too.

At least on my end. I couldn't say for sure how she felt.

Because you're too much of a wuss to listen to that voicemail.

"So, you flew here instead of flying to her and confessing your feelings to her. As if she's Darla and you'll surely find her having relations with some friend of yours."

"You know entirely too much," I mumbled.

"I do. Which is exactly why you came to your mum." She slid my phone back to me and tugged on my fingers. "She's glad, you know. She misses you very much. And those chats we used to have." She drew back her hand, and I gripped my phone to have something to hold onto.

Ivy's laughing eyes taunted me.

"I don't think she's Darla."

"No?"

"No. Okay, not really, in the logical part of my brain. But in the illogical part, I wonder if it's so overwhelming because it was so fast. We haven't spent much time together and distance makes it all more romantic."

"There was a saying I loved. That distance extinguishes a small flame and inflames the great. Paraphrasing of course. Do you feel extinguished?" Her bland smile told me she knew my answer even before I voiced it.

"No, but her feelings matter too."

"They do, aye. You should find out what they are then, shouldn't you?"

I grinned. "Do you make house calls?"

"Absolutely. But you've never invited me to your home."

My grin faded. "Surely I have—" Then I fell silent. "You're probably right. It was an oversight. I would love for you to come. You and Da. And Thomas and Maureen and her...belly."

My mum chuckled drily. "She has a fiancé now too."

"Him too. You're all invited. There's room. Unless—"

I broke off. Frowned. Likely would've choked again if I had anything in my throat but air.

Even that threatened to kill me.

"Unless what?"

"What if I got a place in Crescent Cove? I mean, if it worked out. If she hasn't found someone else. If she still wants to see me again."

"A lot of what ifs and just plain ifs. Seems to me you need to start asking some questions and listening—really listening—to the answers."

"Yes, I do." I wiped my mouth with my napkin and sat back in my chair. "I suppose I need to do that with you and Da too. I always assumed he was glad I'd gone."

"Oh, my sweet boy. You couldn't be more wrong. He believes you were glad to be rid of us." She pushed aside her half-eaten stew. I hoped I hadn't been the cause of her lackluster appetite, but I had to wonder. "I have to admit, the thought has crossed my mind too."

"Never. I swear." I reached for her hand and cupped it between both of mine. "That was the other reason I came here. You're right. I've focused on work to the exclusion of all else. And I've made great strides, but I'm alone." The word felt like a razor against my vocal cords. I could barely get it out. "I always liked my solitude."

"Until now."

Wordlessly, I nodded.

"Love changes everything. Opens up your eyes to what you've deliberately looked away from." She squeezed my hand. "Like how you never could catch a decent fish."

I laughed softly and met her unwavering gaze. "I'm so glad I came, Ma."

Her eyes dampened for just a second before they were clear and true once again. "I am too, sweetheart. Now tell me you'll stay for more than a few days."

I nodded. I hadn't planned on staying long, but it looked as if I'd be extending my visit a bit.

Once I returned to the States, I would be going back to Ivy.

Whatever that meant.

NINETEEN

Two weeks later

I DID TWO THINGS UPON ARRIVING IN NEW YORK AFTER MY visit with my folks.

And Thomas, my smart-mouthed little brother who thought he was teaching *me* something when he offered to take me to some gentleman's club he had discovered. And Maureen, my now sizable younger sister with her equally sizable rock on her hand and her far too smiley husband. And the town at large, meeting friends old and new.

Leaving had been surprisingly difficult. I'd never wanted to stay as much as I did this time. Partly because my village—my family— seemed more welcoming than I remembered. Partly because I didn't want to deal with what might be waiting for me on the other side of the pond.

But all good things came to an end, and I left promising to return soon. I even meant it.

Possibly even with Ivy.

Lots of possibilities there, and just as many chances for failure. I just couldn't dwell on those now.

The trip back to the States was long and tiring. I was restless and couldn't settle, never mind sleep. At least they didn't lose my luggage, a minor miracle. I'd worn the fisherman's sweater my mum had knitted me just in case.

The one she'd whipped up like a damn demon for Ivy was tucked away in my pack, along with the piece of jewelry I'd picked up for her on a whim in a small shop in Belfast. My sister was always one for shopping, and when she'd heard I had a "stór", she'd taken me to all the best places featuring handcrafted pieces.

I'd tried to explain my relationship with Ivy was complicated, but she wouldn't hear it. To her, the world was a rosy bowl of happiness.

It had to be the hormones swimming through her veins. No one had cause to be *that* happy. Pregnancy glow or not.

Now all of that was behind me, and the gifts I'd possibly foolishly brought home for Ivy were safe in my luggage.

Unlike me. I'd cast safety to the wind.

I rubbed my chest where I'd inked part of my soul. Dramatic? A bit. But an Irishman was entitled to some poetry when he'd found the love of his life.

Perhaps I was reclaiming that side of myself as well.

All that remained before I completed the final leg of my journey was to snip off two dangling threads.

The first was to open the mail Ian had sent me over in Ireland. I didn't know how it had arrived so quickly. He must've paid a mint.

But when I pulled out the seemingly old-fashioned tape recorder —that somehow had a Bluetooth connection I could hook up in my rental car, whom I was now calling Silver Bullet of Despair after our multiple trips together—and slipped in the cassette tape he'd included, I understood why he'd paid extra.

His and Kellan's voices soared from the tinny speakers. The sound quality of the machine wasn't the best, but it didn't matter. The combination of Ian's rafter-raising voice with Kellan's grittier one was an oddly interesting juxtaposition. And their song was bloody good too, even if I was already finding ways I would arrange it differently.

I grabbed my phone to jot some things down as I listened half a dozen times. Strings sooner, rather than starting with the piano. The piano coming in on the bridge. Adding a touch of broken glass sound effects to the very end, when the man with the crushed spirit was walking away.

In the song, Ian was basically the more hopeful half of the guy who had just endured a failed romance. Kellan was the voice in the back of his head saying not to bother. Why try when everything always turns out the same anyway in the end?

It could've been a chaotic mess yet the result so far was a kind of crazy poetry.

My hands tingled as I typed out the last of my first impressions and sent them over to Ian. I added a line at the end to make him laugh.

> A tape recorder? Really? It's not the 80s anymore. Also, I think Anthony Robbins has taken over your psyche.

It made *me* laugh, which was saying a lot since I'd just spent weeks with my family, more time than I had in years. Yet my mood was surprisingly buoyant.

I'd made some mistakes. Pushed people away unnecessarily. Not unlike the pessimistic bloke in Kellan and Ian's song. Except today I was drowning out the negative voice in the back of my head.

Mostly.

At least until I took a deep breath and played Ivy's voicemail. Make that two voicemails. She'd left them three days apart and I hadn't replied or even nutted up enough to listen to them.

I was now.

Finally.

They said variations of the same thing. *I need to talk to you. It's really important. In person would be best, but I know you're booked. So...call me.*

I drove away from the rental place and hopped on the Interstate almost without noticing the signs. This trip was already becoming familiar. Good thing, because I scarcely heard the instructions from the GPS or the whistles on my phone that signaled Ian's texts.

My entire focus was Ivy.

I wish I could've said my first worry was illness or a death in the family or some other catastrophic condition. That concern was in there too, but it was beneath the gut punch that she'd found someone else.

Maybe she hadn't. Two messages and that was it. No texts, and I'd checked.

Of course I hadn't texted her again after mine had gone unanswered.

Until she'd called...

Gripping the wheel, I squinted into the sun and blew out a long, slow breath. It was the middle of June. No threat of snow now. Instead, the heat index was climbing higher by the minute, and I was sweating through my short-sleeved button down. Humidity was a bitch.

Unless I was sweating for other reasons. And not even ones like having to meet her older brother.

Before, that had seemed problematic. I'd just chosen to focus on that rather than the content of her voicemails. I knew full well I might not want to hear what she had to say.

I could call. That would be easier. Less traumatic. For her, I mean. I was a strong, tough guy. It wasn't as if her news would destroy me. I was just worried because I couldn't get a refund on the white gold bracelet I'd bought for her.

Right.

And if she'd contacted me because of something serious going on in her life—sickness in her family or job woes or God knows what else

—most likely, she wouldn't want to hear from me now. I hadn't been there for her when she needed me.

I was a bastard. More concerned about myself than her possible tragedies.

Now I would own up to what I'd done. And what I hadn't.

Let the chips fall where they may.

I found a spot down the block from the duplex Ivy shared with her brother. I went up to the door and hit the bell, then tucked my hands in the pockets of my trousers. My palms were actually damp.

Was this what it was like to meet the parents, so to speak? I hadn't done it since Darla. It wasn't an experience I was looking to repeat.

Yet if Ivy wasn't with someone new—and didn't want to maim me with her ice cream scoop—I would be doing it again with her actual parents at some point. She also had another brother.

Bloody big families. Another reason I wasn't cut out for the coupled up way of life.

Almost on cue, Ian's singsongy voice echoed in my head.

IAN

Anthony says what you focus on
determines your results. Focus on what you
love about your family. When bad thoughts
creep in, smack your wrist to break the
chain of negativity.

The asshole had actually said that to me in a text the other day. I'd wanted to kick his arse, but I'd actually found myself doing just as he suggested more than once.

If I ended up slapping myself a lot while talking to...Auggie? Was that what Ivy had called him? If I ended up slapping myself a lot while talking to him, maybe he'd think I had a twitch.

Or that I was a man in a strange land. I could use that excuse for any number of things.

The door swung open on my third ring of the bell. The guy was tall and well-built, the sort of fellow who wore T-shirts that nearly ripped at the seams from his flexed muscles. And in my case, the expansion of his chest as he stared me down.

"It's you?"

I didn't know how to answer that question. I looked over my shoulder. No one else on the porch. Just me.

I took off my mirrored sunglasses as I attempted a smile. "Hello… Auggie." Sweat trickled down my temple and I rubbed it away. "I'm Rory. Is your sister around?"

"Auggie?" He smirked. "No, she isn't. Can't you use her name? Do you even know it?"

He stomped down the hallway, leaving the door open for me to follow. Probably hoping I would so he could spring out and strangle me.

Carefully, I walked into their living room and sat on the first piece of furniture that would hold me.

Auggie—not a fitting name, by the way—pushed a hand through his shaggy hair. It was cut short in back, longer in front, but from the way he was plowing through it, he might be bald soon.

"I'm guessing you'd prefer if I didn't call you Auggie. So, August, is it?"

"I don't give two shits what you call me. What's important is what you call my sister." He turned and crossed his arms over his bullish chest. "What's your story?"

"Story?"

"Yes. Do you have a job? A dozen other children in other states? A record?"

"My own? No, not yet, although I've considered doing one as Carlos did, bringing in a variety of guest singers while I play the guitar. Of course I'd bring in other musicians too. I know my way around an acoustic, but I also know some very talented—" I broke off at August's hard stare. "I'm guessing you didn't mean that kind of record."

"What are you blathering about?"

"She didn't tell you about me?" It hurt more than I would have expected, although how could I expect her to tell everyone about us when I'd done little more than breeze in and out of her life?

I hadn't earned my spot. I was just an occasional visitor in her world.

"What she told me could fit on the head of a pin. You play guitar? You realize that's not exactly a stable job when it comes to having a woman and a family."

I cleared my throat. How best to say this without sounding like a douche? "I do okay, no worries there. Not that Ivy and I have made it to the family stage yet."

August narrowed his eyes. "You got a problem with stepping up and being a man?"

I took a quick glance between my spread legs. "Best as I can tell, I am one, mate, so if you have a problem with me, maybe you should just spell it out."

"I'm not your mate, son." He stepped forward and flexed his hands. I wouldn't have been surprised if he dragged me up by the shoulders and showed me his opinion of me with his fists. But I was scrappier than I looked and wouldn't back down from a fight.

Even if I had no clue why he was so angry. Yes, I hadn't been back to see Ivy in a couple of months, but as long as she was okay...

"Is she all right?" I rose. "Look, I don't have time for pissing matches with you, especially if there is something wrong with Ivy."

"Oh, no, there is nothing wrong with my sister. She's bright and beautiful and funny and far too good for the likes of you."

I couldn't argue with that. "You're right."

He crossed his arms again. "If I'm right, why the hell haven't you stuck around? Sure you don't have that other family or record I asked you about?"

"I live in California. For work. I do not have a wife or children or a police record. Other records, yes, there are many with my name listed as producer. I will agree that I could have done better by your sister. That's why I'm here. To rectify things." I exhaled and turned to head toward the front door. "Since I'm sure you won't point me in her direction, I'll find her myself. I should've tried the diner first anyway."

"So, why didn't you?"

Good question. It hadn't even occurred to me. I'd been pulled toward her flat and clearly, that had been a mistake. I'd been lectured since I stepped onto the stoop.

Worst of all, I didn't even know why.

"I don't know," I said finally, shifting back to face August. "Something told me to come here. Stupid, really, since it's daytime and Ivy is always working."

"You're right, she is working, but not at the diner." Before I could question that, he moved into my space. I held my ground and that seemed to soften some of the glint in his intense green eyes.

That could've been wishful thinking.

"My sister has a soft heart. Swing into town and give her a story about how you play guitars for a living and work with famous people, and her romantic heart probably kicked into gear. Not because she wants fame or money. She'd just see the artistic side of that and not the seedy fucking underbelly."

"I didn't give her a story about my work. In fact, I didn't tell her a whit about what I do until my second trip to see her. Then I brought her to meet my friends at Happy Acres. She met them. Spent the day with them and their significant others. I can guarantee I'm not making up some farfetched nonsense to get into her panties."

August's jaw firmed. "No, you've done that already, haven't you?"

Awkward. "Did Ivy tell you that?"

I didn't know what it said if she'd told her brother we'd been intimate yet hadn't mentioned my music career. Did that mean my prowess in bed was legendary? I'd always suspected I was better than the average bear, but I'd never had verification of the fact.

"Whatever she said, it's all true," I added, preening a little.

A muscle ticked in his temple. "Dude, I have no idea what's spinning around in your head right now, but she's my sister. Gross as fuck."

"Oh. Right. Yes. Of course."

"But even if I wasn't her older brother, she definitely didn't say anything complimentary about you. Short of you being a one-minute man. In and out. Wham. Bam. Done."

I cocked my head. "I highly doubt she said that, since my staying power is—"

He pointed at the door. "Get out."

"You're a bloody rude sot." I stopped in the doorway then turned to find August right behind me with blood in his eye. *My* blood. I could only imagine the vicious things he would do to me for daring to soil his beloved sister.

I couldn't even blame him.

I also couldn't let things stand on such awful terms. If Ivy didn't plan on dumping me for some local yuppie with a Harvard business degree, I'd be seeing August again. He was her family, and they lived together. She obviously adored her brother, and from all I'd seen, Ivy had good judgment.

Most likely, August was a decent bloke under the bluster and brotherly threats of violence. Both implied and otherwise.

"Look, we got off on the wrong foot." I held up my hands palms out. "I only came here to make things right with Ivy. I never meant to hurt her or cause her a moment's unhappiness, but from your attitude, clearly, I must have."

"My 'attitude' is the least of what you deserve, pal. She isn't a truck stop for you."

I nodded. "I understand that, and I regret deeply if my behavior indicated to her I didn't...care for her."

"Care for her?" He cocked a brow. "Gee, don't be so effusive. Vowels are free, just in case you missed the memo. And did it ever occur to you maybe she moved on?"

The pang in my chest nearly knocked me back a step. Was this the confirmation I'd feared? Perhaps that was exactly why I'd chosen to come here rather than to look for her at the diner.

This way, there was a chance that August would clue me in that Ivy was no longer interested. I hadn't consciously expected him to be home on a weekday afternoon, but maybe I'd been hoping to be let down easier.

Except this wasn't that. Not even close. Nothing could be easier when it came to Ivy—*my* Ivy—finding someone else. Especially now that I'd finally manned up and decided I wanted to claim her.

Not like a trophy or a prize, but as the gift she was. I wanted the world to know she was mine. I wanted her to know that too.

I'd had time to think and rethink my actions. All I knew was she made me a better man. With her, I was happy. Hopeful. We had fun together and Christ almighty, she made me crazy. In every possible way.

If she allowed me back into her life, I would be a lucky man indeed.

"Yes, it occurred to me. I can't imagine the amount of men who must want her."

August's face reddened. "You are a vile human. Seriously."

It made me laugh, when I didn't think I still could. "I'm sorry. Not appropriate considering. I'm just saying she's a wonderful woman, and any man would be honored to have her at his side."

August crossed his arms again and lifted a brow, clearly waiting.

"I did everything all wrong with her. Not by design. I came here for work and never expected to meet Ivy. I haven't—" I blew out a breath. "I haven't had many relationships, and I don't have a clue how to do them."

"That's the first sensible thing you've said since you came in here."

"Well, it's brutal truth. I didn't come to Crescent Cove looking for a girlfriend. I bitterly resented having to come here at all. But meeting Ivy is the best thing that has ever happened to me." Shaking my head, I smiled ruefully. "Just goes to show, doesn't it?"

"You really mean that?"

I nodded because I couldn't speak.

"She's a sweet woman and I don't want her to be hurt. She thinks she's so tough—and she is, believe you me—but she's vulnerable too. Especially now."

I frowned. "Why especially now? Because of me?"

God, I hated the thought of that. Hurting Ivy for even a second didn't sit well with me. She'd given me nothing but joy.

August's lips quirked. Not in a smile exactly, or a frown. More like a combination of the two. "You could say that."

"Whatever I've done, I'll make it up to her. I promise. I've come here with new resolve."

"Uh-huh. Because a ladybug changes her spots."

He had a good point. I was determined to do right by Ivy, but maybe I wasn't capable of more. I'd been alone for so long, and I liked my life as it was. Perhaps this was all I could hope to have—

I slapped my wrist. August's eyes widened.

Jesus H, I was going to kill Ian for making me look like even more of an arse. Although the slap had helped to redirect my thoughts.

So, maybe it wasn't so bad.

"I brought her a sweater from Ireland." Only once the words were out of my mouth did I realize how foolish they sounded. "My mum made it. For Ivy. Once I told her I was in love with—"

August held up his hand. "You're in love with her?"

My first inclination was to deny and escape while my stones were still intact. But I couldn't do that to Ivy. Or to myself. The love I felt for her was so new, like a tender shoot climbing out of a crack in the sidewalk. I couldn't stomp on it with my boot or it might break.

Ivy could still break it. But I wouldn't do the honors for her.

"Yes." I swallowed deeply. "Very much so."

"And your mother made her a sweater."

I nodded. "I think she wants grandbabies, although that's not on the schedule. You know how mums are."

"Oh, you'd be surprised." Before I could question him further, he slid his hands in his back pockets. "She's working on Main Street. You know your way around?"

"Yes. The diner—"

"No, not at the diner. She's next to Brewed Awakening."

It was my turn to frown. "Next to the coffee shop?"

"Yes. If you want to see her so bad, go take a good look. See what that woman is made of and what she deserves." He inclined his chin toward the door. "And if you tell her the details of this conversation, I will kick your ass so hard your mother's hand will tingle in Kilkenny."

"Malahide actually, but point taken." I shifted toward the door and twisted the knob, pulling it open.

It was still sunny outside. Freedom was just a few steps away.

I had survived my first official meeting with the older brother. It could only go up from here.

"Thanks, Auggie," I said, just to get some of my own back.

"You're welcome, Rormeister. Now scram."

I was laughing as I walked down the steps.

My smile still hadn't faded by the time I reached town. Granted, it wasn't a long trip. Even so, hope now bloomed in my chest where before there had only been ashes. I'd been so certain she'd called to tell me we were through. Perhaps that wasn't the case.

Although that raised a good question. If her family was okay—and I had to hope August would've told me if they weren't—and she herself was all right, and there wasn't a new man on the horizon, why had she called those two times, sounding desperate?

Better question, why weren't you man enough to listen to her messages when they came in and call her back?

I parked in Brewed Awakening's lot and got out to look around. I'd noticed before I turned off the car that the building next to the coffee shop appeared to be vacant. A *sold* sign had been planted on its tidy strip of lawn.

Something new would be moving in soon. But if Ivy was next to Brewed Awakening, where the hell was she?

Then I saw the truck parked between the two buildings. I didn't know how I'd missed it on the way in. I'd come in on the opposite side of the building, for one, and the alley was surprisingly shady for this time of day.

Better to keep the ice cream from melting.

Ivy's ice cream.

She'd done it.

The truck was like a rainbow. It practically fucking sparkled as I hurried across the lot and examined it from top to bottom. I couldn't inhale all the details fast enough, much the same way as I reacted with my ginger fairy's creations.

She'd done the truck in a jukebox theme. And on the slats where the songs would go on the juke, there was room for flavors. So many flavors. Not all the spots were filled in yet but the ones already there made me grin.

Heart of Choc & Roll

Bon Bon Jovi

Back in Blackberry Pie

Under my Plum

Sweet Child of Mint

All You Need is Lemon

If that wasn't enough, the name of the truck stretched across the top made me grin until my cheeks hurt.

Rolling Cones.

It was bloody perfect. Just like Ivy.

She'd set up the truck in a music theme and she was bringing her dream to life. Best of all, her dream was something we could share. Because she'd made it mine too. She'd combined both of our loves into this incredible thing.

My mouth was already watering for a taste of her Peppermint Patty.

And that wasn't a euphemism.

Probably.

This was why she'd called me. To tell me about what she'd accomplished so we could celebrate together.

Oh, how we would fucking celebrate.

The door to the interior was open. I rushed over to it and bounded up the stairs, not concerned about stealth or making an entrance. Or hell, even being able to breathe in that sauna-like truck.

I didn't care about anything but lifting her up in my arms for a spin. I wanted to laugh with her and kiss her and shower her in the praise she deserved for all she'd built.

Best of all, this was just the beginning.

She stood with her back to me at the sink. I waited for her to turn, to acknowledge me at all. I couldn't seem to speak. She had on heeled shoes that made her legs look miles long and a plaid miniskirt that caused me to think very unchaste thoughts. Her hair was in braids again, and she wore a white top that barely seemed to contain her curves.

She shifted and I had to swallow a groan. Holy fuck, there were a lot of them. Even more so than when I'd seen her last.

Her full breasts pressed against her tight T-shirt with its broken heart and the word *Rebound* written across it.

I frowned. Well, that was worrisome, wasn't it?

But I was here. I could make everything up to her. Ideally, before any rebounds took place.

Let's hope.

I couldn't stop staring at her, sucking down every bit of her as if she was oxygen. The shirt's hem flirted with her navel, until she shifted just a bit more and it lifted enough for me to fully glimpse her belly.

Her *swollen* belly.

Christ, what was I seeing? It couldn't be what I thought. It simply could not.

My knees turned to liquid, and I gripped the doorframe. Spots danced at the edges of my vision.

I was suffering heat stroke. Or worse. So much worse.

Just then, she yanked out her Air Pods and turned her head toward me. Her mouth rounded in shock.

She wasn't the only one currently experiencing that emotion. I could only manage one word.

"Ivy."

TWENTY

 IVY

I STARED AT MY PAINT-SPLATTERED HANDS, STILL UNDER WATER in the sink. I'd been washing my brushes, completely in my own world, focused on the Halestorm blaring in my ears. I wasn't full of rage right now, but I was all about female empowerment anthems at the moment.

Until I'd caught a glimpse of a ghost out of the corner of my eye and that stupidly sexy voice had said my name.

For a second, I'd forgotten I was pregnant.

Forgotten that I wasn't supposed to feel this wild hope in my chest when I knew Rory was near. The instant that mix of leather and woodsmoke hit me, I was helpless not to smile. To turn to him as if I'd been doing exactly that all my life.

But I wasn't just thinking of me now. Even if I wanted to run to him and embrace him despite being pissed and hurt he hadn't called me back, I couldn't. I had someone else to think about now.

The someone else he was examining via my stomach as if he couldn't tear his gaze away.

"The truck," he said hoarsely, still not looking from my belly. It was rather eye-catching since none of my clothes fit right. "You did it."

"I did." Every part of me was trembling, but I still threw back my shoulders. "I'm damn proud of it."

I wasn't only talking about the truck. I was talking about our—my —baby too. No, I hadn't planned on it. Certainly not in this circumstance. I definitely hadn't worked my mind around all the changes my body and my life would go through. But I was still happy. Still glad my baby was here.

If I had to be happy alone, I would be. I'd be happy enough for two people.

Hell, a whole army.

Almost daring him to speak, I cupped my belly. Although the gesture was still foreign, it was becoming more natural every day.

He watched my fingers spread over that growing life inside me and his mouth drew into a tight line. "Is it mine?"

I couldn't have heard him correctly. It was not possible that this jackass I'd slept with enough times to make a baby—to make half a dozen babies truthfully—was asking if I'd slept with another man.

To my credit, I attempted to answer like a rational person. A simple "yes" would've sufficed.

Instead, I picked up the beautiful bouquet of flowers my brother had bought me to celebrate the truck and tossed them at Rory's head, vase and all.

He ducked. Just barely. And when I let out a sob at what I'd done to my gorgeous flowers, he moved forward to collect them off the ground for me. His pants were wet. Petals clung to his shoes, his shirt. But he still bent to collect them all, holding up a hand when I stepped forward to help.

So, I buried my face in my hands and wept like an idiot.

I was still crying when I heard the clink of the vase being set aside and the thud of his footsteps. I didn't fight him when he enveloped me in his arms, because that was where I most wanted to be.

Always.

At night in bed, when I was alone and terrified, in the morning when I woke and wasn't sure how I'd ever be enough for not only myself but a baby who would depend on me for everything. Every time I looked at the door of the diner and hoped he would walk in so I wouldn't feel so hollow inside.

These crazy, confusing emotions were my daily reality now. Wanting him with me. Missing him. Wishing I wasn't so foolish to fall for a guy who couldn't—wouldn't—fall back.

"I'm sorry. I'm sorry," he murmured, brushing kisses over my hair.

Even that made me react. My body was traitorous and not to be trusted. It was as if I'd become hardwired to respond to his voice. His touch. Those shockingly gentle blue eyes trained on mine as I finally lifted my head.

I moved back because I had to. Keeping my distance was the only way I'd get through this.

"I can't believe you."

He scraped a hand through his longer-than-usual hair, the gold and red highlights shimmering from the sun coming through the windows. "I can't believe me right now either. First time up at bat in how long and I made a baby?"

I narrowed my eyes. "*We* made a baby. If my eggs weren't fresh like a prize hen's, your swimmers would've died a fiery death."

His mouth curved and I thought he might laugh. If he had, I probably would have clocked him with the vase alone this time, sparing the innocent flowers.

"I shouldn't have asked if it was mine."

"No kidding."

"It's just been months and you called to let me down easy—"

"Oh, no, buster, I did not call to let you down easy. This is your baby as much as mine." I stepped forward and poked him in the chest. "I don't want your stupid money for me, but you will provide for your child if there are things that I can't. Though I'm going to try. I'm going to try to give him or her the fucking world." I dashed at the tears dripping down my chin yet again with my other hand, smacking at them to make them disappear.

I was not some weak woman who couldn't take care of her business. I was just so freaking irritated right now that I probably could've castrated him with my ice cream scoop and not even felt guilty.

At least until tomorrow.

He gripped my hand and held it tight while his gaze locked on mine. Only then did I see the deep lines around his eyes as if he hadn't been sleeping well. And the way his shirt hung on him looser than it had in the past.

Had to be my imagination. I was the one who'd suffered during our separation.

Not him. He was the freewheeling playboy living the California lifestyle with all his rocker pals. Being the big shot and spending money while I scrambled for tips at the diner.

"Of course I'll do my part. I would never shirk my responsibility." The indignation in his tone soothed the side of me that had worried my income wouldn't be enough to provide for my child.

No matter how hard I worked, I was starting a new business. Most businesses lost money the first few years, if they even survived. I liked to wear my rose-colored glasses, but I couldn't right now. Not when I had a baby to consider.

Knowing Rory would be there financially if needed was a relief.

"Thank you."

"You don't have to thank me."

"You're damn right I don't. It's your responsibility, as you just said. We were both reckless, but I wasn't reckless alone."

"Reckless by even having sex at all? We were careful—" He broke off and wiped his hand down the side of his face. "Except that one time I forgot, but I blame the copper for that."

"How exactly is it fault of the 'copper' when we were mid-sex when he arrived?"

"I didn't even finish!"

"Someone missed their high school health classes. You can get knocked up without the full explosion."

"There wasn't even a partial explosion," he muttered. "I barely got off three strokes."

"As much as I love this trip down memory lane, that wasn't when. We timed where I was in my cycle and the baby's progress and it probably happened the first night we met. If not, certainly the next afternoon. So, you could've gotten off eighteen strokes bare, and it wouldn't have mattered."

He smacked the inside of his wrist and I jumped. "Bug?" I craned my neck to peer around the ceiling. "Are there bugs in here?"

"No." His smile was sheepish. "Sorry. It's this thing Ian taught me to divert—oh, never mind. It sounds even more ridiculous when I say it out loud."

I said nothing.

He exhaled and dipped his hands into his pockets. "So, you're well then?"

I braced my hand against the aching small of my back, which was more from all the work I'd been doing than my pea-sized baby. "We're doing fine."

"Yes. Of course. Both of you. That's what I meant." He rubbed his hand over his mouth and went back to staring at my belly as if it was radioactive and might spew at any time.

Rolling my eyes, I turned away and returned to my paintbrushes in the sink.

"So, that's it then? You're just going to ignore me until I leave?" He swore under his breath. "Can you really blame me for thinking you'd be calling to sever all ties? You gave me your word—"

I whirled to face him with dripping paintbrushes gripped in my fists like swords. "I gave you my word I would tell you if I moved on. I didn't say I would only call if that was the case."

He started to argue then fell silent. "Hmm. I guess that's true then, isn't it?"

"Bloody idiot." I turned away from him and went back to rinsing before the urge to commit violence overtook me once again.

"Bloody? My influence is rubbing off."

He sounded so pleased with himself. So normal. As if this was an everyday conversation.

We hadn't made a life between us who would need to be fed and clothed. Nope, we could just keep meeting every other month or two until I couldn't bend over to tie my shoes, never mind kneel to suck his damn dick.

"I get as much influence from *Lucifer* reruns as I do from you. You know why? Because I can hit play on that show any day I want and he's in my living room. And you are not. You haven't been here and you won't be here." I ran out of steam at the end, staring blindly at the bubbles in the sink while my throat ached and my eyes burned. But at least no more tears fell.

Small favors.

"I came back for you, Ivy. That's why I'm here. Not because of Kellan or Ian or anyone other than you."

I bowed my head. "Don't say that."

"It's sterling truth. Have I ever lied to you before?"

"Does that include you leaving out the part about you being in the music business?"

"Yes." That he acted like that was no big thing just gave me more fuel for my fire. Too bad it was dangerously close to sputtering out.

"I'm not denying you may have flown here solely for me, but it wasn't because you were here to pledge your undying love."

"How do you know that?" he snapped. "Suddenly, you're an expert on me now? You know all my thoughts and feelings?"

"I know what you've shown me, and only that." I dropped a clean brush in a pail and wiped my sweaty forehead with the back of my hand. "If you came here for some reason other than us getting naked in the closest vehicle, yay. That's very sweet. I'd probably be flattered if I wasn't facing my future head-on."

"Considering I just found out you're carrying my child, I think I'm doing quite well."

"Of course you are, because you know exactly where to find the door."

"Goddammit, woman, will you listen to me?" He stepped forward and gripped my shoulders in his strong hands, shaking me just enough to make me grit my teeth. "I'm trying to say I want to be part of this. I *have* to be part of this."

Even as hope surged in my chest, I squashed it. I couldn't afford to wish on any more shooting stars.

Or any more disappearing rockstars.

"That's just it," I whispered. "You're a *part* of it. It's all happening inside of me. I've been here every day, doing all of this alone. Can you get that?"

"I get it." He wrapped himself around me, crossing his arms over my chest until I was completely surrounded in his warmth and comforting smell. "I regret you had to do any of this alone. That I missed even a minute. I wish to God I'd picked up those calls. But there's something I haven't told you about a situation in my past—"

"A woman."

His lack of answer was answer enough.

I swallowed deeply and stared straight ahead until the bright swirls of paint on the brushes in the sink blurred together. I wanted to curl into him and never, ever leave. But somehow, I stood strong. "I can't hear about any of that today."

"Okay. Whatever you need."

"Right now, I need you to go," I said brokenly. I hated that I was on the verge of tears again. Still. I also hated like hell to let him out of my sight for a second.

What if this was the last time I ever saw him? Would I survive it?

But if he stayed, I would crumble. He would sneak his way under my defenses, and I needed to do what was best for my child—not me. It would never be about just me and my needs again. It was one thing if he breezed in and out of my life. Quite another if he did the same thing with my baby.

"Ivy, baby, please." His husky voice against my ear was nearly my undoing. "Let me stay and make this up—"

I let out a dry laugh. "We can't make this up in bed like we did everything else."

"Christ, I didn't mean like that—"

"Rory, just go. Please." The shuddering breath he released made me toss him a bone. "We'll talk tomorrow."

If you're still around.

He didn't answer for a minute or more. All he did was hold me and let out more of those shaky, pain-filled breaths. Each one tore through me.

I came so close to turning and taking it all back. All I wanted was for him to stay. For real. Not just for me, but for the baby. For love, not only responsibility. It was all too soon, I knew, and I was expecting far too much. I wanted the fairy tale, and he was a flesh and blood man.

Except he'd been the reason I'd dreamed so big in the first place. Because deep down, I knew we could live that life. It wouldn't be perfect, but we could be happy together.

All three of us could be.

Or we could have been if he wasn't so attached to escape routes. And a rockstar never changed his spots, did he?

When Rory finally let me go, I wanted to sob. Yet somehow my eyes stayed dry.

"For you, I'll go. Not for me. If it was up to me, I'd sleep on this truck floor if necessary. If that's what it would take to prove to you I'm not going anywhere. You're the one making me go, not me."

He walked to the door and took a step down, then another before stopping and turning back. "I'll be back tomorrow, bright and early. Make sure you rest. And dream of me, as I dream of you."

The last bit I wasn't sure if I'd heard or imagined. He was gone before I could ask.

I squeezed my eyes closed and let out a tired laugh.

Big surprise there.

TWENTY-ONE

 IVY

I TUGGED THE BRIM OF MY PINK BASEBALL HAT LOWER OVER MY eyes. The sun was brutal and my to-do list seemed never ending. I was ticking things off on my app on my phone, the letters jittering a little as I walked.

I missed my coffee so damn much.

The measly eight ounces a day I was allowed per my doctor seemed more like a tease. Who could survive on that? Especially when sleep had been non-existent in my life.

All night long, the shock and panic in his eyes were replaying on a loop.

Rory was back.

Rory staring at my belly like it was an alien followed directly by him asking who the father was.

Yeah, that part was the suck and I still couldn't get my anger in check about it. How dare he think that?

I smoothed my hand over my little bump. Almost four months along and I was already starting to show, thank you very much short torso.

Did he know me at all?

No.

I ignored the little voice. He damn well should.

How would he know? You guys hung out no more than a week total.

Shut up.

I wasn't sure which was worse, him coming back to the Cove, or him never showing his face again. At least his absence meant I could push thoughts of him out of my brain and concentrate on the things I could control.

Doctor's appointments and my ice cream truck.

I stuffed my phone into the front pocket of my overalls. I was trying out one of the shirts for Rolling Cones and it was too freaking small. I didn't have any other shirts that were clean and actually fit because I was still in denial that my clothes were too tight.

And I had a shift at the diner that afternoon. Those shirts didn't fit either. Neither did my pants. The little button extender trick wasn't working anymore, and Kinleigh had let my last few pairs out as far as possible.

I had new ones on order.

For now, I had the trusty OshKosh B'gosh looking overalls that made me look like a damn toddler. But they were roomy. I looked down at the slight swell pushing at the denim. At least they were roomy for now. I'd probably have to get a new pair of these as well.

Or you could get maternity clothes.

No.

All the things I'd looked at were either a summer tent or tight on purpose which showed off every new bump and hump in my repertoire. I was not one of those yoga moms who barely looked pregnant. Or adorable like Zoe.

I dragged my hand against my cheeks and groaned. Stupid tears on top off it all.

Nope, I was curving everywhere, due to a little extra ice cream consumption. I'd already busted out of two new bras, dammit.

"There you are."

I turned at Kinleigh's voice. "Hey. What are you doing out here? Don't you have a shipment coming in?"

She caught up to me on the sidewalk. "I'm not sure how you can outwalk me with that cute little waddle."

"Shut up."

She slid her arm through mine. "Are you okay?"

"I'm fine." I'd called her after Rory left last night and had imbibed another pint of Mintnight in Paris—my new flavor of mint with a dark chocolate swirl—with her at the store. I ate, she mended a new dress she'd bought on eBay.

"Uh huh. That's why your hair isn't washed?"

"I don't wash it every day." I'd create my own landfill with shampoo bottles if I did that. Long, thick hair wasn't easy to maintain. However, she was correct I hadn't gotten into the shower. I'd finally dozed off around the time of birds started chirping this morning.

Could I call it training for the sleepless nights coming my way with the baby?

Probably not.

She didn't answer. In true Kinleigh fashion, she waited me out. I blew out a breath. "I'm fine, just irritable."

"You should be. That asshat showed up and totally acted like a punk."

I swallowed a laugh. "A punk? Really?"

"Shut up. You know what I mean." She laced her fingers with mine. "I'm just worried about you."

"I'm fine."

"That's what you always say."

"I'm fat."

"You are not. You barely have a baby bump. If you looked at you from the back, you wouldn't even know you were preggers."

"Yeah, that's a lie. My ass is expanding, thanks to my addiction to my own ice cream. You'd think I would be tired of it since I've been making vats of it for the last few weeks."

"That baby is going to come out mint-flavored."

"Better than vanilla." That still sent me to the bathroom to hurl faster than any other flavor in my arsenal. However, there were far too many people who liked vanilla as a base for tons of different flavors so I still had to make it. However, my brother and Kinleigh got to test those.

I fussed with the buckle on my overalls, sliding it back up over my shoulder.

"Here." Kinleigh stopped me. She fixed the strap, tightened it and twisted it so it wouldn't fall down. "Girl, you are a mess. What is that under there?" She peeked into the open button along my side.

I slapped her hand away. "It's one of my shirts."

She snapped the mixed material. It had a little stretch to it so the shirt wouldn't be shapeless. I'd ordered them when I still had a figure. "Polyester? Have I taught you nothing?"

"It's easy to clean."

She rolled her eyes. "We need to get you some new clothes."

"Nothing fits. And everything feels weird. Oh, and pregnancy clothes suck."

She frowned. "Hmm."

"Hmm?"

She tapped her lip with one lilac-colored nail. "We'll see."

"Those cute clothes you have up there are not maternity wear."

"We'll see." She curved her arm around my back to my hip.

I shook my head. I didn't have it in me to ask what she meant. Besides, when she got that lost look in her eyes, there were measurements and ideas flinging around that I didn't understand. Same as she didn't understand my recipes.

We didn't question it, things just were.

"It's too hot for you to be out here all day. Promise me you'll go into Brewed Awakening to cool off."

"I promise."

She halted outside Brewed Awakening. "I do have a truck to meet, but I need coffee."

"Ugh. I hate you."

"I don't see why you don't have a cup of coffee. Plenty of pregnant women don't follow that rule."

"Not this one." My coffee addiction would not be the reason my child had some issue during delivery or during gestation, or a host of other horrifying things I'd read in the baby books.

"Suit yourself." She smiled at me, then her gaze slid past me to my ice cream truck. "What the hell are you doing here?"

I closed my eyes. "No way." He'd told me he was going to come back, but I didn't really believe him. Part of me assumed he'd just disappear and send me checks monthly like a car payment.

She gripped my hand again. "Do you want me to get rid of him?"

"I just want to talk, fairy queen." His voice slid down my spine like a caress.

I turned. "You don't get to call me that anymore, Rory."

He winced as if I'd taken aim at him. Again.

"Right. I'm sorry, Ivy Rose."

I flattened my lips and saw red. It was my name, but it sounded far different coming out of him. That lilt of Ireland and sadness. I shouldn't be affected by it. He was an utter shit.

"She doesn't want to talk to you. Why don't you scram? It's what you're best at." Kinleigh's strawberry curls floated around her head in the summer breeze. She was wearing a blue sundress with tiny roses all over it. Her wild blue eyes were fierce and she looked like she was heading into battle. All she needed was her trusty baseball bat from upstairs.

I'd seen her wield it. It was fairly impressive.

"I'm not running anymore." Rory's voice was strong and sure.

"If you say so." I was tired and there was still so much to do on the truck. August would be by in the afternoon to help, but for now, I was on my own.

By the time I'd gotten home last night, August had already been asleep in front of the TV. His own hours were just as wicked as mine.

I brushed by Rory and unlocked the back of the truck then climbed up.

Rory hovered outside the doorway, flicking his finger over the flap on his reusable coffee cup. He cleared his throat. "I got you a coffee."

"I can't drink that. Pregnant, remember?"

He swallowed and pulled off his aviator sunglasses to tuck into the neck of his shirt. "Right. It's decaf, but it's your flavors. Mint and chocolate."

"Should have just gotten me a hot chocolate. Oh, wait, it's ninety degrees out."

He ran the palm of his hand along the back of his neck. "Right. It's iced."

"Oh."

I turned to see the chocolate confection sitting on the counter of the receiving window. I hadn't bothered to put the shutters down last night since a layer of paint needed to dry before I took another crack at it today.

I was tired of painting.

For such a small truck, it was surprisingly difficult for me to get to every corner due to my newly added belly as well as being vertically challenged. But there were many years of abuse that needed to be covered. I'd had the entire truck powder coated on the outside, but it wasn't quite as easy to do inside.

Especially with all the equipment I had.

The genius lightbulb moment Kinleigh had for the name of the truck had also changed half of my ideas. It was so much snappier. I wish I'd thought of it. But I knew it was a goldmine when I told Macy the new name of the truck.

Ivy's Sweets had been cute. So had the turquoise and pink effects. However, Rolling Cones was catchy and perfect to use for social media blasts. I had dozens of names for flavors with the new musical slant.

We'd come up with a jukebox theme, and it had just exploded after that. So much that I couldn't keep up with all the ideas.

"May I come onboard?"

"Do I look like a captain?"

He set his coffee just inside the door then jammed his hands into his pockets as he moved back again. "A little. Change out the pink hat for an old-timey conductor stripe and you'd be right there. Kind of."

I looked down at my overalls. "Are you making a crack?"

His almost smile vanished. "No."

I shrugged. "It was almost a good joke." I sighed. "Are you just going to stand there and stare at me?"

"You could put me to work."

I put my hands on my hips. "Sure about that?"

He lifted his chin. "I want to help."

"Why?"

"Because it's important to you."

I narrowed my eyes. "Don't talk sweet, L—Rory."

His eyes flared to life, then shuttered. "I'm not. I swear it. I'm proud of all of this. Proud of you for what you're doing."

I didn't want the flare of pleasure to hit me so hard, but it did. It was amazing, and I'd done it on my own after saving for years. A bit of help from friends and family—even Caleb had helped me scrub the insides after a freezer malfunction.

Everyone was behind me.

It was the only thing that had kept me sane after I'd found out I was pregnant. But now here was my other half of this baby-making craziness. I didn't want to rely on him. Not again. Not anymore.

I had more than enough people in my life. "I don't need your help."

"Of course you don't. Doesn't mean I won't be giving it. No matter what you want."

I stalked toward the door. "This is my truck. What I say goes."

He took a step closer, but didn't come up the stairs yet. Our gazes met, and I glimpsed all the different shades of blue in his eyes. All the pieces of him that I'd just started memorizing before he left.

Again.

I had to remember that part.

He always left.

But at least he could help me paint in this blasted heat.

"Suit yourself." I toed the paint can tucked under the small seat just inside the door. "Touch up all the royal blue paint inside the truck."

He came up the stairs. I moved back immediately as he peered around the truck. "That's a lot of blue."

"Can't handle it?"

"Got another one of those hats?"

I opened a cabinet under the customer window and took out the rainbow cap with my new logo on it. "Sure do."

He paused ever so slightly, then took the hat and set it on his head backwards. "Where are the paintbrushes?"

I expected him to balk. Moreover, I figured he'd be a crap painter. I wasn't sure he'd ever picked up a paintbrush in his life.

I was very wrong. He was meticulous and methodical. He even asked me if he could add a white pinstripe around the cupboards. He used my chalkboard paint on the inside of the door to keep track of supplies.

When he was done with that, he disappeared. I figured that would be the last of him. Nope. He came back with a light lunch that wouldn't be too heavy in the heat and a large reusable cup full of lemonade.

And he didn't say a word.

The longer he worked, the harder it was to stay mad at him.

He forced me to take breaks. Hell, he even walked me over to the café to sit down in the air conditioning. He even hovered over me, worrying a bit. Then again, I was getting used to that. August was the same in that regard.

Each time Rory finished a thing on my to-do list, I gave him another and he completed it without complaint.

The sun was well past midday when my brother showed up. He climbed into the truck, his shoulders filling the space. His eyes widened as he took in the mostly finished truck. "Guess you don't need me."

I glanced over my shoulder at Rory. Paint dotted his cargo shorts and probably very expensive polo shirt. He even had a streak of chalk paint across his forehead. I had to force myself not to laugh.

I turned back to my brother. "I'm assuming you were the one to tell him where I was yesterday?"

August crossed his arms over his chest. "You're lucky I didn't pull his legs off."

Rory cleared his throat. "Your brother may have left a little detail out before sending me to you yesterday."

I pointed an accusing finger at him. "Wouldn't have been an issue if you'd contacted me like I asked, now would it?"

Rory's molars snapped together and he looked down at his feet.

I folded my arms. "Evidently, I have a slave. For today anyway."

"I'll be here as long as you need me."

I didn't turn to acknowledge Rory's words. I didn't want to fight with him in front of my brother. I was tired and sweaty and so very ready to go home and take a cool shower and fall on my face.

Unfortunately, I also had a shift at the diner to deal with.

"I appreciate you taking a shift, Aug, but I think we're good for the day." Me. *I* was good for the day. Where the hell had the *we* come from?

And I knew my brother had caught the pronoun since his eyebrow spiked and his gaze narrowed. I stalked toward him and pushed him back outside.

Thankfully, Rory didn't follow me. He was probably still worried about losing a limb.

I didn't mind him living in fear.

"I can't believe you."

"I tried to stay up and talk to you last night."

"It was already too late. You sicced him on me without any warning."

"Actually, it was more for him to catch a frigging clue. And you know he needed to know. I can't believe you didn't tell him."

"I tried," I whispered furiously.

"Yeah, well, you didn't let me in on that particular detail. I thought the fucker knew."

"It's none of your business."

The quick flash of hurt in my brother's eyes made me wince. He'd been nothing but amazing since I'd figured out I was pregnant. Kinleigh and August had even both been with me for my first few doctor's appointments.

"I'm sorry."

He waved me off. "Don't worry about it. It's been a helluva day." He raked his hands through his hair. "Is he bothering you? I can get rid of him."

"No."

Aug's eyebrows shot up. "Quick to forgive."

"There's no forgiving because there's no us." My chest tightened even saying it, but it was the truth. There was barely anything between us other than sex and a baby.

Liar.

I folded my arms over my little bump and lifted my chin at my brother.

He huffed out a breath. "Look, the guy came to the house and was distraught."

My mouth dropped open. "Are you defending him?"

"Jesus, no. Just...well, don't write him off completely. He hasn't had any time to figure this out yet."

"I can't believe you. You were just willing to castrate him if I asked you to."

"And I still would. The fact that he touched you is enough for me to kill him."

"August, you're not my dad. I have one of those." One who wasn't exactly speaking to me right now. I'd told my folks and they were supportive under duress. My dad was disappointed though. He didn't exactly say it, but it was pretty apparent since he left the room every time I came home.

This baby was supposed to be a happy thing. And nothing really made sense. I'd been prepared to do this alone all along, but now I just wasn't sure. Unfortunately, Rory being an inadvertent sperm donor didn't mean he was automatically cut out to be a father. No matter how much I wished it to be so.

It wasn't like I hadn't known that from the jump.

Everything felt different now that the reality was upon me. The shocked look on his face, the furtive glances all day. The worst part was the determination in his eyes.

Hope was not my friend.

August snapped his fingers in front of my face. "Earth to Ivy."

I smacked his hand away. "I have a lot on my mind. I just want to get this truck done. That's all I can concentrate on right now."

"Does he know that?"

I looked over my shoulder at Rory blatantly listening in the doorway. "What do you think?"

August's gaze crashed into Rory's. "Say the word and I'll make sure no one finds the body."

I dropped my arms and moved to my brother. "Thanks, Aug."

He hugged me with a sigh. "I'll see you tonight?"

"After my shift."

"Text me if you need anything."

I stepped back. "I will."

With a curt nod, he headed back across the street to his store.

I turned back to Rory, who was gripping the edges of the doorway. "He was kidding, right?"

"About which part?"

He swallowed. "The body."

"No." I brushed by him to grab my purse. "I have to lock up."

"All right. Do you have any cling wrap?"

I looped my strap over my shoulder. "What? Why?"

"Keeps the brush wet."

"Why don't you just wash it?"

"Because you're obviously in a rush. And I have to finish the other doors tomorrow." He closed the paint can with deliberate taps from a hammer.

"So, you *have* painted before?" I would not concentrate on the part where he said he'd be back the next day.

He shrugged. "My ma likes a tidy house. I've painted my fair share of shutters and walls for sure."

"Right, well, that's good. I have to go to work."

"Now? You've been working in this heat all day."

"Actually, you haven't let me do too much, but I still need to pay my bills."

"No, you don't. You have me."

The fact that he was still so blind made me want to rip my hair out. "I really don't." The stricken look on his face almost stopped me. "Goodnight, Rory."

"I'll be here tomorrow."

I didn't reply. What could I say? I just needed to get away from him. I'd used up a lifetime of tears on him already. "Lock up before you leave. I'm going to be late."

At the diner, I'd be too busy to think about us. Thank God.

Counting on him was too dangerous. For my baby *and* me.

I needed to remember that.

TWENTY-TWO

I was going to be a father.

Me. The guy who'd killed a plant labeled "basically indestructible."

The last day was basically a haze in my mind. I'd had more than twenty-four hours to come to terms with the idea yet I was still wandering around like a zombie. I could walk and carry on a semblance of a conversation, but my head was abuzz with white noise and panicked shouts that amounted to little more than...

Holy fucking shit.

After seeing Ivy at her truck and getting the news—and an almost concussion from attempted homicide via vase—I'd driven around for hours in a stupor. I'd stopped in some pinprick-sized town and had waffles at a no name diner. They hadn't had any taste and the texture had been like sandpaper, but that probably had more to do with my mental state than the quality of the food.

Then I'd driven to the nearest city and found a club. I was desperate for music. For something to fill my head that wasn't those same panicked shouts.

Turned out the hysteria was better, since the music had been terrible techno crap and I'd snapped at every woman who had dared to approach me. I'd gotten down half a Guinness before I found my way to the door.

I almost called my mum. Almost called Ian. Hell, even Kellan with his gruff amusement or Flynn with his no-nonsense views on life might've helped me set my head back on straight.

In the end, I sneaked back into the bed and breakfast where I'd yet again booked a room and darted up the stairs like an escaped convict. If Sage had asked me more probing, borderline inappropriate questions, I would've broken like a burnt cookie. She would've heard all about how the needs of my loins had led me to early fatherhood with a woman who now thought I was equivalent to sewer sludge.

I didn't blame Ivy for thinking the way she did. I hadn't replied to her calls because of my own hang-ups. She'd wanted to tell me so we could handle the situation maturely.

Meanwhile, I'd hidden my head under the pillows to avoid finding out she'd dumped me for some guy named Ax who could've taken down her hulking brother without batting a...deltoid.

Sleeping off my misery was all I could do.

I'd gone to Ivy's truck this morning full of resolve. I would help Ivy ready it for her opening day, which I gathered was soon. I would show her I could be depended on, despite my previous track record.

Sure, she knew me as the guy who rolled into town for sex and good times then rolled back out with little contact, but I had another side to me. I could be counted on.

Lo and behold, doing a day of backbreaking painting and cleaning tasks had proven shit to her. She said goodbye to me as if it would be the last one—and I wasn't even sure she'd mind.

I suspected she had feelings for me. She'd enjoyed having sex with me at the very least, which was the source of our troubles. We'd enjoyed it a little too much and too often.

Already I wanted to get my hands on her again. It made me a caveman. A pig. I had no right to want to explore her new curves with my tongue. Yet I did. Even though I had not one clue what to do about the baby, I still wanted to be with Ivy and figure it all out on a path strewn with orgasms.

Good luck there, boyo.

I drove away from my first day helping Ivy with her truck feeling dejected. Probably rejected too. I understood she had a higher responsibility to someone other than herself now, but God, that only made me want her more.

That was my child she was fighting to protect.

My child she cared about more than her own needs—assuming she still had some in my direction.

All right, caveman, cool it. It's her child too.

Our baby she was working so hard to provide for.

If she thought shoving a paintbrush in my hand was enough to drive me back to California, she was sorely mistaken. I was only digging in my heels more.

I didn't have one clue how to be a parent to a child. But others did it every day. Including people I never would've guessed would have wanted that role so soon in life.

Not everything occurred on schedules. Sometimes timetables were moved up and you had to deal.

So, I could learn too. On the fly if need be. And I was heading out right now for some on-the-job training.

Oddly, I wasn't in the mood for music. I could count on one hand the times I could've said that. Even after Darla, I'd filled my world with sound so I could try to forget.

With Ivy, I'd quickly realized no wall of words and melodies could drown her out inside me.

I didn't want them to.

It took me the better part of an hour to reach Happy Acres. I'd taken a meandering route on purpose. I didn't know exactly how to tell Ian what I'd done. What *we'd* done. I'd given him so much grief about knocking up Zoe shortly after they'd gotten back together, but he'd been so certain.

When you know, you know. And too fast doesn't exist.

I understood now what he meant and that scared me fucking senseless. Even the baby thing, while unexpected, didn't seem out of place. I didn't know the first thing what to do with a kid, but all of our timetables had been on hyper-speed since day one. Why should this be any different?

That didn't mean I was going to tell Ian he was right. He was arrogant enough already. I'd just slide in and observe what worked best with Zoe in her maternal state. I needed help.

Lots and lots of tips.

I pulled up the gravel driveway that led to the huge parking lot closest to the main store. I made myself get right out because it would've been too easy to sit in that relentless sun, ruminating. Trying to come up with a plan of attack for how to tell Ian and still not look like a jackass without a clue. But being with Ivy had taught me sometimes spur-of-the-moment was best.

School was newly out for summer, so the place was teeming with parents and children. So many little ones. All crying and yelling and laughing and wanting things. Piggyback rides—I could handle that—and cotton candy—still okay—and a turn on the pony—say what?

Then there were bathroom requests and petty squabbles with siblings, which I'd had my own fair share of as a child. My da hadn't put up with backtalk, however, and these children seemed born to backtalk.

Would mine be that way? Probably. I wasn't exactly the conformist type myself.

I finally made it through the crowd and opened the front door to the store. I'd assumed I would have to go looking for Ian and Zoe.

No, sirree. They were holding court right on the main floor.

Zoe stomped past me, her silver braid flying. She didn't even notice me in her annoyance. "Did I not tell you I didn't want to talk right now? Go away."

Ian didn't look my way either as he followed. "You know better than getting up on that ladder, Magic. If I hadn't been there, you could've fallen and—"

"I didn't fall until you startled me with your shrieking about my tendency to fall. Pain in the as—" She broke off and cleared her throat, apparently recalling children were nearby. "Rear that you are." She whirled and gave him a shove not befitting two happily engaged parents-to-be.

Then I saw the sparkler on her hand and was nearly permanently blinded.

"My God, you finally manned up."

Neither of them appeared to hear me. I hadn't spoken very loudly. The place was full of customers and everyone was laughing, talking, and generally making noise. So, I tried again.

"I did it to Ivy."

It was probably my imagination that all conversation ceased. That couldn't have been possible. But it definitely lessened in our little area.

Ian and Zoe stopped squabbling and stared at me. Ian grinned widely, then frowned as if he'd just fully heard what I'd said.

"You did what, exactly, to Ivy?"

My powers of speech had vanished. In lieu of them, I pointed at Zoe. More precisely, Zoe's belly.

They both looked down at her bump and then back at me with twin horrified expressions. I couldn't help it. I started to laugh.

If it sounded a little hysterical, that was probably due to imminent heat stroke.

"Can you get him some tea?" Ian asked Zoe, already moving toward me.

"With a shot of brandy."

Zoe nodded, eagerly scurrying away.

"Make that two shots," Ian called after her. He turned back to me and hauled me in for one of his standard bear hugs.

Ian Kagan didn't do anything halfway, and that included greeting someone. Didn't matter if it had been a day or two months since the last time. His difficult home environment had left some lasting scars, and he didn't take anything for granted.

Unlike me, he'd evolved from what he'd come from. Me? I'd made mountains from tiny piles of rice.

My parents were good people. Quiet, stoic, and sometimes uncommunicative and undemonstrative, yes. But I couldn't keep blaming them for everything. They'd done the best they knew how to do, as we all did.

And yes, Darla had fucked me over, as had my former friend. None of that mattered now. I couldn't keep using them as excuses for why I shoved people away and painted everyone with the same negative hues.

Ian held on for longer than normal, patting my back as he moved back. Then he smacked my cheeks. "You doing okay? You're still upright. That's a good sign."

"I'm fine. Just fine." I wobbled a little on my feet, only partially affecting the stumble.

Ian laughed and gestured toward the little café area off to one side. "Zoe's handling the drinks, so let's sit."

I sat. It was a relief to have something steady beneath me again.

"I'd ask how you are, but that's probably redundant." Ian sat forward in his chair and stretched out his long legs. "Is that why you went right to Ivy from home?"

I shook my head. "I didn't know until I...saw her."

God, that first glimpse of her would never leave my mind. So proud and defiant and beautiful, that was my Ivy. If need be, she'd take on the world alone. And she'd win, because who would dare tell her no?

"She didn't tell you?"

"She tried. She called. Left messages."

"And you didn't reply to them?" Ian stared hard at me, then shook his head with a sigh. "Worse, you didn't even listen to them, did you?"

I scrubbed my hands over my face. "It's complicated."

"Maybe the baby isn't yours?"

I dropped my hands and narrowed my eyes. "You better watch your mouth, arsehole."

Ian laughed and sat back. "Just proving a point, mate. So, if the baby is yours—"

"Can you not shout the news, please? It still hasn't made it to TV."

"Someone is a little full of themselves. Damn shame too, as I thought you were the level-headed one."

"I was, until I procreated."

"You make it sound like a sexually transmitted disease. Babies are lovely. Right, Magic?" Ian smiled up at Zoe as she approached. He took the tray of drinks from her and set it on the low coffee table between us, then patted his lap for Zoe to sit. She arched a brow and sat on the arm of his chair. "In fact, her only regret is that she can't become pregnant again until she has this one." He patted her belly.

She shoved his hand away, but I didn't miss her small smile.

"You two have the oddest relationship." I leaned forward to dump my shot of brandy into the tea. I hadn't truly expected to be served spirits other than their apple wine varieties and moonshine, but then again, the brandy probably had an apple tinge to it.

I didn't care. As long as it took the edge off, sign me up.

"It works for us." Before Zoe could attempt to reach for her own tea, Ian did the honors, stirring in honey and sugar at some precise quantity only they knew. Then he handed it to her and she granted him a rare full smile before she took a sip.

I swallowed some of my own and nearly screamed like a newborn as it scalded my throat.

"Sorry. I should've said it's piping hot." Zoe balanced her tea cup on the swell of her belly. "So, how is Ivy?"

"She's well."

"Gee, so much information. Don't overwhelm me." Zoe drank more of her tea. Her throat must be lined with steel.

"What do you want to know? She's with child. It's mine," I said pointedly to Ian, who held up his hands in the perfect picture of innocence. "She's not doing poorly right now, although it's early days yet."

"I hope she's okay. I should call her." Zoe frowned into her tea. "That day I saw her at Kinleigh's, she indicated she might be, but I was hoping she wasn't for her sake."

"Why would you say that?" I snapped. "Do you really think it's so burdensome to be carrying my child?"

Wonderful. Now I was the one shouting. I wasn't a big deal like Ian in the rock arena, but my name was mentioned often enough in the trades. At the rate I was going, I might as well just phone in a tip to *The Tattler* and pocket the fee myself.

"Oh, I don't know, because you're never around and she's a hometown girl. A very sweet girl who deserves a family if she wants one, not a guy who comes in and out dropping sperm."

"So, now it's all my fault? I did this alone?"

"No. But she's handling it alone, isn't she? You just showed up today."

"Yesterday," I muttered as guilt and shame twined through my stomach. To combat it, I swallowed more tea. It had cooled off, but at that moment, I wouldn't have cared if it burned through to my vocal cords.

Zoe was making too much sense, even if I hadn't known. I only hadn't known because I hadn't stepped up.

My first act as a father had been to duck and weave.

"I can just bet you haven't been going through this with her," Zoe continued. "She's probably working her ass to the bone right now while you've come here to have Ian assuage your guilty conscience."

All at once, the righteous anger bled out of me. "You're right."

"And for another thing—" Zoe blinked. "Huh?"

"You're right. I'm always quick to say I never led her on, but things change. People change. I knew soon enough I was developing feelings for her, and in that, I did lie. Because I'm in love with her and she doesn't know."

One of them gasped. Possibly both. I was too busy tossing back the last of my tea to notice which.

And that brandy went down smooth.

Ian hadn't touched his shot glass so I picked it up and drank it. He laughed and came around the coffee table to slap me on the back. "Well, congratulations then, Daddy-to-be. Looks like I beat you there, but at least you're on the track."

I couldn't do more than smile. Weakly.

I was really going to do this. Invest 110 percent, whatever that meant.

"So, when are you going to propose? If you need help ring shopping, I have some tips now. My brother and—" Ian must've seen my expression, since he put a lid on his mouth.

"Not everyone gets married right away."

"I know that, Magic."

"Some people wait almost the entire *nine months* to officially propose."

Ian rolled his eyes toward the ceiling. "Plant a baby in a woman, pledge undying devotion to her, give her a ring, and it's still never enough."

I had to laugh. A minor miracle, since my throat was now on fire for a completely new reason. "Do you think she expects that? We barely know each other."

"Yet you're in love with her? Unless you think it's one-sided. And if so," Ian patted my shoulder consolingly, "rough road, my friend."

"Oh, for Pete's sake, it's not one-sided. She was fawning over his accent and missing the hell out of him when he was gone."

"Fawning? Really?" I couldn't help preening a bit. Hell, my dented ego needed some stroking occasionally. "Here I thought it was just my skill as a lover that had her smitten."

"No, the accent is actually more useful in getting laid than the dick. Rather lowering to admit, I know, but I came to terms with it some time ago." Ian shrugged and held a hand out to Zoe. "Give me a little of that, Magic. I've a mighty thirst."

"Sorry. Empty. You might have less thirst if you didn't talk so much." She waved him off. "Go get a tea while I talk to Rory."

Ian cast a look between us, but he didn't hesitate to amble off. Running from the scene of the crime, that one.

"I know you don't want children. You've said it flat out to us a time or ten. So, if you're just stringing Ivy along, hoping to let her down easy, don't. Just make a clean break now." She flipped her braid over her shoulder, then immediately brought it forward again, fingering the ends. "I know you'll do right by her financially. I'm not saying you aren't a good guy, deep down. But trying to be someone you're not won't do her any favors in the long run."

"I wouldn't do that."

"Are you sure? Ian has a way of dragging everyone along with his plans. Maybe you see him so happy about a kid, and figure he's got one, so I can too."

"Bloody hell, woman, what kind of bloke do you take me for?" I set the tea cup down with a rattle in the saucer and locked my hands behind my neck. "I'm not faking anything or stringing her along. I have real feelings for her. For God's sake, my mum knitted her a sweater. I brought home a bracelet that says 'my love' in Irish for her. That was before I knew she was pregnant, by the way, in case you missed that while sitting on your throne of judgment."

Zoe's throat bobbed, but she didn't reply.

"I did say I didn't want children. I didn't think I wanted a wife either. I'm not all the way there to marriage in my head yet, but I'm so much closer than I ever was before. Give me—give us—a chance to get the rest of the way there together, yeah?"

Zoe's shoulders lifted as she sucked in a deep breath. Then she flashed me a dazzling smile. "Much, much better. That was the passion I wanted to see from you." She started to jump to her feet as she once had, then screwed up her features and braced herself on the arms of the chair for a giant heave upward. "Lordy, I am so ready to get this kid out of me. I swear, he's gotta be the size of a Beluga."

I hurried forward to help her to her feet. As soon as she was upright, she wrapped her arms around me and gave me a hug much like Ian's. Unreserved, with every ounce of the fire inside her.

Awkwardly, I patted her back and tried not to crush her stomach between us. "You're not so dissimilar, are you?"

She didn't have time to answer, because the baby took that moment to kick hard enough that I felt it. Without thinking, I placed my hand on the side of her belly. The child kicked again.

"Oh, look at that. He likes Uncle Rory."

I was too busy staring at the ripple under my hand. Awe wasn't a strong enough word for the emotion that moved through me. "Mine will do this too?"

"I imagine so. Can't see a baby of yours and Ivy's being a meek sort."

"Right. A baby of mine and Ivy's." I cleared my throat, but it still didn't do a thing to alleviate the grittiness. Nor could I blink fast enough to keep the heat from my eyes.

"Hey." Zoe's voice was gentle. "You know this is going to be okay, right? I know it seems huge and scary right now, but people have been having babies since the beginning of time. It's a natural process."

"Hey, Magic, they have fresh scones. Want one?" Ian called.

She sighed. "He's cute when he's not being a pain in the keister. Sure," she called back. "Your son is hungry. Again."

"Does it hurt?" I slipped my hands into my pockets, but I could still see that mad dancing going on under her skin.

"The kicking? Not always. Now that he's almost full-term though? Yeah. He's a budding footballer for sure."

I smiled. "Ivy is picking up some of our words too."

"And she'll pick up more, if you give her the chance." Zoe shocked me into silence by gripping my wrist, hard. "The biggest gift you can give her is your presence. Not fancy bracelets or knitted sweaters. Those are nice too. But she wants you with her. Even when she says she doesn't. Even when she threatens to make you sterile. She doesn't mean it. Probably."

Ian strolled over with his plate of baked goods. "I saw you feeling around on my wife. I hope you have good insurance, son."

"Almost wife." She nudged him in the gut and thieved his plate, smiling up at him. "I'm going to have a little lie down. I'll be taking these with me."

Ian let out a long breath. "See? I live to do her bidding and she leaves me with crumbs." He hauled her in for an embarrassingly long kiss. I turned my head away and still, it went on and on.

But I found myself smiling just the same. This—some variation of this anyway—could be Ivy and me. And yes, it was scary. Yes, it was overwhelming.

More than anything, it was amazing.

A moment later, Zoe wandered off, scones in hand. Ian had snagged two, one of which he offered me. "So, what are you going to do?"

"I'm going to prove to her I will be by her side for every step of this."

"And the baby?"

I crunched into the scone. All of a sudden, I was ravenous. Were pregnancy cravings kicking in for me as well? "The same goes for him or her. God, there's a him or her."

"Unless there's two." Ian's eyes twinkled. "Or three. Sometimes there's even four or five or six..."

I pointed at him. "You're not even funny."

"Sure I am. I'm irresistible in all ways. Besides, you're most likely safe on that score." He paused to chew his scone. "Probably."

TWENTY-THREE

 IVY

NO MATTER HOW EARLY I SHOWED UP AT THE TRUCK, HE WAS there waiting for me.

Every damn day.

We'd gotten past the painting to the pure muscle portion of the truck prep. Rory showed up with more bandages on his fingers than skin some days, but he showed up. And never complained. No matter what I threw at him.

He even went to the hardware store and bought a drill and tool belt which I had a hard time not laughing at. Followed directly by drooling because he kinda looked hot with the whole workman thing going on.

That of course put me in a bad mood for two days straight.

His next task was more creative. He went across the street and set up on the grass to do some crazy masking tape tricks to paint the faux jukebox sandwich board sign. He wouldn't let me help because of the chemicals. Personally, I was pretty sure he just wanted to play perfectionist with the jukebox colors. He had a host of spray paints in his arsenal along with a ridiculous face mask to combat the breeze coming off the water.

He'd come back this morning looking for chalkboard paint so the center of his genius mini jukebox could be changed like the song strips on the truck. The fact that he was a very good artist on top of all the other things he could do pissed me off way more than it should have.

Then again, him breathing pissed me off lately.

But he'd been with me every step of the way for the last week. Bringing me lunches, drinks, making me take breaks.

"Ivy Rose, come out here and take a look."

I sighed and gripped the counter inside the truck. I didn't want to go out there. And I wasn't sure which was worse—Rory saying the nickname that followed me into dreams or Ivy Rose.

Couldn't I just stay in here and ignore him? Besides, it was a million times more bearable thanks to the trio of fans Rory had set up around the window. I didn't even know there were fans with clips on them, but he found them.

He'd thought about me and my comfort and the fact that I was in a tin can in the dead of summer.

And I was weakening like a chump.

Because he looked so earnest with everything he did to help me. Other than a grudging thank you every day, I'd barely spoken to him other than to give him some sort of direction.

It didn't take much. He took ideas and ran with them. He was naturally creative in ways I hadn't even imagined.

Especially with titles for the ice cream flavors. Kinleigh and I had come up with a ton of them, but his were even more clever. I knew I needed to give him more credit for all the work he was doing, but it felt like I was giving in.

Forgiving him.

And I didn't want to forgive him. Because if I forgave him, I'd let him back in.

I slipped out of the back of the truck and around the side to where he was standing. The pure joy on his face made my chest hurt.

He was wearing the rainbow hat. It was sprinkled in paint fingerprints and splatter. Even his scruffy face was smeared with mint paint.

He was stupidly adorable and I wanted nothing more than to go over there and hug him.

He pushed his hat back and looked up, his face split with a rare smile. "What do you think?"

I blinked at him for a moment. I didn't think I'd ever seen him so happy. I followed his gaze. "What did you do to my truck?"

His grin slipped away. "I added speakers."

"I see that." The speakers were not on my itemized list of things I'd bought. "I didn't buy them."

"I did."

"I didn't ask you to." My fingers were fisted and I was ready to swing.

His larger one came around mine. He brought it up to his mouth and kissed it lightly. "I wanted to. You've been working so hard—"

"I have. And I did it all on my own. Well, until you came to help, but I could have done it."

"I'm not saying you couldn't have, love."

I hissed out a breath. "Don't call me that."

"I'm sorry. And I can take it down, but it's a gift. Can't you see that? I just wanted to—"

"What? My ideas aren't good enough?"

"Dammit, Ivy. It's not that." He dropped my hand and paced away from me, tunneling his fingers under his hat and through his overgrown hair. "I was trying to do something for you. That's all."

"I don't want you to." My voice was loud enough that a few people twisted to look at us from Brewed Awakening's outdoor tables. I brought it down an octave or three. "I'm fine with my plans. I've been building on them for years, Rory. *Years*." Horrified by the wash of tears threatening, I twisted away from him.

His hands gripped my arms as he crowded behind me. "You're

amazing and this whole production is incredible. You have a rock-themed truck with no music. It just seemed like the perfect cherry on the sundae as it were."

I froze up under his touch. We'd been so careful not to get into each other's space this whole week. I knew it was a perfect touch. It was thoughtful and generous and all the things Rory could be when he wanted to. But it was too much. And it had been in my plans for the future, after I brought some money in and could allow the expense.

Building up my business, one step at a time.

He slid one arm around me, tentative fingers curving around the little bump I was sporting. "I'd do anything for you. For both of you." He tipped his head to touch mine, his lips so close to my ear. "I don't want to make you upset, *a ghrá*."

Another one of those words I didn't understand. It was rare, but even on that first night, they'd tumbled from his mouth at the oddest times. In my heart, I knew he was trying, that this was how he showed me he wanted to do something for me. But I didn't want his money or his gifts.

I covered his hand on the side of my belly, squeezed lightly before slipping away from him. I crossed my arms and turned around. "You didn't even ask."

He looked down. "You're right. I just got excited. You didn't even look at them."

I gave him a huge sigh and turned to look at them. "Where did you order them from?"

He moved next to me. "That's the thing. They were just regular speakers. Nothing special. At least not until I talked to your brother. He helped make them match the look. He built little boxes around them so they looked like the same speakers in the diner." He rubbed the back of his neck. "We went and took pictures the other night."

"August helped you?"

"Don't sound so surprised."

"I was pretty sure my brother was going to castrate you."

"Oh, I'm not entirely sure he still won't, but he wanted to do something for your truck as well. Especially with the juke theme going on. He got all into it." He shrugged. "I'm the music man. I can wire anything into any board you give me. Even a taco truck from the nineties."

I let out a laugh. "And you guys did this for me?" The tears were close again. I didn't know what was up with these baby hormones, but I was not a fan of the plethora of tears that were always so close to the surface.

"We did, yeah." He shoved his hands in his pockets.

I blew out a slow breath and hooked my fingers around his wrist. "I'm sorry. They're really great. Amazing actually." They were almost seamlessly integrated with the scrolling top of the truck with my company name. Peeking out at each end with the same curve of the Rolling Cones font.

The fact that he'd gone to my brother made me feel even worse.

He nodded. "I'm sorry I didn't tell you." He pulled his hand out of his pocket and laced his fingers with mine. His blue eyes were earnest and clouded with doubt. "We've been texting about it all day. I didn't think."

"No, you didn't." My words were still harsh, but my voice was less certain. I didn't know how to feel. I'd been doing everything alone and I was so afraid to count on him in any way.

So afraid to want—to need—him to stay.

He turned me to face him. "We weren't trying to be high-handed. I honestly just thought you'd be happy. That's all we want for you, Ivy. All *I* want."

I nodded. "I love it. I do."

"Good." He pulled his phone out of his pocket. "I bastardized an app a mate of mine created. It works with your truck's stereo."

"How? The radio is a tape deck."

"Believe me, it took some working. I'll rip out the—"

At my look, he cleared his throat. "If you'd like, I'll replace the stereo in the future."

If he was going to be around to do that was the better question, but I simply nodded. "Better."

"Right. Well, I rigged the speakers to the truck and found a tape adapter that actually worked with Bluetooth."

"Really?"

"It's not perfect, but..." He pressed a few buttons, frowned, and fiddled with his phone. "Stupid piece of shite."

I snorted.

"Just wait, fairy queen and you'll see."

I opened my mouth to correct him. To demand he call me Ivy. Even Ivy Rose, but I just couldn't. Not when he was licking the corner of his mouth as he frowned over his phone.

Suddenly "Born to Be Wild" came blaring out of my speakers.

"Fuck, yeah. I knew it was going to work." He grinned down at me then pointed to the sign. "Born to be Wildberry, yeah?"

I laughed. "I got it."

"I have a playlist with all the flavors we have listed. See, right here I've got 'Purple Rain' for your icee flavor."

He was so excited and his eyes were shining with delight.

I didn't even think. I simply rose on my toes and kissed his cheek. He immediately stopped what he was doing and shoved his phone into his pocket. "Ivy."

I lowered myself back onto my heels. "Thank you."

"Right. You're welcome." He stared at my mouth and it took everything in me not to kiss him. It would be so easy to do that. To throw myself at him. Even with this baby bump in the way, it would be so easy to walk right into his arms.

I took a step back.

Too easy.

I cleared my throat. "We're almost done."

"That we are."

"Ahead of schedule, thanks to you."

"Too little, too late if you ask me."

"No. I really appreciate all you've done to make this truck come in under budget and early."

"It's my pleasure."

I laughed. "I'm sure it hasn't been. Your poor hands aren't used to this kind of work, music man."

"No, but I don't mind."

We stood together in the waning light of the evening. I'd worked the day shift at the diner, but it was June and the days were longer now. It was a good quiet between us. As quiet as Crescent Cove could be in the hours just past dinner anyway.

"Can I take you out, Ivy Rose?"

My gaze shot to his. "What?"

"On a date. A proper date."

"You want to take me out?"

"It's occurred to me that we've skipped all the steps that come with getting to know one another. Let me take you to dinner. Not at the diner. To a place that has a bread basket and a dessert cart that will make you feel decadent."

I couldn't stop the smile. "You mean like a restaurant where I have to dress up?"

"If you like. I don't care what you wear. You can wear your smashing overalls if you want. I just want a night with you."

I looked at my paint-splattered sneakers. "A night with you got me into this little predicament."

"No sex."

I shot him a look. "No?"

His neck reddened. "Well, I'm always wanting to get skin to skin with you, but for now, I just want the pleasure of your company. Across a table."

"I'd like that."

"Yeah? Tonight?"

I shook my head. "No."

"Oh."

"Tomorrow all right? I actually have a day off."

"And you'd spend it with me?"

"It looks like it."

His smile widened. "It's a date."

"I guess it is."

I hoped like hell I wasn't making a huge mistake.

TWENTY-FOUR

 IVY

"I'm insane."

"No, you love him. Now stop moving."

I twisted my head around. "I never said that."

Kinleigh grabbed my hips and twisted me straight. "If you don't stop squirming, I'm going to stick you," she mumbled around a pin in her mouth.

I blew out a breath and straightened up. When I'd come to her crying about my clothing predicament—again—she'd set me in front of the mirror with a dress she'd obviously been working on.

A dress made for my additional curves.

I fluffed the fluid middle of the pastel blue dress. It had tiny violets on it and fit like a dream.

"You know you could make bank in this town making cute pregnancy outfits. We all seem to be knocked up."

Kinleigh laughed and tucked her chin on my shoulder. "I was thinking precisely the same thing. I stole some of the material from the hem on this dress. Shortened it a few inches." She slid a pin along the seam at my hip. "Luckily, you have nice legs, so it worked out."

She unzipped the dress. "Step out and I'll do some of my magic sewing."

I let it shimmy to my ankles, then I wandered over to the rolling rack and flipped through the hangers of clothing as the soothing sound of Kinleigh's sewing machine played accompaniment to the chamber music she had playing today. You never knew what kind of music would be playing. It usually matched her outfit.

Steam punk meets corset was on the menu today—with a side of dramatic flair because of her newly pink hair. Had to love my bestie. Life was never boring with her in my life for sure.

Thank God for her and my brother, especially with the little one I was carrying around. My hand slid to my belly absently. Nothing was kicking around in there yet. According to my baby books, it would start in a few weeks—if I was lucky. Sometimes not until past the halfway mark.

Halfway. It didn't even compute. The weeks were bleeding away so fast, then other days it felt like no time had passed at all.

The bell for Kinleigh's front door jangled and I zipped behind the trifold screen in the dressing area. Hanging out in my bra and granny panties was all right with Kinleigh, not so much for anyone else.

"You're early." Kinleigh's voice was flat with displeasure.

"I know it. I was worried I'd be late and well, I'm very early."

"She's not ready."

"It's all right. I'll wait." His voice was a little nervy, the Irish a bit thicker than it usually was. I remembered the way his voice changed when he was with me. While he was inside me. The way his Irish flowed as well as his hips.

Cripes.

Halt. Reverse. Put away that line of thinking, young lady.

Oh, who was I kidding? I peered around the screen.

He was wearing black dress pants and a fitted summer weight shirt in a light blue. His brown hair was in that messy tumble of amber and copper streaks from the sun. He wasn't the type to use a lot of product, but it was obvious he'd made an effort to dress up.

For me.

I swallowed down a lump.

He spotted me and I tried to duck back, but too late. He was headed my way.

"Dammit," I muttered. Usually, Kinleigh had a dozen silky robes back here to shrug on between outfits. "Not a single one? Really?"

"Ivy?"

"Naked," I blurted out.

His dress shoes stopped clicking on the hardwoods, then he started walking again.

"Did you hear me?"

"I did, yes."

"That means you stop walking, LC."

He paused again, but then his stride lengthened.

Shit, I didn't mean to let his nickname fly free. It was so ingrained from the time we'd spent together.

He hovered just outside of the screen. "May I come back there?"

"No."

"Fairy queen." His voice was cajoling. The heaviness in the air made all those fluttery feelings come alive in my belly, in my chest, and along my fingertips. The lust part was easy. If we had any hope of becoming more than *this*—more than just a pair of lusty strangers—then we needed to do this the right way.

"Third date, Rory."

There was a beat of silence. "Excuse me?"

"Third date is when you get to see skin."

"I've tasted every part of you, love. And I do mean every."

My skin flushed. That was very true, but I had to believe there was more to us. More to me and him as a... God, a unit? More than just parents to a little miracle. An untimely one, but still a miracle.

"I do not need to know all the particulars between you, thanks."

Kinleigh bustled over and flipped the finished dress over the top of the screen. "Ready."

I quickly pulled the dress down and slid it over my head. It fell around my midsection as soft as a sigh then swished around my knees. "Oh, Kin."

"I know. It's glorious."

I laughed. My bestie didn't have any self-esteem problems when it came to the clothes she chose or altered. And I couldn't fault her. I twisted in the mirror and smoothed my hand over the gentle curve of my middle. It didn't hide it, but it didn't showcase it like some things I'd tried on in stores. The dress was pure comfort in every way.

"I left a cute pair of boots out here, as well as a pair of sandals. Whichever your feet are into."

I slowly came out from the dressing area. Kinleigh knew me well. Some days it was all about the swollen feet, some days it was everything was too hot. Today, those cowboy boots would be perfect.

Especially with the cool breeze coming off the water that day. I could feel a storm in the air. It seemed fitting for our official first date. Handily, I'd always been good at facing storms.

It remained to be seen if Rory was as well.

"You're stunning." Rory's eyes were hooded in that bedroom way that made me want to drag him back to the room at the Hummingbird. Where everything was easy and life didn't intrude.

But that wasn't what this date was about.

I straightened the skirt of my dress. "You're not so bad yourself." I snagged the boots, then plucked out a pair of socks from my bag. He watched me move to the large ottoman in the middle of the dressing area. I didn't hop around the room putting my socks on anymore.

I was too worried about losing my balance.

He waited patiently for me, then held his hand out. "Now you're stunning with a side of perfect."

"Laying it on thick, buddy."

"Never. Just speaking truth."

I narrowed my gaze, but took his hand. "Is this all right for your plans?"

"More than."

I turned to Kinleigh. "It's perfect."

"It'll do for my first preggers dress."

I laughed and rushed to her, releasing Rory's hand. I gave her a hard hug.

"Are you sure?" she whispered into my ear.

I nodded. I had to give us a try. Even if the smart half of me said I should be sprinting for the door. There was a smaller, more fragile piece of me that wanted to lean into the hope. To lean into the love that was already building inside me. And not just the baby.

I backed away and relinked my fingers with Rory's. "Ready?"

He nodded. "So much."

"Thanks, Kin." I smiled back at her. Her posture wasn't as sure, but she'd pasted a smile onto her face. I appreciated her protective nature. I'd taken comfort from it over the past few weeks. Maybe too much.

Rory led me down the stairs out into the blustery sunshine. The heat of the day was mixed with a charged air that lifted the hairs on my arms. His trusty sedan was parked right outside the building.

I could feel eyes on me. I turned to find my brother in the window of his shop on the bottom floor. His arms were crossed over his chest, and there was more than worry etched on his face. Not exactly menace, but I didn't really need to poke the bear either.

Rory opened the passenger car door and helped me inside. I let him, because he seemed to need it. Even on that first night, there had been a bit of an old world gentleman inside him that was missing from most men. When he went for my seatbelt, I gave him a bland look.

"Right. Sorry. All tucked in?"

"As much as I'm ever going to be." I placed a hand over my belly. The longing in his face made me reach for him. At least that was what I told myself when I settled his hand where mine had been. "There's no kicking yet."

"Right. Not for some weeks, yeah?" His blue eyes seemed even bluer today. Stormy as the air sitting over the town.

The reverence in his voice made my eyes sting. His touch was gentle, but there was no end to the wonder there.

His large hand smoothed over my new curves, the side of his fingers bumping along the edge of my bra. I resisted the urge to shiver, but it was way more difficult than I wanted to admit. For once, I was pretty sure he wasn't trying to seduce. There was too much concentration on his face for that.

"I've wanted to ask questions, but didn't want to overstep."

"I wasn't exactly in the correct state of mind to talk."

"I don't blame you, Ivy." His gaze lifted to mine once more. "I behaved badly. All I'm asking is that you give me a chance to make it up to you."

"Then you better feed me. That's a good first step."

"Right. We have reservations."

"Where?" I snapped my belt into place.

"It's a surprise." He grinned down at me and closed the door.

I frowned out the window as he headed toward the edge of town. "We're not staying in Crescent Cove?"

"No. We're going somewhere special."

I gave him a side eye. "Crescent Cove is special."

"There are things beyond the Cove, my ginger fairy."

My belly flipped at him using the shortened version of the town name that few people used other than residents. I opened my mouth to dissuade him from using his nickname for me, but it just didn't seem worth it at this point.

Not if I was sitting here next to him on a damn date.

Suddenly, the idea of things beyond Crescent Cove became a little more daunting. Because that was where my life was. Where I wanted to raise my child—*our* child. But it wasn't exactly the best place for someone like Rory. It wasn't a hub for musicians. Sure, Ian and Kellan were close by, but they were a little different.

They were in a band, not locked in to working with others. Not scheduling around musicians.

Scheduling around me.

"You're thinking mighty loud."

"Have you thought about what this means?"

"This?"

"Us. Me and you. Even if you wanted to make this work."

"If *we* do?"

I rolled my eyes. "Yes. But my life is here. Yours is so big, so much more than what I can offer you." It nearly killed me to say it, but it was the truth. I only had an ice cream truck and a baby to offer him. Even if my truck took off, it would be a seasonal staple in town.

And the baby was going to change everything.

"I've never cared about anything enough to want roots. I got out of Ireland as soon as humanly possible. I've split my time between New York and Los Angeles for most of my career."

I swallowed. "I understand."

"You misunderstand, Ivy Rose. I was speaking in past tense. Now there's a whole world I need to figure out. You and the baby are only part of that. You may have believed that my absence was all about running. I won't lie, some of it was. But only because what was happening between us rocked me. It obliterated my foundation."

I turned in my seat a little. "We've only known each other for a short time."

"That's the heart of it, isn't it? Why do you think it well and truly fucked me up?"

His accent was so thick I almost couldn't follow him. "I'm sorry."

"Don't be sorry, dammit." He blew out a breath and pulled off the side of the road onto the wide shoulder. It also happened to be near one of the walking paths that led to the lake.

I gave him a startled glance. "Don't we have reservations to get to?"

"Fuck the reservations." He pushed open his door.

I looked over my shoulder at the road. "Okay then." I opened my door and followed him to the stone wall at the far edge of the shoulder. When I got to him, I tugged on his shirt to keep him walking. "There's a path this way."

He frowned. "You make me crazy."

"Feeling is mutual. Let's take a walk. This conversation obviously shouldn't take place in a restaurant."

"So you can toss me into the sea?"

"Lake."

He rubbed the back of his neck. "Whatever. You know what I mean."

I held out my hand. "I'm not in your will yet, Rory. You're safe."

"Nice to know there's a few reasons to keep me around."

I laughed. "Come on." I held onto his arm a little more than I usually would. The cowboy boots were super cute, but not really cut out for the rocky path.

"Maybe we should turn back."

"The view is worth it." A distant roll of thunder heightened the moment. As if the sky was just as stirred up as both of us.

"All right, just hold onto me."

It was a short path to the rocky beach. The water was a bit wild from the wind kicking up. Small waves held more whitecaps than usual, and the air was sharp with brine and the heaviness of impending rain.

We stood together looking out over the water. I could tell he needed to talk. Part of me still didn't want to listen. It was easier to stay wrapped up tight in my anger and hurt.

But I had to give him a chance or tell him goodbye. It was as simple as that.

"Where have you been, Rory?"

He lifted our joined hands to his lips, but he didn't look away from the water. "Home."

"You ignored my calls."

"I did. I wish I could say it was for a good reason, but it really was just because I couldn't bear to let you go."

"That is the definition of faulty logic."

He gave a humorless laugh and drew me in front of him so we both faced the water. He linked his hands over my middle, drawing me back until we were flush. He brushed his cheek against mine. He had well past a bit of scruff after working with me for the last week. It was just long enough to be soft and not scratchy.

"When I left, I made you promise to let me go if you found someone. I didn't believe I deserved a girl—no, a woman—like you. I still don't, but I want it more than there are words inside of me. And for a man who lives by finding the right combination of words and notes, that was a scary thing."

I stilled against him. I wanted to spin in his arms, to see the truth in his eyes, but the fact that he wasn't looking at me seemed to be giving him the courage to talk.

"I went home to Ireland."

I twisted enough to look up at him. "Ireland?"

"I've been a loner all my life, but I think it was self-inflicted now that I've done some soul-searching. I assumed that the life my parents had was full of duty and unhappiness. I didn't want any part of that."

"And your trip changed that?"

His voice was low in my ear. "So much. I think my glasses might be Ivy colored instead of rose. Or maybe it's Ivy Rose-colored."

I laughed. "Dork."

He hugged me tighter, his fingers lightly playing over the curve of my belly. "And there it is. The venom I crave like a favorite wine."

I elbowed him. "I only speak truth."

"That's the heart of it. I needed your truth, not the foggy and worn out prescription of my own."

He told me about his brother and sister, about the new baby coming into his own family. The townsfolk he'd taken a little time to get to know again.

The music of his voice comforted. And there was no boredom in the telling.

I didn't even feel the need to insert my own familial anecdotes. It was rare for him to share things with me. There was work of course, and I'd seen him in his element at the orchard, but he was different. He *felt* different.

"I told my ma about you."

I turned in his arms, my heart racing. "You what?"

"I did. She knew it even before I opened my bleedin' mouth. We spoke of you and all the feelings you churned up inside of me. The way I'd distanced myself from everyone to focus on work. She even poked a few wounds I didn't want to face."

I had so many questions, but what I saw when I twisted again to look into his eyes made everything go still inside me. "Another woman."

He nodded slowly. "Quite a while ago. There hasn't been anyone for me in so long that she kind of became this festering scab that never quite healed. I can't say I was a total monk, but in my line of work, it was probably pretty close."

I touched his chin. The hair there was nearing a beard. "Did you love her?"

"It was young love, but felt real enough to me. Obviously, she didn't feel the same since she cheated on me."

"Oh, God."

"With my best mate."

"That fucking whore."

"Whoa." He laughed and linked his hands at my lower back. "There's my ginger fairy queen."

"There's no excuse for cheating. Ever. Fucking man up and break things off, but to do that—God, I can't."

He laughed and kissed me at the same time. The kiss was as sweet and wild as the breakers behind us. It had the potential for more, but he seemed to pull himself back as if he wanted to keep the moment light and soft.

I gripped his shirt, the simple vee of it stretching with my touch. I frowned as black ink peeked out of the place where whorls of hair used to be. "Did you get a tattoo?"

His neck flushed and his cheeks reddened. "Maybe."

I pulled until the words came clear. "You don't have any ink."

"I didn't used to have a fiery redhead in my life either. Things change."

I traced my fingers over the words.

Tomorrow I'll be on a plane
Gone far away
A lock of flame in my pocket
The words I couldn't say

The song he'd written and sang to me in the clearing at Happy Acres. The words were heavier now that I knew his truth. And that he'd come back for me even though he'd practically dared the worst to happen between us by ignoring my call.

So much made sense now. To lose your girl and your best friend was a lot for anyone. I looked up at him and his eyes softened.

"Don't cry for me, Ivy Rose."

I dashed at the tears. "I blame the baby. I've never cried so much in my life as I have since this little bit of news."

"Scary news for sure, but good."

My eyes stung again. "Yeah?"

"Maybe a bit out of order with how I'd figured things would go. And boy, is my mum going to flip. She's excited to meet you simply for the fact that you brought her boy home. Her words, not mine. Now? Well, let's just say the good graces train is covered with hearts and flowers."

"Rory..." My voice trailed off. That was heavy and huge. I'd concentrated so hard about how I could move on without him, that this about-face was messing with my head.

He cupped my jaw and tipped it up so our gazes locked. I

couldn't look away. Not from the urgency there in his hurricane wild blue eyes. "A ghrá, you have no idea the happiness you'll bring my family. And have already done with me."

I curled my fingers around his wrist. "I—"

The crack of lightning breaking the sky made us both jump. We'd been so focused on talking that the storm that had been in the far distance was sitting on top of us. Thunder followed almost immediately. Close didn't even cover it.

And with it came sheets of rain as if the heavens opened up with buckets of it and some hail for good measure.

Was this an omen?

He practically dragged me away from the waterline and up the path. "Come on," he shouted.

His hand was clamped around mine, drawing me to the far path.

"Rory, there's a closer one," I yelled over the whipping wind. Another slice of lightning lit the roiling sky, and the boom of thunder seemed to disperse the sharp scent of ozone in the air.

"Are you daft? All those trees? I'm not risking you or the baby."

My chest tightened and seemed to crack. I didn't even mind getting thoroughly soaked because of his plan. I was too focused on the fact that his sole focus was safety for us.

Thanks to the rocky path, it wasn't too muddy and we both managed to climb without falling. By the end of it, we were laughing. My dress was completely see-through at that point, and I was shivering.

His hair was plastered to his forehead as was his shirt. I swallowed thickly. And mercy, so were his pants. He raked his hands through his hair to slick it back and finally got a good look at me.

"You are a vision."

"Drowned rats are your jam?" The rain lightened to a soaking instead of a deluge. I quickly twisted my thick ropes of hair into a braid and flipped it over my shoulder.

He stepped forward, wrapping my braid around his hand. "I have dreams of this fiery hair. Some nights it's wrapped around me like chains."

"You think I'm trying to trap you."

His other hand came up to my face. "No. It's the kind of chains I want. The kind that makes me sit still and stop fucking running. You're everything I've ever wanted, Ivy Rose Beck."

My heart skipped. The way he said it sounded so big and profound. I opened my mouth, but no sound came out. I wanted to give the same back to him, but a little part of me was still so unsure.

We were so new. There was so much unknown between us.

Instead of holding my silence against me, he fused our mouths together. *This* I understood. The passion and the sparring that was so much a part of us.

I gripped his shoulders and leaned into the tempest between us that matched the one around us.

It felt like it had been forever since he'd touched me. And everything was different. My body, my hormones, my emotions— everything was heightened.

The tight hold on my braid loosened, and his kiss softened. "As much as I love the taste of you in the rain, I need to get you back to the car."

I nodded. "Right. And I'm freezing."

"We'll get you home and dry."

"So much for our date."

He laughed. "Better than you getting sick. Or the wee one."

"Think he or she is all toasty in there. Me? I'm frozen."

"Right." He took my hand and we circumnavigated the stone wall to the road. We both slowed at the flashing lights. "Well, shit."

I laughed, because honestly, this was our luck.

The sheriff car was pulled up behind Rory's car.

"Seriously?" Rory's voice was exasperated. He picked up his pace and dragged me behind him.

The town sheriff climbed out of the car. His usual laid-back uniform shirt and jeans were made a little more formal with a hat against the elements. With it on, the already imposing Jared Brooks seemed just a touch more intense.

Especially when his face tightened. "Problem, folks?"

"No, Sheriff."

"Did we do anything wrong?" Rory interrupted.

I resisted the urge to hide my head in my hands. "What he means is, we're sorry, Sheriff Brooks. We were..." Having a make-up session that started with an argument. Like our entire lives.

His gaze dropped to my middle. It wasn't exactly a secret in town that I was pregnant, but I hadn't taken out a billboard either. "I don't have to add another incident of public indecency to your tally, do I?"

Rory stiffened at my side. Evidently, Sheriff Brooks remembered our lovely meeting in the spring. It was kind of surprising since half of Jared's job consisted of breaking up clinches at the various make-out points around town. The other half was picking up drunk and disorderlies at The Spinning Wheel and traffic stops.

We weren't exactly a hotbed of crime in Crescent Cove.

Then again, Jared Brooks was best friends with Gina, my coworker. But my shifts at the diner had become less and less as I got the truck ready. I wasn't sure he'd really seen me in all my popping glory yet.

"Can I get her into the car at least?" Rory asked. "Then you can write your citation."

The sheriff's brows rose. "Getting your sweetheart pregnant isn't a crime in this town. At least not yet."

Rory wiped his hand down his face. "Right. Apologies. I just wasn't expecting—"

A loud chime and buzz went off. Immediately, Rory's hand went to his pocket, but he didn't go for the phone. When it sounded another series of chimes, he winced. "Sorry." He reached for it and Jared's hand slid to his side arm. Rory raised his hands. "Just my phone."

Sheriff Brooks gave him a bland stare.

The chimes went off again.

"It's Ian," he said to me out of the side of his mouth.

"Oh." At his worried glance, I turned to Jared. Ian and Zoe were due soon. "Oh, that might be something important. Can he check it? Please?"

Jared sighed. "Yeah. Keep your movements slow."

Rory shook his head. "Not sure you know, but where I come from, we don't have guns. Not even the coppers."

"Yes, well, you're not in England."

"Ireland," Rory spat.

I hid a laugh.

The phone sounded another series of tones as Rory pulled it out. "Shit. Shit. Holy shit, it's time. Oh, God. I promised him I wouldn't let him be alone for this."

"Of course, go. Jared can take me back to town."

"No."

"No?" The sheriff frowned. "I'm not going to put her in the back of the truck. This time, you have your clothes on. You technically didn't do anything other than show bad judgment in the rain, Mr. Ferguson."

Man, he even remembered Rory's name. I cleared my throat and crossed my arms over my very see-through dress. "Do you have a jacket in the car?"

"No." Rory frowned. "But I have something." He rushed to the trunk and Jared followed.

"I'm not quite sure who you think I am, sir. But I'm no criminal. The only thing you'll find in my trunk are instruments and a few bags."

"Ever seen *Desperado*?"

Rory laughed. "Actually, I have. Cool movie. No impressive guitar case for me though. Unless you count the signed slider from B. B. King inside mine."

Jared hooked his thumb in the belt loop in front of his gun. "Wouldn't mind seeing that."

"Freezing," I called out.

"Right." Rory popped the trunk and rummaged in a small suitcase. "Here." He flashed the cream sweater at Jared then brought it over to me. "I've been trying to find a way to give this to you."

It was cloud-soft and intricately patterned in a way that only a handmade sweater could be. I recognized it because every woman in a cold climate like Crescent Cove lived for a cozy sweater. Especially the famous Irish fisherman's sweater that wasn't easy to find or afford. "Oh, Rory."

"My ma made it for you."

"What?" I brought it to my face, then instantly pulled it over my head. It felt like a dream. While I was still soaked, at least my purple bra wasn't on display anymore.

Rory's phone chimed again, and he took it out to look. "Ian's in full meltdown status."

"Is it okay if we go, Jar—Sheriff Brooks?" I burrowed my face into the neck of the sweater.

The sheriff rolled his eyes. "Just get out of here."

Rory opened the door for me and got me settled before rounding the hood and opening his own door.

"Slowly, Mr. Ferguson."

"Of course." He got into the car.

"I can seriously go home with Jared."

Rory turned to me, his hand already on the gear shift. "I'd like you with me if you're not too tired."

"Oh." The comforting sweater and his little confession warmed me right up. I swallowed against the knot in my throat and turned up the heat. "Yes. I'd like to go with you."

"Good." He leaned over and kissed me hard on the mouth. "Good. Thank you." He handed me his phone. "Now can you text Ian that I'm on my way so the sheriff doesn't send out the state cops?"

I laughed. "Yes, I can do that."

It felt far too easy to do such a relationship-ish thing for him. Not the least bit scary at all.

Maybe I could do this.

I slid a smile at Rory before sending the text. Maybe *we* could.

TWENTY-FIVE

 **Rory**

It felt like it took forever to get to Happy Acres, and of course the storm seemed to be chasing us out there. From the information relayed by each successive rant and panic induced text from Ian, Zoe had decided to use a doula and have a home birth.

Without machines and doctors and drugs.

Horrific.

"You're not doing this doula thing, right?"

"Maybe." Ivy didn't look up from my phone as her fingers flew.

The windshield washers squeaked against the incessant rain and it took me a moment to find my voice. My knuckles went white on the steering wheel. "What?"

She shot me a look. "Relax, Rory. I'm all about the drugs and doctors. No home births for this girl."

"Sweet Jesus." Blood began to circulate in my fingers again as I relaxed my grip. "Don't scare me like that."

She giggled and curled deeper into her sweater. I was roasting my balls off, but I'd sit on hot coals before I asked her to turn the heat down. She was the mother of my child and she'd been wet to the skin. Whatever she wanted, she got.

Finally, the sign for the orchard came into view. "Where are we going?"

"She's set up in the barn it says."

"What is she Mother Mary, for feck's sake?"

"Is there going to be a manger?" She glanced at me and snorted. "I'm kidding, Rory."

"I don't know how this works. But the barn has some significance for them, that I do know." I was pretty sure they had actually lived in it at one time, but it sounded almost too ridiculous to say that out loud.

"Barn it is." She pointed to the far building close to the taproom we'd been to in the spring. "I think that's the barn. Zoe mentioned she uses it as a studio most of the time."

"Fecking baby in a goddamn art barn," I muttered as I parked.

"Your Irish is intense today."

I arched my eyebrow. "I'm Irish every day."

"As well as intense at times." She laughed. "It's not a bad thing. I'm just saying your accent is thicker."

"Welcome to me and stress, ginger fairy."

"Well, let's go see our friends."

It warmed me that she called them her friends too. I came around and opened the door for her and we both trudged through the canopy of trees to the large structure.

Three men paced outside. Her brothers. Beckett, the eldest one I knew the least, was smoking a cigarette as he paced. A motorcycle helmet was clutched in his other hand like an extension of him. And quite possibly a pseudo club.

A shout from inside made us both pick up the pace.

"Go in there at your own risk." Hayes held up a flask, then took a long drink. The fact that he swayed a little freaked me out. Firstly, Hayes had the tolerance of an eighty-seven-year-old career drinker with an eighteen-year-old liver, so that was alarming in its own right. And second, he wasn't one to imbibe in the middle of the day.

"Magic, you're doing amazing." Ian's voice floated out into the rain.

"Shove your amazing up your ass!" Zoe screeched.

I turned to Ivy, backing up a few steps. She spun me back around, put both hands on my back, and shoved me forward. "Nope. In you go."

"I don't—"

"You do need to go inside. All the way, there you go."

The barn doors were wide open and there was a section along the back draped in a rainbow of colored sheets. Wall-sized canvases peeked from the sheets. Her studio?

Well, if that didn't suit them, I wasn't sure what did.

In the middle of it was Zoe and another woman who reminded me of a darker-haired version of her. A little more wizened, less frazzled than the mother-to-be, and holding a cup of ice chips.

It was a fucking stage.

Well, the bed area looked like one anyway. Okay, technically it was more like a dais with the three stairs to reach the wide pallet of blankets and pillows. Music, full of chimes and chants, filled the air and Ian was wearing about three different religions worth of medallions on his person.

Were those linen pants?

He looked like he was getting ready to go on vacation, for feck's sake. What the sweet Jesus?

"There you are, mate." Ian's false cheer was strained around his eyes and his smile was a little manic. He tucked a sweaty lock of lightning-colored hair behind Zoe's ear. "She's doing amazing."

"If you say amazing one more time, I'm going to rip your lips off your face."

"See?" The smile cracked a little. "Last time she said she was going to rip my—" He glanced at Zoe's mother. "Well, it was an unmentionable part of my anatomy."

"It was the part that got me in this state!" Zoe seethed as another contraction hit her. She grabbed for Ian's hand and raked her nails down his arm. "I hate you so much right now."

"Okay, Zoe, just breathe slowly." The soothing voice of a third woman in the room seemed to instantly calm Zoe. Where Zoe was rounded with the end-stages of pregnancy and her hair was a wild mass of braids and curls, the other woman had sharp features and black hair shorn close to her skull. She wore scrubs like a true medical professional, which was soothing for me.

Not that it was of importance at this juncture, but it felt less like they were going to break out the crystals and start chanting to a goddess. Maybe Ian would be. He looked as if he'd escaped from the new age store and taken a side trip to Hawaii.

Zoe suddenly collapsed back against the pillows propped up behind her.

The woman in the scrubs checked under the sheet and I slammed my eyes shut. "There we go. Your contractions are getting closer."

"Ya think." Zoe grabbed a handful of ice chips and shoved them in her mouth and crunched loudly.

The woman just laughed. "Not too long now. Just take a breather."

Ian kissed Zoe's forehead. "I love you so much."

"I'm going to murder you in your sleep."

Ian sat on the edge of her bed and wrapped his arm around her. "It's our love language."

Zoe shoved him off and he fell onto the floor. "Go away for a few minutes."

He popped back up, but instead of looking wounded—emotionally or otherwise—he kissed her again. This time, Zoe leaned in for a moment before pushing him away. "I love you too. Maybe. Just give me a second."

Ian nodded. "Right. I'll be right there."

"I'm sure you will be." Zoe leaned back into the pillows, holding her mother's hand.

Ian rushed down the stairs and gave me a chest-cracking hug. "Thanks for coming, man. I'm so glad you're here. Simon, Margo, and Raine are coming out on the next flight. They weren't supposed to fly out until this weekend but the baby had other plans."

I hugged him back. "You seem to have things under control here." Sort of. My back was either still wet from the rain or slick with sweat for my friend. Or my future on display right before my eyes like a friggin' play on a stage.

"She's amazing. Anna got here a few hours ago and she's kept us from killing one another. The first hour of labor was cake. This last one," he glanced over his shoulder at Zoe who seemed to be sleeping, "Christ, I'm freaking out here." He held out a shaking hand.

Impulsively, I gripped his hand to stabilize it. "Impatient much? I hear it takes a little while for a baby to come." I tried not to look at Zoe and her setup. She was fully hidden from prying eyes, but it was still way too intimate for my taste.

I wasn't sure how all this stuff worked yet. I only had movies to go by and I was the first to know that Hollywood took some liberties there. And I hadn't gotten to this chapter in the baby book.

At all.

In fact, for my own sanity, I kept skipping the bad pages. The ones that explained complications and side effects because that rabbit hole was scary and I knew I'd never return with my psyche intact.

At least not yet.

I needed the sweet and wondrous part.

This was not the sweet and wondrous part going on right now.

Zoe made a seething groan. Ian turned to go to her, but my Ivy grabbed his wrist.

"Let me take a turn."

Ian gave her a grateful smile. "She's ready to kill me, but I don't know what else to do for her."

Ivy patted his chest. "You're doing it. Just by being here, I promise."

Ian's eyes got a suspicious sheen and he only nodded. The fact that Ian was speechless told me volumes about his fear. The man never shut up.

"Thanks for coming, man."

"Of course. I'm not sure what I can do or if Zoe wants me here..."

"She wants to burn the entire world at the moment. My fiancée is a scary one for sure. But such a warrior."

I glanced over Ian's shoulder to the two women huddled together. Ivy had her hand wrapped around Zoe's as they both laughed through the contraction.

Laughed.

Dear God. The black spots forming in my vision weren't from a stroke, right?

Ian punched me lightly in the gut. "Breathe, mate."

I blew out a slow breath. "That's my future right there."

"It sure is. It's beautiful and terrifying."

"Fuckbeast!" Zoe's shout filled the rafters.

"Right, I better get up there."

"I'll be right here."

Ian gripped my upper arm. "Thanks. Really." He ran back to the mother of his impending child.

The next hour was more of the same. Furtive glances from Zoe's brothers outside who hovered but wouldn't come into the barn. I paced while Ivy took turns with Ian sitting beside Zoe.

The storm raged outside. Rain slashed at the roof and thunder rolled ominously.

"Okay, Zoe it's time to give me the goods, all right?" Anna's voice was calm and sure. The only calm one in the room at that point.

Ian was stationed behind Zoe now, supporting her as contraction after contraction zapped all of her energy. Suddenly, Zoe slumped in his arms and Ian tried to lift her back to a seated position. "Magic? We're almost there, love." His panicked expression made me cross my metaphorical line and move into the birthing area.

Anna moved quickly, coming to check on Zoe. Anna checked her stats, lifted her eyelids, and checked the small machine set up beside her bed. She moved quickly and efficiently back to where the sheet was draped over Zoe. She ripped it back and I staggered back out of the way.

"Zoe?" Her mother rushed forward; her voice shrill. "What's wrong?"

"Just her blood pressure dropped. She's fine. No internal hemorrhaging or anything. Everything's... There we go. Welcome back, Zoe."

Zoe's eyelids fluttered open. "Ian?"

"Here, love. I'm right here."

Ivy came up next to me, her fingers lacing with mine.

"Scared us a little, Zoe. How about we not do that again?"

"Are you kidding me?"

"Just a little fainting."

She dragged Ian down to meet her eyes by his hair. "If you tell my brothers, I will kill you."

"You mean kiss me." The color returned to Ian's face. He touched his forehead to hers. "And don't you fucking go anywhere. I need you. This baby needs you."

She nodded. "I'm not. I swear, I'm okay. Just tired."

Anna kept looking at the monitor beside the bed, but the frown lines around her eyes eased. "Okay, I need you to give me deep, even breaths and push."

I closed my eyes against the savagery. Ivy wrapped her arms around me.

And we waited while Zoe pushed and pushed.

Suddenly, there was an almighty cry then the shriek of a baby and relieved laughter.

"There we go." Ivy sighed and smiled up at me. "Perfect and howling like the very best baby ever."

"He's perfect." Ian's shocked and tear-filled eyes met mine for a moment before he turned back to his girl and his little one like they were his entire world. "You're perfect, Magic."

I backed out of the room. I needed air.

There was too much emotion and chaos in there. From laughter to tears, the voices were now bright and full of love.

Zoe's brothers and father pushed by me to get in as I fought the tide of testosterone to get out. Guilt sat on my shoulders, but I still needed air.

"Rory?" She chased me out the door into the clearing. The rain had stopped. Sun was bleeding into the violent storm clouds racing out of the area to the next town. "You're leaving at the best part. Isn't he beautiful?" Her voice was filled with wonder and light. Much like the room full of people I'd had to escape. "I mean, I only got a little glimpse, but that part's not for us. It's for them."

"I just need a minute." All I could keep seeing was Zoe going limp. How wrong it could have gone. "That was a lot to take in. This isn't my kind of scene."

"Well, you better get used to it." The teasing glint drained out of her voice. "It's going to be your scene in about five months." She pushed by me and hurried toward the copse of trees heavy with new baby apples.

Even the trees were ready to give birth, for God's sake.

I quickly followed her. Christ, I'd stepped in it. Would I ever learn to shut my stupid mouth? "Ivy, wait."

She was stalking away from me at an alarming rate.

I grabbed her hand and stopped her. "I'm just freaking out a little, all right? This is why I don't let people in." If I let them in, I could lose them.

I could lose *her* to some freak medical emergency.

She gripped the front of my shirt. "I know this whole letting people get closer to you thing is going to take some time to get used to, but he's your best friend. You need to get back into that barn and congratulate him."

"Of course I am. I just don't *want* to."

"Why the hell not?"

"You know why not." I'd explained my past to her and I thought she'd understood.

"I get it. You had a friend betray you once. But hey, guess what? You did the same to me."

"I did not." My stomach bottomed out.

"You didn't cheat, but you left. And to be honest, I didn't know if you had a woman in every damn city from here to Los Angeles. We barely know one another."

"We're fixing that. And I didn't. There's only ever been you."

Flashes of Zoe losing all her color and collapsing in Ian's arms played like a reel on a loop. How the hell was I going to be enough for Ivy? I wasn't equipped for that kind of loss.

Not of Ivy.

"Yeah, except did you forget the part where you went near radio silent on me in the middle of the scariest time of my life?"

Finally, the reel snapped and stopped. Panic for what could happen superimposed itself on the woman before me. That I could lose her because I couldn't face this fucking fear. I took a step toward her, but she held up a hand.

"No, you got a chance to say your peace. Now here's mine."

Her hair was falling out of its messy braid and was curling in the humidity that was quickly replacing the storm. Whatever makeup she'd been wearing had been washed away. Even in her anger, she was so goddamn beautiful it hurt me to my bones knowing I'd almost lost her.

And still could.

"I don't know anything for sure, but I'm here, Rory. I'm trusting that you won't hurt me again. That what you said on that beach today was true."

Her voice wobbled and I couldn't stay away from her. I twisted my fingers around hers, holding tight. "It was. I swear it. I want this. I want us." I pressed our tangled hands to her belly. "Both of you."

"I want to believe you."

"I just..." I squeezed my eyes shut for a moment and blew out a slow breath. Letting her see everything was the only way to keep her. And God, I wanted that more than the breath in my body. "I watched that one split second where Ian almost lost her and I just…" I cupped her face. "I can't lose you. I can't. I love you too much."

"What?" Her huge brown eyes locked with mine. "What did you say?"

"I love you, Ivy Rose. So fucking much. I know it doesn't make sense. But I'm not wrong here, right? You feel it too? I know I have no right to ask—"

She went on her toes and slammed her mouth over mine, then jerked back. "You love me?"

"I do, yes." I wrapped her in my arms. The echo chamber that used to be my chest suddenly filled as she laughed. Tears blurred her perfect eyes and I frowned. "That's good, right?"

"So good. I love you too."

"Oh, thank God. I'd wait for it if necessary. For the right to have a woman like you love me—"

"Rory, stop. You're everything I want. You're a complete pain in my ass sometimes, but I love you. I do."

"Thanks, I think."

She laughed and dashed away the tears. "It happened so fast. I was afraid that it was too fast."

"You? I'm the one who thought I was literally going mad, a ghrá."

"You keep saying that. What does it mean?"

"It's Irish."

"I figured." She drilled her finger into my chest. "What does it mean?"

"My love."

"Oh." Her eyes filled again. "You've been saying it to me for so long and I didn't even know." She fisted my shirt. "You did it on purpose."

I laughed. "Maybe a little. It kept popping out, no matter how hard I tried to tell myself that I didn't need you. I didn't need the complications of love. Work was such a haven for me."

"You mean a place to hide."

I tipped my forehead to hers. "Yes, I suppose it was. But there's no hiding now."

"Because of the baby?" Her voice sounded uncertain.

"No, the baby is just a bonus. It's always been about you, Ivy. Always will be. Now it's all just going a bit faster. We Irish know how to do the baby thing once we get going."

"Is that right?"

I cupped her little bump where my entire future was growing. "This little one is a blessing and simply put our lives on fast forward. We would have gotten here no matter what. I believe that with my whole heart."

"You really know how to say the right thing when you get out of your own way, Rory Ferguson."

"Words are my thing, my sweet ginger fairy." I bent down to kiss her. In the dappled sunlight, there was nothing but her minty scent and soft mouth meeting mine. I slipped my hands under her sweater to get to her curves.

She pushed me back to get the sweater up and off of her. "My sweater is glorious and I don't really want to take it off, but I'm sweltering."

"I'll be sure to let my ma know." I drew her deeper into the trees and out of view of the people who seemed to be materializing by the dozen.

It seemed like there was quite the party forming now that the baby had made his arrival.

"Actually, maybe you better tell yourself. When I take you to meet my family."

Her dark eyes widened as she tied the sweater around her waist. I leaned down to take her mouth again, but she wasn't responding. "Meet your..." She pushed me back. "Me?"

"Well, you are carrying their grandchild. I'm pretty sure they need to at least meet you. And to be honest, I'd already planned on asking you to come to Malahide with me."

"Malahide?" she repeated.

I nodded and stared at her mouth, my thumbs drawing little circles along the sides of her breasts. "Where I'm from." I nibbled on her lower lip. "A little town just outside of Dublin."

"I can't think when you do that."

"Good." I covered her mouth, our tongues tangling. The craziness of the day, the euphoria of her saying she loved me back, the months in which I hadn't touched her—they all coalesced until we were wild for one another.

I lifted her leg up so I could get closer to her. To fit my aching length against the softness I craved.

"I'd really like that," she said against my mouth.

"What? Me inside you again? Me too," I said as I nipped her lower lip.

"No."

"No?" I drew back a little, though my hips still undulated against her.

She dug her fingernails into my belly. "Yes. I mean all of that, yes, God, it's been so long. I mean, I want to go to Ireland and meet your family."

"Oh, right. Of course. My ma is dying to meet you. Think we can talk about that later though? Talking about my mother while I'm trying to get into your pants is confusing and hurts my head."

She laughed. "We can't do that out here."

"Right." I held her tighter and pressed my cock to her warmth. "Of course not."

"We have to go back and see Ian and Zoe." She went for my zipper.

"Of course we do."

"Maybe in a minute."

"I've never been a minute man, Ivy." She fisted her hand around me and I groaned. "I could be, but it's a point of pride."

"Stuff your pride inside me, Rory Ferguson."

"Jesus, you are a dirty little fairy." I pushed her panties aside and slid inside of her with a low groan. "I didn't want to do this for the first time here."

"That little bump between us belies a first time for anything."

I laughed. "I meant without a condom. For real. Not the tease in the car so long ago. But sinking into your sweet," I groaned, "perfect body." The warm clasp of her after months without her just about put me on my knees. "Jesus, you are like heaven."

Her nails dug into my ass. "Chase heaven faster before someone comes."

"Someone or me?"

She laughed and then groaned when I thrust into her again. "As long as I get to come too, I don't really care."

My eyes crossed as she squeezed me with all those glorious internal female muscles. "You feel even more amazing. I didn't think that was possible."

"Perks of pregnancy." She dug harder into my ass. "Harder, LC."

My thighs burned as I lowered myself enough to match up with her. "I don't want to nail you to a tree, dammit."

"We'll do it up proper when we get home. Just please. Now." Her dark eyes were full of love and lust in equal measure.

I prayed that the sweater wrapped around her would survive us. I lifted her enough to get her legs around me and slid home again and again. I swallowed her cries, growled against the release chasing me like a rabid dog.

When she sunk her teeth into my shoulder, I finally let go. I held her tight to me as I came. My world went silent for a moment. In its wake was my heartbeat thundering in my ears with the overwhelming love I couldn't quite contain.

We kissed as the sunlight beamed and birds chirped around us.

Laughter bled into the moment I'd forever hold inside me as I lowered her to her feet and stuffed my cock back into my jeans. "People sound really close."

"Let them watch," she said with a sigh.

I scraped my teeth down her neck. "That sight is only for me."

"Is that right?"

"Yes."

She grinned up at me as she fixed her dress. She winced a little. "How bad do I look."

Her hair was wild and there was a rip in the shoulder of her dress. "You look perfect."

She rolled her eyes. "I look just fucked, don't I?"

"Maybe a little. We can stop at the car. I have some clothes in the trunk." I held her hand and led her to my car then grabbed the bag still in the boot.

People passed us by as more and more cars parked. The taproom was overflowing with people as the new baby became a reason to celebrate. We stopped in to use the bathroom to clean up the best we could.

When I swapped out my own ravaged sweater for a T-shirt, I found the little black jeweler box beside my toiletry case. The bracelet I'd bought with my sister nestled inside.

I tucked it into my pocket before zipping my suitcase closed.

I met her by the bar. She had a can of diet soda in her hand and was filling a bowl full of fruit. Ivy's outfit had been a lost cause, but she was still tiny enough to use one of my gray button down shirts as a replacement. It even looked like the style was on purpose with the little violet sash from her ruined dress.

She'd even managed to get her hair into a braid. She was a damn vision.

And she was all mine.

She smiled up at me. "Feel a bit more human?" She tucked a piece of watermelon into her mouth.

I nodded.

"I do too. Though I'm pretty sure I'll be sleeping like drunken frat boy soon. I'm whipped."

"We can go."

"No, we are going to meet the baby, then we'll go."

I sighed. "All right." I stole a piece of pineapple. "If we must."

There was a line of people waiting to see the new family. We finished our food and drinks while we waited. Ian was preening as he held the baby in his arms. He was holding his phone up and speaking. Probably talking to his brother.

I pulled Ivy aside. "Before we go in."

"Again?"

"No. Even I'm not that bad."

"Oh."

She looked disappointed enough to make my nerves even out. "I know it's not the time, but I have something for you."

Her eyebrows shot up as I pulled the box from my pocket. "Rory."

I flipped it open. "Not quite that ill-timed, love."

"Oh." Again, the bit of disappointment made my heart race. Had she been hoping for a ring?

Did I dare hope to be able to ask her? It was just a matter of connecting the dots in my mind. Owning up to loving her was far scarier a prospect than forever as odd as that may be.

"I got it in Ireland. I was going to give it to you later, but it seemed fitting to give it to you here."

She traced her fingers over the little white gold beads and bars of the bracelet. "It's lovely."

"Lots of little shops in Ireland, but this one spelled out words using Morse code."

Her eyes went misty as she looked up from the box to me. "What does it say?"

"A ghrá."

"Oh, Rory. Before you even told me."

"The words have been sitting in my chest since I met you. Seemed a special—oof."

She flung her arms around me. "I love it. It's so perfect. So different." She stepped back and held out her wrist. "Put it on, please."

I smiled down at her. The clasp was small as hell and I fumbled it twice before finally setting it to rights on her wrist. "There."

"Thank you," she whispered and went onto her toes to kiss me.

"Have you hidden yourselves away long enough? We have a baby to introduce you to."

Ian's voice made me turn. My fingers grazed down Ivy's arm to link our hands. "Thought you and Zoe might need a minute."

"More likely that the two of you needed one." He tipped his head. "You look...at ease." He rocked the baby in his arms lightly. "Did you go off and get laid while my wife-to-be toiled through afterbirth and learning to breastfeed?"

I coughed. "Jesus, Ian."

"What? Get used to it, bub. This is going to be your life too."

I smiled down at Ivy. "Yeah, it is."

"Oh, well, will you look at you? Totally at ease with the miracle of childbirth now. You were pretty green a little bit ago. White as a sheet."

"Like you noticed." I stepped forward to look at the tightly wrapped baby. A shock of dark hair whorled around the front of his head. "Wow. That's a lot of hair."

"I know, right? Takes after his da, right, little man?" Ian nuzzled the baby's cheek. The baby let out a squall. Ian sighed. "He keeps doing that."

Ivy crowded in next to me. "Babies cry. Don't they?" Her voice was gentle and easy with almost a song-like quality to it. The baby settled and tried to drag her finger into his mouth. "Hungry little— what's his name?" She peered up at Ian.

"Elvis." Ian's smile was wide and proud.

"Pardon?"

"It took some doing, but Zoe finally capitulated. I mean, how can he not have such a rock and roll name, right? Especially with this pompadour."

"You named your child Elvis?" I slowed my words to make sure I had that right.

"Yeah." Ian's eyebrows waggled. "It's perfect."

I looked down at the little bundle of pink in the muslin blankets. "Of course it is."

"Right? Simon is still making fun of me, but he's coming around." Ian swayed back and forth in that way people had when they held a baby. The baby started to fuss then Ian sighed. "Come on, come see the one who created this little miracle."

We followed him back into the barn and Zoe was now settled into an oversized leather chair with a huge sandwich half eaten in front of her. "Have you finally brought my child back to me?"

"I was showing him off."

"As if you did any of the work." She pushed the small table to the side and held her hands out.

"He's beautiful, guys." Ivy was smiling as she gripped my hand tightly.

"Yes, utterly perfect. The name though."

Zoe sighed. "I tried to fight him on it, but the hair."

"You do know Elvis was a blond."

She laughed and smoothed the baby's hair back. "I know, but the hair really cinched it. Even I couldn't deny this idiot his request."

"The baby will hate you."

Zoe grinned up at me. "I know. Isn't it great?"

"You two are very odd."

Ian laid a gentle hand on Zoe's shoulder. "Yeah, we know. But we're never boring."

I couldn't fault them there. "That's the truth." I cleared my throat at Ivy's sudden death grip. Right, being a best friend. I cleared my throat. "Thanks for letting me be a little part of this."

Ian came around and hugged me hard. "Of course. You helped me so much."

"I didn't do a damn thing." But I hugged him back.

He eased back and slapped me in the arm. "It's called moral support."

"Right." I guess that was exactly what it was. "Just so you know, I'll need it in return."

"As if you had a choice in it, mate."

I laughed. No, I guess I didn't.

We spent a little more time with them, but it had been a damn long day and I was anxious to get my woman home. We had much to discuss and I had a lot of plans to make.

This was just our beginning.

IVY

CHAPTER 26

July 4ᵗʰ

It had been a whirlwind week. After we got back from the orchard, we were consumed with ice cream truck preparations.

The bonus? Long, hot nights at Rory's room at the Hummingbird's Nest. He'd even stopped hiding from Sage. Sort of.

We spoke of the future and the past.

I learned about his family and his childhood.

I introduced him to my parents—yeah, that was a rough afternoon. But my mom and dad were surprisingly good with him. My mother was fascinated with his accent. My brother Caleb kept trying to get Rory to give him Gaelic words to use for picking up women.

August was reserved.

He didn't like that things were still so nebulous when it came to the future. We didn't know where we were going to live yet. Rory was forever on the phone trying to rearrange his schedule and work with clients over Skype.

I knew that would need to be figured out. There were almost five months to go in this pregnancy, and he had to leave me eventually. Even if it was for a few days to get his affairs in order.

But right now, it was all about Rolling Cones.

We'd had the soft opening for the employees of Brewed Awakening as a trial run. I might have had a meltdown in the middle of the truck when we ran out of *It's Only Rock n' Raspberry.*

Rory had dusted me off and helped me make a batch of it that night for the opening. He was good at being level-headed even when I was spinning out with stress and nerves. He was also good at distracting me when I couldn't sleep.

Really good.

And today was the grand opening. I could hear children's laughter across the way in the park. It was the holiday weekend and there would be fireworks over the lake. But for now, the sun was shining and the light breeze off the water kept my truck from being a complete oven.

"What are you thinking, ginger fairy?"

I turned toward Rory's voice. He was standing at the opening of the back of my truck, outfitted in the rainbow ball cap with my logo on it. The new logo he'd put a rush on for the opening. I didn't even want to think about how much he'd paid.

I let it go. It was a gift.

I didn't have to do all of this alone.

I'd been better at asking for help. August had hauled over my backup trays of ice cream and my newly tested custard I'd decided to offer as a surprise for the afternoon crowd.

Everything was in order.

My family was taking turns doing shifts today in the truck, but Rory was there for the first one.

His smile was full of pride. "What are you thinking right now?"

I tied my apron strings behind me. "I'm thinking how excited I am to do this for real."

"You're amazing. The whole town will be knocking at your window. In fact…" He crooked his finger at me. "Have a look."

"Rory, I'm opening in an hour."

"I know. Which is why this is such a wonder and you need to see it with your own eyes."

I sighed. "If this is to look at your cock, we're going to end up in a fight."

He laughed. "You already had a view of my cock this morning. And I appreciate being your cure for insomnia at three am."

I blushed. "Orgasms put me to sleep."

"Say it a little louder, love. I don't think the whole of the town heard you."

"No one—wow." I stepped down to see a line of people waiting on the sidewalk. In fact, the line was around the building Macy was renovating for her new secret project and past the stationery store. "They're waiting for me?"

"Yep."

"But I don't open for another hour."

"I know."

"Should I open early?"

"Nah, let them wait." He lowered his mouth to mine in a sweet kiss. "Gives me a minute to be selfish."

I grinned into his kiss. "I like when you're selfish."

"I hope so."

I cupped his face. The scruff was becoming a part of him. Not quite a beard, but definitely not as Los Angeles as he'd been when I first met him. The little smile lines next to his eyes were blooming and his skin was getting tan from working on the truck during the long summer days.

"I love you."

"Ah, fairy queen. I'll never tire of hearing that. In fact, I'm certain of it." He dropped to one knee and my stomach went into a free-fall.

"Oh my God."

"I know today is your day and God knows I've tried to figure out the perfect time to do this, but in the end, all I can think about is getting my ring on your finger. I love you madly, completely, and with everything in me." He pulled a black box out of his pocket and flipped it open. "Marry me, Ivy Rose Beck."

The ring was...huge.

"Holy shit."

Epically huge with the widest diamond I'd ever seen in all my life.

"Big ring for a big love, right?"

"Rory, my God." I didn't even know what to do with a ring like that.

"You're killing me here."

"Yes!" I crouched in front of him and wobbled a little, thanks to a baby screwing with my center of gravity. "Yes, a million times yes. I'll marry you."

He slid the ring on my finger and I was literally blinded. Tears made it shine even brighter, if that was possible. I wrapped my arms around him.

Someone in the line must have figured out there was a proposal going on. The clapping started and wolf whistles followed as he helped me up.

"All right, thank you." Rory waved and ducked his head.

"You're the one who asked me in front of the whole town."

"Yeah, it seemed better in my head than the reality of it."

I stared down at my hand. "Yes, well, the reality of it is crazy and," I sniffled, "Rory Ferguson, you surprise me every damn day."

"That's a good thing, right? I know today is your day and all. And I shouldn't have horned in."

"No." I went up on my toes and kissed him. "No, it's absolutely perfect." I stared at the ring and had to use my pinky to straighten it since the stone was so large it kept twisting.

"Besides, I want the whole town to see a ring on your finger.

Once they start tasting your ice cream, they're going to try to steal you from me."

I laughed. "Never."

"That's what I like to hear. Now maybe we open a little early?"

I looked down at my watch. It was just after eleven. "Ice cream for breakfast isn't a bad thing, right?"

He rubbed his belly. "I know it works for me." He walked around to the front of the truck and waited at the edge of the shutters we'd put up to keep some of the details a secret. Most of the town knew, but we'd added a few new flavors after some taste-testing.

I went to the other end and we lifted them up, securing them with the huge hooks August had installed for me.

After jogging to the front of the truck, I turned on the music, using the app on my phone that Rory had made work with the ancient radio. I pressed play on "Start Me Up" and it blared out of the speakers.

I slipped into the back of the truck and opened the window to peek out. "Rolling Cones is open for business."

I turned to find Rory next to me, ice cream scooper at the ready.

"I'd like a banana split, please."

I laughed out loud at my brother's voice. He and Kinleigh were waiting in front of the window.

"You know we had to be your first customers." Kinleigh put her hand on August's shoulder to boost herself up a little. "I'd like a *Paint It Black Cherry* cone please. You know, in honor of the Stones."

"Coming right up."

"What would you like for your flavors on the banana split, sir?"

August's lips twitched. "Traditional. I'm that kind of guy." He smiled down at Kinleigh, who quickly removed her hand.

"Boring. Look at all those flavors."

"I like what I like."

Hmm, that was odd. Kinleigh and August's teasing had an extra layer of snark today, and the look they exchanged had been almost... sparky.

What the hell?

I didn't have time to think about it. The orders came fast and furious after that. I scooped so much ice cream that my shoulders ached. More sprinkles and caramel got caught in my ring than anything.

And everyone asked about it. Including my brother when he wound back around later in the afternoon.

He was happy for me—for us. But there was more than a little sibling worry in there too.

I barely had time to focus on his concern with all the scooping and squealing from the patrons. The rock of Gibraltar I was wearing was the talk of the town as much as my flavors.

Rory made me take a break at dinner and handed me a hamburger from the cookout going on over on the pier. I might've almost eaten my own fingers with how fast I wolfed it down.

August worked the dinner shift, and my mother came to help for the evening. She *oohed* and *aahed* over the ring and teared up a little and hugged Rory. All very good signs. My dad was supposed to take a last shift before the fireworks, but I ran out of ice cream.

Literally, all of it—gone.

I couldn't even count the gallons of ice cream, crushed ice, and custard I'd sold. Even my backups I'd had stashed at August's house and in Macy's freezer were gone.

"I can't believe it."

Rory sat next to me under the three fans. "Can't believe what? That you're marrying the most attractive Irishman in town?"

"Well, you're the only man actually from Ireland in town. Though quite a few like to pretend they're full Irish in the month of March."

"Imposters.

I laughed. "No, that I sold everything." I looked down at my ring. "But the marrying you is pretty awesome too."

"Gee, thanks."

I swallowed and twisted my ring back and forth. "Rory?"

"Yeah?"

"Would you be frightfully offended if I wore your ring on a chain while I'm working?"

"You know you can't take it off once I put it on that finger."

My eyes blurred. "I'm afraid I'm going to lose it. And I'm getting it ruined with all the sticky sauces and whipped cream. I just don't know what I'd do if I lost it."

"Ah, love. Don't worry about it."

"No, I will worry."

"I mean, you can wear it on a chain."

"Oh, good. It's so gorgeous, but it's...really big."

"That's what she said."

I elbowed him. "You're hanging out with Ian too much."

"I'm learning how to change nappies. You should be excited."

"Oh, I am." I leaned my head on his shoulder. "I really am."

"Come on. Let's go sit in the gazebo and watch the boats until the fireworks start."

"That sounds amazing."

He stood and took a bottle of water from under the counter and handed it to me. I had a lot of ice cream to make tonight. But for now, I was going to enjoy some time with my fiancé.

We'd put up the *closed* sign half an hour ago, but people kept walking by hopefully to see if we changed our minds. We put the shutters down, then walked over to the gazebo hand in hand.

I was a sticky mess and needed a shower, but it had been a pretty perfect day.

Surprisingly, the gazebo wasn't overrun with people. It was usually the best place to watch the fireworks. The closer we got to the stairs, the more I saw why.

"What did you do?"

"Well, I asked people to let me use this just for a few minutes. When I explained the reason, they were all too happy to give me a moment with you in here alone."

"On the Fourth of July?"

"Yes. Just for a few minutes."

He drew me in to sit on the bench. There were balloons all over the gazebo with the names *Rory and Ivy* on them. Streamers flowed and little sparklers were set to be lit.

It was perfect and sweet.

I turned to find him on his knee again.

My vision swam. "I think you already asked this question."

"I did. And I'm sorry I've had a bit of fun with you today. You should have seen your face when you saw that piece of glass."

"Glass?" I looked down at my ring.

"I'm a wealthy man, Ivy, but I'm not sure even Gates could afford that rock."

"He probably could."

He laughed and opened his hand to reveal a small blue box. "I love you madly, and I would never give you a ring that didn't suit you."

My eyes overflowed as I took in the much smaller vintage-style setting with its trio of diamonds. The bottom one was longer and pointed, and the other two were smaller and round—

"Oh my God. It's an ice cream cone." I covered my mouth. "You gave me ice cream."

He grinned. "Only fitting since you gave me the world. There's something else you gave me too. Someone." He tapped the ring. "Three stones there. One longer than the others—"

"That's what he said."

His grin turned into laughter. "That one was for our baby, you perv. The cornerstone of our life now."

I couldn't stop the happy tears. "Oh, Rory."

"Will you be my wife, Ivy Rose?"

"Yes. If you'll be my husband, Rory Michael." I'd only just learned his middle name, and this seemed like a fine time to use it.

He slid the gorgeous ring on my finger, and I leaned forward to kiss him, long and sweet.

Our happily ever after started now.

FOR AN EXTRA SPECIAL BONUS EPILOGUE...
Go to our website: tarynquinn.com

Wondering who our next dad is? How about one who's been keeping it
a secret?

Next up is Gideon & Macy's story!

Gideon and Macy have been dancing around each other forever, but she's been pretty outspoken about her feelings on kids—a hard no thanks! During the remodel of her new Halloween themed restaurant everything explodes, including finding out Gideon has been hiding a daughter.

For character charts, reading order list across all of our series—including spoiler free versions—please visit our website at tarynquinn.com.

We appreciate our readers so much!
If you loved the book please let your friends know. If you're extra awesome, we'd love a review on your favorite book site.

Now...turn the page for a special sneak peek of DADDY in DISGUISE now.

MACY

DADDY IN DISGUISE

Sometimes the universe just did not see fit to provide what you wanted. In this case, I wanted to be alone.

"Are you sure you don't want me to stay and help clean up?"

"Go." If I had to watch my frighteningly pregnant friend—and original employee—teeter around the café any more tonight, I was going to have a damn nervous breakdown. "Moose has texted me no less than three times looking for you."

Veronica Masterson, café baker extraordinaire and wife of Murphy aka Moose, sighed. "He's always worried."

"Considering you barely fit behind the wheel of your huge-ass SUV, it's not shocking." Because, of course, Vee had to overachieve in all ways, including babies. One wasn't enough. Which, hey, I got it. Baby fever was at an all-time high in Crescent Cove. But man, twins right after having a baby?

Yeah. No thank you very much times a billion.

"Give Bray a big smacking kiss for me." Okay, yes, I was soft on her little boy. I couldn't help it. Every time he saw me, he suction-cupped himself to me like an octopus. And he was just as leggy as one, thanks to his huge dad.

"I will. Murphy said he was conning him into another bedtime read."

"*Llama, Llama?*"

"Is there any other book these days?"

I hid a smile. I rather liked that one myself—enough to give it to most of the kids in the ever-expanding baby-crazy group of women who kept taking over my café, Brewed Awakening.

I steered her toward the door. "It was a light evening. Cleanup will be a snap."

"But Clara already left. She had that test—"

"Vee, I'm a big girl. I've been closing this place for well over two years now." And as sweet as my server was, I was a helluva lot faster than Clara anyway.

"Almost three, actually."

My heart did a little twist in my chest. "Yes, three." I wasn't exactly sure where the whole of the summer went, but my anniversary was coming up again. Which just happened to coincide with Halloween, my favorite time of year.

"I don't want to leave you here alone."

"What exactly is going to happen in the Cove?"

"You don't know. Serial killers love to use small towns because it's least expected."

I sighed as I nudged her toward the door. "You gotta stop listening to those podcasts."

Vee gave me some side-eye. "You love horror movies, and yet you won't look at the realistic parts of the world."

"I don't need to. Shit is hard enough. Besides, I like the pretend kind of murder and mayhem where I know the killer is going to get his comeuppance." That wasn't exactly true. At least in the good kinds of horror movies, the bad guy had to come back at the end.

However, my favorite worrywart had to be on her way. And thankfully, she wasn't into watching scary flicks, so she was none the wiser.

"Is Gideon next door at least?" Vee hung her cross-body purse over her head and swung it around to the back since, surprise, it didn't fit in the front.

I jumped back a step before I got smacked with some sort of the baby paraphernalia that was forever spilling out of that thing. "I'm not sure. I'm not his keeper."

Okay, so that sounded a little bitchy. I was definitely *not* his keeper. Even if I kept sneaking over there to see what was what. However, it wasn't because of the man.

Not exactly.

Nope, it was because he and his crew were working on my newest acquisition, The Haunt. A restaurant that combined my two favorite things, food and horror movie memorabilia. I'd managed to procure a good mix of employees from the café who wanted to do something different as well as bring in some fresh blood—pun intended.

Not only did I have an anniversary deal to figure out for Brewed Awakening, this year, I was adding another whole business to that annual event. And my nerves were at an all-time high. At this point, I didn't even know if the restaurant was going to be ready.

Mostly because my favorite carpenter-slash-contractor wouldn't give me a straight answer about what was going on next door. In fact, he kept barring me from going over there. Oh, he gave me really good explanations as to why I couldn't. Insurance and safety and blah, blah, blah.

But I was going crazy. I needed to freaking know how far off schedule he was. Surely, he wouldn't keep putting me off unless that was the case. Guys needed that ego stroke. He'd want to show it off.

Then again, Gideon never quite reacted how I expected. I knew from experience his work was beyond compare. He'd remodeled the café exactly how I wanted it with a few detours I hadn't known I needed. I trusted him. At least when it came to the things in his tool belt.

Under the belt? Well, that was debatable.

I mean, how many times had we almost kissed in two years? A

damn fuckton, that was how many. And he never sealed the deal. So, either he wasn't that into me or...

I didn't have the mental bandwidth to figure out the or.

Vee turned around just as I towed her through the door. "I'll just sit down in the corner. I won't make a sound."

"Creampuff, you don't know the definition of not making a sound."

She huffed out a breath, blowing a blond curl out of her softly rounded face. "Text me when you're done."

"I never leave, remember? My apartment is literally upstairs. I'll be fine. I'll even lock the door right after you."

Her huge blue eyes were about three minutes from full-blown tears. Preggo hormones must be wreaking havoc today. I so could not deal with that. I pushed the door open and unclipped her keys from the bag of death. "Take these," I handed them to her, "and go home to your husband."

"But—"

"Goodnight. Go cuddle your men." I closed the door and dug out my own keys and jangled them in the window. "Go."

She finally turned toward her car. Her dejected eyes almost made me waver. Almost. Finally, she waved, and I saw just how tired she was when she sighed and got in her car.

I snicked the lock and even typed my code into the security panel. I was from Chicago. Security was automatic for me, regardless of the ultra-safe small town I'd ended up in. I'd needed a change after...well, just after everything.

I'd literally thrown a dart at the state of New York and ended up moving my entire life to Crescent Cove. That was after I'd played a drunken game of pin the tail on my future. A bastardized version of the childhood game with a map of the United States instead of a cartoon donkey.

The map had been pinned to the ectoplasm green wall in my old house. A color I would never have chosen but had happily painted to make Malcolm happy. Hey, he was a kid. Made sense. But me? I might as well have been one too.

Back then, I'd been young, eager, and stupid. Back then, I'd thought I was building toward a future.

Then I'd learned the truth and there had been much Jack Daniels. I'd needed a fresh start.

While I was drunk, I found New York.

When I sobered up and stopped crying about shit that would never change, I got angry. And that was when I'd gone into research mode. I sold my house and my coffee truck for a sizable figure and started over.

And here I was, taking another gamble with my savings. This time, my emotions were in check. This time, I'd created a business plan and had taken steps to correctly position myself for success. Not the blind luck I'd backed into with the café. I'd grown quickly and invested wisely, but it was still insane to open a restaurant. I was gambling on the small town's upward climb. More people were moving in and Crescent Cove was ever expanding with its epic baby boom.

Maybe I should have gone with baby-centric themes instead of the life-sized animatronic Michael Myers I'd sunk an absurd amount of money in. Whatever. It was too late now.

I was banking on my style.

It had worked for Brewed Awakening. The coffee shop was full of pieces straight from horror movie culture. Rylee had been right about pushing forward with the movie idea with viewing parties and specialized popcorn and treats. Money was pouring into the bank. Enough that I'd added a banquet room to The Haunt for gatherings and bigger viewing parties.

There just wasn't much to do for people in this town. They were starving for fun.

And I was going to give it to them. If John Gideon and his crew actually ever finished the damn restaurant.

Maybe I'd just take a little peek. It was my place, after all.

I scrubbed my palm down my jeans as I made my way to the connecting doors. A huge eyesore in the form of a piece of plywood had been taped over the double doors. Not only was it taped, but Gideon's crew had added a few nailed pieces of wood to keep me out.

I pried my fingers under one of the planks until the nail wiggled enough for me to pull it free. The nail at the top of the two-by-four allowed me to swing it down to rest against the wall. I winced at the scratch I made in the toffee-colored paint. That was what touch-up paint was for, right?

Now there was just enough room for me to duck behind the huge sheet of plywood.

I'd sneaked in last night, but I'd been waylaid by Lucky, one of Gideon's employees. He was the one who'd tacked up the extra wood.

Like a few pieces of soft pine were going to stop me.

I slipped inside and the scent of stain with a sawdust chaser nearly knocked me over. Drop-cloths were draped over everything, leaving ghost-like figures that could be booths or tables or monsters. With my place, it really was a crapshoot which you'd find.

I'd won an auction for a replica of the 80's movie version of *Swamp Thing* last month. It had been delivered to much fanfare during the week. I wondered which lump was the former Dr. Holland.

I made it to what should be the main dining area and the low murmur of voices had me scrambling back behind a—*son of a bitch*. I clipped my pinkie toe on the carved foot of a booth. Goddammit. I spun around in circles and resisted the urge to howl.

The only things not draped were the sawhorses Gideon was forever using to cut stacks of lumber. I gripped the top of it and touched my forehead to it as the stars and black spots receded.

Fuck.

When the pain lessened, dialogue from *Halloween* dented the quiet of the night. The telltale piano and spine-tingling strings were broken up by the lame love scene. I knew this movie by heart.

I hobbled my way to the back of the dining area to the bar. A ridiculously large laptop was sitting on the half-covered bar top. The low light from the screen flickered in the near dark.

A LED lamp threw the band of carved wood along the front in stark relief. The closer I got, the louder the movie became. Then I noticed the tick of shavings hitting the floor around a very familiar pair of Timberlands.

John Gideon. It couldn't be Lucky or Frank. Nope, it had to be the man himself. And it had been a damn long day. That was the only reason I let myself do a nice long perusal of all six-feet-three inches of him.

Sure.

That's the reason. Tell yourself another lie.

He had his yellow safety glasses on as he used the world's smallest chisel to carve into the corner of my bar. His dark hair was slicked back, but the ends were curling up. He tried so hard to keep a smooth, well-groomed look but his hair just wouldn't be tamed.

I didn't mind. I liked it a little wild.

I always mourned his hair when he actually remembered to go to the lone hairdresser in the Cove. The town barber had retired to Florida. Many men had learned the fine art of hair products this past year. John Gideon included, damn him.

I frowned as more shavings came pinging over his shoulder.

What was he doing?

I dared to creep a little closer. It seemed like a lot more delicate work than just a regular corner finishing. I was well-versed in Gideon's woodworking capabilities. Brewed Awakening was full of his innovative shelves and benches.

He didn't take the time to do intricate work very often. Every once in a while, I caught him doing something special, but he was often rushing to do five different jobs in and around town. The citizens of the Cove kept him very busy.

"Well, come on. Take a look then. Damn woman, always ruining any surprises."

I jumped. "Shit, Gideon."

He glanced over his shoulder. "I told you to keep out of here until we were further along."

I put my hands on my hips. Now I didn't want to look, dammit.

Liar. You want to see it so bad that you can taste it.

"It's my place. I should be able to come in and take a look around."

He swiped at his forehead with his forearm, leaving behind a trail of sawdust. My lips twitched. And okay, I couldn't stop myself from trying to see what he was blocking. Too bad his rather delicious ass was throwing a shadow over it.

I did love a man who had a little junk in his trunk. So many didn't. Not that I had a huge amount of knowledge there, but I'd done enough soul-searching—read, stupid hookups—in my twenties. As thirty approached, I'd become a little more discerning.

Evidently, a lot more. Cobwebs had been growing in my lingerie drawer since I moved to the Cove.

"You trusted me to take on this job, so trust me to finish it."

I crossed my arms over my traitorous tits. The deep timbre of his voice always activated my stupid nipples. It was like they were damn divining rods to our very favorite water source. "It's not a matter of trust."

"Isn't it though?"

"We open in six weeks, Gideon. I need to train people in here, get the bar set up. I've had the liquor license forever and the booze is sitting in my backroom gathering dust."

Mostly because I'd heard horror stories about the liquor license process in New York. Late night forums and Googling were my life. I didn't know how to sleep. Caffeine was my friend for more than one reason.

"And if you'd stop sneaking back here every hour and distracting my guys, we'd be further a-fucking-long." He raked his fingers through his hair and the sawdust doubled.

"If you'd bring me up to speed, then I wouldn't have to fucking sneak back here." I knew I was shouting, and I didn't even care.

Frustration and stress had been eating at me for weeks—months—now. Not to mention the tension caused by my ever-growing personal sexual desert.

He stalked by me and whipped off one of the coverings behind me. A darkly stained booth came into shadowy view. He slapped his hand against a panel and a low hanging pendant light flicked on. The booths were obviously not in the right spot yet. His shoulder brushed the stained glass hood and it swayed, throwing light all over the room.

Deep red paint with a super subtle darker stripe coated the walls. The dizzy beam of light threw the corner into relief. There was something akin to blood splatter along the walls. It was a trick of the light with some sort of clear paint to create the effect, but it was breath-stealing. A poster of Dracula leaned against the rich, midnight stain of the bead-board that covered the lower half of the wall. Kickplates were half installed as well as jet black vents piled against the freshly painted trim.

My gaze bounced around the room. The booths matched the stain of the bead-board. It was a simple style, but the high, arched back had a relief carving of a raven. He whipped off another sheet to show the same booth style, this one with a bat mid-flight.

I spun around to get a look at each one he revealed. Some were achingly chilling, some were funny—all captured everything I didn't even know I wanted.

As always.

I reached out a shaking hand to touch the bat. The light was still dancing since Gideon was stalking around the room, flicking drop-cloths to the floor. Sawdust and other sundry construction dust floated in the pale shafts of light. I was trying to bring it all into focus, and my heart was racing like I'd run down Main Street. It was too much to take in without proper light, but it was even better than I could have ever imagined.

Finally, I turned to him. His hazel eyes were angry and wild. They were bloodshot with fatigue and something else. The thing that always arced between us like electricity from the climax of a vintage monster movie. Dr. Frankenstein and his creation had nothing on us.

It was terrifying and electrifying.

My fight or flight response kicked into gear. Part of me wanted to run, and the other half of me wanted to stay. To demand he finally fucking man up and touch me.

My heart raced, and I dragged in deep breaths. Black dots danced around my periphery. I didn't know if it was the adrenaline or the shadows being thrown from the little Tiffany pendant light.

As I stepped closer, my pulse tripped at the madness flickering in his eyes. Every muscle bulged in his forearms, shoulders, and all those little ones in between that climbed up his arms. The ones I didn't know the names for but made my mouth water every time he lifted something heavy.

Jesus, he was fucking hot.

He opened his arms, his ever-present white T-shirt stretching tight across his broad chest. A stub of a pencil was tucked behind his ear, peeking out from the flipped-up ends of his hair.

His chest heaved as he stared me down. "Well? Are you happy now?"

I took another step closer, my heart slamming so hard against the walls of my chest I couldn't hear anything else in the room. Even the chilling soundtrack from the climax of *Halloween* couldn't dent the heaviness vibrating between us.

I grabbed his shirt and dragged him down to me. His mouth crashed onto mine and there was barely a breath of shock before his arms went around me and crushed me to him.

He tasted like my coffee—the special blend of chicory and dark chocolate I'd created just for him. That I brewed for no one else. That maybe, just maybe, I drank when the nights got too lonely. It burned my tongue as he invaded my mouth. His kiss was just as quietly overwhelming as the man himself.

No gentle first kiss between us. Nope. There was only lust unlocked.

And I was fucking here for it in every goddamn way.

Here in the place that I'd been dreaming about since I purchased the dilapidated building last year. Coffee was what I knew. What flowed in my veins, but I wanted more. I always wanted more. I was forever stretching past the boundaries set on me.

Even here in this sometimes stifling town, I wanted to demand more. Make my space more than just a pit stop in someone's day. Why I pushed myself to create drinks for strangers. To unlock their hearts and make them feel special for a second.

No one knew that but me.

But maybe this man knew a little bit of what I felt. I could see it in the details he'd brought to this project. Maybe it wasn't just a job.

Hope fluttered in my chest as I savored the long, slow, and dizzying way he kissed me. Like I was the best part of his day.

Then my phone buzzed against his thigh. Insistently.

"Do you have a vibrator in your pocket, Mace?" he asked against my mouth. "I'd figure you'd be less surly if you had a pocket rocket."

I dug my fingers into his stupidly firm pecs. "Shut up. Ignore it and go back to kissing me like you mean it."

He laughed into my mouth and cupped my face, but the stupid phone started up again. I was prepared to ignore it. Brewed Awakening was fucking closed.

"Do you need to get that?"

"Nope," I mumbled against his mouth and pulled my phone out to silence it.

He grinned and looked down. "Shit. Is that the time?"

"Got somewhere to be?" I took a step back. The phone went silent again.

Gideon shoved his hands into his hair. "Shit." He dug into his pocket then frowned and went back to the bar. He did something on his phone, and suddenly, it started buzzing and ringing as well.

My little bit of happiness and hope popped like a soap bubble at the way his face went from smiling and sexy to serious.

"Hello? Karen? Is everything all right?" He turned away from me.

Actually, he may as well have planted one of his big boots into my now too tight chest. Something was very wrong. Who the freaking fuck was Karen?

He listened for a second, his big shoulders sagging as he tunneled his fingers through his hair. He shifted around and those worried eyes caught mine.

Dear God, not again.

This could not be happening to me again.

NOW AVAILABLE!
Ebook, Print, & Audio

Check out our website: tarynquinn.com

CRESCENT COVE

For more information about our books visit

www.tarynquinn.com

For more information about our books visit

www.tarynquinn.com

USA Today bestselling author, Taryn Quinn, is the bestie combo of bestselling authors Taryn Elliott and Cari Quinn. We've been writing together for years and decided to combine forces under one name.

Do you like…

✓ Ultra sexy romance with a side of sweet and funny.
✓ Quirky characters.
✓ RomCom shenanigans that usually involve crazy families.
✓ A crazy baby town that has exploded into a few side series.
✓ Office romance.
✓ Rockstar romance.
✓ And one BIG promise. If you love found families, you're guaranteed to find ones you wish were your own by the end of our books.

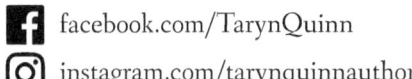 Pour a cup of coffee and join us. We're glad you're here.

For more information about our books visit
www.tarynquinn.com
Email us: tq@tarynquinn.com

facebook.com/TarynQuinn
instagram.com/tarynquinnauthor